MASTERS OF
ROME
RISE OF EMPERORS

The Rise of Emperors Series
Sons of Rome
Masters of Rome
Gods of Rome

Also by Gordon Doherty

The Legionary Series
Legionary
Viper of the North
Land of the Sacred Fire
The Scourge of Thracia
Gods and Emperors
Empire of Shades
The Blood Road
Dark Eagle

The Strategos Trilogy
Born in the Borderlands
Rise of the Golden Heart
Island in the Storm

The Empires of Bronze Series
Son of Ishtar
Dawn of War
Thunder at Kadesh

Also by Simon Turney

The Damned Emperors Series
Caligula
Commodus

The Marius' Mules Series
The Invasion of Gaul
The Belgae
Gallia Invicta
Conspiracy of Eagles
Hades' Gate
Caesar's Vow
Prelude to War
The Great Revolt
Sons of Taranis
Pax Gallica
Fields of Mars
Tides of War

Sands of Egypt
Civil War

The Praetorian Series
The Great Game
The Price of Treason
Eagles of Dacia
Lions of Rome
The Cleansing Fire

Roman Adventures
Crocodile Legion
Pirate Legion

Collaborations
A Year of Ravens
A Song of War
Rubicon

MASTERS OF
ROME

RISE OF EMPERORS:
BOOK TWO

DOHERTY
& TURNEY

HEAD
ᵒᶠ ZEUS

An Aries Book

First published in the UK in 2021 by Head of Zeus Ltd
This paperback edition first published in the UK in 2022 by Head of Zeus Ltd,
part of Bloomsbury Publishing Plc

9 7 5 3 1 2 4 6 8

A catalogue record for this book is available from
the British Library.

ISBN (PB): 9781800242050
ISBN (E): 9781800242104

Typeset by Divaddict Publishing Solutions Ltd

Printed and bound in Great Britain by
CPI Group (UK) Ltd, Croydon CR0 4YY

Head of Zeus Ltd
5–8 Hardwick Street
London EC1R 4RG

WWW.HEADOFZEUS.COM

MASTERS OF
ROME
RISE OF EMPERORS

EBORACUM

COLONIA AGRIP

TREVERORUM

MEDIOLANUM

PC

TERRITORY OF CONSTANTINE

MASSILIA

ROME

CARTHAGE

TERRITORY OF MAXENTIUS

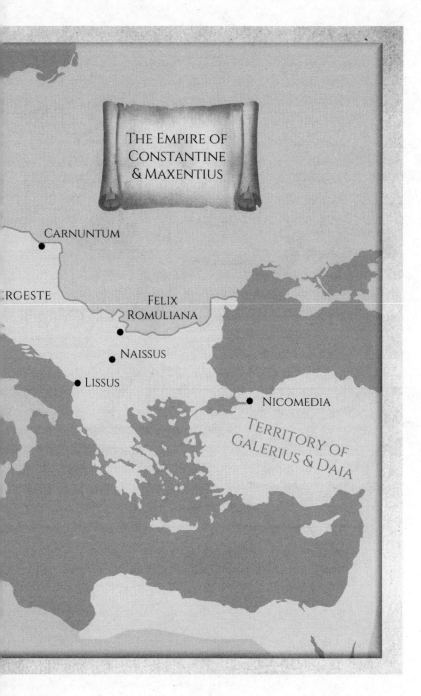

THE EMPIRE OF
CONSTANTINE
& MAXENTIUS

CARNUNTUM

RGESTE

FELIX
ROMULIANA

NAISSUS

LISSUS

NICOMEDIA

TERRITORY OF
GALERIUS & DAIA

ROME
306AD

VIA FLAMINIA

VIA SALARIA

SEPTEM BALNEA

MILVIAN BRIDGE

R. TIBER

R. ANIO

ROME

PRAETORIAN FORTRESS

VIA FLAMINIA

VIA SALARIA

VIA LATA

NEW BATHS OF DIOCLETIAN

CAMPUS MARTIUS

QUIRINAL HILL & BATH HOUSE

THEATRE OF POMPEY

SUBURA

CAPITOLINE HILL

OPPIAN HILL

GARDENS OF TORQUATAS

FORUM

FLAVIAN AMPHITHEATRE

LUDUS MAGNUS

VIA CAELEMONTANA

VIA PRAENESTINA

DISUSED IMPERIAL PALACE

VIA LABICANA

PALATINE

TIBER

CIRCUS MAXIMUS

CASTRA PEREGRINA

IMPERIAL HORSEGUARD BARRACKS

VILLA OF MAXENTIUS

RIVER PORT

AVENTINE HILL

HORREA GALBAE

VIA APPIA

TO VILLA OF HERODES ATTICUS

PART 1

Gradus est statione minus libertatis
(The higher your station, the fewer your liberties)
Gaius Sallustius Crispus

1

CONSTANTINE

The greatest affront happened at the imperial river city of Carnuntum. That day, in those marbled halls, the Lords of the Tetrarchy assumed they could strip me of my station. I had rebuffed their attempts and let them know in no uncertain terms that I was Constantine and I would remain Augustus of the West, heir to my father's realm. A mere month had passed since that grand congress and my stubborn refusal. I must admit it had fired my pride to assert myself so and witness them gasping in ire. Yet what might those curs think were they to see me now: crouched in the musty ferns of a Germanian hillside nook like an outlaw, my bear pelt and black leather cuirass blending into the earthy hillside like my dirt-streaked face in the half-light of this sullen winter's day?

A few shafts of watery sunlight penetrated the sea of freezing mist around me, illuminating the semi-frozen hillside: strewn with a frosty carpet of leaves, dotted with dark green spruce and skeletal brown larch. The valley floor below – the one clear path through these roughs – was carpeted with bracken. The cold gnawed on my skin and stung my nostrils,

3

but not so much as to mask that ubiquitous musty stink of the Germanian woods. Hardy ravens cawed somewhere in the skies above the sea of mist, as if to remind me just how far I was from home, yet all down here was still and silent... eerily silent. Then the sudden, hollow drumming of an unseen woodpecker nearby sent an invisible lance of ice through my breast. With a puff of breath I cursed the winged menace, as if it were scouting for the enemy who had drawn me out here.

The Bructeri – one of the many tribes in the Frankish confederation – were on the move. Coming this way to cross the Rhenus and pour once more into Gaul... *my* realm. I only had myself to blame, for early last year I had put two of their many kings to death in Treverorum's arena. Yes, it was in the name of vengeance that the tribes had mobilised. But now, of all times? *Marching to war in the grip of winter?* I seethed. *And you wonder why we Romans call you barbarians!*

I could not ignore the tribal threat, yet equally I could ill afford to be here. For back across the river and all over imperial lands, the hearsay and consequences of Carnuntum were already spreading like a plague. A chatter rose within my mind, each voice urgent and shrill, like hooks being dragged through my head, all demanding attention...

I closed my eyes and pressed the tip of my forefinger to my thumb. I fought at first to steady my angry breath. Soon, it slowed. The only noise now was that of gentle birdsong somewhere beyond the hills, and the distant gurgle of the Rhenus. I unlocked a precious vault of distant memories then; of Mother coddling me as a boy. Of Minervina, my sweet wife for precious few years before she had died in childbirth. The two people in my life with whom I had known complete peace. No, I corrected myself, for there was a third. His face ranged alongside those of the other two: *Maxentius*.

I thought of times long gone: the boyhood days when first he and I had met at Treverorum; Maxentius' wedding celebrations at Sirmium – eventful to say the least; our paths crossing in Antioch and again in Nicomedia where our families spent a whole spring and summer as one. Golden times. Gone now… like our friendship. My eyes peeled open, a sour taste rising from the back of my throat.

Maxentius, I mouthed, bitterly this time. These days, there remained only two strands of commonality between us: our estrangement from the Tetrarchy – me as the 'False Augustus' and him declared as an outright enemy of Rome – and our will to each make the West our own. Yet it was duly mine. How could the man who had once been like a brother to me stubbornly believe it was his? How?!

An animal howl penetrated the fog from somewhere down on the bracken-strewn path: lasting, guttural and untamed, my thoughts scattering like birds.

A loquacious man once told me that a soldier is but a man with a sword. Well, just as a man stirs when the sun rises, and hungers when his belly grows empty, a soldier becomes an altered beast when he hears the savage harbingers of battle. My shoulders stiffened, my mouth drained of moisture and my eyes grew keen like a hawk's, sensing every lick of fog that moved down there, hearing the blood crashing in my ears like a war drum.

When they came, it was as if they had leapt from my nightmares. The curtain of fog split and the dark shapes spewed forth like a murky, distended torrent along the valley floor. Like heralds from *Tartarus*, they were: fire in their eyes and flowing red locks and beards to match. They wore wolfskins on their heads, complete with fangs and glaring glass eyes as if to exaggerate their ferocity… as if they needed to! I counted as best I could as they ran through the semi-frozen mud: hundreds, a thousand... nearly two thousand, clutching sharpened steel and cajoling each other with gruff, guttural chants and cries cast from snarling mouths. Even the verbose fool with the low opinion of soldiers could not have mistaken such a sight: the Bructeri were coming to war.

From my refuge among the ferns, I twisted to look over my shoulder. Nothing... nothing to be seen. My cohort were well placed and well hidden along the crests this side of the vale. Just two cohorts – one of the Minervia and one of the Cornuti – merely nine hundred men against at least twice that number, for it was all I could spare. Every other force of mine was stretched thinly across my eastern and southern borders – hastened there as soon as I had returned from Carnuntum. After that I had barely enough time to rouse the Cornuti from Treverorum, and these hardy Minervia ranks from the river fortress at Bonna, and bring them here.

I caught sight of one hiding centurion, his head rising above a tuft of long grass and the whites of his eyes wide at the sight of the Bructeri. His gaze flicked from the flood of warriors along the valley floor to me and back again. He wore dark leather armour, just as I had demanded of the rest of his comrades. Dark, like these infernal woods. Black, like the clash that was to come. I saw his chest rising and falling, his tongue darting out to dampen his lips. He and every other legionary waited not on the right moment; they waited on me. But damn, they would have risen and charged down those valley sides onto sharpened stakes for me, so fiercely loyal were they.

I placed a hand on the hilt of my *spatha*, watching the passing Bructeri. My gaze latched on to one tall, broad warrior in the midst of their procession. This was their leader,

Hisarnis – instantly recognisable from his flowing iron-grey hair and braided beard – a wily general. He cajoled his men by beating his well-honed *francisca* axe against the boss of his shield – painted gold and adorned with the emblem of a blood-red winged demon – and bellowing out some homily. It was time. I shot up to my full height and tore the blade from my scabbard with a steely *zing*, thrusting it overhead. 'Minervia, *rise!*'

At once, a trio of *buccinae* blared, the wail of the horns filling the vale. The valley sides came alive: a line of my legionaries rose up on this ridge from their hiding places, clad in a hard carapace of black armour and carrying dark green shields, glistening like giant scarabs. Across the void rose a line of leather-armoured Cornuti bearing twin feathers on their helms. This regiment had once been a Frankish tribe. Now, they served as a fine bodyguard. Leading them was big Batius, my one-time childhood mentor, now *Tribunus* of the Cornuti and more than a brother to me. A bull of a man with an oversized jaw permanently shaded in stubble who had never once shown a hint of fear despite the many wars we had been through. I saw him hold his sword aloft like me, and as I chopped my blade down like an accusing finger towards the valley floor, so did he.

'*Advance!*' I roared.

'*Advance!*' Batius echoed, the back of his throat as red as the twin serpents on his Cornuti shield and the twin feathers jutting from the sides of his helm shuddering.

The two parties of my men unleashed a cry and surged downhill, boots snapping and crunching through bracken and undergrowth, each line converging on the valley floor like the jaws of a wolf. I slid on my plumed helm, wrenched the chinstrap tight and surged after them. I took a place on the right of the line and rapped my sword on my iron shield boss, urging those running with me to do likewise with their spears, ushering a din of iron over the valley. The valley floor jostled before me as I charged, my bear pelt rippling in my wake. Again I thought of the fat, slovenly whoresons in Carnuntum. *If only they could see me now,* I thought again, this time with a feverish grin, *look me in the eye and tell me I am not Protector of the West.*

The torrent of Bructeri fighters stumbled and slowed, their heads switching this way and that, mouths agape as they beheld the waves of imperial soldiers haring down towards them from either side. Hisarnis yelled some command to the man by his side who blew into a war horn furiously, again and again, the wail rising high into the air and no doubt sailing over the forest for many miles, then the Bructeri leader howled to his rough column of men to draw together, the front and rear contracting into the middle and forming a packed oval. They passed shields to those on the edges and those within the oval hoisted more shields overhead, obeying Hisarnis' frantic orders and taking the shape of a *testudo*-like formation they had picked up from centuries of fighting against the legions.

'Don't let them gather!' I snarled across the line of legionaries as we ran.

My Minervia officers pounced on this. '*Spiculae!*' they bellowed as we came to within fifty paces of the valley floor. I heard the same cry echoing from Batius' lot descending the opposite slope. The legionaries slowed a fraction and raised their javelins, before hurling them like swooping broods of raptors down onto the packed Bructeri. The breath stilled in my lungs: battle, you see, trades in a currency of heartbeats. A moment sooner, and the spiculae would have riven the

Bructeri warriors and might even have ended this before swords could clash. But the Bructeri presented their screen of shields and a thick rattle of steel striking wood rang out as the javelins quivered – nine in every ten blocked. Yes, a swathe of these forest warriors fell in puffs of blood where their shields crumbled or were held too low, but we had been too slow.

At least the horn-blower with the seemingly bottomless lungs had been struck, I realised. The fellow was gawping, swaying, the horn still at his lips but a spiculum that had plunged into the mouth of the instrument and torn through his throat now jutted from the back of his neck, putting paid to his efforts. A gout of dark blood spat from the horn and he collapsed.

'Onwards!' I bellowed, knowing each man would have seen his javelin strike evaded or blocked and read this as the first signs of reversal. I had seen it before – the tides of combat changing on the natural ebb and flow of a man's courage. Indeed, I too felt a pang of fright at the thought that it could all end here in this filthy wilderness: the dogs from Carnuntum would surely laud news of the False Augustus' ignominious death in such a clash and hoot with laughter at the thought of my corpse rotting in the Germanian woods like a parody of Varus. So I raced a few steps ahead of the line, such was my desire to show my ranks that the day could still be ours. 'They march to pillage your homes. They journey to slaughter your families. End their journey here, now!'

It seemed to reignite their spirit, and a fresh roar erupted along the line as we completed our descent then bounded onto the valley floor and came to within thirty paces of the corralled Bructeri.

Hisarnis' mouth stretched wide as he bawled some jagged

cry, flecking the air with spittle. I did not hear the order, but the sight of the Bructeri drawing their francisca axes underarm was a spectacle that any legionary serving on the Rhenus knew well from his blackest nightmares, and I barely needed to shout my next command.

'Shields, low!' I bellowed as the Bructeri hurled the axes across the ground. The weapons skipped and leapt, kicking up shards of bracken and showers of semi-frozen mud. I lowered my shield just before one thwacked into it, burying itself deep into the timber and even part-cleaving the iron boss.

I heard and almost felt the thick crunch of bone by my side as one of my men was too slow, the axe smashing his ankle, sweeping his leg away under him and sending him into the air, head and feet changing places, helmet falling away. He tumbled forward across the ground and another two axes punched into him – one breaching and almost disappearing inside his leather armour and into his chest cavity, the other hammering into his helmetless forehead and casting a pool of dark blood from the deep and instantly mortal wound. From the corner of my eye and in Batius' line opposite I saw plenty more fall. Hisarnis boomed again, and this time the Bructeri hoisted their *ango* javelins overhead. My flesh crept at the sight of these missiles and their viciously barbed heads.

'Shields, *up!*' I cried as the javelins sailed up, then dipped and hurtled down at us. A classic and deadly combination attacking low with the ground axe then high with the spears. As I swept my shield up. I caught sight of the glint in Hisarnis' eye – that look that betrays a man's hubris in sight of victory. The barbed javelins smacked into my two closing lines and I was sure nearly a hundred more of my precious legionaries fell. I saw one pirouette, gawping skywards and along the shaft of the ango that had plunged right through his cheek – now spouting blood. But still my forces ran until there were but paces between us and our foe. I heard Hisarnis roar with his men in defiance, saw them brace, then I leapt at their lines with my shoulder wedged behind my shield.

A great clatter of timber on timber and the rasp of iron striking iron rang out. The breath was forced from my lungs in the shoving that followed. I battered my shield into the face of one foe, breaking his nose, then slid my spatha round and up into the gut of another. Our weaker numbers had somehow upheld the momentum of our charge down the valley and we pushed against Hisarnis' Bructeri pack, Batius' lot pushing likewise on the other side.

'Stay together,' I cried, but within moments, the battle lines crumbled into a frantic melee: legionaries spearing out, slashing with their swords, Bructeri hacking through flesh with their axes and blades, men rolling in the mud, grappling one another, fists and legs flying. Dirt and blood flew up all around me. I blocked the longsword strike of one warrior then ducked what I thought was a flying axe, only to realise it was the cap of one of Batius' men's skulls. The maimed legionary gazed absently at the top of his head, hurtling away at pace like a discus, as runnels of black blood slopped down the sides of his face like a grotesque volcano before he crumpled to the ground.

When another ango javelin hummed past me I pounced upon the thrower, butting at his face and feeling his teeth crack as my brow met his mouth. I ran him through before he could draw his sword, then found myself facing Hisarnis. Now this man was some age, but still he resembled a bull standing on its hind legs. He drew out an axe in each hand and goaded me to come for him.

'Come, then, rogue-emperor!' he snarled, his grey hair plastered to his face with dirt and blood.

News from Carnuntum had obviously travelled far and fast, permeating even across the imperial borders and into this accursed land, I realised, trying as best I could to ignore the insult.

'You must have thought you had us?' he continued, circling. Blades flashed all around me, men falling in swathes. 'But a good general thinks a step ahead, aye?' he said with a throaty chuckle. 'Which is why I split my men. March divided and fight as one... is that not a maxim of your famed legions?'

I noticed him glance past my shoulder to the valley side behind me as he said this. I levelled my sword at him then snatched a look and saw how the fog there swished and swirled again. I thought of the barbarian war horn and those frantic signals.

Hisarnis grinned broadly now, glancing round and seeing how my men were locked in combat, ensnared. 'Now it is just a matter of waiting for them to come...'

I replied as calmly as I could: 'I couldn't agree more.' I watched as his brow knitted in confusion, the hubris clearly fading, then added: 'A good general plans one step ahead. A better one looks beyond.' Now the confusion vanished, replaced with outright horror as he looked again past my shoulder. At the same time, like rodents scattering from a flame, the Bructeri warriors around us drew back from the skirmish and away from that slope, gasps of lament filling the air as they beheld what had appeared up there, while my men erupted in a chorus of victorious cheers.

'*No!*' Hisarnis gasped, staggering back a few steps, his eyes riveted to the brim of the slope behind me.

'Here are your reinforcements, Noble Hisarnis!' a jagged

voice called from the valley top behind me. I did not turn around. I did not need to. A moment of near silence followed, with just the gasping of exhausted men to be heard. Then came the *thud-thud-thud* of something heavy bouncing down the slope. The severed head of Hisarnis' general, still bent in a death rictus, rolled past me and to a halt before the aged chieftain.

Now I turned away from the spluttering Hisarnis to behold the line of hide-armoured, wild-haired men up there who had brought the gruesome gift. These were the Regii, once men of these forests before my late father had recruited them to serve as his bodyguard. A thousand strong, I had made sure never to commit them to any frontier or garrison post. They existed to shield me and edge days like this – days when my legions were thinly stretched. Their leader, Krocus, his auburn, pointed beard and long, bound hair framing a somewhat manic and craggy expression, looked at me like an expectant mastiff at mealtime. It would have been so easy to let him and his warriors loose upon the Bructeri, but I shook my head. With a slight slump of disappointment, Krocus peeled the spiral-etched conical helm from his head and stabbed his sword into the earth.

I turned back to Hisarnis. 'Now, unless you have anticipated my ruse and have another wing of men on their way, I believe this fight is over.'

The clatter of enemy weapons being thrown to the ground was answer enough.

Fires crackled all over the encampment we made that night – a sturdy ditch and palisade that claimed a patch of those damned lands as our own – fending off the fierce cold that came with a cloudless sky streaked with stars. The Minervia cohort had lost nearly a third of their number that day and the Cornuti had counted one hundred and seven dead, but they talked with great cheer, grinding their grain, baking bread, cooking meat and supping watered wine as they spoke of the lost fondly. The fallen would never leave them; it was the soldier's way.

Sitting on a stool in the half-light from a torch on one of the watchtowers, I tipped a small clay vial until a droplet of oil splashed onto my already-cleaned sword. With a rag, I wiped it again. I saw myself in the blade: broad, flat features and flaxen – albeit dirt-streaked – hair that hung in gentle curls on my brow. It was how I remembered myself as a boy... but for the distant look in my eyes: azure like a summer sky, Mother used to say; cobalt like wintry ice, these days. The foul respite of battle over, the chatter had returned to my mind. It was almost time to leave this dank wilderness, cross the Rhenus and return to imperial lands, to the nest of problems... so many problems.

It had been less than a month since Carnuntum, yet already the empire bubbled and seethed from within. The Tetrarchy – Diocletian's great dream of four emperors – was bursting at the seams with rival claimants and barely bridled hatred. Before I had even returned from the conference I heard word that they had enforced a trade embargo on Gaul, Hispania and Britannia – my heartlands. Thus, my coffers would soon begin to dwindle and my people would be quick to voice their discontent. The armies I had raised in the last few years, which had once seemed numerous, now appeared fragile and thinly stretched when faced with the forces of the quarrelsome east.

'They,' I said aloud with a wry snort. It was not *they*, but *him*. Galerius. The Herdsman. The serpent who had slithered up the Tetrarchic hierarchy, playing Emperor Diocletian then taking the post as senior Augustus for himself. Parthicus Maximus, Gothicus Maximus, sired by Mars, the cur claimed of himself. He was still the foulest creature I had yet endured. I recalled the moment in Carnuntum when Galerius' lackeys had been proclaimed in the Tetrarchy – Maximinus Daia as Caesar of the East and Licinius snatching my post as Augustus of the West. The Herdsman had seemed triumphant, knowing he had me cornered. I could have accepted the decree and died a slow political death, but he knew I would not. He knew the announcement would give him the war against me he craved. Once again my thoughts turned to the other in this great game.

Maxentius.

The young leader who sat in Rome had plentiful armies and far fewer borders to protect with them. With Africa under his rule he also had control of the majority of the West's grain. How long before he imposed an embargo of his own – on grain shipments from Africa to my northern lands? I stabbed the clean blade into the dirt, rested my elbows on my knees and let my head slump. *Damn you, Maxentius.*

Crunching footsteps scattered my spiralling thoughts. Batius came over and sat beside me, tugging at a strip of glistening, freshly roasted meat with his teeth. 'I still think you made the wrong choice,' he said.

I raised my head and cast him a sour look. The big man responded with a disarming smile. He was one of the few who knew how to deal with my foul moods. 'Which of my recent dreadful decisions are you referring to?'

'Hisarnis,' he replied. 'What's to stop one of his lot deciding he's not up to leading them?' He sucked on a wineskin as if to punctuate his argument. 'They might knife him tonight and turn their horde around – head straight back for the fording point upriver.'

When I reached out to take the wineskin, he withdrew it and offered me a mere water skin instead.

'Damn you, Batius. Damn everyone!' I groaned, waving the water away. But he was right to be concerned. Yes, we had made Hisarnis swear an oath and we had stripped his surviving Bructeri warriors of their weapons, but the tribes were notoriously fickle and quick to raise new chieftains and despatch of old.

'You think he'll keep his word?' Batius asked, carefully pouring a measure of wine into the water skin.

I nodded, taking this tincture and slaking my thirst, enjoying the sourness but slightly disappointed at its lack of potency. 'Hisarnis knows he was beaten today and beaten well. He'll deliver the silver I asked of him.' It had been a knife-edge choice. I could have ordered the Bructeri slain to a man earlier that day. Indeed, had circumstance allowed, I would have. Instead, I demanded coin from them, taking three of Hisarnis' brothers as hostage to ensure the payment would be delivered by the ides of the month. Those tribal siblings sat silently, roped together and well guarded at the heart of the camp. 'Coin it must be,' I sighed. Coin I would soon need once the trade embargo took hold. Coin I had to obtain were I to uphold my current armies, let alone raise the extra number I desperately needed. I could count upon nearly ninety thousand men. Some might think only a deranged leader would crave more spears and horse than this, but then my armies were dwarfed by the Italian and African forces of Maxentius – almost twice as strong as mine since he had acquired the conquered armies of Severus and many regiments of Galerius – and even more so by the legions of the East.

'Coin,' Batius repeated mutedly.

I detected an edge in his tone. 'Batius?'

He failed to meet my eye and muttered something. 'Bloody pointy-bearded, tree-worshipping arsehole… found something… thinks he's clever,' he said, jabbing a thumb over towards the campfire where the Regii were cooking a spitted boar. Krocus was regaling them with some ribald tale, making a pelvic thrusting motion into some invisible protagonist.

I noticed Batius fiddling with some object in his palm. 'Hand it over,' I insisted.

The big man reluctantly dropped it into my outstretched hand.

I stared at it for some time, not quite wanting to believe. The gold coin bore the haughty relief of Galerius upon it – the Herdsman's blocky, shapeless face rendered somewhat more agreeable than in real life by the mint's sculptor. It had been struck very, very recently. 'You say Krocus found this—'

'—in the purse of one of the dead Bructeri,' Batius finished for me.

The crescendo of chatter rose once more inside my head. The Bructeri had not set out across the icy lands in some blood feud to avenge their fallen kings. They had mobilised against me because Galerius had paid them to do so. I clasped my fingers over the coin and my fist shook, the nails digging into my palm.

War was not a matter of if, but of when…

…and with whom.

2

MAXENTIUS

ROME, 5TH DECEMBER 308 AD

I was the *enemy* of Rome. I was its master, but apparently also its enemy. I found it rather distasteful that men who cared not a wet slap for Rome, and who had never even visited the place, could take its name in defiance of me.

I stood at the balustrade, looking down into the crisp, frost-whitened grass of the stadium garden, built by that most loathed of emperors: Domitian, and found myself wondering idly whether perhaps history had abused that man's reputation and that mayhap he had been in truth just a Roman trying to maintain order in a chaotic world. Certainly my *peers* in the wide empire would cast me as a creature lower even than Domitian, for all my good intentions. All those preening dogs of the Tetrarchy who yapped and growled, and who had declared to the world my illegitimacy: Galerius, Licinius and Daia, even the retired Diocletian and my own father. Of the whole barking pack, only my onetime friend Constantine did not drag my name through the mud, though nor did he champion it, while he vented his frustration by breaking barbarian heads across the Rhenus. Still, at least while he concentrated on that troubled border he was not challenging me over my domain.

At one end of the peaceful garden, bathed in its glittering wintry sheen, the emperor Septimius Severus had converted the apsidal curve into a small arena for private displays, and today it held a martial contest for the first time in many years. My son Romulus – the light in my darkness and the whole of my heart – sparred with heavy wooden practice swords against Ruricius Pompeianus. He was surprisingly good, holding his own despite the decades of military service his opponent could claim. It alleviated a little of my panic at the thought of my dear son serving in the military. Not enough, but a little.

In contrast to their measured, careful, even stately dance of martial skill, the real fight was going on a dozen paces along the balustrade where Anullinus – my Praetorian Prefect and the man who had propelled me to the throne in the first place – unleashed his verbal artillery in a shower of brutal barbed invective against his enemy Volusianus, the former Governor of Africa who had brought me that province and saved me from destruction at such an early stage of my career. Two men who had made me. One had lifted me up and the other had sheltered me. I owed them both a debt too large for one life. Oddly, I owed them far more than I ever felt I owed my own suppurating boil of a father. And yet they remained permanently at odds, arguing so often over so little that I spent my time wanting to crack their heads together and remind them that they were noble Romans, imperial advisors and, most importantly, grown men.

'You are the commander of the Praetorian Guard,' spat Volusianus angrily. 'You may be brave and strategically minded, but the fact remains that you are little more than a glorified legionary, with no business airing his thoughts on the running of an empire. Leave that to those of us who have at least governed a province and have the faintest idea how to handle administration.'

I pinched the bridge of my nose, bitter experience telling me that listening to much more of this was going to bring on a headache of Herculean proportions. Off to my left, even with my eyes squeezed shut, I could picture Anullinus reddening and gasping with indignation.

'Remember, Volusianus, that some of us were administering Rome and dealing with its multitude of problems even before the emperor took the purple, while your experience keeping the border safe from a few camel-humpers and working through the troubling problems of one of the richest, calmest, most well-fed provinces in the empire qualifies you at best to oversee the imperial gardens.'

I pinched tighter as Volusianus resorted to name-calling, intimating that a rather far-fetched and fanciful selection of animals had had a hand in his opposite number's ancestry. I stopped listening at *camelopardalis*, walking swiftly along the balustrade away from the exchange, knowing that even the clonking and grunting and the rhythmic calls of numbered moves from the friendly combat below would be a balm after listening to my two chief advisors tearing holes in each other. Anullinus's brother Gaius had been the governor of Africa before Volusianus, and somehow, despite the fact that Anullinus and his brother were in no way close, it seemed that Volusianus extended the blame for the mess he had been forced to put right in Africa to Anullinus himself. The Praetorian Prefect had been tarred with the same brush as his imprudent sibling, and in return, Anullinus clearly resented the importance Volusianus had managed to secure in my court in such a short time. One day they would simply kill each other, I thought sourly.

Romulus executed a rather interesting manoeuvre as I watched, leaping back out of the way of Ruricius' thrust, using his left foot to launch himself into the air and his right to change his direction of movement on the raised stones at the arena edge so that he spun and came down close to his teacher, delivering a swipe to Ruricius' upper arm that hurt enough to make him drop his sword. Romulus laughed lightly as he picked up the practice weapon and handed it back to his appreciative teacher. Perhaps he *would* make a good military man. Despite my fears that my son was too mollycoddled and juvenile, always wanting to play his games, all those adventurous activities had made him strong, lithe and fearless.

I resolved to take him to the races again at the next event. Not that he didn't go often enough. In fact, in the past month he had rather taken to the racing, showing his imperial favour to the white team – the city's true sporting underdogs – in a manner that I found endearing. But while he enthused about the racing and now, on occasion, even socialised with some of their racers, I rarely had the opportunity to accompany him, for Rome was a beast with a thousand black mouths, all lashing out with needs to be met. And the gods knew I could hardly leave Volusianus and Anullinus to feed the beast.

My eyes strayed past Romulus to where my younger son – Aurelius – sat, painfully contorted with his deformities, wrapped in a blanket against the cold as he applauded to the best of his ability his brother's efforts. Romulus turned with a wide grin and saluted his poor younger sibling with his sword, spinning back sharply to catch Ruricius' blow just before it hit his leg.

Rising, my eyes caught a flash of white in the apsed viewing box across the stadium garden. My wife, who kept herself separate from me in the Severan wing, all solitude and disdain and as icy cold as the December weather could hope to become. Who had she been watching? *Not I* was the only clear answer, for our arranged and enforced marriage against which she had railed from the beginning had never had her feeling more trapped than now, shackled to an enemy of Rome while her father barraged me with barbed accusations. Our world was one of silent and cold co-existence, and I could see no future in which it might be me she was looking for while her father and I remained at war.

'*Domine?*'

I glanced around and found one of the palace's senior slaves waiting patiently, head bowed in respect. I tried to recall the man's name, but it escaped me. The staff of the Palatine palace were too numerous to keep track of, and as soon as my new villa on the Via Appia was habitable I would be moving there with my own people and leaving this place of nightmare histories and wickedness to Volusianus and Anullinus, long may they argue over it. The latter had a house down at the corner of the place, opposite the great amphitheatre and his ready access to my apartments was starting to wear on me. Where Volusianus lived, I couldn't recall. Seemingly under my feet, from the feel of things.

I gestured at the slave. 'Yes?'

The man moved a few paces closer, still bowed. 'Domine, the deputation you were expecting has arrived.'

I frowned. I couldn't remember anything on my schedule this morning, but it wouldn't be empty. It never was. 'Remind me?' I prompted.

'Ah... the Christians, Domine.'

'Oh yes. Good. You have them in the *aula regia*?'

'Yes, Domine.'

'How many?'

'There are but three men, Domine. They have been checked for weapons and six of the Praetorians watch over them.'

'Good.' I was fairly sure I was under no threat of violence from Christians, who by their professed beliefs could not kill lest their God punish them for it. And yet I remembered those dreadful days back in Nicomedia with my friend Constantine... with Constantine *when he had been my friend*... in which the Christians had risen in ire and burned buildings and killed soldiers. They may *claim* to be so pacific that they melt in the presence of violence, but I knew them for bloody-minded, resilient and desperate creatures. I would never underestimate the strength of Christians. Even the relatively quiet and downtrodden variety we had in Rome.

'Stay here, and when my son finishes his practice see that he spends some time cooling down in the baths rather than going straight out and cavorting with his racing friends. Let him know where I am if he needs me.'

I became aware that Volusianus and Anullinus had finally broken off their argument at this new interruption and were making for me. I held up my hand to halt them in their tracks – I had had quite enough of their bickering today. 'I am in quiet discussion with three holy men, not running into battle against slavering Franks. If I need you, I will send for you.'

Turning my back on their disapproving faces I made my way through the private rooms of the palace, out across the immaculately tended and crisp white peristyle garden that separated my temporary residence from the public rooms of state, and in through one of the twin rear doors of my audience chamber. The aula regia was three storeys high yet a single room, designed by that same damned emperor Domitian to impress his guests. Constructed of a dozen different-coloured marbles and with the finest painted walls in the city, it dazzled in the light cast by the high windows that surrounded it. At the lowest level, each alcove held a statue of a great emperor, the ones who had eventually become unpopular being replaced by their successors as time progressed. Augustus and Vespasian, Trajan and Marcus Aurelius scoured the room with coloured marble eyes, and the nearest of the twin alcoves? They held myself, of course, and the man with whom I had come so far only to find a broken bridge between us: Constantine.

In one of their rare subjects of complete agreement, Volusianus and Anullinus had urged me to pull that statue down and replace it with someone less hostile to my realm. But I somehow couldn't pull down his statue. It would be like admitting defeat. Like admitting that we were enemies and there was no healing the open wound that divided us. Indeed, there were as many statues of him in the city as of me. I was never a great one for self-aggrandisement, and I had commissioned many likenesses of my old friend when he and my sister married, hoping that my brother-in-law and I would create a new Rome together.

An impossible dream.

As the guard at the entrance quietly closed the door behind me and I looked back and forth between those two statues, my gaze also fell upon the side door to the Palatine basilica. I had not entered that room since the awful reading of entrails less than a month ago – was that all it was? I could not go in – just the thought made me shudder. I could hardly wait to move out of this place and into my new villa. Even as I put on my most imperial mask and walked benevolently towards the deputation of Christians, I promised myself I would spare an hour later to hound my master builders for a completion date.

'Good morning, gentlemen.'

Normally I would have entered the room with my *lictors* and attendants, my guards, my advisors and even a musician who would provide the fanfare before the proclaiming of my many titles. But the Christians were a strange, mistrustful lot and treating them to a little show of munificence in the form of more personal attention seemed a cheap way to build bridges.

The three men bowed deeply and I allowed a little genuineness into my smile at that. A gesture of respect. Their sort would never worship an emperor, but so long as I had their respect and their loyalty, they could babble to their Judean god as much as they liked.

'Greetings, Imperator. We are truly grateful for your time in this matter.'

I nodded an acknowledgement and settled into my seat as the three stood before me like some parody of the Capitoline triad. The two Praetorian guardsmen at my shoulders shuffled slightly as they tensed, ready for any trouble from these odd cultists. But as I looked into the men's eyes I saw no malice towards me. Just hope... and a little too much zeal if I am honest. The one at the centre of the triad, the Jove figure in my own little private joke, was the speaker and clearly the senior. I gestured to him.

'I understand you crave an imperial boon?'

Jove glanced at Juno and Minerva to his sides and I had to fight to stifle a chuckle as I imagined the two serious Christian clerics in women's garb. I kept my visage austere while the leader replied.

'As Your Majesty will be aware, the Church of our Saviour

in the city has a long and proud history of supreme *pontifices* that stretches back to the noble and holy Peter, whom the damned tyrant Nero brutally murdered.'

I had to hand it to the man. He had just stated the power of his claim and the centuries-old lineage of his cult while insulting the emperor of the time and all without actually saying anything that might give me reason for offence. After all, Nero *was* a damned tyrant. And he *did* murder their first senior pontifex. I saw Minerva by his side – all wisdom of course – nodding his agreement.

'I am aware of this,' I replied. 'I am also aware that the great Diocletian ended the line of your high priests some six years ago now. I forget… did he have the last one burned or crucified?' It was an offhand question. Cruel, really, but I didn't like being played by this man and I felt the need to shake him and put myself on top again. He recoiled slightly. My words had hit him just as I had intended.

'Both, Your Majesty. As well as the hook and the sword. He died hard for what he believed. For what we *all* believe.'

'All?' I prompted with a raised eyebrow.

'All Christians,' sighed the man, aware that he was losing his edge. Good. My turn.

'And because Diocletian has retired and I rule in Rome, and because you know, as does everyone, that I hold little regard for his successor, and most of all because I have stopped the persecution of your sect in my city, you think I will change things?'

The man nodded and cast his gaze downwards meekly. I smiled. Back in command, I could afford to be generous.

'You wish to reinstate the supreme pontifex of your cult without bringing down imperial anger?'

'Yes, Majesty.'

My eyes rose at the sound of a gentle click to see a side door open and admit a single figure. Zenas. The praetor in command of my Urban Cohorts and an unabashed Christian himself, he had unrestricted access to all the public areas of my palace, and much of the private wing too. No great shock that he might show up for this particular meeting. In fact, I had been quite surprised that he hadn't been there waiting with them.

'Do you even need such a man?' I asked. 'If your sect has survived these past six years – and even grown, if I am to believe my advisors – without one, why do you need him?'

The third of the triad – Juno, of course – now spoke. 'In the absence of a supreme pontifex, Marcellus here has been tending to his duties.' He gestured to the man in the centre. Naturally. He was the leader. I was enjoying toying with them.

'So despite the ban on your post and the execution of your predecessor under proper Roman law, you, Marcellus, have been a hidden high priest, defying imperial authority?'

Marcellus was looking a lot less like mighty Jove now as his eyes took on a wild look. I laughed lightly and gestured with both hands to encompass the entire triad. 'I jest with you. Am I to understand that you would wish this secret priest to be ratified and to be able to lead your cult in the open air without fear of persecution or prosecution?'

The men on either side nodded hopefully, while Marcellus himself kept his face lowered, all respect. I looked up at Zenas, who was standing silently at the side of the hall, almost a direct copy of the great Trajan who loomed in cold marble behind him. An accident? I wouldn't put it past Zenas to stand there on purpose, acquiring an air of ancient nobility from the long-dead hero emperor behind him.

'What say you?'

Zenas frowned. 'Domine?'

'You are familiar with the problems of governance in my city, being one of my most senior officers, but you are also aware of these men and the needs of their sect, since you are one of them, are you not? What say you to this Marcellus?'

Zenas padded across the room towards me, stopping equidistant between myself and my visitors. 'Marcellus has carried out the duties of the Roman Pope very efficiently in the absence of an official incumbent. He is popular in our community. I would give him my support.'

I nodded. In fairness, I had intended to say yes from the start, but a show of consideration always makes a decision look more thorough. I knew little about their cult's workings and cared even less, but I did want them on my side. And I wanted peace.

'Very well. I agree to your request. You may crown – or invest, or whatever it is you do – this man as your high priest, with the blessings of the emperor and freedom of worship in my lands.'

I held up my hand in a gesture of benevolence as the three men smiled in relief. 'I would like a few moments of your new pontifex's time in private, if I may. He will join you in the courtyard shortly.'

Summarily dismissed, the other two Christians glanced nervously at their new chief priest, clearly worried that I planned to throw them out and then crucify the man in their absence. Marcellus gave them reassuring looks and told them he would meet them outside. To add weight to his words, Zenas stepped protectively close. Still unhappy, the other two priests left the room and walked out into the winter sun.

I waited until the door clicked shut and I was alone with just the new Christian Pope, my Urban Cohort commander and half a dozen Praetorians. Then I rose and stepped down to face Marcellus, lifting his chin so that his gaze met mine.

'I am pleased that you have come to me to ratify this officially, Pontifex Marcellus. Know that I am no enemy of your faith, for all I cannot fathom its point.' I allowed my light tone to darken and take on an air of threat. 'Know also that I will not tolerate unrest or discord in my realm, whether it comes from cobblers, chandlers or Christians. I do not know what your role entails within your Church but I hereby add to your burdens the following task: keep your people content and peaceful. You can call yourself what you wish and pray however you like as long as your Christians are also Romans and they cause me no trouble.'

My somewhat rocky but generally peaceful history with that peculiar sect began in earnest that day and for all the difficulties I might encounter, for now all was good.

The new Christian leader was escorted from the room, bowing as he went, and my eyes slid again to the statue of my adversary, all cold marble stoicism in his alcove. Constantine would have known better than I what to do here. His family had prepared him for this strange sect. In a huff with myself, I pulled my gaze back. Maybe I should have let Volusianus and Anullinus, my warring twins, tear down that statue after all.

3

CONSTANTINE

AUGUSTA TREVERORUM, 14TH DECEMBER 308 AD

After days of chasing down recalcitrant tribes and retreating when they massed against us, the gruelling struggle with the Franks lessened. It was merely a hiatus – only a fool would believe otherwise – but welcome all the same. We left behind those grim forests, crossed the Rhenus and returned to the empire once more. It was a mercy that we did so, a mercy that several hundred of my men would never enjoy. The sight of their graves, back in the woods, never left me. Every dead comrade, every pyre and every burial is with me, even to this day – from that clash and the many others. But the soldier's way is to laugh off grief, or at least to make it appear that way.

In my wake, the legionaries of the Minervia sang as they marched, breaths puffing in the icy air, their ribald tunes seeking to outdo those of Krocus and his Regii. I heard Batius lead them in a spirited line about a barbarian's personal hygiene. There followed a chorus of spluttering disbelief from Krocus, who replied with a feisty verse comparing the length of a legionary's appendage unfavourably to that of a mouse's.

I chuckled, guiding Celeritas, my faithful dappled-grey

stallion, across a short stretch of meadow – speckled silver with frost – and rode down the hillside that led into the Mosella valley. A look at the mid-morning sun and the meandering river ahead reminded me of the many times I had ridden this path. 'By noonday we will be home,' I called over my shoulder. They cheered, distracted from their filthy – if thoroughly entertaining – songs.

Home. A simple, solitary word. A place of sanctuary, warmth and love. For most men, aye. Me? I had called many places my home over the years: Naissus, Salona, Nicomedia, Alexandria, Eboracum, Antioch and others. A soldier's life had ensured that I never rested in one place too long. Never in any of those fine cities did I truly feel I was in my rightful place. But in Augusta Treverorum, that had changed.

As I rode, I watched the bends of the river peel back before me until I caught sight of the stoutly walled city that had finally granted me a modicum of sanctuary. The towers commanded a fine view along the valley and over the surrounding countryside and the battlements were studded with silvery helms. Red-tiled domes and marble halls – scaffolded and specked with the tiny forms of workers – were taking shape from within as my programme to aggrandise the city's northern quarter continued. Smoke rose lazily from the countless dwellings within and the sharp, fresh air was suddenly spiced with the scent of it all: baking bread, cooking fish and woodsmoke.

The men saw it too and cheered again. Sighting us, the watch atop the great, smoke-stained eastern gate heralded our return, sounding a trio of *cornua*, the G-shaped brass horns filling the Mosella valley with a paean that suggested we had not only beaten back the Franks but vanquished them entirely.

We passed under the shadow of the gatehouse and made our way towards the palace. A crowd had gathered on the main avenue and now the pleasant aromas were mixed with the ones that come with any congestion of people: dung, sweat and stale wine to name but a few. They drank and cheered as they tossed petals over us. I could not help but notice the throng was seemingly endless, stretching even beyond the well-wishers. Everywhere I looked, the streets were packed. And I was sure there were even more of those damned timber shacks along the base of every temple, hall and *insula*. Grubby and gaunt faces everywhere.

The war with the Franks had been devastating. The farmers and land workers had been terrorised by the Frankish raiding parties that had penetrated my lands all too often. Many had abandoned their crops and their homes and fled for the cities. Many – too many – had come here in search of salvation. How could I explain to them that without their hard work in the fields, there would be no grain to feed the many mouths of my realm? And if I could not adequately protect them out there, what right did I have to demand anything of them? I sighed. That was one of the myriad problems I would have to tackle now the business of battle had receded.

Over the cries of adulation though, I heard their laments. Some cried out to me, pleading for food, begging me for coin. Others, however, cried out not to me, but to their gods. Some offered prayer to Ceres, Goddess of the Harvest, at smoke-stained shrines on street corners. Others sang Christian songs together. United in their will, I thought, but then I saw two groups scuffling by one shrine: fighting over a half loaf of bread. A cursed scrap of bread!

'The gods shun us because you and your followers dishonour them!' one wild-eyed agitator by the shrine of

Ceres snarled, spittle flecking the air as he howled at the Christians. He cradled the bread scrap he had wrested from one Christian and backed away, only for a young man to try and wrest it back.

His friends tried to pull the young one from the confrontation. 'It is not God's way, brother,' they tried to calm him.

'And *that*,' the wild-eyed one rasped, 'is why you are a pox on the empire: you'd rather fall to your knees and pray than take up a sword and shield!'

I snorted at this. The Christians were in the main reluctant to resort to violence, but a fair few had rationalised the word of their God with the reality of their world. Christians served in my legions, no doubt. I recalled then the boyhood memory of that lone Christian legionary on the walls of Naissus.

My thoughts were scattered when the young lad threw his friends off and lunged at the wild-eyed fellow with the bread. In moments, fists were flying and I saw a flash of steel as one man near the shrine of Ceres leapt in with a knife. The sight of faith-fuelled hatred sent a shiver through me – so reminiscent of the persecutions in the East that had brought the great cities there to their knees. Not in my realm, I avowed, not in my city... not in my home. I turned to nod over my shoulder. Batius read the signal and dispatched twelve Cornuti men, who swiftly broke up the trouble.

On we rode and I cast a cold eye at the old basilica as we passed it: the place where my journey had begun, all those years ago on the day my father had chosen to marry into the line of succession. It was something my rivals were keen to remind me of: Constantine the beggar, with not a drop of true imperial blood in his veins. It was with a wry smile that I beheld the roped-off ruin. For only the façade of the old place remained, you see, with a new, grander hall being constructed behind it. A glorious structure that would smother those foul rumours about my worthiness. We passed the huge wool mill, the arms fabrica, the baths and the amphitheatre, then came to the city barracks.

Batius and Krocus had the men fall out here, where they were to see out the rest of the winter. The heaving crowds thinned a little and the three of us then proceeded to the foot of the palace complex: a vast, rectangular peristyle enclosing gardens and orchards. In the centre, like a marble mountain rising from a sea of green, stood a stack of vaulted, red-roofed halls, the tallest of which stood nearly twice as high as the city walls. The two Cornuti standing watch at the entrance to the peristyle stiffened and saluted, clacking their amber shields to their leather-armoured chests, the winter breeze ruffling the feathers they wore either side of their helms.

They parted and we entered the palace gardens, the air thick with the scent of winter blooms. Fountains babbled and birds trilled, hopping from the branches of poplar trees to the beds of pink cyclamen and yellow mimosa. I eyed the palace high sides, etched with tendrils of ivy and beautified with tessellated balconies and gently billowing silken drapes.

Home. My lips played with a smile. For it was only now, freed from the travels of a mere soldier, shorn of the bonds of foul masters and with this marvel of a city to call my own, that I realised it all meant so little: all the broad streets and fine towers, every gilded statue and magnificent hall. I would have been happy with a bare room in a listing insula. Home, you see, is not a matter of mortar, stone or fineries – such things are inconsequential. Home is the place where your loved ones await you. And when they appeared on the steps, I swear my heart swelled against my ribs.

'Father!' Crispus cried, skipping down the stairs and crunching across the gravel, his curls bouncing in his wake. I leapt down from Celeritas' back and crouched, arms extended to catch him. He thudded into me and I stood, lifting him in my embrace. Such moments a man must savour, especially when he is oft apart from his family. Indeed, in my boy's five summers, I had seen all too little of him. Perhaps it was a penance I inflicted upon myself: part of me still believed it had been my fault his mother had died. Sweet Minervina, my first love, had breathed her last as he had breathed his first... and I was not there to save her.

Upon his neck I caught scent of rosewater, and this sped the dark memory from my mind before it could fully form. More, it conjured a joyous grin on my face.

'You grew tired of eating raw boar in the woods?' Fausta said, striding over in Crispus' wake, a stronger waft of the rosewater perfume she wore coming with her.

Some called my marriage to Fausta a political investment, a desperate attempt to buy legitimacy and noble blood. But I had agreed to marry Maxentius' sister not to play the game of power, but because I enjoyed her company, because I trusted her. In truth, part of me did believe our marriage might heal the rift between me and her brother, but is it purely cold and political to desire renewed peace with a one-time friend? In any case, I feared that such hopes were all but faded. Still, Fausta was mine and I hers. She was a fine mother to Crispus too. Just thirteen years old, we had yet to share a bed. She was showing the signs of womanhood, and had taken to wearing kohl and ochre on her fine-boned face, her dark curls bunched on top of her head and spiralling down to her waist: a true beauty. But in truth I craved her company and conversation more than anything else, for she was a shrewd one for her age – always challenging my thoughts, slapping down my hubris when it threatened to veil my wisdom and simply... being there.

My bond with Fausta was but one link to Maxentius' family, and a fine one at that. The other one... not so.

'Ach, there's always one thing to spoil a perfectly good day,' Batius groaned under his breath, squinting at the steps and the shaded arched doorway of the palace.

'Hmm,' Krocus agreed, 'you may have the cock of a mouse and the brain of an ox, but I'll agree with you on that.'

Krocus and Batius in grudging agreement? That meant only one thing: a common threat. I looked over to the steps with them and I must admit my heart sank a little. The portly, waddling figure who lumbered down the steps reeked of many things: wine and meat, usually, but always, *always*, trouble.

'Maximian,' I hailed him, the tenor in my voice underlining my feelings.

'Constantine,' he replied, those hooded green eyes appraising as always. Such a different creature to Fausta. Where his daughter sought truce and tranquillity, Maximian craved strife and friction – enough at least to create a gap into which he could barge uninvited.

He was ruddy-faced, overweight and somewhat unkempt with a bushy, silver-flecked beard and swirl of hair. Now, you might ask why I, Master of the West, might mistrust such a fellow? Well, for one thing he was none other than Maxentius' estranged father: banished from Italia by his son, the man had come grovelling to me, as his daughter's husband, for succour. Crucially though, he was no mere outcast parent, oh no: in times past, this one had been Augustus of the West. Behind the affable and harmless appearance lay a quicksilver mind, bred on the game of power. So why did I endure his presence in my home, my sanctuary?

Fausta squeezed my hand. My heart grew warm. Is that answer enough?

An uneven crunching on the gravel alerted me to the presence of another, approaching from the maze of paths within the gardens. I turned to the pair shuffling towards me: Mother, lined with age and yet still such a beauty. Her eyes, azure like mine, sparkled like the Christian *Chi-Rho* on her neck chain. 'My boy,' she said in a frail voice, 'my dear boy.'

Linking arms with her was a shrivelled, white-haired and bearded old man shuffling with the aid of a cane. He seemed more absorbed with the butterfly resting on his forefinger than with my arrival.

'Isn't it a marvel?' Lactantius cooed at the patterns on the creature's wings. 'And just last moon, it was another thing entirely. It makes you wonder what truly happens inside the chrysalis, to change a creature so entirely.'

Now he looked up at me, a canny glint in his eyes. 'One has to wonder: can a man do the same? Change his entire being, his beliefs... his faith, even?'

I stared at my old tutor in disbelief, then roared with laughter. 'By all the gods, man, you will turn any conversation to your faith, won't you?'

The Chi-Rho on his necklace – just like Mother's – sparkled as if in tacit reply. He flicked his finger gently, sending the butterfly fluttering off back to the gardens. 'Well, there has to be room to talk of faith amid all else that goes on,' he reasoned.

'Aye, perhaps. And there is much talking to be done,' I agreed, looking to the mid-level of the palace. It was here that

I received dignitaries, assigned legions and drew up plans. I would be spending much time there in the coming days.

Not long after dusk, two days later, the sky over Treverorum was inky black and strewn with a silvery sand of stars. I could still hear the people down on the streets, beseeching me for grain and coin or trading barbed insults. They were restless – a microcosm of the empire, almost. I shut out the clamour and fixed my attentions on the squabbling mass before me instead.

The great meeting chamber was like a beacon in the night, its arched windows open to the elements. A fire roared at the far end, its light dancing on the marble floor, the frescoed walls and the high, gold-veined ceiling. The sides of the room were lined with marble steps – like a mini amphitheatre – and a collection of advisors, dignitaries and notable figures were gathered upon them. Sixty or more voices squabbling like the throngs outside. Lactantius stood near the Christian bishops I had invited along: Maternus of Colonia Agrippina, Reticius of Augustodunum, Marinus of Arelate and Ossius of Colonia Patricia; four men made from the same mould as Lactantius by the looks of it – aged, too shrewd for their own good and wearing the same righteous expression.

I thought that perhaps they might help strengthen my reputation if they were to hear my plans to resist any invasion effort from Galerius, the great persecutor. Deliberately placed on the far side of the room were the priests and leaders of the imperial cults: a cluster of *haruspices*, the diviners of the future; the hooded *Rex Sacrorum*, master of sacrifice; and a number of pontifices and temple keepers too. Acting as something of a breakwater in between stood a collection of noblemen, equestrians who had served my father well, and the best officers from my legions. With them, of course, were Batius and Krocus, each of them looking askance at Maximian, who stood nearby.

Some said I had dared to form a senate of sorts within the lofty halls of my palace. I looked upon it as pure necessity, for the empire was on the brink of war. I *had* to know everything there was to know.

'Domine?' a voice said, scattering my thoughts. It was the shaven-headed Prefect Baudio, leader of the Second Italica legion. They were stationed right now in the eye of the storm: on the hills of Noricum where my realm met that claimed by Maxentius in the south and the dominion of Galerius and his underlings in the East. 'You asked me to bring word of the borders?'

There was no urgency in his tone, so no imminent danger, I surmised. But there was something about his inability to hold my gaze that told me he had displeasing news to impart. 'Please, tell all.'

'The hill forts are complete and they will hold back all but the stoutest of attacks,' he said. 'But... but there have been issues with the garrison.'

'Issues?'

He gulped and nodded. 'Some men have deserted – fled south over the mountains and into Italia. One cohort has lost over forty men.'

I sat forward in my chair, my searing look enough of a prompt for him to continue.

'Some believe... wrongly... that the emperor in Rome holds greater claim to the West.' A bead of sweat darted down his face. 'They say Maxentius is... is of the nobler blood.'

It was like a dagger to my breast. Heat spread over my

face and chest and I wanted to break something – something hard – over the man's skull. It ushered back memories of that childhood day in this very city, when Father had abandoned Mother, marrying into the Tetrarchy and rendering me – in some people's eyes – as nothing but a bastard son. Such slurs had followed me since that day and there were some in my own realm, and outwith, who revelled in repeating them.

A concerned murmur spread over the crowd, and I was sure I saw a few of the nobles smirking. *I will watch these ones closely,* I decided privately. Maximian was the only one to react blithely.

'Nonsense!' he boomed, stepping forward onto the floor. 'My son is but a shadow of the rightful emperor who raised him.' He gestured at himself as he said this. I saw Krocus and Batius roll their eyes. He strolled down from the opposite stair, across the floor and up the steps to stand behind my chair, resting a sage hand on the back of it. 'Rumour spreads about his clumsy handling of the Christians within Rome's walls. Any troops who flee south to his heel will quickly realise they are better off back here. Need the people of the West look any further than this city for leadership? *I* stand by Constantine's side as a vouchsafe for his fittingness and nobil—'

'And what of the other legions?' I cut in, stopping Maximian's restless tongue, casting my eyes across the other commanders.

'The Eighth Augusta are loyal to you, utterly,' one grey-haired, lithe officer shouted confidently, slapping a fist to his chest.

'As are the Thirtieth Ulpia Victrix,' said another.

'The Seventh Gemina will march into the jaws of Cerberus on your word, Domine,' another cried, outdoing the others.

Suddenly, the room was alive with shouts as my legionary commanders avowed their loyalty. Still, though, I noticed a few who had not spoken.

My eyes turned to slits as I imagined their inner thoughts. It had confirmed what I had always suspected: I would have to continue the legacy of Diocletian's military reforms. The old Augustus had begun breaking up the ancient legions – most five thousand strong – into smaller units, a thousand men in each. By doing this he had diluted the power of any one unit, while giving himself many more of these smaller legions to station around trouble spots on the borders and, crucially, gathering the most loyal of these new-style regiments around him as a *Comitatus* – a central reserve of crack brigades, a private army, even. A voice within spat horrible abuse at me for treading in the footsteps of that old tyrant, but was it anything other than prudent?

I realised the claims of loyalty had ebbed and all waited on my response. 'Your fidelity is noted. Stay vigilant, for war might break out on any given day.'

I then looked to the men of opposing faiths on each side of the hall. Here, equidistant between them, I wondered at Mother's advice to me as a boy: that every man must journey to find his own god. Father had worshipped Mars and I had followed in his tradition. Damn, I had spent most of my life at war, so it seemed apt that I should offer tribute to this awesome and ancient divinity. Was Mars my god? I did not know, then. I only knew for certain that I was still on my journey, yet to reach my destination. My thoughts settled and returned to the matter in hand. 'And now I must turn my attentions to the strife within. This city knows no restrictions on what god a man can worship, yet I saw blood spilled between warring faiths on my streets.'

Bishop Marinus – the man who had given a Christian blessing to my marriage with Fausta – spoke first. 'Your toleration is acclaimed, Domine. While my fellow Christians might choose not to worship an emperor, they venerate you for your kindness. From the Rhenus to the far corners of Hispania, they speak your name with bright hearts.'

I snorted. 'Don't speak my name... *honour* me! Quell the people's ire!' I looked from the bishops to the temple priests of the old gods, my hands extended. 'Tell me what can be done to assuage the unrest?'

Silence. Then the Rex Sacrorum spoke through taut lips, raising and pointing a shaking finger at the Christian bishops: 'They are a blight on the strength and fibre of your realm, Domine. They know nothing of the virtues that saw Rome blossom and claim the world as its own. While the mortal sons of Sol Invictus seek to solve the famine and overcrowding in this city... *they* rest on their knees, meekly praying, assuming their God will grant them bread from nothing. While the worshippers of Mars enlist in your legions and aid the fight to drive back the Franks so the crops can be re-established, *they* cower, happy to let us risk our lives.'

I arched an eyebrow at this. It stoked that childhood memory again. 'When I was a boy, I once saw a legionary on the walls of Naissus, braving the wrath of a foul storm while his comrades ran for cover. A *Christian* legionary.' A series of muted gasps sounded. 'Such a thing exists, you see.' I even noticed a few of the legionary commanders look around nervously, hoping no eyes were upon them. 'The persecutions were brutal, and many of the faith still choose to conceal it.' I stood, casting my hands in the air. 'Fighting, distrust, suspicion... I want an end to it. As I call upon my legionary commanders to watch my borders, I also call upon you—'

I addressed both religious parties '—to find a way to bring harmony to my cities.'

Such a short series of words for such a lofty demand. But one I had to designate. I could not be in all of the cities in my realm at once. These men ruled the hearts of the populace in a way I never could. They had to find appeasement between themselves and their clashing faiths and teach their followers that such was the way. The bishops and the temple priests bowed and genuflected, pledging to do what they could. I wanted to believe in them, I truly did, but something within told me I would have to find an answer myself. At that moment, such a challenge felt akin to donning a blindfold and rummaging in a sack of snakes to find a rope.

Wine, bread, meat and fruit were brought in and on we talked until only a few hours remained before dawn. I dissolved the council and sat alone for some time, mulling over the mixture of offences and platitudes that had come out of it all. My head was pounding. No grain, civil strife, the cursed trade embargo… and my coffers, surely they were all but drained. How much longer could I afford to pay the legions? Soon I would see more desertions… but on a massive scale.

Footsteps sounded. A messenger was shown into the hall. Nervously, he came to me and bowed. I recognised him: a rider from the legionary fortress at Bonna. It threw me back to our recent foray in the tribal lands. The frost, the mud, the stink of blood – it all came blasting at me like a blizzard of icy needles. The flurry of memories eased, and I recalled how one of those early battles had ended… the oath. Hisarnis' pledge. The ransom of tribal silver. Enough to part-fill the drained coffers. Enough perhaps to fund my armies into next summer. That was why the rider was here! For a moment I was like a boy, roused with optimism. The ides of the month had been and gone and this man had come to tell me that Hisarnis had delivered his promised bounty. And then the manic thoughts crumbled when I remembered the twist in that tale: the imperial coin of Galerius in the dead tribesman's purse. The oath had been a lie.

'The Frankish treasure wagons were due three days ago, yet none have arrived, Domine. Hisarnis of the Bructeri has reneged on his—'

'Of course he has,' I cut him off with an angry growl and a humourless laugh. I took a deep drink of wine, gulped and sighed. My thoughts creaked this way and that, chained as always by the pressures of state and power. I had almost forgotten about the two tribal wretches we had brought back from the forest campaign, and at first when I remembered them, they were a distraction. But the image of them sitting chained below the palace kept returning to me unbidden. Slowly, however, I realised that those two might just unlock the promised silver after all.

'In the morning, go back to Bonna Fortress,' I instructed the messenger. 'Tell the garrison there to expect my return, and soon. Tell them to prepare to march once more into the woods.'

'To battle the tribes again?' the man said, paling.

I leaned forward, smiling the fiercest of smiles. 'No. This time we go straight to Chief Hisarnis, to his village.'

'Domine,' the man croaked, the word inflected with doubt, 'his village is set deep, deep in the forests, well protected by the terrain and outlying settlements.'

'If Hisarnis wants his brothers back alive, then we will meet no resistance. I will sit at his table and he will give me the answers he owes me. This time, he will pay with the promised silver... or his family's blood.'

4

ROME, 18TH DECEMBER 308 AD

It was an informal council in the cosy library, not a grand meeting of minds in the curia or my aula regia. I had foregone my toga despite the winter chill that infected the very bones of the Palatine, and sat in a heavy wool tunic with my legs crossed, thick socks keeping the cold from my toes. There were only four of us, and we were well acquainted, after all, so there was little need to stand on ceremony.

Anullinus was decked out in a military tunic and long trousers with heavy soldier's boots, his snow-speckled cloak across his knees, the flakes rapidly melting into wet spots in the wool as the roaring fire did its work.

Across from him sat Volusianus in a dark blue tunic all but buried beneath his senatorial toga, the pair of them like gladiators sizing one another up.

My third guest – a necessity to help hold back the headache that the presence of my two oldest advisors always brought forth – sat in a simple tunic, much like my own, though less expensive and with no gold thread woven cunningly into the material. Zenas, commander of my Urban Cohorts. Somehow his presence always felt soothing.

'I gather we have updates from Treverorum?' I began.

Volusianus turned to me, still shaking off the cold and warming to the cosy environment of my Palatine library. 'Constantine continues to struggle with sparring tribes and troublesome conditions. Treverorum is overcrowded, and sustenance in scarce supply, and your father remains in Constantine's court, advising him and cheapening your name and position. Unless something changes radically he is no threat for now, embroiled as he is in local affairs.'

'Good. I have enough enemies for now without counting former friends among them.'

And fathers...

'I have had correspondence from Lucius Domitius Alexander in Carthage,' I said, changing the subject now. 'He has reaffirmed his oath of allegiance and that of Africa and the legions, as we requested, but he also has entreaties.'

All three men looked at me expectantly.

'He says that he requires considerable extra funding for the Third Augusta and also requests permission to grant citizenship to a number of migrant border tribes in order to create an adequate pool for recruitment to the legions. Thoughts, gentlemen?'

'What does he need more men for?' Anullinus frowned. 'He's professed his loyalty and it's not as if there's been war in Africa.'

'There is *always* war in Africa,' Volusianus grumbled. 'Never on a grand scale, but the borders are mutable and the nomad tribes forever restless. A level of annual attrition among the military in the southern *limes* is standard. I say it is an inflammatory request from a dangerous man, and should be refused. He's almost as bad as this one's brother was.' He snorted, gesturing at Anullinus.

The Praetorian Prefect rounded on him with a snarl. 'Oh stop overdramatising everything. Such attrition is normal across the empire and too small to account for such requests. There must be something else – some danger to the borders of which we are unaware. Majesty, we cannot ignore his request as Volusianus suggests.'

'Nevertheless, the fact remains…'

Anullinus raised his voice to cut off Volusianus. 'You simply *cannot* let any subject past without having a damned opinion to voice, can you?'

I pinched the bridge of my nose. Why did two such intelligent, reasonable and serene men turn onto six-year-olds whenever they spoke face to face? As the pair began to heat up and Zenas made fruitless conciliatory noises, I took a deep breath.

'Shut up!'

'Majesty…'

'No. Just be silent. New rule for this particular meeting: none of you will address each other directly. You will all direct your speech to me and I will reply. For the love of Jove, it's like sitting on the dock at Ostia surrounded by competing gulls.'

A taut silence descended on the room, though my two senior advisors continued to hurl insults with their eyes.

'Governor Alexander informs me that the summer and autumn have been disastrous for the African grain farmers. Flash floods have destroyed terracing, dams have been breached, irrigation systems broken and aqueducts cracked and shattered. He has had most of the men of the Third Augusta spread across the countryside repairing the damage, but it is a costly business, and he rather tactfully reminded me that two-thirds of his standing manpower are now on Italian soil at my request.'

A thought occurred to me momentarily. 'Volusianus, are convoys of grain from Africa still supplying Gaul and Hispania?'

'They are, Domine.'

'Is it wise with a land struggling with its agriculture to still send grain to mouths that are Constantine's to feed? Perhaps we should concentrate on our own and let his people go hungry?' *And with any luck my cursed wine-sack of a father, hanging on Constantine's tunic hem while he further ruined my reputation, would dwindle away to nothing along with them, though the bloated old fool would take a few years to starve.*

Volusianus gestured, and I nodded.

'Domine, just because the population of Gaul do not live in Rome does not make them non-Romans. These people, for all they follow Constantine, are the citizens of the Western imperial lands. Correct me if I am wrong, but it is your intent to be Emperor of the West. Unless you wish to be emperor of the world's biggest cemetery, you must let the grain shipments continue.'

I nodded again. Of course. It was hardly the fault of Ausax the Gallic wheelwright that Constantine was his master, any more than it had been our fault back in Nicomedia that Diocletian had been ours. I could hardly starve the servant for the faults of his master.

'Fair enough. Alexander makes good points, really, and yet we are not so wealthy here that we can afford to send much remuneration to the provinces arbitrarily. And I fear the inevitable backlash from the senate if I inform them that I have added barbarian nomads who speak not a word of a civilised tongue to the august citizenship of Rome. Moreover, it concerns me that, given the entire population of the province of Africa, he cannot bring up the manpower for a legion.'

Anullinus turned to me and raised a finger. I nodded.

'Africa is more sparsely populated than the northern provinces, Majesty, and the vast majority of its yeomanry is dedicated to agriculture and infrastructure. In times past when there have been large recruitment drives following troubles, the men taken for the legions have left Africa's farms undermanned.'

'Yes,' grunted Volusianus, 'when your short-sighted idiot brother was in charge.'

Anullinus gave his opposite a stare that could cut through steel as he continued to address me. 'Given the fact that the province supplies Rome's bread almost in entirety, I can understand why Alexander is taking great care.'

'Alexander is an untrustworthy snake,' Volusianus retorted, carefully directing his face to me, while his words were clearly meant for Anullinus. I also noted how he had not asked for permission to speak. A twitch began in my upper lip and I had to force myself not to shout again.

'You do not trust Domitius Alexander?' I prompted.

Volusianus almost snarled. 'The man is the lowest, basest rat. No. Not a rat. Rats are just unpleasant. Alexander is a polecat. He is vicious and untameable as well as unpleasant. If he is trying to increase his military, look to his objectives. If you recall, I put forward three names for my successor when I came here, Majesty, all men I have known for over twenty years since my first tenure in the province. I cannot imagine why you set them all aside and granted the position to that animal.'

I let my disapproving eyebrow rule the conversation for a moment, and then spoke slowly and steadily. 'All your replacement suggestions were men who owed their advancement to Galerius. I cannot put Africa in the hands of a man who might still be loyal to my enemy. Domitius Alexander owes his own advancement to the divine Constantius.'

'Also the father of an enemy,' Volusianus pointed out.

'Perhaps so, but less invested in my downfall than the man who made me an enemy of my own city, I would say.'

'Majesty,' Volusianus said, with exaggerated patience, 'I know Alexander of old. I have served with him and above him, and I can tell you that no good will come of his controlling Africa. I highly recommend that you remove him from the role and promote someone else.'

I sighed, unconvinced.

You see, the great problem with such groups of counsellors is in knowing who to trust over negative voices. In the early days of my reign I placed an unfounded level of confidence in Anullinus, and I still found his advice to be largely good. But his ongoing feud with Volusianus led me often to wonder how much was genuine opinion and how much simply gainsaying for the sake of argument. And a similar issue plagued me with Volusianus. He had brought me Africa and legitimised my reign, and his words were often true. But how much of his advice was born from simple refuting of whatever his opposite number held to be true.

'Anullinus? Your opinion?'

My Praetorian Prefect shrugged. 'Alexander has a record as a competent officer and administrator. He's never spoken against you as far as I am aware, and there have been no rumours of trouble through the *frumentarii*. Ancharius Pansa has been very much at the centre of things in Africa recently and is reliable, and he reckons Alexander to be capable and dependable. Added to this, Alexander is popular with the African troops. Turning on him could damage your relationship with the army.'

I could read Volusianus' response in his eyes, though he was holding his tongue with difficulty. I nodded to him and he spoke in strained, careful tones.

'I *know* Africa, Majesty. I governed the place… *twice* thanks to the failures of the elder Anullinus. I know Africa's soldiers, as I've commanded them myself. And I know Alexander, and would not trust him to prop up a table, let alone govern your most important province.'

I nodded and gestured to Zenas, my mediator in these arguments. 'What is your opinion?'

'I have no precise evidence with which to support my judgement, Majesty, but I am inclined to support Volusianus in this matter. Better to remove a potential threat and risk wasting a good man than to leave him in power and learn the hard way that he is an enemy.'

Anullinus, this time failing to raise a finger, glared at Zenas as he addressed me. 'Majesty, Zenas' views can hardly be considered objective. Alexander is renowned for being one of the worst perpetrators of the persecution of Christians, and it is hardly a secret that Zenas here follows that sect in his heart. He would *naturally* wish to see such a man removed for his own personal reasons. But Alexander's former zeal in those persecutions does not preclude his ability to govern.'

Despite my express command that all present direct their words to me, the room suddenly exploded into a furore of accusations and bile as my two oldest advisors laid into each other again, but now with the usually calm Zenas slinging as strident an insult as any, a reminder that Anullinus' brother in his time in Africa had also been a zealous persecutor of Christians, fanning the flames. I sat silent amid the row, wincing at the familiar throbbing rising in the base of my skull. I counted under my breath, and when I had reached twenty and the argument still showed no sign of abating, I let out a shout that had all three sitting bolt upright and silent, the blood draining from their faces. I cannot for the life of me recall precisely what I shouted, but it shocked them and a heartbeat later both doors to my chamber were flung open as guards rushed in. I waved them away, my face purple with anger.

'If you continue to behave like this, I will send you all to Africa to dig irrigation trenches. Am I clear?'

A chorus of silent, contrite nods greeted me, and I sat back, counted to ten and let the colour retreat from my face before continuing. 'I do not have such a wealth of good administrators that I can afford to waste them, and Alexander's only potential loyalty other than me would be to Constantine, whose father was his patron. Constantine is far away to the north and likely is unaware that Alexander even exists, and thus I wish Lucius Domitius Alexander to continue in his role, but I am also receptive to your valued opinions. If Alexander cannot be wholly trusted, and we cannot *buy* his trust for fear he use that money to further his own goals, then we must achieve a degree of leverage over him.'

Volusianus narrowed his eyes, and Anullinus was openly nodding. Good. Perhaps I had a solution.

'I seem to remember that Alexander has a son, yes? Not old enough to take the *toga virilis* but very close with his father?'

Volusianus nodded. 'He is ten summers, I think, Majesty.'

I smiled at him. 'Good. Send a cohort of your best men to Carthage with a chest of gold for the repairs to the province and permission for Alexander to draw men from Sicilia and southern Italia to bolster his forces. *Invite* Alexander to send his son with them back to Rome. Here he can further his education in the imperial court with the best of tutors in the greatest city in the world – a coup for any ambitious nobleman.'

'A hostage, Majesty?' asked Zenas uncertainly.

'A *guest*. A ward of the palace, if you like. Alexander will not refuse. He cannot. And unless he has no care for his own progeny, that should buy his allegiance.'

Volusianus was nodding again. 'I will do so in the morning, Majesty.'

Anullinus was clearly struggling with the idea and when I gestured to him, he cleared his throat. 'I worry that, if the man *is* the polecat that Volusianus believes, poking him might elicit just the reaction you were hoping to avoid?'

I frowned. Did my oldest advisor have a point? Galerius had once pushed Constantine into a corner, expecting to crush him, and instead had driven him to Britannia and to claiming the purple himself. Was I now risking doing the same? But I could not simply hand out money and hope he did not use it against me, and merely removing him would leave me with a number of headaches. It was a gamble. I looked up at Anullinus. 'Like Caesar of old, I must cast the dice and let them fall as they may.'

5

THE GREAT HALL OF THE BRUCTERI,
22ND DECEMBER 308 AD

Some men find respite from their troubles in the oddest of places, but few, surely, in the heart of their enemy's realm. Yet I must admit that as I sat in Hisarnis' mighty lodge at the heart of the Bructeri stronghold, deep within the Frankish forest on the day of the winter solstice, I did find an odd sense of calm. Perhaps it was the simple relief of rest after a gruelling march and ride through the woods to get here, churning knee and fetlock deep through the heavy snowfall. Maybe it was the distance from the strife at Augusta Treverorum. Conceivably it was because while Hisarnis was undoubtedly a threat, he was not my darkest foe. Or perchance it because I was on my third cup of the robust barley ale. I wetted my lips with the effervescent nectar once more and looked around.

The hall was as tall and magnificent as anything in the imperial cities, but that was where the similarities ended. Instead of limestone blocks, the walls were made of thick wattle and daub, washed in off-white. There were no frescoes or niches bearing statues on the walls, just magnificently decorated circular shields mounted there like giant, burnished studs, with age-old swords and spears crossed behind them. In place of porphyry or marble columns to support the high ceiling, two ancient, gnarled oaks wound from the packed-dirt floor to the apex of the pitched roof – thick and thatched. The fire in the open hearth roared and crackled, mocking the bitter, late afternoon chill outside. The wooden doors on the western wall were open to the elements, giving a fine view of the snow-blanketed lower town that ringed the mound upon which this great hall sat. A skirl of pipes filled the hot air and all around me Hisarnis' bearded, plaid-cloaked noblemen chattered and laughed, cups clacking, their cheeks as rosy as their moods.

In my present condition I probably looked like one of them, with my bear pelt wrapped around my shoulders hiding most of my bronze vest, the dirt of the journey still smeared on my face and my untended stubble. Boar and bread loaves filled the long table before me – and my belly too, and the sweet aroma of cooking meat and roots filled the hall, part-disguising an underlying musty odour.

Hisarnis sat opposite me, clad in a brown and yellow plaid cloak fastened at the right breast by a silver brooch in the shape of a wolf's head, the eyes picked out with small, green gemstones. His iron-grey hair was neatly combed and tied back in a tail, and his hoary beard was carefully braided. Without his armour, his twin axes or that fierce look he had worn at the forest battle, he seemed smaller, gentler. My sense of calm rose just a fraction, but I was quick to check it. How many chieftains had he entertained like this, plying them with boar and ale?

I had heard tales of the strife in these dark woods, yarns about how the tribes settled their grievances. They had battles, yes, but they also understood that most scores could be settled with just a single death. Many warlords, would-be kings and upstarts had met their ends at gatherings like these – a mouthful of ale one moment then a throatful of sharpened steel the next. Suddenly, I could not help but think of that time in Galerius' company in Nicomedia, when the demon had tried to kill me as I ate. Perhaps unwisely, I glanced behind me: no assassins, just drunk Franks engaging in some kind of belching contest.

Besides, three cohorts of legionaries waited outside the village, under strict instruction to kill Hisarnis' brothers and raze the place into the miserable, frozen dirt if I failed to return to them before dark. I caught Batius' eye. Standing near the open door, he was agitated – partly because he was excluded from the ale-drinking, and partly because the late afternoon sky was quickly darkening, a crisp sapphire twilight taking its place. Orange bubbles of torchlight had appeared in the many small, thatched dwellings down in the lower town. Batius made a face that suggested he had accidentally caught his manhood in his spatha sheath, and tilted his head towards the sky and then towards Hisarnis. *Get on with it,* he mouthed. I gave him a placatory nod.

Conveniently, Hisarnis noticed our tacit exchange. He clapped his hands and the sound echoed around the hall. With a series of groans, the skirling pipes tailed off, cups were drained and the babble ebbed as the Franks traipsed from the hall, crunching out across the hardened snow and back to their homes. Soon, there were just a pair of guards by the door, and Batius, the three locked in a 'withering gaze' competition.

Satisfied that we were as alone as Hisarnis would allow, I swirled my cup and sighed. 'You promised me silver and gold. Where is it?' I reckoned there was no point in any more pleasantries. The twilight was growing impatient.

Hisarnis issued a short, barking laugh. 'Treasure? What riches we possessed were spent long ago.'

I bridled at this, recalling the coin Batius had found on the forest floor, freshly minted with the profile of the scowling, blocky-faced Galerius. 'The emperor of the East has sent you no more?'

Hisarnis' lips grew thin and bloodless. 'We would have raided your lands regardless of the coins from Nicomedia.' He shrugged and snorted. 'A thirsty man makes his way to a lake. On the way, a stranger offers him a golden chalice to drink with. Cup or no cup, the man is still going to the lake. And he would be a fool not to take the cup anyway.'

I almost smiled at the plain logic. And I noticed, not for the first time, the dark, decorative boar hide stretched out on a frame behind Hisarnis. A simple, saffron-yellow Chi-Rho was painted upon it. Galerius, the great persecutor, had paid these Franks to be his allies. Did he realise that some of them were now Christianised? It mattered not, for the Herdsman wouldn't let such a small technicality get in the way of his greater designs: to sweep me from power – to sweep *everyone* but himself from the board. I shuffled to sit straighter and rested my cup on the table. 'If you have no more gold then why did you agree to the terms in the first place? You must have known I would not forget such a slight.'

'Oh yes, I know you, *Domine*,' Hisarnis said archly, his eyes tapering. A log snapped on the fire as if to punctuate the abstruse words. 'When I first heard reports that you were coming here, I did not want to receive you empty-handed. Indeed, I hoped you would not have to come here at all... though I am honoured to have you in my hall,' he added quickly. 'I tried and failed to reap tribute from the rest of the tribes.' He held out his hands, palms upturned, his face lengthening. 'Once, they would have been swift to obey. Now, they talk of how I was crushed in the woods by you and your regiments, and they fear me no longer. They have cut me adrift, it seems.'

I glanced to the doorway and onwards past the wooden stakes that ringed the lower town. Just a thin band of dark blue hung on the western horizon now, the last vestiges of day. My cohorts would be readying their artillery and honing their blades. Hisarnis' brothers would be on their knees, the edges of executioners' blades at their necks. 'So what am I to do? Nothing has changed: you must uphold the terms of our agreement, else *my* authority will be brought into question.'

There was a moment of affinity. Both of us began to look at each other differently. I wanted to tell this fellow – who had treated me well since we arrived at his home – that I had no wish to kill his siblings. *Give me something, man!*

Maybe his gods were listening and passed on my thoughts. For a few moments later, Hisarnis lifted a small chest from the floor by his side and pushed it across the table to me. I opened the lid to find a treasure of sorts. Not coin, but a fine iron helm, coated in a silver-gilt sheathing to give it the lustre of pure gold. It was inlaid with green and red gems and sported a studded ridge running from the back of the neck to the centre of the brow. Where the ridge ended, a thick nose guard struck down like the tip of a spatha blade, and cheek guards on either side almost met with this, leaving openings for little other than eyes and mouth.

'It is mine. It was my father's and his father's before him,' Hisarnis said. 'Now... it is yours.'

'You would give me this?' I replied.

Hisarnis sighed. 'I know it is not even close to the value of gold we agreed but it—'

'—is worth so much more,' I finished for him. He seemed taken aback. 'Price and value are two very different beasts. Thank you.' I nodded, placing the helm back in the chest. 'But my men would never respect me were I content to take a personal gift in place of the coins they expect – coins I need to stabilise my realm.'

Hisarnis steepled his fingers and rested his bearded chin upon the apex. 'Gold I cannot give you. You could lay waste to my village, turn over every home, yet you would find few coins. But there is another currency.'

My eyes narrowed a little.

'I know of the dark pall of trouble that gathers over your empire. Factions forming. Armies swelling. A storm of war is coming.' He said this in the most confident drawl, drumming his fingers once on the table, then leaned forward. 'I cannot give you treasure to pay your legions, but I can offer you my warriors.' His eyes sparkled in the firelight and he seemed to be weighing up his next words.

It was an unexpected twist. I thumbed my cup, turning it slowly where it sat on the table. 'What makes you think I need them?'

Hisarnis seemed hesitant to reply, but noticed my continual glances to the door and the retreating daylight. 'Rumour has it that you need more regiments... desperately.'

I arched an eyebrow.

'Passing merchants say that Galerius' eastern armies grow with every passing month,' he continued. 'They also talk of the young prince in the south: Maxentius, Master of Africa and Italia and general of the mighty armies of those lands... growing too as regiments flock to his cause.'

Master of Africa, I think not, I mused with a hint of a smirk. If anything, that region and its troubled farming lands was becoming a bane for my one-time friend. 'And what do they say of me?' I snapped.

Hisarnis hesitated, and his gaze fell, his confidence plummeting too. 'We could have raided Galerius' lands or Maxentius'. But we did not. Instead, we chose to attack the… the…' his words faltered, as if he feared that they might be the death of him '…the weakest realm.'

Now many from my court – slaves and attendants, generals, loved ones, even – have come to know that my temper is foul at times: broken tables, smashed windows and ruined furnishings were commonplace in Augusta Treverorum. I felt those fiery talons rise within me as Hisarnis' words echoed in my ears, taking on a mocking edge. Yet try as I might, I could not refute his argument. I needed soldiers, badly. I took a draught of beer to cool my emotions, planting the empty cup down. 'You will pledge your allegiance – come from the forests and to my side when I call upon you?'

Hisarnis shook his head. 'The fate of my tribesmen is written in the frozen dirt: the other tribes of the Frankish confederation see us as outsiders now. Were we to make such a pledge then we would become their enemy. It would be they who would line up outside the village walls next.' He leaned forward. 'The Regii once roamed these woods, yet now they are part of your army. The Cornuti too – and they even dress in imperial armour, proud to call themselves Romans.' He paused for breath, nodding to himself in the way a man does before making in irreversible decision. 'When you return to the Rhenus and cross back into the empire, take my people with you. Arm them and they will fight for you as a true Roman regiment.'

'Will they?' I gasped, the talons of rage withdrawing. 'After what I did?' I was already replaying the memory in my mind.

That day when I had ordered the pair of Frankish kings to be mauled in the arena by lions.

Hisarnis cocked his head to one side. 'Ah, the two lords you executed? Merogaisus and Ascaric?' he said, understanding my point. He stroked at his beard for a time. 'And how do you feel now about what you did that day?'

'Justified,' I said. 'One was a snake and the other a degenerate. You know what the most upsetting part about that day was? It was afterwards, when I found out the lions had been killed by their handlers.'

Hisarnis stared at me as if a hawk had just flown from my mouth. And then his face creased up and he doubled over, broken with laughter. It took him a time to recover. 'You knew those two well enough, I would say,' he said in between fading chuckles. 'Many here too were overjoyed to be rid of that pair.'

His mirth was welcome. Yet my eyes drifted to the hide Chi-Rho again. I remembered the truth: yes, some of my people had cheered as they watched the lions ripping apart the Frankish Kings. However, the Christians within the crowd had appealed for mercy. Lactantius too. Mother's reaction had hurt most of all. She simply fell into a silence that lasted months. Every time I tried to speak to her she had closed her eyes and bowed her head, bringing her Chi-Rho necklace to her lips. There is no lesson quite so acerbic as a mother's scorn. 'In truth... I sometimes feel shame for what I subjected them to,' I said. 'The two kings, aye, they were cretins. But what does it say about me as a leader when I could not bring myself to offer them a nobler end? Men and animals dying in the arena upon my word – that is the way of Galerius and Diocletian. It is time for the empire to shed that grim mantle.'

Hisarnis' gaze crept to the open door and out across the darkening, endless forest, no doubt thinking of the many tribes who had ostracised him. 'So, will you accept my offer? Will you lead my people back to your empire with you?'

I thought of the brigade I could possibly fashion from Hisarnis' warriors. It would take time and money to do so, but another hardy central regiment – like the Cornuti and the Regii – was an appealing prospect. Another force bound by oath directly to me. Another part of my Comitatus? Yet many families would come with them too. Many more mouths to feed from swiftly dwindling grain silos. However, quite simply, there was no alternative. I could not return to my cohorts outside the village with nothing.

'Have them prepare to travel west,' I said. 'And bring what grain and fodder you have – all of it.'

Hisarnis' eyes brightened. 'Thank you, Domine,' he said, releasing a long-held breath in relief. 'We will serve you well.' Then he pushed the chest with the jewelled helm over to me once more. 'And this, please accept it as a personal token of my loyalty and to seal our pact.'

I gave him a slight but earnest nod of gratitude and took the gift as it was intended.

Suddenly, an urgent voice disturbed us. 'Sir!' Batius hissed.

I turned to see him gesticulating wildly at the now almost pure-black sky. From beyond the town's walls I heard shouts of legionaries and the distinctive call of a *ballista* commander ordering ammunition to be brought to him. 'Give the signal,' I said.

Without delay, Batius fumbled with the bow on his back, bringing a pitch-soaked arrow to a sconce to light it then nocking, drawing and loosing the blazing missile. The flaming arrow streaked across the almost-dark sky. There was a tense hiatus before the legionary shouts outside the town ebbed, spotting the signal to stand down.

Batius' shoulders slumped in relief and he swung away from the doorway, stomped over to the table and took an abandoned but full ale cup and downed the lot. 'Talk about cutting it fine,' he gasped, wiping foam from his lips with the back of his hand.

6

MAXENTIUS

ROME, 30TH DECEMBER 308 AD

The afternoon had begun with excitement. After a morning of lesser races, a fifth of a million people now watched as we bounced around in that uncomfortable, bone-shaking contraption to mark the start of the important afternoon races. Around the elongated track in the bloodied sands of the circus, where eight men and sixteen horses risked their lives for financial gain every few heartbeats, we raced.

It was Saturnalia, and as part of the festivities there were races in the circus. I had flat refused when my advisors had suggested it: a glorious ride around the sands in a racing *biga*, dressed in purple and gold, to the acclaim of the crowd. Good for public morale, apparently. Bad for the knees and the lungs was my personal opinion, only halfway through the lap, as my legs turned further to jelly with each bounce and my lungs sought air in the freezing, dust-laden atmosphere.

But at least I wasn't driving. No. For Romulus had been so insistent that he take the reins. I had flat refused that too, but like all my arguments it was brushed aside with the force of the point raised by Volusianus and my son. I needed to be seen by the people and to be a figure of power and glory to them, and this was a huge opportunity for just that. And so there I was bouncing, lurching, feeling as though the soles of my feet were being pulled up through my body into my head, wondering how good for public morale it would be when I was sick over the side of the chariot.

Romulus was probably a good driver by racing standards. He seemed to know what he was doing, but he also equally cared little for comfort or stability as the wretched thing bounced and shook and once – unbelievably – actually touched the spina wall and careered off it. He would never make a coach driver for the rich, that much was certain. One look at the sheer joy on his face as he drove us, though, was enough to still my harsh words. Racing was his love. I had him. He had his chariots. How could I deny him what he gave me?

We rounded the last turn, lurching, jumping and scraping through the grit until we slewed to a halt and my son threw up his hands in victory as though he'd been racing against heroes. The crowd seemed pleased, breaking their gloomy demeanour and cheering the display. I can only assume they were lauding Romulus and not me, since I dropped from the vehicle like a lead weight, was a little bit sick on my own sandal, and then swayed and wobbled all the way to the exit, waving a hand expansively as I tried to remain upright.

I recovered my wits slowly as we made our way up to the *pulvinar* to watch the rest of the day's entertainment. A day of races for the most beloved festival in the Roman year.

Saturnalia that winter had been a slightly more subdued affair than in previous years, prompting such lunacy as this publicity stunt from the mouth of Volusianus. Perhaps it was a sign of Rome's weariness of war and uncertainty. Two years ago, the great festival had followed my raising to the purple and, despite the desperation of our collective situation, the mood had been one of hope reborn and of the overwhelming value of Rome, as befits such a celebration. And last year, against all expectations, we had fought off the great incursions by Severus and Galerius, leaving Rome triumphant and in a mood of great joy.

By this year, though, the abundant hope at the start of my reign seemed to have diminished somewhat and elation at our victories had been eroded by the inescapable recognition of the fact that we remained isolated and pressed from all sides by long-term enemies and dangerous former friends. The pressure was beginning to tell among the populace. Violence became a commonplace thing. And not the regular organised violence of the city's criminal brotherhoods, nor the random sporadic violence of the opportunistic felon, nor even the surges of bloodshed that followed riots and civil disorder. This was more the sort of sullen background violence that nibbles at the edges of a city's collective patience – a viciousness born of fatigue and doubt, like a lidded pot left to boil too long on a high flame.

Saturnalia saw an increase in spirits and mood as always, but now instead of taking a dour populace and making them content, it took a tense populace and made them dour.

Indeed, as I stood amid the purple and white drapes embroidered with slogans and eagles in the pulvinar of the city's great race track, where generations of emperors had watched the games, I could almost feel the tautness of the spectators in the myriad subdued voices that thrummed across the circus. They had cheered my son, but little in the following display similarly caught their enthusiasm. Against the backdrop of thundering hooves from the track, six Praetorians held silent position at strategic points around the box as a deterrent against any poor idiot who might try and climb into this lofty eyrie of extravagance. Other than them, though, only Romulus shared this great state occasion with me, my invitation having been politely declined by my various acquaintances, each of whom was busy even at this celebration time. I had even extended the invitation to Valeria, though I'd known she would not come. Short of an imperial command, nothing seemed likely to draw her to my side.

Over recent months, my boy's attention to the regular gladiatorial contests of the city had waned to be replaced by a growing fascination with the races. The young are ever wont to change their tastes with surprising regularity, though indeed the whole of Rome seemed to be shifting their favour from the bloodshed of the arena – perhaps an all too obvious simile for life as a Roman these days – to the breakneck excitement of the chariots.

Today was an *exceptional* circus day, too. The Greens and the Blues who dominated the races on every occasion, and who were recognised by high and low as the masters of the circus, had suffered several fatal calamities early in the morning races, losing a number of very famous and very popular racers. Consequently, their chances of securing any kind of victory this afternoon were slim at best, and the lesser racers of the Whites and Reds, familiar with collecting runner-up prizes, suddenly found themselves within sight of the wreath of victory.

It was recognised by those in the know as one of the best days of racing in living memory, and still the crowd languished in a dreary mood, even the roars at a fall or a surprise cut short, seeming somehow subdued and cheerless.

Perhaps, in retrospect, I was projecting my own fears upon the people. Perhaps they were not quite as miserable as they seemed, and I just saw them that way. The past is a nebulous thing, and the moods of others even more so.

Whatever the case, my beloved son seemed unaffected. He still wore the *bulla* that marked him as a boy, though I had agreed with him that he would take the toga virilis in the summer when the weather was better, and when, hopefully, the villa on the Via Appia was complete enough to host a celebration. I had held him under my wing as a boy too long, in truth – he should have been his own man by now. I am unapologetic for that, though. I had little in my life that I felt true love for: my boys, my sisters and my city. Young Aurelius would never be able to live a normal life, for all that I loved his sad, twisted little form.

My stepsister Theodora had taken herself off to a family holding in Campania following her brief time in Rome, her concern with court life having seemingly died along with her husband. The same villa, in fact, in which my father had drunk himself to sleep night after night, when the reins of power had been ripped from his hands. My mother was also there now, sent there by Father to keep her out of the way, and I had given thought to bringing her to Rome. But why would I launch her into this world, when in truth I rather envied her rustic peace? Fausta was married to my friend – my enemy? – Constantine, and remained at his court along with our treacherous father where they gathered barbarians to build a new army. And my city was a troublesome beast to ride these days, seemingly trying to buck and throw me at regular intervals.

All the things I loved seemed to twist and writhe and try to squirm from my grasp except Romulus, who went on bright and wonderful as always.

The bronze dolphin dipped on the rack, indicating the last

lap, and the remaining three chariots hurtled around the end of the track, trying to stay as close to the spina as they could in dangerously tight turns, partially to improve their chances of victory, but mostly to avoid the deadly tangles of splintered timber and twisted equines where the less fortunate drivers had ended their race in disaster. Every lap, slaves had run out to clear as much wreckage as they could, and they had kept a wide enough channel unobstructed for those still racing, but there was simply too much to completely clear in time.

The remaining man of the Blues was one of their lesser drivers and was struggling to keep up with those leaders of Red and White who jostled for first place even now as they raced along the straight. The poor Blue failed to recover from his too-tight corner and his *quadriga* veered off sharply to the right. The four horses, clearly strong and well trained and alert even at this stage, leapt over a piece of abandoned chariot and continued to thunder on, but as the wheels of the vehicle hit the wreckage and bounced mightily into the air, the driver was wrenched back and somehow the leather rein wrapped around his wrist for security broke free. As the vehicle hit the sand hard and lurched this way and that at the horses' whim, the rider sailed through the air with a shriek, arms flailing until he hit the ground, bounced twice and slid agonisingly to a halt in a twisted shape, convulsing rhythmically.

Even this, which would normally have the spectators on their feet roaring, elicited little more than a collective groan.

I sank into some sort of internal peace, trying not to think about the crowd or the city to which it belonged. Trying not to think about anything at all, if I am honest. I let the rest of the race – the last race of the day and of the festival – wash over me as I drifted in a mental fog. I registered in passing a win for the Whites and the shape of the Blues' driver being carried away with the team's official mourners in tow, wailing for appropriate remuneration. I watched the Priest of Saturn shower the victor with praise and grant him a wreath, along with other more tangible prizes. On other occasions such rewards might have come from my own imperial hand, but on this occasion it was the task of the priest of great Saturn, in line with the festival.

Respectfully, the crowd waited for my hand to be raised in benediction as I stood and exited the imperial box. Again it struck me that there was no roar from the throng in appreciation of the win and of my largesse, which had paid for the whole damned thing, but then neither was there a wave of violence and bloodshed that might be expected to follow the loss of the big team to their smaller cousin. A strange feeling in all.

Leaving the crowd behind to their sombre revelry, I stalked through the corridors back up from the pulvinar and into the Palatine complex, through corridors painted to the tastes of dozens of emperors, filled with busts of the better among them. Beside me, Romulus chattered away about what the various racers had done right and wrong, sounding surprisingly knowledgeable. The six Praetorian guardsmen, joined by the two who had stood outside the pulvinar's door, marched both ahead and behind, their eyes watchful, their ears alert. More than one ruler of Rome had come to an inglorious end in these corridors and despite three centuries of making and breaking emperors and being untrustworthy to a man, the Praetorian Guard and I were as closely linked as could be, both of us condemned by the 'legitimate' emperors, bound together in defiance. The world was full of enemies for me, but the Guard was not one of them.

I felt the men at the front tense even before they stopped

and held up a silent hand in signal for me to wait. Then I also heard the approaching footsteps. In other parts of the palace, such a sound was perfectly normal. Here, though, in the private route from the palace's residential area to the imperial box at the Circus Maximus, no one else should be expected. I stood, tense, Romulus at my side, as two of the four men behind us joined their fellows ahead, hands on sword hilts and blades drawn just a hand's breadth in preparation.

There was a palpable sense of relaxation as the footsteps reached a crescendo and the figure of one of my senior freedmen appeared, unarmed and puffing, around the corner. The guards stood down, returning their blades to their scabbards and moving back into a four-four formation. The freedman – Callisto, who was the functionary in charge of my appointments – took a deep breath as he bowed low.

'Domine, forgive my intrusion, but I have been sent to find you and deliver grave tidings.'

I felt the chill settle on me. Somehow, I think I'd felt bad news coming in the general grey sullenness of the world around me. I had expected *something*. Of course, woes are sociable things and rarely travel alone, and my day held more of them for me yet.

It was odd, I thought, that I had never once set foot inside this house in all the time I had known its owner, yet *he* had been in *my* house seemingly on a daily basis. The atrium was everything I would have expected it to be – austere, ascetic even. The single floor mosaic was monochrome and old-fashioned, not like the great coloured efforts prevalent these days. The fountain in the central pool was plain and simple, the walls decorated in a red and white pattern that had been scoffed at as out-of-date for generations. This was an old house, harkening back to the days of the great early emperors with few changes across the decades. Somehow it perfectly suited its owner.

Ahead, the member of the Urban Cohorts who had first come across the scene gestured for us to follow and my guards stepped through cautiously, blades drawn even within the *pomerium* – Rome's sacred heart, where ancient law forbade weapons of war. We passed into a peristyle garden and the plain, light grey sky above was dominated by the vertiginous Palatine hill that rose beside the house on my right. I could just see the upper curve of the great Flavian amphitheatre above the opposite corner, for this house stood below the palace and across the square from the arena on some of the most expensive land in the city.

I was concentrating on minutiae, logging everything I saw and weighing it up, and I knew in my heart that this was just an attempt to keep my mind from the reason I was seeing it all.

We were led by a soldier, whose voice was thick with some southern accent reminiscent of Sicilian, into a small bath complex across the peristyle, where I could hear the sounds of others in quiet discussion. Oil lamps blazed in every niche, illuminating the building, and the time for deliberate distractions was over. I held my breath. Somehow, I had not quite believed the tidings brought to me in that access corridor or the scant details Callisto had to hand when questioned on our journey across the hill. But now that I was here, there would be no more doubt. There could be no more denial.

I waved the Praetorians aside, which made them frown with disapproval, but they were loyal veterans and did so neatly, keeping out of the way yet close, should I require them. With Romulus at my heel and the soldier ahead, I moved into the *apodyterium* – the changing room of the baths. The first thing that struck me was the quantity of blood. I had experienced battle and personal combat more than once in my time, and I had witnessed the spilling of lifeblood in the arena and the circus on plenty of occasions. And I was not squeamish, I might add. I had vowed more than once that if I ever again laid my hands upon my father I would kill him myself, with blade and spike and a vicious sense of retribution.

But was it possible that one human could contain so much blood? I felt a chill run through me at the sight and knowledge of what it meant.

The floor was deep with it, though it had been cooling for some time now and was tacky, making my sandals cling and lift with an unpleasant tearing sound as I stepped closer. My eyes darted around the room. The clothes niches were all empty, but not a single one had escaped the spray of blood that had also spattered over the painted fish designs on the walls. It looked like the scene of a massacre, and yet it had all come from just one man.

Publius Anullinus lay at the heart of that lake of dark red, his plain white tunic little more than strips of rag wound around his waxy, grey flesh, though both white tunic and grey flesh were more crimson than anything else, so soaked were they in blood. My Praetorian Prefect had been killed in the most brutal fashion. In fact, the way he lay there on his side, bloodied and rent, with an outstretched, imploring arm, reminded me so much of the reports of the death of Julius Caesar that it was difficult not to see him that same way and to feel appropriately aggrieved for the state.

So many wounds…

'Tell me,' I said, my voice as level as I could manage while I addressed the three members of the Urban Cohorts in the room. I did not look up at them, could not tear my eyes from that horrifying sight. Anullinus, a man who had *made* me in many ways. More of a father, perhaps, than that bloated villain who now sat at Constantine's right hand. Even as the soldier began to answer, already my mind was working. What would I do without him?

'I was on patrol, Domine,' said the man who had ushered me in. 'My route takes me around Titus' arch and the temple of Venus and Rome, and this building, of course, falls in my path. I noted that the door to the house was open, and with this being such a generally busy area, that struck me as odd. I hadn't realised who lived here, Domine, but it was clearly a man of note, since there are no shopfronts built into the walls. I took it upon myself to enquire, so I knocked at the door. Receiving no answer, I stepped inside and searched the house, finding no servants or slaves. The whole place was deserted. I was all but ready to send for someone in higher authority when I came to the baths and found this.'

'You did well to check. Many of your peers in older days would have shrugged and walked on.' *Would that whoever was responsible for the thing on the floor had done so.*

The man nodded professionally. The Urban Cohorts were good men these days under Zenas' control, not the dissolute waste they had previously been. I peered at the body. I felt that I should be angry. I should be shaking and demanding heads to roll and the like. Yet despite a chill that encompassed me and a vague sense of incomprehensible loss, I could not quite feel much, other than numbness. It was like waking to find you were missing an arm. Too big to take in right now.

The enormity of it and the grief it would bring would hit me later, and I knew that on some level, but at the time I simply examined my old friend, the man who had brought me to power and protected me as best he could.

It occurred to me that despite all the recent friction between Anullinus and Volusianus and the almost childish way they bickered, my reign would have been cut short long ago without either of them to support me.

'What can you tell me of the attack?' *So much blood…*

'We have discounted the possibility of numerous assailants, Domine,' another soldier said quietly, busily marking things down on a wax tablet. 'The wounds are consistent with overhand blows from the same blade, which was a pugio of standard military shape and size. The medicus who just left was convinced that the blows had all been struck by the same man – same hand used, same amount of weight behind them, and all struck within a matter of heartbeats. It was a quick, brutal, frenzied attack.'

'And the killer?' *Killer. Killer of my friend…*

'Someone crazed I'd say, Domine. This was not the work of thieves or random attackers. This was a concerted effort to destroy the prefect carried out by one assailant. The medicus was of the opinion that the killer was probably a military man. Quite apart from the dagger used, the medicus thought he'd identified the initial blow, which was up between the ribs in the back and straight into the heart. The victim was dying from the first strike. We believe that the additional repeated stabbings were a work of frenzy.'

'Or an attempt to make it look like the work of a madman, or more than one killer,' I added quietly, a suspicion forming in my mind, and seizing upon it in a new attempt to drag myself from stupefied numbness.

'That is possible, Domine, yes.'

I took in the shape of Anullinus in that lake and clasped my hands behind my back to stop them shaking.

Volusianus had not been at the games either. Anullinus had cried off, claiming he had too much to occupy his time, but Volusianus had also declined my invitation, muttering about work. It was appalling to think of it, but I could find no other potential culprit in my mind than my remaining staunch advisor. Surely he was above this sort of thing? The pair had been at one another's throats almost since they'd met, but neither had ever shown any hint of violence towards the other, for all their verbal attacks.

'Do you think it was agents of Galerius, Father?'

I had almost forgotten that Romulus was with me and as I turned to him I bit my cheek at the madness of having brought him here. He was pale and clearly worried. And trying to find a simple solution where there was none. If the enemies of my realm were to go to the Herculean efforts of sending assassins, I'm sure that they would have been a lot more subtle than this, and they would probably have come for me, and not my prefect.

No. This was something closer to home.

The soldier was speaking again. 'I have to advise you, sadly, Domine, that there is next to no chance of us identifying the killer unless he happens to wander into one of our barracks covered in blood.'

I nodded, fairly certain that such a thing would not happen, for the killer was closer to home than that. Who else hated Anullinus enough for this? Who else would have such ease of access? The man was built like a soldier too, and would know how to use such a knife and where to drive it for a kill. It *had* to be Volusianus.

I still hoped it wasn't, and that one of these men would suddenly rise from searching a corner with some evidence that shifted the blame, but in truth I could picture no other suspect. I would have to watch him carefully in the coming days and see if I could trip him up and...

And what?

What would I do if I discovered beyond doubt that my *Dux Militum* had murdered my Praetorian Prefect? Hardly could I have him tried and punished. I was now missing one of my closest advisors. To lose the other to the executioner's blade in retribution for the first would be idiocy.

Closing my eyes and biting my lip, I sighed, my clasped hands white with the pressure of my grip.

'Learn what you can, and then tidy up the body and prepare it. I will arrange the appropriate rites and the funeral at the city's expense, since he has served it so faithfully. And have someone clean up the house and locate the servants and slaves. He has no close kin, so the palace will administer his property. Anullinus must have been alone, else there would be other bodies, so you'll likely find that the staff are all dead and heaped in an alley somewhere close by, but we still cannot discount the *possibility* that this was the work of one furious slave.'

It wasn't. The military man who had performed the deed had cleared the house of servants somehow and I knew they would all be found dead, if they were found at all. But the loose threads needed tying up anyway.

'Come, Romulus. You will join my circle of advisors soon, when you take the man's toga and before you disappear on some prefect's posting, and it will do you good to sit in on our meetings before then to prepare you for such times. I have an appointment with my council this afternoon. Anullinus may be absent but the rest will still attend and you can fill the spare place.'

I was ready for Volusianus. In the hours before the meeting I had disappeared into a small room deep in the bowels of the palace, where I had allowed all that I had dammed up inside at the bathhouse to break free. I had railed against fate and the gods, had shed tears and punched the wall until my knuckles were black. And then I had taken a deep breath, cleaned myself up and returned to the world, ready for what was to come next. I had taken great pains to carefully prepare the room. My chair was higher and more comfortable than the others – something I generally abhorred as vainglorious, but right now I wanted to remind Volusianus of our relative positions. Romulus sat at my left, while the empty chair that was habitually taken by Anullinus lay to my right hand. All very meaningful. Volusianus' usual chair, decorated with his exotic African animal pelts, sat directly opposite, where I could bolt him to the seat with my gaze.

It had been a matter of hours since I had stood in that claustrophobic room in the blood of my right-hand man and I was sure of Volusianus' guilt. Though I could ill afford to do anything about it, I wanted to be certain. And once I was, I wanted him to know it.

I was prepared.

Perhaps Volusianus was too, for he was late to the meeting, which was unprecedented. For a heart-stopping moment, I considered the possibility that someone had done away with *both* my closest aides in one swoop, but I quickly shoved away that idea.

Aurelius Zenas, my urban prefect, had arrived and taken

his seat along with Ruricius Pompeianus, the imperial Horse Guard commander, Sempronius Clemens of the frumentarii and two men of the senate I had come to consider worthy of at least seeking their opinion – Ovinius Gallicanus and Antonius Caecinius Sabinus. I'd greeted each as they entered and sat, either with a nod or a word or two. And each one had visibly noted and understood the arrangement of seating, for news of Anullinus' death would have spread across the city like wild fire in a summer grass.

I was starting to become irritated at my Dux Militum. Not only was I fairly sure he had brutally murdered his opposite number among the Praetorians, but now he was late for a meeting and was making me wait. I would tear a strip off him for all of this. As soon as I looked into those eyes and confirmed his guilt, I would make him sweat. For no man who had committed such a crime and still clung to any kind of conscience would be able to avoid guilt filling his gaze.

I was actually rapping a beringed finger on the arm of my chair and about to call the meeting off when the door opened and Volusianus entered with a quick nod of the head in greeting. His eyes were down, hooded beneath beetled brows as he scurried across the room with an armful of scroll cases and slumped into the chair, apparently not even noticing my careful placing of everyone.

I felt suddenly unsure. Volusianus did not have the *bearing* of a guilt-ridden man.

Then he glanced up.

And I went cold.

The look in his eyes swept away everything, for his expression was dark with foreboding. He bore news, and his demeanour alone told me that Anullinus was a subject that would have to wait.

'You're late,' I said flatly.

'I warned you,' Volusianus said quietly, not smug, but rather with a hint of nerves.

'What?'

'Africa. I warned you about Domitius Alexander. I told you to replace him, but Anullinus counselled you to caution.'

My mind flapped about like a loose sail. Alexander? What had he done?

'The governor has refused to send his son to Rome. His cronies in Carthage have proclaimed him emperor and several of the military units still based over there have thrown their support behind him. My deputation were stripped of their weapons and uniforms and put on a ship straight back here, bearing the head of their commander in an oiled-skin bag as a token of their resistance. I brought you Africa, Domine, and Anullinus' recommendations have lost it again for you.'

I felt my senses reeling.

Africa.

The source of so much of my army, my money, my grain. I could not afford to lose Africa. If I let Africa rebel, I would not be able to support the enormous army I had amassed in Italia in defence against the other claimants. To lose Africa was, in effect, to lose the whole game. I felt lost and directionless. Damn it, but now I needed Anullinus more than ever. I noticed Volusianus looking at my bruised knuckles and swiftly hid the hand from view. Something in his expression shifted at the sight, and peering through his eyes into his soul I saw the guilt swimming in him. I was right. It had been him. And as his gaze leapt away from me, I felt certain that he was now aware that I knew. Allowing my lip to curl very slightly in subtle disgust, I addressed the gathering while still looking directly at Volusianus.

'What do we do?'

'Invade,' said Clemens quickly, unaware of what had just passed between the Dux Militum and I. 'We have a massive army in Italia. Send a sizeable part of it to Africa and *conquer* the place.'

Volusianus shook his head, turning to Clemens and avoiding my gaze as he focused on the matter at hand. 'To diminish the Italian army so much is to invite invasion by Galerius or Constantine. Anyway, this is a task for a careful strike aimed at the heart of the trouble – like an arrow shot – not flattening a mostly loyal province with a blunt hammer.' *A careful strike to the heart, eh? He still would not look me in the eye.* 'Had we removed Alexander from position at the start, there would be no revolt. This needs to be done carefully but quickly. And I should be the one to do it. I know Africa. I know those people in power who are supporting Alexander, and I know how to turn them. Africa was *my* province, and I can bring it back to you. I will take four cohorts. That should be enough.'

I suddenly realised I was shaking my head, though I had been fully intending to nod. How odd, for it all made sense. Volusianus could do the job, I was certain – there was surely no better choice in all of Rome for the task. Yet I was shaking my head, and the reason quickly rose to my conscious thought.

'Domine?' Finally Volusianus met my gaze again, and this time he flinched very slightly.

'No,' I commanded. 'Anullinus is gone, and he was ever my close advisor and counsel. You have also played that role since you first arrived in the city, and I cannot afford to lose both of you. I cannot do without you here. And your job as Dux Militum is to control this vast force we have assembled. You cannot be spared for a job that another able commander and diplomat can do. We will send someone else.'

'Domine,' Volusianus cautioned, 'no one else here knows the place like me.'

'I do,' said a quiet voice. The assembled faces turned to young Zenas, who was sitting forward.

'What?'

'*I* know Africa. I grew up in Uthina, not far from Carthage. I know the big families, and what needs doing, and I am an able commander as you know. I have rebuilt your Urban Cohorts into a fearsome force, but now I sit idle commanding them. I can be of greater use in Africa, and you know that.'

And now I was nodding. I had come to trust Zenas as one of the highest members of my council. Only one thing niggled at me.

'Can you do that?'

He looked at me in incomprehension and I tapped my temple thoughtfully.

'You are one of the Nazarenes, yes? A follower of the Christ God?'

Zenas was still frowning his lack of understanding. 'Yes, Domine?'

'Well aren't you supposed to abhor violence? You will have to not only command in battle, but also condemn a man to death and see that he meets Elysium swiftly. I remember men of your sect standing peacefully in Nicomedia while they were beheaded and burned, with no hint of fight in them. *Can* you execute a man?'

It was perhaps harsher than I had intended, my suppressed anger at Volusianus being displaced to my trusted friend, but I need not have worried. Zenas gave a strange smirk and raised a quizzical eyebrow. 'I'm a Christian, Domine, not an idiot.'

I looked deep into his eyes and saw no doubt. Just resolution. I had long held that the sheer willpower of which these Christians seemed possessed could be a powerful resource, but never before had I considered wagering my future on one. Could Zenas bring me Africa again?

'Go. Take a legion – a veteran one, and one from the south that is used to warmer conditions. Bring me Africa and bring me Alexander's head.'

PART 2

Nil agit exemplum, litem quod lite resolvit
(Worthless is an example that solves one
problem with another)
– *Horace*

7

CONSTANTINE

GAUL, LATE MARCH 309 AD

Winter was fierce and unrelenting. Blizzards and deathly cold winds held sway for months. I spent the start of the year locked in my planning chambers – glowing in the merciful heat of a well-stocked fire. I grew weary of the map that dominated these discussions: a yellowing, huge map, unfurled on the planning table and held in place by two silver weights in the form of resting lions. Upon it were dozens of carved wooden legionary figurines. Each piece resembled a regiment, and to a passing eye, it might have resembled a mighty army, but in truth, it was not big enough – not even close.

The regions of Gaul, Hispania and Britannia sported just a few figurines each, because the vast majority of them were engaged elsewhere. Many were dotted along the jagged line that demarcated my southern borders – locked there in case my rivals thought to march into my realm. Just as many again were strewn along my eastern frontier – at the River Rhenus where the many still-hostile tribes of the cursed Frankish federation had spent all winter probing and prodding, eager to break into my lands and renew the slaughter and pillage.

But as the month of March drew to a close I started to believe we might just have survived the winter threat from the Franks. I longed for spring to come – a chance to ramp up trade, swell my coffers and perhaps recruit new legions. I was a fool for allowing myself to think of the new season... for winter was not over yet.

As I trudged from the planning room one night, I stopped by Crispus' room, finding him asleep there, Fausta cradling him and slumbering too. I kissed them both on the head and crept to my own sleeping chamber. I think I must have fallen asleep but a moment after lying down in that warm comfort. It was a deep, dreamless sleep that nourished my tired mind. Until I was awoken by the clatter of boots, echoing into my chamber.

Never wake a soldier abruptly, Batius once told me, and now I understood why. I fell from my bed, landing in a crouch, grabbing and unsheathing the dagger I kept nearby in one fluid motion. The two feather-helmed Cornuti flanked a single, panting messenger, swaddled in a thick cape and spattered with semi-frozen mud from what must have been a hasty ride.

I rose and sheathed my dagger, noticing the Cornuti pair gulping slightly at my reaction, then I flicked my head, indicating that the messenger should speak.

'The gods have forsaken us, Domine,' he gasped, falling to his knees on the marble floor. 'A winter bridge has sprouted across the Rhenus – a frozen crossing.'

Instantly, my blood was awash with ice and fire. 'Where?'

The messenger's eyes answered before he spoke. 'At the forsaken gap, Domine.'

For a moment, I longed to suddenly awake from this nightmarish moment. I had endured foul dreams of this very news. My mind swiftly conjured an image of that damned map. The 'forsaken gap' was the stretch of the Rhenus frontier – over fifty miles – where no legion was stationed. It was a narrow but ferocious section of the river with tumultuous rapids. Due to our manpower shortage, I had taken the calculated risk of leaving that area undefended – employing just a few messenger scouts like this man before me to monitor the banks. Now, all I could see was an unchecked flood of Frankish tribesmen pouring across it, spilling into my realm.

'Summon Batius and Krocus,' I said, throwing on a thick woollen tunic, trousers and cloak. As I helped to saddle Celeritas in the chilly grounds of the palace stables, I turned my mind to exactly how I was going to tackle this threat. I needed men. I could not strip Treverorum of its garrison – not with the ever-present strife in those streets – yet I could not ride to the great river with just my two officers.

When Batius and Krocus arrived, offering each other no more than a grudging flick of the head in greeting, I consulted them. Baleful but vital, they had been present in every planning session.

'The Primigenia are more than two days' march away, in western Gaul,' Batius muttered. 'Every other legion—' he started, then stopped and shook his head, extending his arms, palms upturned.

'My men move swiftly, Domine,' Krocus added, then slumped, 'but they are at least seven days away, at the southern forts, watching Italia.'

Not quite the close-to-hand Comitatus I had envisaged, reprimanding myself for letting the bulk of the Regii be drawn to the ever-threatened borders.

'There is one other option,' Batius muttered grudgingly.

I looked at him, my eyes shrinking to slits. 'They are not ready, surely?'

'Yet they are the only force we can call upon,' he reasoned.

With a stiff sigh and a puff of icy breath, I climbed into my saddle. 'Very well.'

So, Batius, Krocus and I set off northwards, accompanied by the twelve Regii still stationed at Treverorum. We rode at haste, knuckles and faces turning blue with the chill gale. Batius and Krocus wore scowls befitting both the cold and the presence of each other. The wind howled relentlessly, furring the tall grass ahead. The land was still streaked with the white veins of remnant winter snow, and the night sky was starless, as if threatening one last blizzard like the many that had battered my realm for months.

We reached a stretch of frost-speckled heathland at dawn. These once bleak fallow lands were now a patchwork of gold and green winter crops, with a few early risers already at work on them. A sea of timber huts and a few newly constructed stone villas hemmed one edge of this tract of farmland. The gentle clucking of hens and the lowing of cattle were at odds with the storm of worries in my mind.

As we slowed to a canter and then a walk, I heard a shout, heralding our arrival. A moment later, a clutch of figures emerged from one of the villas. Hisarnis of the Bructeri and his bodyguards walked towards us. I hadn't visited this settlement since bringing him and his people here in December, and I had left their bedding in to my subordinates. Those obsequious individuals had given me the usual honey-coated updates that might have mollified a weaker emperor. Yet I had had little time to even think about it; the best I had been able do was to send Batius to observe affairs here – back in February.

'Tell me again how they are progressing?' I said to him under my breath so Hisarnis – still a good way away – would not hear.

Batius stroked his anvil jaw and tilted his head this way and that. 'The families – I'd say they have taken to imperial life with ease. Those crop fields are the work of a contented lot.'

The word absent from the end of his sentence pealed like a bell in my head. 'But?'

One edge of his lips lifted a little in amusement. 'But... the fighting men: they're finding it a little harder to adapt. Roman military training is proving to be something of a challenge.'

'How so?' I replied, giving him a sideways look.

'Formations – not too bad. *Ambulatum* exercises are pretty good – they know how to spring an ambush and work a flanking manoeuvre. And *armatura* sessions with sword, javelin and shield are actually quite encouraging too. But you know as well as I do – is any army just men, armour and weapons?' he said, arching an eyebrow.

I let a short, barking laugh escape my lips. 'No more than a tavern is just bricks and mortar.'

The big man nodded. 'That's just it. They lack spirit and camaraderie. When I was here last month we issued them with their Roman tunics. But apparently they were too itchy, and that's all I heard all day – grumbling and *scratch-scratch-scratch*. They spent the day plodding about with their faces tripping them. And there's some sort of infighting going on among them – some of them are refusing to take part in the training at all. I'm not sure what to make of that. One of the buggers lost an eye in some sort of scuffle.'

I sighed. 'Barbarian tribes pressing from the east. The Herdsman and his innumerable legions poised to the south-east. Maxentius...' I paused, a needling heat spreading across my chest '...lodged in the southern half of my realm... with armies that dwarf mine and have none of the tribes to contend with.' I chuckled mirthlessly. 'And then we have... itchy tunics. Is there no limit to my concerns?'

The question was left unanswered as we drew up next to Hisarnis. The aged Bructeri chieftain had dispensed with his plaid and now donned an off-white tunic and thick, brown cloak. He had even trimmed his braided beard short, to little more than stubble – were it not for his flowing, hoary locks, he might even have passed as an old Roman landholder. I also noticed how he walked with the aid of a cane, nursing some leg injury.

'Domine,' he said with a half-bow. It was a warm greeting that was reflected in his eyes and melted the chilly tension. A flock of women and youngsters began to assemble behind him, gawping up at me and my small escort.

I nodded in reply, then cast my eyes over the settlement behind him. Closer, I could see some of the structures more clearly. One squat, timber hall bore a Chi-Rho above the door. A temple of sorts, I reckoned. I noticed that some of his people loitered near this building, faces wrinkled, some muttering curses at those entering and leaving. These ones were quick to turn their sour gazes upon me and upon the back of their chieftain too. An understanding of what was going on here – the unrest Batius had described – began to form. Was this place a microcosm of the strife in Treverorum and so many other cities across my lands – a battle of faiths, fuelled by hunger and poverty? I rid myself of that perpetual, nagging problem and returned my thoughts to this one, reverting my eyes to Hisarnis. 'As part of the treaty that saw you and your people settled here, you agreed to provide me with men.'

The warmth in Hisarnis' eyes faded just a fraction. 'The Bructeri will march as part of your Comitatus, Domine.' I noticed the lines on his brow deepen. 'I don't know what you've heard, but I can assure you that come autumn, they will be ready.'

So the troubles within this tribe were on Hisarnis' mind too, I realised. 'Autumn, we agreed,' I sighed, 'but events dictate that I will need them sooner.'

A flurry of whispers and gasps rang out from the crowd. 'Sooner?' Hisarnis said.

'Today,' I clarified.

Now the gasps rang out loud and clear.

Hisarnis' head darted to those behind him, as if he was unsettled by the sound. He returned his gaze to me at last. 'Domine, I...'

'I would not ask this of you were the situation not... pressing.' I gave him a look as I said this, a look I hoped would transcend words and convince him this was no showy display of my power – some deliberate violation of the treaty terms to put him in his place. When at last he nodded, I released the captive breath in my lungs and felt the tension ease once more.

'Domine, while I have almost two thousand men of fighting age, less than half of them are...' he hesitated, glancing over his shoulder towards the shack with the Christian icon '... ready.'

'Give me what you can – that is all I ask,' I replied.

As the dawn sun rose and the morning began in earnest, I watched two cohorts' worth of Bructeri forming up before me. They had been issued oval Roman shields, painted gold with a scarlet, winged victory in the centre. Most heads were crowned with the simple oval ridge-helms bolstered by iron rivets and nose and cheek guards I had commissioned for them. Some wore their old, tribal furs under imperial-issue mail shirts. A few of them had even donned those wretched itchy tunics under their armour. Some still sported long, braided hair and shaggy beards or moustaches.

I rode across their front, eyeing each of them. To my relief, I noticed none of the baleful glares worn by those lurking within the dirt streets of the settlement. 'I hear you have worked hard since you came here: marching and duelling as well as any of my legions.' I thought it best to steer clear of the mixed reports Batius had given me – for now at least. I scanned the nine hundred or so faces, wondering as to the wisdom of what I was about to do. 'Now, I call upon you to march with me, and march at haste. For at the great river, I need you to stand with me, to protect this realm. My country, your country... *our* country.'

Silence. I doubted myself for that instant. But men of the tribes are raised on the need for war, and these fellows had been starved of it since entering the empire. So the silence was brief, shattering as they exploded in a roar of agreement, gruff and guttural.

As they hoisted their packs and weapons, Batius spoke to me in a whisper. 'Nine hundred? That is not enough. If the tribes come for the forsaken gap as I expect, that is not *nearly* enough.'

'I agree entirely,' I said flatly. I felt his uncomprehending stare on the side of my face as I watched the Bructeri assembling into a legionary marching line. 'And that is why we must make a stop along the way, at Mogontiacum.'

Batius' face creased further. 'Mogontiacum? Domine, the garrison there is threadbare. A century of men and no more – you cannot strip them from the city.'

'It is not Mogontiacum's soldiers I need, Batius,' I mused, gazing east.

Three days of marching followed, feet crunching through the snow and ice that clung to the land. The two Bructeri 'cohorts' marched well. We swept by Mogontiacum, stopping not for shelter or rest, but merely to requisition what I needed. With a perplexed frown, Batius watched the train of mules the city governor sent out for us. 'Mules?' he said, scratching his stubbled jaw. Conversely, Krocus's face lit up in understanding and he took great delight in glorying over Batius' bewilderment.

We moved on at haste. By late afternoon on the third day we came to a patch of white-coated flatland that led us to the Rhenus and the forsaken gap: the river was narrow here – about a hundred paces from west bank to east. The thrashing waters tussled and threw up columns of spray that caught the sunlight in a medley of iridescent haloes. A fierce river, but not fierce enough to break the sparkling ice bridge winter had cast across it. The winter ford, stubborn and mocking, straddled the waterway like a good marching road – maybe seventy paces wide. There were no signs of boot or hoof prints in the frost or earth on this side of the ford, I realised. Good, we had triumphed in the race to get here before the enemy on the other side, it seemed.

I slid from my saddle and strode towards the waterline, Batius and Krocus either side of me. There, I looked to the far banks, shrouded in a forest of frost-speckled pines. Three squat and bare peaks stood proud of these thick woods, each capped with remnant snow that sparkled like white flame in the dying light, the lofty breeze up there blowing a mist of ice particles across the orange sky. But it was the woods that I feared. I gazed into the darkness of the treeline, my mind showing me an army of shadows within.

'We have not a heartbeat to lose,' I realised.

And then I heard the faintest but most marrow-chilling howl from somewhere over there. A wolf-like call. The call of a tribesman.

'Domine, perhaps it is time for the mules?' Krocus said.

Batius shot him a foul look. 'What?'

But I had no time to discuss the matter. 'Bring the mules forward.'

'Domine, what is he talking about, why—' Batius started, but the crunch of the pack animals' hooves in the snow drowned him out. The mule-handlers took the rough sacks from the backs of the beasts, and scampered with the weighty burdens out onto the ice bridge under Krocus' direction. They slit the bottoms of the sacks with knives, and white powder tumbled onto the mid-section of the bridge in thick piles – the men walking back and forth, all the while their eyes shooting to the foreign banks of the river and the dark forest.

'Salt,' Batius said, his expression falling blank, then a craggy grin rising. 'Salt!' He slapped his leg and roared with laughter. 'I watched all the tricks your father pulled, but this beats any—'

He fell silent as a *hiss* sounded from across the river. All eyes shot that way. A single pine over there shivered, shedding its veil of frost. My body tensed. The salt-spreaders froze too. Then I heard the rapping of hooves on semi-frozen ground.

The tribes?

Batius, Krocus and I exchanged a look that only close comrades can – a tacit language learned from years together on the battlefield. It was too late to wait on the salt to do its work. I sucked in a breath to call out in alarm... to draw back the mule-handlers out on the bridge, when a slingshot spat from somewhere deep in the trees and took one poor fellow in the eye – a burst of blood erupting from the back of his head. The rest of the mule-handlers scattered off the bridge and past me in panic.

'Together!' I roared, beckoning the Bructeri into a line. A cool wind furred my bear pelt and searched inside my bronze scale corselet as I gazed around the modest force that collected either side of me. The nine hundred would have to do. One Bructeri warrior brought me my jewelled, golden helm – the gift from Hisarnis. Then I saw the shadows among the trees writhing, growing... innumerable. '*Together!*'

The breath was almost pushed from my lungs as we crushed together. Batius had my right, while Hisarnis and Krocus were by my left. Just as the young warriors in line with us had been trained to in these last months, we bore our spears in the wall of shields that plugged the western end of the ice ford.

The tribesmen emerged like a mist of wraiths. And in moments the far bank was swollen with them. Thousands, maybe five of them for each of my men.

'The Chatti,' the Bructeri men whispered in terror. I had only heard of these deep-forest dwellers before. They were wan-skinned, some with their faces or bare chests painted white – as if borne by winter itself. Their pale golden hair was shaped into jutting peaks. They stalked forward, lithe and ready, spears levelled, glacial eyes glinting. And the eeriest thing about them was how they moved with almost no sound at all. No clamour, no songs, no curses – just a deadly, resolute rumble of feet advancing.

They halted when their leader – a broad, stocky type

with a wolfskin on his head, the lifeless beast's eyes staring and the fangs striking down his forehead – raised a hand. The chieftain then barged through to stand on the far end of the ice ford and beheld us with a disdainful, sweeping gaze. He erupted in a forced, booming laugh, seemingly unimpressed by the resistance we presented. A moment later, the innumerable warriors with him joined in, their baritone laughter shaking the air. The chieftain then took to aiming some trilling diatribe at us.

'What is he saying?' I grunted to Hisarnis.

'He's calling us motherless pigs. He says we spit in Wodin's eye for standing with the enemy.'

I felt a breath of doubt pass over my skin. What was to stop these tribesmen, who just months ago counted the Chatti as their allies, from turning upon Batius, Krocus and I and butchering us, then joining the Chatti to raid and slaughter across Gaul?

From the corner of my eye, I caught Hisarnis' shark-like grin. 'But I've never liked him or his kin. I think I will send him to talk with Wodin today.'

I could have laughed aloud had we not been facing such grim odds. Indeed, the breaths of the other Bructeri came and went in short, snatched gasps. I glanced along the line to see their faces, taut and wan with fear at the gargantuan horde facing them. Our ranks were twelve men deep, so there was a chance – just the most tortuously narrow chance – that we might hold them back. But to what end? The Chatti would not relent even if we somehow repelled them once, twice or thrice. And we had no reinforcements to hold out for.

I spotted one of the Bructeri, whispering to himself. No, to his god. Wodin? The Christ? I did not know. But when he was finished, I noticed that the fear was lessened in him. Just like the legionary on the walls of Naissus on the night of the storm from my childhood. The memory brought a renewed streak of determination to my heart.

'Comitatus,' I cried, emphasising the word, underlining their status as one of these, a regiment of my closest, 'stand with me and I will stand with you against these dogs before us – let us keep our dearest ones back in our homes safe from their poison blades. We will not yield. We will *not yield!*'

The line of bearded faces above the wall of shields turned to me. I could see the spark of hope my few words had given them – enough to break the dread spell of the nearby Chatti. As one, they vented and vanquished their fear in an explosive cry, rapping their spears against their shields in a deafening refrain. Batius and I could not help but join in fervidly and the throaty song of defiance utterly trampled the laughing tribesmen across the river.

The Chatti chieftain's face fell and he lifted his spear. He held it there, trembling with rage for what felt like an eternity... then swept it like an accusing finger across the ice ford. With a jagged cry, his army surged forward past him with a crescendo of guttural roars. Those deathly white warriors bounded like hunting cats, faces bent in frenzy, spears raised, eyes affixing their would-be victims.

'Brace!' I howled, my officers yelling in unison in the breath before the Chatti plunged against our lines. The impact was like the kick of a mule and the sounds of their lances battering against our shields was akin to an angry thunderstorm. Enemy spears flashed and clanged against Bructeri helms, gouging chunks from the edges of our shields and sending blood spray into the air where they found faces or gaps in the shield wall. The warrior pressing against my shield panted, teeth clenched, foul breath wafting over me. A manic, yellow-toothed grin was plastered across his white-painted face as he shoved and I shoved back. This close, neither of us could bring our spears to bear and so shove was all we could do. But while there were just eleven ranks behind me in support, there were endless Chatti warriors behind him, eager to win the battle of strength.

Soon, our line buckled into a V, bending at the centre under their weight. Were it to break, we would be done for.

'Dig your boots and spear shafts into the earth!' Batius screamed, leading by example. But even the big man's efforts were in vain – his boots slipping and skidding and his spear shaft driving a rut into the earth as he was forced back.

'We're going to break,' one Bructeri warrior near me quailed.

'We cannot,' I snarled defiantly. But already I heard wet, strangled half-screams, cut short by the tearing of iron across flesh as the Chatti hacked at our collapsing centre, warriors climbing up and over our shield wall and leaping into our ranks. Next, the frightened Bructeri fighter who had spoken crumpled from view in a puff of blood – an enemy club staving in his face. A spear sliced past my neck, nicking my skin, casting my own blood up across my lips, the coppery stink all too familiar. My paltry line of men was set to break apart like a pair of gates.

It was then that I felt a curious calm overcome me. I can only hope to explain it to men who have stood in battle, men driven to find logic amid chaos: it is a sense of acceptance – that what is meant to be will come to pass. If death was my destiny that day, then so be it.

But it was not to be.

A thick, thunderous crack split the air, far louder than the initial clash of shields just moments ago – this was more like the irate lash of a titan's whip. It shook the land and the ground under my feet shuddered with it. It was followed swiftly by another series of seven or eight louder cracks – like the trailing and even more vicious tails of this invisible lash. My body fought on, blocking the blows of the furious warriors before me – but my eyes could not help but shoot to the spectral image that rose up behind our assailants, midway across the river: a vast, jagged shard of ice had broken from the ford and now swung up, tilting like a plate pressed down at one edge. On it, a swathe of screaming Chatti warriors skidded and slid. Hundreds of them slipped helplessly across the smooth surface and plummeted into the freezing river. A few clung to the edges of the broken ice shard, wailing, as it settled again with an almighty splash that washed across the shard and swept them under the rapids.

The salt! I realised, seeing the film of meltwater that rippled on the surface of the shard, my spirits soaring. It had worked!

Those pinning us onto the western banks suddenly found their momentum and sheer weight of number stolen away. They staggered back, eyes swinging to the remaining stretch of ford where thousands more of their comrades had frozen in fright. A moment later, another enraged groan and a sharp, decisive crack echoed across the land. This time the remainder of the ford broke apart under the weight of the huge host upon it, shattering into a thousand pieces. I caught sight of the chieftain's confused face for but a moment before he was gone, pulled into the deadly, glacial river. Men thrashed in their thousands, fighting to survive for moments before falling still and drifting off, face-down with the current like the fragments of the ford.

The ice bridge was gone, and the lucky handful of Chatti stranded on the far banks of the river gawped over at us.

The remnant on this side of the river who had almost broken our lines – suddenly bereft of their many kinsmen – lost their pluck at once.

'Finish them!' I snarled. My beleaguered force clustered together behind a now blood-spattered shield wall, snarling, then slowly pacing towards the marooned Chatti. A few of them screamed and charged towards us, only to be riven with a volley of thrown spiculae. Another bunch charged our right flank, but were rebuffed, many cut down without ceremony.

Then, Hisarnis stepped proud of the line and sneered at them: 'Today, Wodin has shame enough, only for you!' With that, he hoisted his spear, as if ready to wave the lines forward. The fearsome warrior's actions utterly broke the last vestiges of Chatti courage.

An instant later the beaten warriors tossed down their weapons and – with a graceless din of splashing – leapt into the perishing Rhenus in order to swim to safety on the far bank. Most thrashed manfully at first but few even made it halfway before the cold seized their strength and pulled them under. The few left on these banks then fled like frightened deer, bolting north along the riverbank. I let my men see them off with another volley of spiculae.

I stepped forward through the red-streaked mush of ice, earth and blood; past torn bodies of friend and foe until I came to the river's edge. There, I knelt on one knee, transfixed on the jagged ends of the collapsed ford. A broken bridge, an untold number of dead.

Looking back on that day, it makes me weep to think that it was not the last time I would endure such a sight.

★★★

We spent a night at the battle site. Under the stars, Batius, Krocus and I shared a campfire. Batius took great pleasure in accidentally dropping the injured Krocus' share of charred mutton into the dirt, before picking it up and handing it to him with a sickly sweet apology. In return, Krocus 'accidentally' smeared a bloody fingerprint from his freshly dressed shoulder wound on Batius' bread, thus claiming the soiled loaf for himself. That aside, their usual bickering was limited by fatigue.

In any case I barely noticed, for my gaze continuously returned to the now-dark trees across the river. What would become of the Chatti? The horde that had come for us today was vast, but there were seemingly limitless villages dotted out there in the bogs and dark, endless woods – surely brimming with many more young men that the heir to the drowned chieftain could muster to form a new army. Despite our fortuitous victory today, the Chatti were still very much a threat.

'We cannot continue to fight the Franks like this. Our strategy is flawed,' I muttered, thinking aloud. 'We fended off the Chatti today, yet they are but one tribe. What of the Marsi? What of the Tencteri, of the Ubii, of the Mattiachi, of the Sugambri and the Chamavi? While our legions remain pinned on the Rhenus frontier fighting attritive wars, Galerius and Maxentius stockpile weapons and recruit many fresh legions. Our only hope of neutralising the Frankish problem – and swelling our numbers in time to dissuade our imperial rivals from any thoughts of invasion – is to bring more of the tribes into our ranks as we have done with the Bructeri.'

'Fantastic,' Batius said glibly under his breath then almost drained the wineskin before sinking his teeth into a freshly roasted joint of mutton.

'Excellent idea.' Krocus grinned. 'You will send envoys into the Frankish lands, I presume? May I offer my riders to serve as escorts?'

'I already had your men in mind.' I nodded in agreement. 'Having a new strategy in place might at least give me a chance to think of our foes within the empire.'

A silence passed, but I could tell Batius was mulling over whether to say something as he fidgeted. 'Spit it out, big man.'

Batius looked up, bemused, then shrugged. 'The threat from the Eastern Empire – it might not be what it once was. They say Galerius has grown weak with some strange illness.'

I had heard, but largely ignored, such rumours. 'And have his vast armies been stricken too? And his mongrel of a deputy, Licinius?' I snorted.

'Fair point,' Batius agreed, taking a deep gulp of a fresh wineskin to wash his food down. 'But Maxentius certainly has enough troubles to balance with ours.'

'Africa,' Krocus whispered, his gaze lost in the flames. 'They say that without its grain, every soul in Italia will starve.'

'They will,' I said flatly, taking Batius' wineskin and having a long gulp for myself before handing it to the Regii leader. 'And soon after, so will we. The crop fields of Gaul and Hispania alone will not support the many mouths demanding bread. Grain – or lack of it – is about to become our darkest enemy.' I thought of the rich wheat and barley fields of Aegyptus and Syria in the East and stifled another sigh. 'Illness or no illness, Galerius will be the only winner in those stakes, unless...' I fell silent for a moment, the weight of my next words troubling me, 'unless the West can be unified.'

Batius' face fell as he mulled this over. 'After all that has come to pass, do you think such a thing can be achieved,' he asked quietly, '…without bloodshed?'

I gave him a look. Once more, it was that tacit language of comrades.

8

MAXENTIUS

ROME, 18TH APRIL 309 AD

Marcellus – the high priest of the Christians in Rome – looked unbearably smug as he entered my aula regia, though the lackey at his shoulder seemed considerably more subdued, which, while I was still furious, warmed me towards *him* a little at least. If I'd needed to stoke my ire, though, I had only to turn back to the unctuous lunatic I'd had the misfortune to appoint as head of that troublesome sect.

'Majesty,' hissed one of the Praetorians just off to the side, trying to remind me that these visitors were coming perilously close to the imperial person. I had noticed a subtle change in the attitude of the Guard since I had put Volusianus in command of them following the death of his opposite number, Anullinus – nothing *strong*, just a stiffer, more formal manner. Volusianus might have been here with me now, had he not been busy beyond belief administrating at once the vast army, the Praetorians *and* the Urban Cohorts. Zenas, of course, languished in Africa, failing to bring me the conclusive victory over the usurper Alexander for which I had hoped. I tried not to think of Zenas and Africa. I was angry enough right now with those in my own city.

I waved the guardsman back. This was not Constantine's swelling army of Germanic savages, but a pair of pacifist priests. What had I to fear in person from these men? It seemed that they had endless power over their own worshippers, but I was a true son of Jove, not some cultist from a half-desert eastern backwater. I could sense the disapproval of the soldier at my lack of caution, but I *wanted* Marcellus to come close. The closer the better. Real anger is best expressed close and all the worse for being experienced that way.

'Marcellus,' I said, keeping my voice steady. He seemed completely oblivious to my mood in spite of the fact that I had done nothing to hide it, and I was curious despite myself to see how long he could maintain his composure.

'Majesty,' the priest replied with appropriate deference, though his eyes were only cast downwards for a moment, almost as though in recognising my authority he was denying his own God. Hades, how these Christians bothered me sometimes. Intrigued me, to some extent, but still bothered me.

'You seem to be in a jubilant mood,' I prompted. Marcellus's already smug smile broadened, and I was fascinated to note his companion wince. Good. At least one of them knew what was happening.

'There is much to be jubilant about, Majesty.'

'Oh?'

I *knew* I had a dangerous edge to my voice, like the sword of Damocles hanging over the idiot's head.

'Of course, Majesty. The *Lapsi* are returning to the fold of Christ, and their restoration swells the coffers of the holy seat of sainted Petrus. Our numbers grow... while remaining true in our allegiance to your mighty self,' he added quickly, whipping a tongue out to wet his lips. 'And our dilapidated finances are slowly recovering.'

I cocked an eyebrow and almost laughed as the priest behind him shook his head very slightly and put a hand over his eyes.

'Well, Majesty,' Marcellus went on in a conciliatory tone, 'I know that our Church has not always enjoyed the same legitimacy as some of Rome's older... err... faiths... but since our legalisation, surely we should be encouraged to grow and finance ourselves in the same manner as, for instance, the cult of *Sol Invictus*, or the priests of Saturn?'

'I care not, Pope Marcellus, whether you are penniless or rich. Do not think for one moment that I lie awake at night pondering the state of your finances. And as long as your people remain loyal to the throne and to Rome, I could not give two Thracian farts whether there are ten of you or a thousand. I have your people serving in both my court and my army. You may be Christians, but you are also Romans, and I respect that. But *you*, Marcellus, are more than just a Christian. More than a *Roman*. Indeed, you are more even than a high priest to your people.'

Marcellus positively glowed, anticipating my next words. The other Christian priest at his shoulder took a small step backwards, his hand still over his face. My smile turned cold as quickly as a Pannonian winter.

'Indeed, Pope Marcellus. You are *much* more. You, Marcellus, are a moron!'

The priest frowned for a moment in confusion and lifted his face to meet my gaze as I rose slowly from my throne, unfolding like the wrath of Titans.

'You are a *moron*. You are presumptuous, inflammatory, short-sighted, dangerous and hopelessly poor at your occupation.'

Marcellus rocked back. His companion had taken several

more steps away, his gaze flitting to the half dozen Praetorians in the room.

'Majesty, I...'

'Lapsi!' I snarled, leaning into his face. 'It staggers me that you even bother putting a name to such a thing.' The Lapsi were what their people were calling Christians who had recanted their beliefs during the persecutions. To my mind that made them eminently sensible, but apparently to their own Church that made them the lowest of the low.

'The Lapsi are cursed, Majesty. It is the duty of the Church to bring them back to Christ's love.'

'And to make a bucketful of *sesterces* each time for your effort.'

'Majesty?'

I heaved an irritable sigh. 'You actually charge your own people money to be saved from this cursed state. And not just a *small* fee, I am led to believe. I am told that your price for taking back your own worshippers is cripplingly high. So much so that many cannot afford to go back, even if they destitute themselves.'

'They should have thought of their future wellbeing when they sold out their faith for the comfort of their corporeal lives, Majesty. They placed their flesh above their spirit, and now they pay the price.'

'And your Lapsi are causing trouble, Marcellus.'

'Well, Majesty, they...'

'For your continued good health,' I cut him off sharply, 'I heartily recommend that you seal your lips tight and utter no further word until bidden, *Pope* Marcellus,' I snarled.

The other priest was now halfway between his master and the exit. I might have laughed had I not been so caught up in my anger.

I took a step forward, forcing the now-cowering Marcellus to back-step. Each soldier in the room took a pace forward in a tightening circle.

'I raised you to the highest position your cult allows, with *imperial patronage* no less, to solve the problems of restless Christians and to bring peace and order to your people in my realm. I specifically told you *not* to cause any trouble.'

He opened his mouth to argue but, catching the look in my eye, shut it again, prudently sealing in the hasty words.

'And now, because you are oppressing your own people, fining your Lapsi with an o'er heavy hand and generally running your cult as though it were a grocer's shop, with profit and growth your guides, your people revolt.'

'*Revolt* is a strong word, Majesty,' croaked the man halfway to the door, but he was looking deferentially at the floor again before my gaze even struck him. I wrenched my anger back to Marcellus. 'I have reports of angry demonstrations in public on no fewer than six occasions in the past few days. There have been countless injuries, some of which were inflicted upon innocent bystanders. There have been, I believe, three deaths so far, including one of your priests and two of these Lapsi who could not afford to worship their God. One of your own temples lies in smouldering ruins – unpleasantly reminiscent of Nicomedia during the persecutions – and, despite everything else, *that* is the incident that finally broke this for me. I *will* not allow your troubles to risk a fire in my city. You surely know the history of Rome enough to know how devastating fire can be. One Christian church burns and the next thing I know I'm watching whole districts go up in flames, *vigiles* filling the streets with their fire carts, every watch-house full of charred citizens being tended by every surviving medic, from imperial surgeon to horse doctor, and I am being proclaimed the new Nero. DO. YOU. FOLLOW. ME?'

Each of these last words I snapped with such force that Marcellus recoiled as though each were a hammer blow nailing him up to one of his beloved crosses. I thought I smelled urine, though his voluminous robes hid any truth of it from me.

Silence reigned in the aftermath of my tirade.

'You may speak,' I announced very quietly.

He tried several times to do so, managing a hoarse rasp at best. Finally his voice reappeared from somewhere and he managed: 'How can I regain your favour, gracious Majesty?'

I hardened my gaze. 'You can get out of my sight and make sure that I never set eyes upon your infuriating face again.' I stepped forward, raising my hand, and he flinched and cowered back. He must truly have thought I was going to strike him, and in that realisation I was sorely tempted to do so. Instead, I tore at the chain and clasp that held his outer garment of office fastened, and ripped the heavy robe from him, leaving him in a richly embroidered tunic that likely represented a significant slice of their freshly swollen coffers.

Sure enough, the waft of urine heightened with fresh exposure as I dropped my hand to my side, still gripping the robe.

'Get out of my sight, my palace, my city and my realm, you worthless, ungrateful, feckless piece of excrement. Go to Ostia and take ship. I do not care *which* ship, but do not let your name be heard again in Italia or Africa. You are hereby stripped of your position by the same authority with which you agreed your investiture. If you are found in Rome after sunset, things will not go well for you.'

The former Pope, eyes wide and wild and stinking of fear, shuffled backwards slowly. I gestured for the guards to open the door at the end of the room, and as I began to growl slowly like an angry hound, Marcellus turned and fled.

His companion was still standing a little further back, shaking his head. I wondered momentarily whether Constantine was enjoying such difficulties with the Christians of the north, given his familial connection to the strange sect. Probably not, I decided. I'd not heard tidings of such incidents, and things ever seemed to fall easily into place for the man.

'You!' I barked, pointing at the former Pope's lackey, and the man scurried forward and dropped into a bow. 'You are a priest? One of import?'

The man nodded.

'Who are you?'

'My name is Eusebius of Caralis, Majesty, and I have the honour by the grace of God to be the father of one of the larger churches in the city.'

'And your people look up to you?'

The man seemed confused by the question, shrugged, and then nodded. 'I would say so, Majesty.'

'And you can sort out this mess Marcellus created? Stop charging money to the Lapsi so they can return to your *fold* and so on?'

'I believe so, Majesty.'

I smiled. 'Good. Congratulations on your appointment, Pope Eusebius.' I thrust out a hand rather ignobly, proffering the dusty outer robe of office, and Eusebius took it reverently, though with a wrinkled nose. 'Excellent. By the time summer ends I want a peaceful city with a Christian community that pays its taxes, upholds the law, and fails to set fire to anything. That is your task. No more troubles. Understand?'

The new Pope bowed his head. 'I understand, Majesty.'

'Good. Now go and carry out your orders.'

I watched Eusebius leave the room, throwing the robe carefully about his shoulders, and I hoped that with him would go my troubles with that most difficult sect and their God. I might as well have wished for a green sky.

As I sat, recovering my temper, the doors to the chamber remained open and, presumably entirely by chance, the ghost-like figure of Valeria passed by, pausing to frown into the room. I tried to smile at her. Despite everything I always tried to smile, for if I could only melt the ice between us a little, the world could be a much different place, but the meeting I had just endured had left me with only irritation and acerbic wit, and the smile I offered probably contained as much warmth as her own expression, which promptly turned away from me as she walked on out of sight.

I sighed. If only moronic priests were my only worries.

9

CONSTANTINE

GAUL, SPRING 309 AD

As April turned to May, Treverorum hosted the *Ludi Florae*, the spring games, a celebration of fertility, flowers and growth held in honour of the Goddess Flora. With my treasury all but depleted, I funded the whole affair myself, selling armour and trinkets Father had bequeathed to me. In truth they were foul heirlooms, reminding me of the wealth he had enjoyed while Mother and I had been left behind, and I was glad to be rid of them.

The games themselves – races, discus and javelin throwing along with somewhat licentious displays of dancing and acrobatics – were supposed to be a salve to the winter-weary populace, a bold and welcome herald of the warm season. Aye, the people keenly observed the ancient customs, wore bright gowns and vivid wreaths, painted their faces in lurid colours. True enough, the joyous cascade of red and white petals tumbled through the day-by-day more clement air from the top of every high building. Yet I could not fail to recognise the underlying discontent, hidden beneath the paint on those gaunt faces, whispered in snatched, curse-ridden outbursts. They cheered the dancers, aye – though perhaps that was more to do with the rough wine I had commissioned and ordered to be distributed among them, and almost certainly a little to do with the dancers' gradual state of undress. They whooped with delight at the performing trio of elephants – but who would not marvel at such a spectacle? The magnificent beasts marched into the arena and carefully walked up a wooden ramp and along a narrow plank suspended the height of three men above the sandy ground. But despite such marvels, I heard the grumbles of dissatisfaction in between.

On the last day of the games I took my place on the padded couch – purple like my linen cloak – in the *kathisma*, overlooking the great, sun-bathed arena as two teams of mock-gladiators sprinted onto the sand. They were painted like the crowd and dressed even more brightly. They leapt and sprung through the mild sunshine in a carefully choreographed routine, eliciting cheers and gasps as, one by one, they 'killed' one another with their wooden weapons, each kill being met with a dramatic blast from a horn and a rumble from the timpani drummers. Goats and hares sprung nervously between the fighters – the animals probably fearing for their lives, but not today, for they would be released at the end of the festivities as tradition dictated.

In any case, I paid little attention to the entertainment. My eyes scanned the crowd again and again. I must admit to sporting a foul head thanks to an entire flask of the rough wine – unwatered, much to Fausta's chagrin – the night before, and that only heightened my disdain for the people whenever I heard them grumbling.

They lamented the growing threat of civil war, and by all the gods, so did I: my dreams were plagued with images of Maxentius and his swollen ranks in Italia, and Galerius and his gargantuan forces hovering in the East. The realms of the two imperial antagonists touched mine at the Alpes Mountains, as if the pressure of our mutual hostility had thrown up those great, rugged peaks. And now the first move in this great game had been made: according to my agents, Licinius – Galerius' hound – was now mobilising his forces at his Pannonian base, his scouts probing west. Did the cur truly believe he was Augustus of the West as Galerius had proclaimed him? He certainly seemed intent on asserting the claim with brute force. And who would he strike for, Maxentius or me?

My heart swirled with bitter confusion. Maxentius, my old friend, had ridden fortune in his victories over Severus and Galerius. Licinius' mobilisation was surely the start of a third, decisive strike. Was the end coming for Maxentius? But then it would mean Italia, that great peninsula, which was mine by rights – *mine!* – would fall into the hands of Licinius and Galerius.

'The Herdsman will spare none of us when he turns his eye to the north!' said one of my people, seated just below the kathisma and no doubt unaware that I had arrived. I balled a fist and rested my chin upon it, pretending I hadn't heard.

'Or to the south,' the speaker's companion replied. I leant forward on the couch a little, straining to hear the male voice over the cheering of the crowd. 'They say Galerius will be the one to stamp out the African revolt. Perhaps he will – after all, Emperor Constantine has made no move and Maxentius' efforts have so far yielded no victory.'

I sat back with a rumbling sigh, my lips thin. They talked of the disaster in Africa as if I had personally asked that dog, Domitius Alexander, to snatch that land and steal the grain from my people's mouths. I took a deep breath, closed my eyes and pressed forefinger to thumb, seeking calm – a rare commodity when suffering the morning wrath from last night's overindulgence. But, mercifully, a spark of reason illuminated the blackness behind my eyelids. For a moment I imagined the twin problems: Licinius' legions and Alexander's African forces, hovering to the north and south of Maxentius' Italia like open jaws.

Maxentius' problems, I mouthed. Shamefully, it was like a weight toppling from my shoulders. But it was true: my old friend would bear the brunt of these threats before me. More, the beating heart of his realm was in disarray, or so I had heard: Christian Lapsi uprisings in Rome and Popes banished from the city. Now Maxentius had been appalled at the Christian Persecutions as much as I, but I remembered then his rather abrasive opinion on how much – or little – the empire should bend to accommodate the sect. Perhaps his strident approach had stoked those troubles? It worried me that I too had considered banishment of the most troublesome leaders of the faiths – Christian and ancient – from my lands. *How close our paths in life wander, old friend. How entwined our journeys have become,* I mused with a hint of sadness.

The crying of an infant stirred me. I lifted my head and looked over the balustrade to see a mother and baby in the crowd. The mother's face was gaunter than most, and her eyes were black-ringed. She fed a handful of bread scraps to the young one, but it was clear to me even at distance that the meal would be inadequate, and the mother would clearly be going without. Now I sighed the deepest of sighs.

For despite the threat of civil war, despite the disastrous revolt in Africa and the loss of its long-term source of grain, it was the stark and immediate lack of food that hovered over my people like an axe. The lands of Gaul should have been enough to tide us over for a winter or two while the

African situation was dealt with, but the Frankish raids had driven my many farmers from their countryside homes to seek refuge in the painfully overcrowded streets of my capital and the other major walled cities of eastern Gaul. Thus, the croplands out there still lay untended, the silos and grain pits were now perilously vacuous, and there were precious few replete bellies within Treverorum's walls.

A hungry man is quick to bite, they say, and my people were famished. All winter they had quarrelled about the empty ovens as they queued for the few loaves of bread; they squabbled about the gods other men chose to worship; they cursed one another for the winter being too cold and their garments being threadbare. And while idle moaning was one thing, I had witnessed all too often throughout that bleak winter how words could lead to blows and to blood.

On that last day of the games, to the discord of the screaming babe, I now noticed just how many sour faces floated in the crowd, mean eyes laden with intent. I saw a team of emaciated agitators in the throng shouting and spitting at a group of sombre-faced Christians on the seats just below them. The air of discontent thickened as those nearby pitched in with curses and shouts in support of one side or the other; a moment later, nearly one quarter of the crowd on the arena's sloping sides were swaying, turning to the disturbance, snarling and shouting others down. I stood, my heart sinking; for the scene reminded me of the people of Nicomedia in the days of the Great Persecution. So many raised fists, so many snarled threats: all it would take was one spark, and my very own Treverorum might be subjected to large-scale rioting like those foul days in that eastern city.

I gave a Cornuti centurion – standing behind me in the kathisma – a look and the faintest of nods; moments later he

brought another two centuries of his feather-helmed warriors
to the arena. Magically, the group spoiling for a fight lost their
appetite for conflict, and the restless section of the crowd was
quelled, like a knotted rope being loosened. For a short while,
I almost relaxed, until a voice from the other side of the arena
split the air like a cornu.

'You bring the Bructeri invaders into our lands? *Give* them
our soil to farm as their own?' the fellow – tall and lantern-
jawed – screamed up at me, shaking one fist. It was like a glass
shattering in an empty room. The crowd gasped at the man's
daring challenge. Even the mock-gladiators on the arena floor
slowed. His eyes were rolling with the effects of wine as he
continued: 'If you claim to be our emperor, then you owe us
an answer!' The crowd looked to him and then up at me in
the kathisma, knowing that the shout could not be ignored.

I could have had him dragged from the arena – indeed,
two Cornuti soldiers were already barging down through the
crowded terraces towards him. Instead, I stepped towards
the kathisma's marble balustrade. A flick of my hand halted
the pair of Cornuti forging towards him. I met his withering gaze
with one of my own. 'I bring *invaders?*' I boomed. I had heard
mutterings of this along with all the other troubles. Indeed,
some small part of me had longed for a public challenge such
as this – for it was the only way I could set them right on the
matter. 'When a tribesman sets down his sword, removes his
armour and takes up a hoe and a rake, is he still an invader?'

Cornu-voice's shaking fist fell a fraction as he scratched his
head. 'Well I heard the Bructeri are still well acquainted with
their swords. They train in soldiery every day, I am told.'

'Hisarnis and the Bructeri train to serve the empire,' I
replied swiftly. 'Remember, it was they who stood firm at the
Rhenus when the Chatti tried to invade across the ice.'

Cornu-voice's forehead drew tight and he scoffed, momentarily lost for words. 'Franks on our lands,' he muttered after a pause, 'taking up Roman weapons, filling their bellies from crops grown on our soil—'

'There is plentiful soil out there,' I replied briskly, gesturing up over the lip of the arena and towards the city walls. 'The lands have been free of Frankish invaders for over a month.' I pinned him with a fiery look.

A murmur of confusion rattled around the crowd. I had tried – damn them I had tried – to spread word of this truth in the past month, but so few had dared to leave the safety of Treverorum's walls.

'Your name?' I demanded of the heckler.

Cornu-voice hesitated, but realised he had no choice but to reply. 'Noster. Statius Epidius Noster.'

'And what is your trade, Noster?'

Noster shrugged. 'I am a farmer… *was* a farmer.'

'You were chased inside these walls by the Frankish raids?'

He nodded. 'Like so many others; I have lived in the street shacks throughout winter like a beggar.'

I arched an eyebrow, my hand still extended towards the countryside outside the city. 'The raids have been stopped, yet your cheeks grow more gaunt and I'd wager that your belly feels hollower with every passing day.'

'And my three daughters too – ill with hunger, they are,' he said, his voice cracking.

'Then tell me, Farmer, who will till and tend the lands? Who will bring crops to feed you and your girls?'

Noster's vexed features softened just a fraction.

I turned my head slowly to address the entire crowd now: 'The lands of Gaul are safe, from the fort at Bonna in the north to Argentorate in the south. The tribes from across the

Rhenus have been halted.' I couldn't help but add *for the time being* silently, but it was true for now: my cohorts were well stationed – if thinly stretched – to cover the Rhenus frontier, and – praise Sol Invictus, Flora and the pleasant heat of spring – there were no more fears of ice fords and the like. Added to this, two more tribes – the Petulantes and the Ubii – had agreed terms like the Bructeri, and were readying to come to imperial lands in peace. Two more workforces to till the lands and potentially two fresh regiments – regiments that for once might not need to be assigned straight to the borders. Instead I now had the opportunity to build my Comitatus. 'If you fled to this city for protection then I urge you now to go, return to your homes in the country. You will be safe. The crops you planted before you left might yet be salvageable. You will have a chance to address the stark shortage of grain before it becomes a famine.'

Not a soul replied, but I could see the defiance in their eyes gutter and fade, replaced by realisation. A fresh muttering then spread as the people asked one another if it was true, if they could return home. Not that any of them did so – at least not immediately. But a few days later when the first creaky wagons had arrived from Hisarnis' embryonic settlement, laden with cabbages and spelt, the voices fell silent. The many gaunt faces watched this unsolicited tribute as it trundled through Treverorum's streets, the lead Bructeri wagon driver more than a little bemused at the sea of staring eyes.

That night and for days afterwards, my people feasted on the robust but plentiful fare in open taverns around roaring hearths. I heard their chatter change: growing ever warmer and brighter like the month of May. 'If those hairy bastard Bructeri are farming the stinking fens in the north in peace, then perhaps the land *is* safe?' I heard Noster the farmer's familiar cornu-like voice bawl one evening, the words echoing from the streets up to the open, vaulted windows of my palace chambers. In the days that followed, the crush of refugees within Treverorum's avenues eased as streams of them headed out into the countryside to reclaim their lost homes. Messengers took word of this to all of the major Gallic cities afflicted in the same manner as Treverorum.

From the palace's highest chambers, I watched them go and sent with them a prayer – a prayer to all the gods.

It was nearing the end of May when I climbed the stone stairwell in Treverorum's northern gatehouse and emerged onto the paved roof of the fortified tower. Alone, I rested my palms on the silvery stonework of the parapet. The tower afforded me a god-like view of my realm: I could see for miles. I must admit that my spirit soared as the heralds of summer grasped my every sense: the early evening heat, the nutty scent of freshly harvested barley, the dust motes floating idly in the pastoral air. The lands themselves were a patchwork of gold and green fields, streaked with spreading orange light from the dipping sun, speckled with lowing oxen, mules and workers tending the early wheat, planted in the cold season before the Frankish troubles and now almost ready to reap. Up on that tower, far from my bickering court, distant from the hordes of Roman steel I knew I would one day have to face... I think I truly remembered what it was to be joyous. And what man could fail to rejoice when the same word hung on every set of lips – *harvest!*

And this was no commonplace harvest. This was the result of extraordinary endeavour and industry of my people; more, it signalled a rebirth of sorts, a rediscovery of that precious commodity – *hope*.

I watched the wagons – so many of them – trundling in from those fertile meadows towards the four main city gates, laden with early crops: barley, broad beans, carrots, leeks, radishes, beets, asparagus, spinach, turnips, onions, apples, gooseberries, cherries, currants and rhubarb. And as the wagons entered the city, others left, having swapped their bounty for sacks of grain and seed vegetables to sow the next batches. The fare might, *might*, be enough to see us through the summer and the following winter.

I heard the excited chatter of the populace down in the city streets behind me. It was all down to them, you see: for at last my subjects, worshippers of old gods and new, were working together. Why? Some might say that adversity had driven them to it, but I like to think that as their emperor, I played my part in paving the road for the farmers to return to their lands. Fittingly, it was a familiar, cornu-like voice from down on the north road that stirred me from my thoughts.

'Hold the cart! I've got a stone in my boot,' Noster the lantern-jawed giant bellowed, handing the steering pole of the small vehicle heaped with cabbages to one of his three girls. They were heading into Treverorum with the salvaged winter crop like so many others.

In the glare of the evening light, I can't be sure, but I think he might even have looked up at the tower for a moment. Perhaps he saw me. I wondered what he might think of me now. *A worthy emperor?* Had I won the hearts of my people? I smiled at the thought, only for it to be tempered with the contrasting opinions of the few but powerful nobles who still saw me as a false king. Not a soul dared to whisper it, but at the gathering of my council the previous night, I had seen stark disapproval in the eyes of some. They would not be won over by the saving of the harvest. The memory was like the sting of a scorpion, robbing me of my elation. I slumped forward, putting all my weight on my palms and hanging my head. 'Damn you,' I cursed myself. 'You cure one pox only to strengthen another.'

'Domine,' a gentle voice spoke behind me.

I turned my head to see a legionary – one of the Minervia *vexillatio* who garrisoned this gatehouse. He was young, lithe and with nothing but the down of youth on his narrow chin. I realised he must have been there for some time.

'Be wary of the stonework there,' he said, pointing at the limestone block upon which my right hand rested. I noticed how a fine trickle of dust fell from the mortar as the monolith trembled ever so slightly under my weight. Were I twice as heavy – about the size of big Batius – the battlement might have crumbled before me and sent me plunging from the tower. 'It has been due for repair for some time.'

I stood upright and snorted. 'Now's as good a time as any.'

The legionary nodded briskly. 'I'll see it is done, Domine.'

He turned towards the staircase and descended into the tower, when the evening light glinted on something on his collar. 'Spare me one moment,' I said.

He halted, gulping and turning back to me, climbing back up the stairs.

'At ease,' I said, seeing that it was indeed another Chi-Rho amulet – silver but well tarnished – that had caught my attention. I was at once transported back to my childhood, to the storm that rocked Naissus and the one soldier – no doubt long dead by now – who had braved its wrath on the city walls.

He shuffled uncomfortably under my gaze, raising a hand gingerly as if to tuck the piece away inside his mail shirt.

'Come now, soldier. If you truly believe you will be scorned for your faith then I have failed,' I said, somewhat dismayed.

The lad gulped and jabbed out his tongue to dampen his lips. 'But you are emperor, Domine. I heard that none who wear the purple approve of my god.'

I recalled again Maxentius and the Christian troubles in Rome. The thought steered me in my words. 'My mother follows the Christ. You think I would disapprove of her?' I said. 'My father worshipped Mars, and so do I. And in my times on the battlefield, Sol Invictus has guided me, protected me. I am not in the practice of shunning gods, nor suppressing the faiths of others – it is a fool's strategy.' My mind flashed with memories of the persecution riots and the horrible torture-deaths in Nicomedia's arena. 'One I have seen play out in its most horrific form.'

He let his hand fall back to his side. 'Then it is true... they say you were there, in the East, when many of my faith burned.'

My face lengthened. 'I was. I witnessed many Romans die at the hands of other Romans.' I saw the battle of fear and faith in his eyes. 'The persecutions swept the East, but its flames licked at the edges of the West too, did they not?' I asked, knowing that the quarrels I had witnessed in my time in Treverorum were but an aftermath of those days.

The legionary's eyes moistened a little, as if stung by the salt of some distant, painful memory. 'There were incidents,' he said.

I wondered then if his instinctive move to hide his Chi-Rho was a behaviour learned from that time. 'Some say the Christians' greatest weakness is their unwillingness to fight.

Many believe that no Christian will serve in the legions. Yet you stand before me with the symbol of that god over your heart *and* a spear in your hand. And I have seen many more of your kind within my ranks, swaddled in iron.'

He smiled at this. It was a warm, gentle smile that suggested he was no longer nervous. His eyes grew distant and he spoke wistfully: 'Moses carried a rod and Aaron wore a buckle, and John the Baptist is girt with leather and Joshua the son of Nun leads a line of march.' His far-off gaze sharpened upon me. 'It is not about whether we fight… it is about how and why.'

I found his smile infectious. 'By all the gods, soldier – yours, mine and every other – I wish the Persecutors had but a pinch of your wisdom.' I thought of Galerius – that vile, bloated bastard. The Herdsman had so much to answer for. Yet it was *he* who dared to question *me*. I might well have put him in his place the previous winter at the Alpine passes, but as long as he remained Augustus of the East, backed by countless legions, he would pose a perpetual question over me and my station. 'And let us thank all of the gods that those bleak days are over.'

The soldier straightened a little. 'Domine, they are not over. Still the coals of hatred glow. In Africa, it seems that the rebel who has declared himself emperor still sends my like to the arena to be skinned, burned and sawn into pieces for his amusement. They say that in Tingis, when a Christian legionary refused to fight – by setting down his armour and sword in the parade ground and praying instead – he, his wife and his twelve sons were decapitated as punishment.'

I tried but failed to remove the look of revulsion from my face. 'Yet there must be many others like him – Christians who will not fight?'

'Thousands, Domine, in Africa and as many again in this part of Gaul alone,' he replied. 'They are wandering souls.'

'What differs between a man like you and men like them?' I asked, nodding to his spear.

He took a moment to think it over, then answered gently: 'Belief, Domine. They do not believe that an earthly man can lead them. I do.'

Something about the way he held my gaze stoked the most ferocious pride within me. A pride and self-belief I had sought throughout all my years suffering accusations of illegitimacy. Despite the many times I had marched at the head of thousands of men, never, *never*, had I received such a personal, heartfelt acclamation.

I stepped back from the lad, leaning against a sound section of parapet and gazing into the setting sun. A silence ensued. I absently drew a gold coin from my purse and began tilting it over my knuckles, back and forth. I recalled Father's words from his deathbed. *Harnessing the army is like grappling a wolf by the ears. Only a hearty donative of gold brought them to my side.*

'Perhaps it is not always about gold, Father,' I muttered.

'Domine?' the young legionary said, confused.

I looked up. 'My thoughts escape my lips,' I said with a shake of the head. 'Now I will leave you to your shift.' I met his eyes before I turned to head for the stairs. 'Remember that I value men who will fight for me, legionary. I would never ask such a man to hide his faith.'

With that, I descended into the shadows of the stairwell, my thoughts churning. In what had been a day of swinging emotions, my mood once more darkened as I thought over the young legionary's account of the pretender, Domitius Alexander, and his splinter African empire. Alexander had just moved sharply up my long list of enemies. The staunch efforts here in Gaul to bring in the early harvest might have lessened the threat of the African grain shortage, but Alexander's very existence as self-proclaimed emperor of a huge tract of the West – my realm – was an affront to me. And news of the festering remnant of the persecutions in that distant land gave the whole affair an extra, noxious edge.

For just a moment, I found myself aligning with my one-time friend, Maxentius: perhaps it would be best for all if he could topple Alexander from his stolen throne. After all, that would solve the long-term grain crisis, for when he had previously called Africa his own, Maxentius – despite his brazen embargoes on the trade of wool, wax, honey, gemstones and other commodities between his lands and mine – had never stopped African grain from reaching my lands.

And if Alexander fell... it would mean only Maxentius himself remained as a false emperor in my dominion. Just one last foe between me and a unification of the West?

In the space of those few heartbeats, all thoughts of gods and virtue were banished from my mind.

10

There are times when the most important concerns of empire become as insignificant as a frosty breath in a sea of fog. Such was the most dreadful September – the most terrible day – of my life. As with all great tragedies, it began with the mundane.

I looked down at the huge map, painted with great care on the hide of a deer and now spread flat on the table in front of us. Volusianus' face was blank of emotion and etched with only a professional calm, something he now seemed to achieve at all times, withholding any further potential admission of guilt from me. Other than my Dux Militum, who was also my acting Praetorian Prefect, I kept no council that autumn. With Anullinus gone and Zenas still struggling to nail down the traitor Alexander in Africa, I felt unsettled in the presence of the various senators who all had their own agendas, and much as I might condemn Volusianus for what I was certain he had done, I was still heavily reliant upon his abilities and his support.

'Show me,' I said quietly.

Dutifully, Volusianus collected the markers and began to

place them on the map. A wooden soldier with a standard representing Constantine was slid into place at Treverorum where his strength continued to grow worryingly. The black legionary that seemed wholly appropriate for Galerius stood somewhere in northern Moesia, where rumour had it that that swollen nightmare of an emperor had retreated to a private palace he was building. Daia's ivory soldier was placed on Nicomedia, where he was busily doing his best, by all accounts, to rekindle the persecutions despite the laws against it. These were my opponents in the great game of empire. But the one that was still in Volusianus' hand was the one that concerned me right now.

The wooden Licinius hovered over the deerskin for a moment, and then took up position at Sirmium, just a short distance from his evil master in Moesia, but – significantly – a distance *towards* me...

Recently, Licinius had been probing the northern periphery, making his presence felt among barbarian tribes with whom he no doubt felt quite at home. Now he had settled into a strong base in a great imperial city. But worse was yet to come.

I watched, nibbling my lower lip, as Volusianus put marker after marker on the map, each representing an army – not an individual legion, but a gathering of them. Constantine's forces were mostly clustered on the eastern edge of his lands, where the endless hordes of Germanic peoples pressed the limit of empire as always, though now he seemed to be hiring them rather than defending against them. Galerius' forces were spread across the East, as were those of his pet monster, Daia.

My own were largely concentrated in Africa, based on the latest news, though we had a few in northern Italia and some to the south of the peninsula.

Then came Licinius' men. Half his forces, as I had expected, drew a line of steel and muscle along the Danubius to the north, holding back the tribes. The other half, as I had dreaded, were encamped within my territory, but I could not believe how *far* inside. My most important north-eastern garrisons were now his. Pola. Tergeste. Aquileia. Osopus. All places that until recently had been my solid defensive line against any threat from the East. And with my attention – and that of my officers and men – firmly centred on the ongoing disaster that was Africa, Licinius had seen and grasped an opportunity to eat away at my territory.

'I thought you said he'd taken the outposts in Noricum and Raetia?' I gasped, almost breathless.

In response, he placed more of Licinius' markers on Teurnia and Anisus in Noricum and Veldidena in Raetia – once my border – this last perilously close to Constantine's lands, which had given me constant worry. In a way it was comforting to think that Licinius – the *legitimate* Emperor of the West – might soon form a buffer between my old friend and I. Not *that* comforting, though. Along with the troubles in the south, he was beginning to enfold me like a shroud.

'Is there any way we can realistically retake all these places?'

Volusianus pursed his lips and drummed his fingers on the map, making the markers tremble as though the earth itself shook. 'I have already dispatched near seven thousand men from the southern regions of Italia to garrison our second line at Altinum, Tarvisium, Ceneta and Laebactium. They will hold against any further incursions. There are many thousands of men in the north-west keeping an eye on Constantine's borders, too, so they will prevent Licinius surrounding us to the north.'

'That is not what I asked,' I pointed out somewhat peevishly, examining the secondary cordon of defence to our north-east that looked far nearer to home than I would have liked. I wasn't particularly sure that I preferred Constantine surrounding me to the north any more than Licinius. But, I supposed, at least there was still a chance for peace between my old friend and I. The same could not be said for Licinius.

'"No" is the answer to your question, Domine.' Volusianus straightened and folded his arms. 'We have more men we can draw from the south, but they are there in order to supply a reserve against the need for such in Africa. Given the troubles Zenas seems to be encountering, I am loath to reduce his available manpower. Many of our forces are committed in the south, and those we have in the north-west cannot be moved, lest we open the door to Italia and invite Constantine to wipe his feet on our backsides before entering.'

I still couldn't quite bring myself to believe my old friend would yet countenance invading my land, but neither was I foolish enough to disabuse Volusianus of the notion.

'If only Zenas would manage to settle Africa, then we could concentrate on strengthening our northern borders,' I grumbled. 'It is not an enviable position to find oneself in: to have to scrabble about defending ourselves against an aggressor while our own lands burn in revolt.'

'Constantine's armies grow, also,' Volusianus sighed, waving a hand at the concentration of markers on the Rhenus and then tucking it back into the fold of his arms again. 'We cannot afford to concentrate on the south much longer. Zenas may not be up to the task, and if this uprising continues into the new year we will have to find a resolution, Domine, lest while we look south, your northern enemies advance right to the gates of the city unopposed.'

I nodded unhappily. He was right. I had wanted Zenas to achieve his task quickly and efficiently, but it was not happening. Whether or not the fault lay in Zenas' poor choices or abilities or, perhaps more charitably, Domitius Alexander had proved to be more wily and stronger than any of us had expected, we could not maintain a campaign there much longer. Every day it continued to threaten the stability of my domain. At least the Christians seemed to have settled down a little now. Eusebius had apparently renounced the tax on their cultists' return to their churches. Things seemed to be progressing relatively peacefully and, though there were still rumours of troubles, no buildings had burned or riots broken out for almost a month. Now if we could just sort out Africa...

I opened my mouth to say something to Volusianus, but paused at a feverish rapping on the chamber's door. I frowned. No one should be interrupting us here. Two members of the Guard stood outside to prevent such a thing, and nobody in the palace had the authority to stand them down and approach, barring the man already here with me.

'Come.'

Volusianus had also now unfolded his arms and stepped forward.

The door opened, and Phaedrus, one of the senior palace freedmen, entered with his head bowed. Behind him came a young man in a dirty, tattered green tunic, and half a dozen Praetorians. I felt nothing but confusion initially at this odd group, then Phaedrus raised his head, and my blood chilled as I caught sight of his pale, gaunt, haunted expression.

'What is it?'

★ ★ ★

Ravens circled – awful black shapes against a chilling bank of grey that filled the vault of the sky from horizon to horizon.

My joy had ended. In one tumultuous event – one dreadful morning – my life had lost its purpose, its meaning, its direction and its hope.

I stood on the turf, turning a slow circle as if the tidings might change if I found the right angle from which to view them. Here, a mile and a half north of the city walls, even the poor, ramshackle suburbs had petered out, the closest building a large country villa perhaps half a mile away. The great Milvian Bridge that carried the Via Flaminia north arced out across the water, its pylons cutting the fast current of the Tiber into gleaming ribbons that rushed by with a hiss. The river curved downstream from there, around this pleasant meadow, and looped back behind me before snaking its way south and through the city.

Nothing much to see.

A few trees, some areas of undergrowth and a wide expanse of grass. Over at the road itself there were the varied intermittent shapes of the mausolea of countless Roman generations jutting up to the cheerless grey, but I couldn't look at them. Wouldn't look at them.

'Here?' I asked, rather hollowly.

'Yes, Domine,' said the scruffy youth, tear streaks having carved clean lines down his dirty cheeks. It had taken me a long time to recognise the boy, given the state he was in. Young Virius Gallus should have been in a toga, as presentable and austere as his noble line and civic status demanded. I had ranted at him. I had bellowed and screamed in those chambers on the Palatine. I had been so violent in my temper that he had quailed against a wall in desperation. I had even sent for a man to take his head, though Volusianus had talked me out of that, with some difficulty.

I peered around the grass. There were hoof prints everywhere. This was an area of the local countryside where men went hunting and riding every day on both banks of the river. And yet, as luck – luck? – would have it, it took mere moments for one of the Praetorians patrolling the area to pick up the track. He called to me in muted, respectful tones, and I hurried over to him.

There it was.

And now I could see the whole scene in the eye of my mind, just how young Gallus had described it.

Romulus…

I broke down for a while at the mere thought of his name. When Volusianus and one of his men helped me up from the cold turf and I shook them off with muttered nothings, I said it to myself again, a dozen times. A hundred. A thousand. Until it brought only numb horror instead of a hopeless weakening of the knees.

Romulus in his chariot, fuelled by his love of the races. He and Gallus had been re-enacting the recent magnificent win of the Blue hero Thibron over the more experienced Green, Fulvius Primus, which had had all of Rome talking.

The fresh-carved ruts in the grass told the tale in their own gruesome fashion, and with Gallus' account in mind, I began to follow the lines. Two bigae – smaller chariots drawn by a pair of racing steeds – had contested along this stretch of grass side by side, mere feet apart. I could imagine the speed they had reached in their excitement. Here, the two had almost collided. The right-hand chariot – that of Virius Gallus – had momentarily lurched to the left, almost bumping that of his friend.

The two tracks hurtled on towards the riverbank, beyond which I could see the small engineering crew, commandeered from the strengthening of the Porta Flaminia, at work, surrounded by watchful Praetorians.

Walking slowly, like a man lost in a dream, I followed the lines as they weaved and straightened and then finally curved. I could see how it had happened. Even though there was no way from evidence on the ground alone to judge whether the two tracks had been made at the same moment, I could see that Romulus...

Another long, heart-breaking pause...

Romulus had managed to pull ahead of his friend Gallus, perhaps by even more than a length. It came as no surprise. My son was... my son *had been* athletic and brave. He had pulled ahead, but the extra speed had reduced the space available and he had been forced into a nightmarishly tight turn. How Gallus had avoided running straight into him was beyond me, but somehow he had. And here, where the two tracks separated properly, was the evidence that the gods had deserted me. Gallus' tracks disappeared off to the right, away from the river. Romulus' not quite so. I followed the ruts, noting with horror the unbroken turf in sections, where the wheels had bounced and skipped. I could imagine Romulus, now knowing that something was horribly wrong, desperately gripping the reins and holding on as the vehicle bucked and threw him this way and that. I could almost see the panic in his eyes.

I cried again for a while, then.

The turn was too sharp and had put undue stress upon the vehicle.

Through the clearing tears I could see the deep scar in the grass where the pole had broken, leaving poor Romulus in the dire position of riding a chariot no longer attached to its horses, except by the reins in his hands. An experienced rider in the circus would have tied the reins to his wrists or waist for safety, and bore a small knife to cut himself free if the worst should happen. Romulus was not an experienced circus rider. He had seen the danger and had made the wrong choice, letting go of the reins. The horses had thundered off, dragging the stump of the broken pole between them.

But Romulus in his chariot...

The vehicle was light and unstable on its twin wheels with no beasts to guide it. At best it would have tipped over forward or backwards and thrown Romulus out.

The gods had not been kind. Before the chariot had the opportunity to do either, the right-hand wheel had struck a rock. I could see the rock. I could see the score mark across it and the mud where the wheel had hit. And the whole vehicle, along with its driver, had pitched into the air, bounced twice – here, and here – and then plunged into the torrent of the Tiber.

And now I was standing at the river's edge, my heart in tatters, watching as engineers worked feverishly from a raft they had requisitioned. The remains of the chariot were coming out of the water and there... oh, gods preserve us... there was Romulus.

I ran into the water.

I couldn't help myself. I suspect I was crying. No, I *know* I was. I was bellowing my son's name, wading into the deadly Tiber that had claimed a million lives and more in its time, my vision a blur of tears, screaming his name until I was hoarse and rasping, and then still calling for him in whispers in the hope that that pale shape in the blue tunic lying so still on the raft would sit up and wave.

Two Praetorians dragged me back out of the water. They must have been unbelievably brave to wade in after me, given the armour they bore, which could so easily pull a man to his doom in that torrent. I shouted things, but no one could hear, for my voice had rasped and cracked into nothing. I was led to a fallen tree and made to sit, where I shuddered again and again, racked with horror and loss.

At the time, I was so utterly absorbed in my grief that I had entirely forgotten about the others, but now, as I watched the macabre recovery in the water, I saw Valeria out of the corner of my eye, wandering slowly down to the water's edge, her arms folded, and even my ice queen shivered in this cold. She stopped at the bank and I saw her shake once or twice. Then she turned, her face a marble mask of imperious solemnity as she walked away from the scene of our son's death. Not once did she look at me. Nor, I suspect, did she look at Euna, holding the hand of our second boy, who sat, twisted and misshapen in the seat of the small, decorative *pilentum* carriage that habitually conveyed him any distance. At a distorted word and a jerky gesture from Aurelius, the two Numidian slaves drew the vehicle closer to the river.

The raft was nearing the bank now.

I rose from my perch. My knees failed me and I fell back. I shook for some time, in horror and grief and pain, then finally rose once more on unsteady legs, and began to close on the scene. I cannot describe the feelings that flooded me as they lifted Romulus' alabaster body from the raft and carried it across to the litter prepared for it. I only know that I had never known such grief existed. I had never experienced anything approaching it, and I never have since. No one who has not gone through it can comprehend the pain. I have spoken to others who have lost their children and even most of them cannot see it as I did. A few, whose children were their life as Romulus was mine, clearly understood, for they had no words. They said everything that could be said with their eyes alone.

I stood and watched my boy, half expecting him to jump up and laugh at his latest misadventure, but the voice that finally insisted itself upon me came instead from behind.

'Vaaavur.'

Aurelius had said it three times, I think, before I realised my poor, crippled second son had been speaking to me.

'Yes, Aurelius?'

'E own ooof. I own e ooof?'

A fresh agony ran through me and it took me some time to compose myself enough to reply to my innocent little five-year-old's question.

'He cannot move, Aurelius. Romulus is dead.'

There. I had said it.

A name. A condition. Two such I could never have imagined hearing together. Almost automatically, I bent and placed a coin beneath his tongue as Aurelius looked down at his brother – one of few people in the whole world who had looked after him and treated him as a human – and he wept. I had never seen Aurelius weep. Despite everything with which nature and the gods had seen fit to burden the young boy, I had never seen him cry. But, for Romulus, he mourned.

I could not. To mourn would be to accept what had happened and it would be many months before that could happen. For now, it was September in Rome, Africa was still in revolt and Licinius was eating at my borders. And my son was dead.

Romulus was gone.

And the troubles of empire could wait until I was prepared to breathe again.

11

CONSTANTINE

I passed under the low, sturdy limestone walls of Colonia Agrippina's eastern gatehouse, two Cornuti escorting me, leaving the jumble of red-roofed temples, palaces, workshops and houses and the pall of yellow-grey smoke behind. Outside lay the edge of the empire, demarcated by the mighty Rhenus.

It was a cool, overcast day and the water's edge was alive with activity: saws rasped, hammers tapped and chisels chattered as men of the Primigenia legion fashioned timber from the plentiful woods of this region. The fresh, sharp scent of pine and cut wood mixed with the rich aroma of the stews and breads being prepared nearby to keep them nourished and encouraged. I made my way through their midst, the ground growing damp and spongy underfoot as I came to the western bank. The shallows too were packed with men standing knee-deep in the water; further out, anchored galleys of the Classis Germanica and a panoply of rafts rocked and swayed against the Rhenus' fierce and foaming currents.

'Heave!' a booming voice cried from the shallows. Spume-soaked marines groaned under the strain as they hauled at ropes to hoist a titanic shaft of fir from the riverside using a web of hooks and pulleys. The timber, hewn of its bark and fashioned to a flat surface on one side, rose with a ghostly groan under its own weight until it was upright. Then, very slowly, they fed the ropes through their hands and lowered the beam like a drawbridge, out over the water. It dipped until it came within arm's reach of the nearest of the nineteen identical oblong piers that jutted from the furious river like the fins of defiant water demons – cutwaters pointing upstream to break the river's unending assault.

Ten men were clustered atop that nearest pier; they threw up their hands to take hold of the lowered beam and tossed ropes over the end, guiding the timber towards its place on a groove carved into the edge of the pier. The leader of the ten held one hand up to instruct those on the banks to maintain their control over the wood's weight. I smiled the driest of smiles, for he looked like the many brave generals and princes I had stood with on the battlefields, ready to give the signal to attack. But today, there would be no battle. Today, I would take the first steps in the final part of my plan to secure the Rhenus frontier... utterly and forever.

His hand dropped. The tension in the ropes eased. The *clunk* of the wood slotting into position was most satisfying. The first plank had been laid and already the next was being hoisted. The Franks were loath to admit their admiration of the imperial roads, but they would soon marvel at the wonder of my bridge – a bridge that would be firmly under imperial control. Now it was not I who would fear their advance, but they mine.

An odd thing happened then. I noticed something among the activity: not something moving or making some clamour as you might think, but something that stood out for its inertia and silence. A figure. He was a mere onlooker, near the water's edge but standing back from the works. I couldn't see his face, for he wore a wide-brimmed hat that cast his features in shade, and his rustic, full-length grey cloak was wrapped around his body in a way that gave no clue as to his station, occupation, ethnicity or even gender. And when a man has a shadow for a face, none but he alone knows upon what his gaze rests. But I was sure... I was *certain,* that he was staring at me.

The spell was only broken when a voice cooed from behind me. 'So this bridge of yours... *this* is what mistress Fausta derides?'

I swung round. There, shuffling onto the damp silt of the western bank towards me, came old Lactantius, his cane sinking into the wet ground as if to defy him as he picked his way through the squads of workers. I glanced back to the bridge-works. The shadow-man was gone. An odd shiver danced across the nape of my neck; I have learned to trust such misgivings now – and only providence spared me from my ignorance that day. 'Mistress?' I said with a mischievously arched eyebrow as Lactantius shuffled up beside me. 'Indeed, and a savage one at that.'

'You could have had this monstrosity finished by now,' he tutted, still angered by the muddy banking that sucked at his sandals and muddied the hem of his robe, then glanced upriver to a narrower, calmer section of water. It was true: I had chosen a particularly fierce part of the Rhenus to erect my bridge – over five hundred paces of thrashing rapids wide.

'Old friend, your mind and mine are cast from different moulds. If I merely wanted to *cross* this river then a pontoon boat-bridge would have taken just days to organise. But I want to *conquer* this river.' I shook a fist as I said this, and saw Lactantius' disapproving look. But the old man had stood in session with the imperial court often enough to know that this waterway had been a bane of the empire for countless generations. 'What use is a border if you do not control it?'

'What use is a border when you do not intend to stop there?' he shot back immediately, prodding his cane to the far banks. On the raised banking beyond the waterline there, the old, ruined imperial frontier fort – no more than a tumble of bricks and rotting wood, was awash with Primigenia legionaries working tirelessly to dismantle the tumbledown structure in preparation for the construction that would complement the bridge. A thick line of three centuries of fully armoured comrades formed a perimeter around them, watching the eastern woods for any sign of activity. The Franks had not dared interrupt my works so far... but then they had a habit of surprising me.

'Divitia was once an imperial bridgehead, and so it will be again,' I replied a little tersely. The *tink-tink* of stonemasons' tools echoed across the water as if to strengthen my retort, as new, vast blocks brought downriver from the Alpes region were shaped for the fortress I had personally designed. *Thick, rounded and protruding towers and even sturdier walls,* I mouthed. As with every time I thought of such matters, my mind was cast back to my youth and that day I had first met with Maxentius – the boy with the city of wooden blocks... a city with feeble walls. My smile faded, and I don't know why, but I turned my attention back to Lactantius. 'With the new Divitia fortress, the Rhenus will be a strong border – an asset instead of a liability. With an impregnable foothold on the eastern banks, the tribes will not be so quick to foray west and leave their homes unguarded – and then we can afford to reduce the garrisons on the riverbank elsewhere.'

And put them to good use in building my Comitatus, I added privately.

'*Armilustrium* is but six days away,' Lactantius scoffed, 'yet you have your soldiers scurrying to and fro, as active as they would be in the height of campaigning season.'

'You, the first of Christians, fear the wrath of Mars if we do not store our weapons in his honour and in time for the winter?' I said, this time with a devious grin.

'Mars? I, no... gah!' He flapped a hand at me. 'I think I understand Fausta's frustrations with you and your obsession.'

'Every man needs one, does he not? You with your god, me and my bridge?' I laughed and looked up to the grey, late afternoon sky, then scooped an arm around his shoulder and steered him back towards the gates of Agrippina. 'Come, now, let us retire to our quarters, where solid ground and dry shoes await.'

As we walked, I felt that cold, tingling shiver on the back of my neck again, like the winter fingers of a shade stroking my skin.

I *was* being watched.

The fire snapped and crackled, bathing me in warmth as I sat alone by the hearth in Agrippina's imperial villa, the ascetic whitewashed walls uplit by the dancing shadows and the night outside bathed in pale moonlight. I smoothed a hand across the breast of my fresh green linen tunic and stretched my legs, my aching muscles soothed by the heat. I took a long drink of tart and delicious wine. The heady drink and the delicious loaf of fresh, still-warm bread on the small table by my side did a fine job of massaging the incessant chatter out of my mind. The precarious harvests back in central Gaul, the new tribal regiments and my hopes for their ongoing loyalty, and most of all, the great game of empire. Another mouthful of wine ensued. One by one, the thoughts slipped away – even the odd memory of that shadowy figure by the bridge-works on the river earlier in the day.

'I'll have your damned head next time,' I muttered, wishing I had acted upon instinct. For a moment I felt the spark of anger that comes before battle… then I erupted in laughter, putting the wine cup down and nudging it away. 'Fausta is right. Fausta is *always* right. Only a fool sits and drinks cup after cup of poison.'

Silence reigned bar the crackle of the fire. Then, the oddest sense that once again, I wasn't alone. I turned my head ever so slowly, feeling my skin creep. There, in the blackness of the doorway to the hearth room, was a figure – a shadow – loping towards me. Instinct harnessed my weary body and I leapt from the chair, swinging to face the intruder fully, fists clenched, lungs full, ready to shout for my Cornuti bodyguards. The call never came, the breath spilling back out of my lips as a manic and mirthless, chattering laugh. 'By all the gods, Batius!' I roared as the firelight betrayed the figure as none other than my ox-like comrade.

'A pair of shoes—' I gasped, seeing his bare and silent feet '—a knock upon the door—' I gestured to the entrance through which he had come, then threw my hands up in the air '—a shout… a *belch,* would have served as a nice warning that you were here.'

Batius scowled and looked at his bare feet balefully. 'Shoes? Nah – dropped a bloody axe on my foot today. Blunt side mind you,' he mused, then shook his head and affixed me with an urgent look.

Now this was the Batius I knew, and this was a look of

his I could not mistake. 'Batius?' I said, then saw the message scroll he carried. 'Something has developed?' At once the faces from the fire reappeared in my mind. 'Licinius has struck out north?' I guessed.

Batius shook his head and handed the scroll over. 'This is not a military matter, Domine.'

As I took it, Batius pressed a hand to my shoulder. 'A messenger from Rome brought it in and he gave me the gist of its contents.'

'From Rome?' I said, my voice faint.

Batius drew in a weary breath. 'Aye. And I feel it would be best read alone. I will be downstairs with the guards.'

I barely noticed him leaving, for my eyes were fixed upon the seal – an unmistakeable image: the Goddess Roma, seated in her temple, spear and crested war-helm jutting imperiously. The seal of...

Maxentius?

How long was it since we had last communicated? *Too long,* my mind replied instantly. So many moons of nothing but ruminations over where our friendship had foundered. So many times when I had gloried at his reported troubles and failures. I felt shame then, and for the first time in an age, wished things had not gone so wrong between us.

I broke the red wax disc and unfurled the scroll. My mouth grew dry as I read and recognised his way with words, his modesty, his gentle manner.

I trust life in the north treats you and my sister well? How is young Crispus? Have you taught him how to ride? I often think of big Batius too, and how he must be enjoying the winters there, for he was always complaining about the heat in Antioch!

He asked of old Lactantius and my mother too. This was

the Maxentius of old. Not at all like the clipped, cold missives I had received in the days after Carnuntum. It felt as if... as if something had changed.

And by all the gods it had.

I came to the line that made sense of Batius' recommendation that I read it alone. My heart slowed and my eyes widened as I read it again and again and I swear I felt the icy water of the Rhenus enter my veins.

Times here in Rome have become darker than I could ever have imagined. I speak not of the city or the empire, but of the soul closest to my heart. Romulus, my dear, sweet boy, has perished. He lived the life of a thousand heroes, but his death has condemned me to a life more bleak than all the great tragedies combined. I thought it only fair to reach out to you, old friend, you whom he once thought of as an uncle. I will never forget that day in Nicomedia when you and I rescued him from the silo fire. Gods, if only I could have saved him this time too...

I noticed the darker spots on the scroll. Rainwater from the messenger's journey, I told myself, knowing they were in truth my old friend's dried tears. My throat tightened as I thought back to those days in Nicomedia. Young Romulus had been almost ever-present at my chambers. The affable lad had helped Minervina during her pregnancy, entertaining her with childish games and stories, all the while eager to see Crispus come into the world. I had taught him how to ride at the city stables. He had been a genial youth indeed, unspoilt yet by the black things in life.

I flopped unconsciously back into my seat, dropping the letter and gazing into the dying fire again, thinking of the riots in Nicomedia that day and Romulus trapped in a blazing grain silo. Maxentius and I – presently so set upon quarrel

– had acted in union and without hesitation. We braved the flames, we conquered them... we saved little Romulus. Yes, I had been bitter for a time about it all; for that very day, Minervina had perished giving birth to Crispus, and I had not been by her side because of the riots and the fires. But time had brought me to realise that even if I had been with her, I could not have saved her. It made me wonder if anything I had ever done really mattered. Minervina was gone. And now Maxentius was my enemy, or so the game of empire had dictated. Now Romulus was dead...

I stood, as if to fend off the stinging sensation behind my eyes. I strode to the balcony doors, sweeping them open to walk onto the veranda and lean against the thick, cold grey stone balustrade. From there I could smell the crisp night air, tinged with woodsmoke and the scent of autumn bloom from the courtyard and gardens three storeys below. And I could see across the moonlit, red rooftops of Agrippina: smoke meandered from the chimneys of hundreds of homes, taverns glowed orange, and sentries glinted like argentine shards on the walls. Beyond lay the river. The mighty river, with the reflection of the crescent, waxing moon dancing on its surface like a sharpened sickle. The skeletal outline of my bridge-works was less than impressive in the low light, and in any case, my attentions were on the waters. I could not help but feel Maxentius' pain. In my mind's eye I imagined little Crispus falling into the Rhenus and almost sobbed at the idea of my boy meeting a fate such as Romulus'. I let my head loll forward to compose myself.

'Our choices, our rash words, our pride-fuelled ignorance,' I whispered into the night, 'pales to nothing in the harsh light of a young one lost. What world have we created, old friend, a world where we have refused to sit together since the fires of Nicomedia? Were we not allies back then, united in our loathing of Galerius?'

I wondered what Maxentius' response might be, were he there to give it. Yet once more I could hear nothing but the crackling, dying fire behind me.

And... the faintest sound. A hissing. A drawing of breath.

Right behind me.

Not Batius.

I spun on my heel just as a short, silver, leaf-shaped blade shot through the space I had been occupying, penetrating what would have been my kidneys. There was a minute hiatus where I stared into the shadow-face of the intruder. The wide-brimmed hat; the long, grey robe. I saw but a streak of yellow as a mouth within the shadow, contorted into a snarl, and the silver blade came up for my gut. I slammed a forearm down blocking the strike – sending the blade clattering across the balcony floor where it came to rest somewhere within the shadows.

In reply, the foe bashed both palms against my shoulders, barging me back onto the balustrade. I fell back across the coping stone, arms and legs flailing to balance, then he turned one shoulder to me and rammed it into my raised thigh, toppling me over the edge completely. I cried out, knowing I had no purchase to halt my fall. Time slowed. I clawed uselessly at the night air, sensing the long fall and the cold, hard flagstones below upon which I would surely dash out my brains. I saw only a flurry of movement and torchlight on the balcony as it slipped from my eye line – movement accompanied by a sudden series of barking shouts. Then I plummeted.

Just as I had all but accepted my fate, a ham-like hand grasped my flailing forearm. My shoulder jarred as my fall was halted and I swung against the outside of the balustrade. I looked up, seeing a Cornuti soldier and, on the end of the meaty hand, Batius, his eyes wide.

'Domine,' he grunted as he hauled me back over the balustrade and onto the safety of the balcony floor.

Gasping, I looked around, seeing another Cornuti drawing his sword from the chest of the supine shadow-man. Blood and air escaped the would-be assassin's mortal wound with a hiss, and an oddly incongruous gentle sigh came from the fellow's lips as he expired. The wide-brimmed hat rolled free of his face; he was an ageing man, face lined and pitted with the scars of some pox. He had green eyes and a cruel mouth – albeit locked in a death grimace.

As the Cornuti wiped his sword on a rag, I stood, looking the dead assassin over and over. 'Who is he?' I asked. The Cornuti who had killed him held out his hands.

'I have never seen this one, Domine,' he said. 'Not within this city.'

The other Cornuti agreed.

Batius, however, looked upon the corpse with a lengthening expression, sadness in his eyes. 'It is him,' the big man said, his voice laced with despair.

'Him?' I asked.

Batius looked me in the eye. 'It is the messenger. The messenger from Rome.'

12

MAXENTIUS

ROME, 25TH OCTOBER 309 AD

I sat in the imperial box at the Circus Maximus, watching the chariots thunder around the Tiber turn, narrowly avoiding the wreckage of two vehicles that had collided three laps back and had been dragged to the side but not yet fully removed. The Greens were ascendant, and there was little chance they would lose this race now.

I cared not.

Every time a chariot reached either curved end of the track and careened into the turn, I saw Romulus in the vehicle, his eyes wide with panic as he lost control. Six laps had passed and, even allowing for the various losses that had left us at this last stage with only three remaining racers, I must have seen Romulus die more than fifty times in this past hour. I couldn't smile or cheer. I couldn't take any joy in the race. But neither could I cry, for I was a desiccated, dry husk of a father. Over the past month I had cried until finally not a drop of moisture could pass through my eyes. They felt dry as old parchment and my face ached all the time.

I cared not.

My world had ended that day by the Tiber and I was now a ghost – at best a shadow of myself.

I felt something drip on my foot and I looked down in surprise, missing a spectacular collision as the last Blue rider met with the stone of the spina in a disastrous crash. Small droplets of blood spattered my sandal and the bare foot within. I looked at my hand, white and strained as it clutched something I'd forgotten I was holding. I opened my palm and there was one of my new freshly minted sestertii, clutched so tight that it had cut into my hand in two places and my palm was bleeding. Romulus looked older on the metal disc than I remembered, but then in my mind he had always been a small boy. This Romulus on the coin was a young man. Had I missed him growing up somehow, or had I deliberately ignored it? I would never see him mature. I…

I turned the coin over hurriedly. I couldn't ponder too long on the face, with no tears left to cry. The reverse was no consolation, since it showed my precious son's mausoleum.

My gaze rose from the coin, past the last straight of the race, over the crowd filling the seats on the curved end. Off to the south-east, beyond the circus, I could just see the roofs of the great public baths built by the despised Caracalla, spirals of smoke rising into the grey sky above. And between those curling, ethereal columns, in the distance and past the great gate that my engineers had raised with the defences, I knew there lay the Via Appia, though it was not quite visible from here. On that road, three miles from where I sat, lay my new villa, almost complete. And beside the great road, at the edge of the estate, stood the great heavy drum of the mausoleum I had constructed, planned for myself and to house my dynasty like those great tombs of Augustus and Hadrianus. There would *be* no dynasty. The tomb would only ever contain

Romulus, his brother, and myself. And my beautiful, lively boy was the first to inhabit it, not me.

My eyes dropped once more to the coin in my hand and the image of that very mausoleum. I dropped the coin as though discarding it would allow me to shed some of the sorrow. I reached into the small purse at my side and drew out another. The same design. I threw it away. A third. Another design, but still Romulus. I rid myself. Another. Romulus. Discard. Another. Romulus. Discard.

How many coins had I minted that every one I picked up bore my son's face?

Rome was full of him.

The temple to the Penates in the forum that he had loved had been rededicated to my son on the orders of Volusianus. He thought to please me with the gesture, but now I could not look at the forum without flinching. And Fortunatianus, the governor of Sardinia, had paid for and dedicated a colossal statue to my boy below the Capitol and close to the senate house. So now I couldn't look at the Capitol without wincing.

One of the Praetorians on guard in the box hurried over to gather up the coins for me and I lifted a snarl to him.

'Leave them!'

The soldier recoiled and took up his post once more, pale-faced and trembling.

I cared not.

The race ended to thunderous applause and great clamour. The Greens secured their place. Already I could see at the *carceres* the circus staff beginning preparations for the second race. Could I make it through another race? Every turn was a fresh hell for me, and there were twenty-four races scheduled for the day. Eight drivers in each race. Seven laps. Two curves. I would watch Romulus die over a thousand times today.

Could I do it?

I had almost declined to attend altogether, but Volusianus had persuaded me. They were, after all, Romulus' funeral games. The races were in his honour; in his memory; in very poor taste, to my mind. But he would have loved them, and in his honour I would make it through as many as I could before I crumbled to dust and blew away in a breath of grief.

In the distance I could hear the crowd at the great amphitheatre yelling wildly at the fights and beast hunts there. Rome mourned in its usual way, with lakes of blood and sporting wagers.

I cared not.

Romulus would have loved this race.

If only he were here…

I glanced across at Valeria. She never went anywhere with me anymore. We had not spoken civilly in years. We lived a sham of a marriage, tied together against our will, and had done for almost all our joined lives. But today she was in the imperial box with me. For Romulus. It struck me as odd that she seemed to care more now that he had gone than she ever had while he'd lived. Her face had lost the ubiquitous sneer of haughty ire to be replaced by a blank visage, like an unpainted marble bust.

I had not known she was capable of grief.

Had I not been wallowing so deep in my own, I might have actually felt for her.

The seat that lay between us was empty, with just Romulus' circlet of bronze on a purple cushion. Was he here in spirit? He would have so loved to be here.

'I shall build you a circus,' I whispered under my breath to the shade of my son. Valeria flicked a look at me, then returned her cold gaze to the track.

'I shall build a circus as grand as this at the villa, beside your tomb so that you can watch every race. And I shall hold games every year on your naming day, and races whenever I am there, and you can watch them with me from your mausoleum.'

Because *that* I cared about.

That night, the busy day of games done, I sat in my private retreat, the Palatine library, staring into the room's darkest corner in my latest fit of hollow anguish. A hiss drew my attention to the brazier that kept the room warm as a large piece of charcoal released a breath and settled. Flames. I remembered again that day in Nicomedia – the burning granary from which Constantine and I had saved Romulus.

Glorious days, in retrospect, despite the evils of the time, for my boy had still lived and my old friend and I had shared a closeness that had somehow in so few years become a gulf the size of an ocean, rolling between us.

Odd that I was thinking of Constantine at that moment – a prescient thing perhaps, for there came three gentle raps on the door before it opened – a sign that Volusianus had arrived.

I turned to see my only remaining close advisor fully clothed against the late autumn weather. Even though the business of state seemed now such a pointless thing to me, I couldn't help but think that he finally brought news of Africa. Had Alexander fallen? Had Zenas? Were we a reunited domain at last?

Whatever it was, the news did not appear to be good. Volusianus' face was dark.

'What is it? Africa?'

He shook his head. 'The messenger has returned from Germania.'

I felt a tiny flicker in my heart. An ember of life remained, apparently. I had managed, even in my sea of grief, to pen a letter to my old friend. With the icy wall between Valeria and I, I'd concluded that only Constantine might understand what I was going through, and despite all that had happened, he remained the man who had saved Romulus from the fire. Though the world would never be good again, perhaps Constantine and I could still be reconciled. Just that one weak ray of light might come out of this great tragedy. 'Constantine?' I said. 'He has replied? I wondered if he might come in person.'

Volusianus' face remained immobile. 'The messenger returned in a box, Maxentius.'

Maxentius? Not majesty, or imperator, or domine, but just a name. At other times I might have exploded with rage. But I was too drained to feel anything these days.

'What happened?'

'The messenger failed.'

I frowned. How could a messenger fail?

'You've lost me, Volusianus. Did Constantine read my message? Did he reply?'

The prefect rolled his eyes and folded his arms. 'Will you forget the letter? It was the *real* message that failed.'

'Will you speak plainly, Volusianus. I am too tired for your riddles.'

'Clemens failed. His blade was sent back in the same box, snapped off at the hilt.'

I frowned still for a moment, and then realisation struck me and my eyes widened.

'His *blade*? Why would the messenger carry a blade into...

no! Surely not?' My eyes searched Volusianus for some sign I had assumed wrongly. They found none. 'You tried to have Constantine *killed*?'

'Of course,' sighed Volusianus. 'Was that not the whole purpose of your letter?'

I stared in disbelief. 'My letter was to inform an old friend of Romulus' death, and instead you take one tragedy and try to use it to forge another?' My heart was pounding with a heady mix of ire and fear, such as I had felt that day I chased Severus' forces over the causeway at Septem Balnea. But this was no battle. This was…

'Your enemy's death would be a blessing, Domine, not a tragedy.'

I almost exploded, such was my incredulity and my fury.

'How *dare* you use my correspondence to conceal your clandestine activities? How dare you try and take the life of my old friend without my permission? I am incensed! I am…'

'Permission?' snorted Volusianus. 'Domine, I sought your permission the only way I could. Do you not recall me asking if I should send *Clemens*, since he would likely make it into Constantine's presence?'

'Well, yes…'

'*Clemens*, Domine. The master of the frumentarii. If the point had just been a letter we could have sent a courier, not a killer.'

I boggled. Clemens *was* a killer, trained and by trade. He was just such an important one that I often forgot that and saw him instead as an officer, advisor and administrator. Why *had* we sent the head of the imperial spies and assassins with the letter if not to kill my old friend? Simply: I had not realised I had agreed to it. Volusianus had been subtle and circumspect in the matter, for it would not do for an emperor to order an assassination. It would ruin my reputation, and so Volusianus thought he had secured my consent without a direct approval. I had been so lost in my grief I had not noticed.

'We must send another message,' I hissed.

'Yes. With a swifter knife,' added Volusianus.

I growled quietly. 'Not another killer. Another *letter*. Explaining that the last visitor was a mistake and should not have happened. An apology, even.'

'Domine, that would be foolish and pointless.'

'Oh? How so?'

'Foolish because while you cling to this fallacy that Constantine is your friend and that somehow the gods will make everything right between you; that time has long passed. There is no reconciliation in your future. There can only be a reckoning, and one of you will not walk away from that confrontation. Foolish because if a single blade in the night can end Constantine then we might be able to avoid a vast war of territory and *imperium* that will tear the West apart and leave the whole empire as carrion to be picked over by Galerius and his pets. Foolish because we should not apologise for an act of war, because we are at war with Constantine, no matter what you think. The first battle has not been fought yet, but we are at war.'

I shook my head. It couldn't be true. Constantine would never come for me, and despite the gulf between us, I would never go for him. There would be another solution. There had to be.

'And pointless, Domine, because Constantine would not accept an apology. He would not believe it, or would twist it into some oath of subordination. We have struck at him, and he will not shake your hand after that. Pointless because we were just lucky enough to get our assassin to him before he got around to sending one for you. Pointless because Clemens will not be the last man I send. I would send the whole of the frumentarii if I thought it might save us a war.'

'He will reconcile. I know it.'

'No, Domine, he won't. And soon Licinius will forge further west, either for Constantine or for you. And looking at his troop dispositions and gains in north-eastern Italia, the clever money is on you as his target. Only with a combined West can any man hope to defeat an invasion from the East. With our army and Constantine's new German regiments together, we could defeat Licinius. But Constantine will never join us to fight our enemy, for you and he claim the same imperium. Licinius can only be beaten if either you or Constantine alone control all the military power of the West, and it is my job to make sure that it is *you* who achieves that, not him.'

'I will not be party to assassinations.'

'No, Domine. You won't. For I shall not ask permission next time.'

I stared at the man. How did he believe he had the authority for such a thing? Had I still any doubt that Volusianus had been the man who wielded the blade against my other advisor in that bathhouse, it would have melted away now. If my Dux Militum could blithely decide to kill my oldest friend, then how difficult would it have been for him to remove a personal opponent? If I had not needed him so much, his head would have rolled away many times by now. In the end I simply glared in silence, and finally, after a dangerous pause, Volusianus bowed and retreated from the room, closing the door.

How had it come to this?

Somehow this room now felt tainted, as though it held

assassins and murderers in the shadowed corners. Suppressing a shiver, I left the library. Volusianus had gone and the corridors were empty, even of slaves and guards. I felt alone. Totally alone.

I wandered for some time, calling in to see my poor boy Aurelius. He was my son and I loved him, even though he could never be Romulus. He would grow older yet, but the best physicians in Rome were all agreed that in his condition he would be lucky to live to manhood, and would certainly perish soon after if he did. And he would never address the senate. And he would never marry and sire me a grandson. I loved him, but even from the beginning I had hardened myself – prepared myself for the inevitable day that I would lose him. His presence, sleeping curled up in his room, stoked another tiny ember in my heart. Would such a tiny glow in such a dark place allow me to go on, I wondered? Would that I had the strength of spirit these Christians seemed to have, then I might be able to face my loss with less pain. Perhaps they are stronger than us in the end.

Sometime later I found myself approaching Romulus' room and I almost turned away. I only went there when I felt strong enough, which was rarely the case. But for some reason there was a flicker of light coming from his room. I felt my heart leap with joy and hope for a moment, but I stamped down on it, forcing that false hope away. My boy was gone and there was no changing that.

I padded softly down the corridor and turned into the doorway.

Valeria stood in the centre of the room, an oil lamp in her hand. She had her back to me, and arrayed on the floor before her were Romulus' favourite toys.

'Valeria?'

I said it softly, soothingly.

She turned, that marble mask of cold dispassion still on her face, and without acknowledging my presence she walked past me and away from the chamber, leaving me standing in the darkness in our son's room amid his toys.

And I discovered then that my well of tears had not run dry after all.

PART 3

Inimicum quamvis humilem metuendum est
(An enemy, however small, should be feared)
– *Publilius Syrus*

13

CONSTANTINE

THE GREAT FORTRESS OF DIVITIA, 1ST APRIL 310 AD

A fresh breeze furrowed my hair as I flitted up the winding broad stone steps – still pristine and bearing remnant dust from the stonemasons' chisels – and onto the wide eastern battlements atop Divitia's colossal walls. I acknowledged the stiff and prideful salutes of the Second Italica sentries up there. I gazed east as I walked along the parapet; outside, green forests and grey mountains stretched to the horizon – but not one peak or tree rivalled Divitia, my five-storey limestone giant on the Rhenus' eastern banks. Bulging, rounded towers adorned the corners and punctuated the curtain walls of the square bastion, and the eastern and western walls were embellished with monumental gatehouses.

The fortress had been declared complete eight days ago, just prior to the ceremony of *Tubilustrium*, the celebration that marked the army's awakening after a cold, hard winter. In truth my legions had been busy throughout those frozen months, not in military matters but in quarrying, shaping and hauling stone, mixing mortar, hewing scaffolds and laying flagstones.

I passed through the cool, stony shade of the eastern

gatehouse's nearest tower room, stocked with spears, bows, quivers and swords, then out onto the parapet again across the backbone of the fortified gateway. I paused for a moment up there to gaze at the forest again. I saw no movement but the odd rustle of branches where a flight of tree swallows were swooping and darting in and out of view. Apart from their chattering and gurgling, and the spring song of the other birds and animals in that great, dense woodland, I heard nothing.

A dry smile played with one side of my lips. No raids for months, not a single tribesman had dared to approach. A warmth swaddled me – security such as this the Rhenus frontier had never before known.

I turned to look across the fortress, over the serried ranks of red-tiled barrack houses, to the western entrance – a reflection of this eastern one. Beyond those towering, iron-strapped gates, the mighty bridge stretched across the Rhenus, back to Colonia Agrippina on the western banks. That city, once a majestic stone and marble pearl in this green wilderness, was now the envious sibling of my creation. Divitia was no mere bridgehead on the Germanian side of the river; it was a great stele of my overlordship.

While legions were the mainstay of my army and the muscle behind my building works, it was the ranks of engineers who had designed the fortress and the bridge and overseen their construction. And as this thought crossed my mind, the central section of the bridge shuddered and moved – orchestrated by a chorus of cries and hoisted ropes and pulleys – opening ever so slowly like a set of gates to allow a patrol flotilla of biremes from the Classis Germanica to row upriver. I watched, transfixed, until the bridge gate was hauled shut once more nearly a half hour later.

What a wonder my people had constructed here, a wonder fitting of an emperor. And to think the bastard Galerius sneered at my claims to the Western throne. My teeth ground as my eyes lifted beyond the bridge and beyond Agrippina, to the south-western horizon... to think Maxentius, the cur lodged in Rome like a tick on a man's neck, had dared to send a hired blade to cut me down. Ideas struck through my mind like tongues of fire: I had established my own school of agents – winter-cold assassins who could travel to Rome and do what Maxentius' agent could not. I could order them to make it slow and painful. I could...

The swallows sped overhead, singing, their melody incongruous with my thoughts.

I stopped, sighed and partially doused the fiery notions by dropping my head and pinching thumb and forefinger together, that old trick that used to scatter my troubled thoughts – not so now.

It cannot have been Maxentius who sent that cut-throat. Unless... unless he has changed beyond all recognition?

The anger swelled again. I swung to face the north and stomped on through the second tower house, leaving the gate complex and going on along the eastern battlements towards the mid-tower and then the giant, bulging north-eastern corner tower. I thought my anger could not be topped, but then I heard a cry that dispelled that notion.

'*Bastard!*'

My brow tightened and I hopped up the few steps to come onto the circular, flagstoned roof of the corner tower. Three ballistae were mounted there, peeking over the sturdy parapet like hawks' beaks, and the bull-like form of Batius was huddled over the central bolt thrower. The big man's body jolted.

Whoosh! Thud!

'Wodin's balls! You massive bastard!' a jagged shout came again from somewhere down on the ground outside the fort.

I strode up to the wall's edge and peered down over the crenellations.

Krocus stood down there on the patch of ground cleared of trees. He wore a ruddy streak across his nose and cheeks like warpaint. Around him, three thick and lengthy ballistae bolts jutted proudly from the earth, the latest one still quivering where it had plunged into the soil, just a stride to Krocus' left.

Batius' face split into a haggard smile as he adjusted the angle of the huge ballista and winked to ensure the Regii leader was now firmly in his sights. 'Heheh, you hairy, stinking, tree-shagging arsehole,' Batius muttered under his breath.

I noticed that Krocus carried a handful of short sticks, each with a knotted coloured rag tied to it, in his hand. 'Sighting and distance marking?' I guessed. Batius turned, only now aware of my presence, and nodded. I cocked my head to one side. 'Usually the practice involves letting the poor sod on the ground plant the sticks before you shoot.'

'Usually,' Batius grunted. 'Thought this might save time, though. Look, we're nearly done. But we can test it once more?' he said, turning to me with the look of an excited – if grossly overgrown – boy.

'One more bolt,' I sighed as if speaking to little Crispus.

Batius poked his tongue between his teeth gleefully, his hand hovering over the holding peg. For a moment, Krocus' eyes bulged and he flapped his hands before him like a shield. 'What are you doing, you dog-ugly maniac?' he squealed.

Batius chuckled again, then shifted the device on its rollers just a finger-width to the right. His hand dropped, knocking the holding peg free.

Whoosh! Thud!

What came from Krocus' mouth next nearly peeled the paint from the shields of the legionaries lining Divitia's curtain wall.

'...and I'll come up there, rip your bloody balls off and cook them in front of you...'

On it went.

Those watching and unfamiliar with this pair might well have expected blows to be traded – or worse. Their rivalry had certainly become ingrained – insults used by way of standard greeting, each slandering the other's gods as if passing comment on the weather. Mars had become a curse-word to Krocus and Wodin likewise to Batius. I, being so close to both men – each of whom was a most trusted general – had seen more than the average passer-by. I saw their snatched glances at one another after battle or at the end of a hard day's march. Admiration, respect... albeit loathingly offered. They were almost an illustration of my burgeoning army: heterogonous, embryonic... volatile.

Hooves clopping on timber yanked me from my musings. I turned to see two green-cloaked messenger-riders cantering across the bridge from Agrippina.

'I'll deal with this one, Domine,' he said in a low drawl.

I blinked, seeing the riders enter the fort via the western gates. Dismounting, one of the fellows remained with the horses, hooded, while the other was led by two of my legionaries across to the foot of this tower before he disappeared into the stairwell.

Batius patted his scabbard and the dagger tucked into his boot. All messengers were put under extreme scrutiny now. My heart hardened at the thought that this might be another blade from Maxentius. *You wouldn't dare, cur.*

The weak-chinned messenger rose from the darkness of the stairwell and stepped onto the rooftop, his face ruddy with the exertion of the five-storey climb. As well as the two legionaries flanking him, Krocus had come up too, his ire at Batius forgotten, his eyes hard upon the messenger.

'Domine,' the messenger gasped, stepping proud of his two-man escort and falling to one knee then flinching as Batius and Krocus stepped towards him and clasped their hands to their sword hilts. Looking up at the pair with wide eyes and a bulging Adam's apple, he held out a scroll. 'A message...' he began.

My eyes tapered. From Rome?

'From the East,' he finished.

My eyes met with Batius' and Krocus'. I had received not a word of communication from the East since my defiance of the proclamation of Carnuntum, since I rejected Galerius' carefully worked calls for me to abdicate. Silence... apart from the slow, steady crunch, crunch of hobnailed boots as his puppet, Licinius, moved into position along my south-eastern borders. Where the Germanic threat ended, the Herdsman's armies now swelled like wolves, some even spilling deep into Italia.

I could not stop one side of my top lip from flinching in hatred for all that bloated whoreson had done. I snorted mockingly, snatched the scroll from the messenger's hand and unfurled it without ceremony, primed to be angered, certain it would be some demand for my throne and a threat of imminent invasion was I not to comply. It had been coming, after all, ever since Carnuntum.

But my eyes dragged across the script, the letters not matching my expectations. Not at all.

My flesh is weak and my time is short. I fear I may not

see another summer after this one. I call upon you before the darkness claims me. Come, Constantine, Warden of the West, and speak with me. I wish to bring peace upon the empire. Let there be one last, amicable meeting...

'You mean to trick me? You think me so gullible?' I spat. But the wording was striking, more for the phrases that were absent: no self-proclamations as Parthicus Maximus, Gothicus Maximus, sired by Mars.

'This is no trick, Domine,' the messenger pleaded. 'The Great Augustus has a short time to live. He is in torment, both from the agony of his condition and, and... from the memories that plague him.'

I showed the scroll to Batius and Krocus and strode round the kneeling herald. Batius let out a single, barking laugh. Krocus hitched himself, snorted and spat phlegm by the kneeling man's side. I bored a fiery look into the rider. 'Galerius calls me to the East, and he expects me to run to him like a dog?'

The messenger nodded. 'He does, and he knew you would spurn his invite.'

I scoffed without a hint of mirth: 'Galerius could send me his own mother as proof of his geniality and I would still not believe him.'

'He knew it would take much for you to trust him,' the messenger said, then stood – gingerly to appease Krocus and Batius – and waved down at his fellow rider on the fort floor.

My two generals looked with me, confused.

The man down there saw the signal, and drew down his hood to reveal a pale, gaunt and war-hardened face, ice-bright eyes, lips tight as a drawn bow, and thin, straight hair combed forward ascetically.

'Glaucus!' Batius and I half-whispered, half-gasped.

★ ★ ★

The fires in Divitia's praetorium lit the austere grey room with a troop of dancing shadows. I had barely touched my meal of goose and leek stew. I had drained three cups of unwatered wine, however, and was eager for the slaves to return with more. I looked across the table at Glaucus again, my eyes narrowed as if sure that from a certain aspect I would see through his words. But the notion was absurd.

The centurion had served under me in the East, in the wars against the Goths and in the Persian struggle. A Christian, he had been one of the few to remain in Nicomedia, the epicentre of Galerius' persecutions, while so many others fled. A man who hated the Herdsman with all of his being.

'It is as the scroll suggests, Domine,' Glaucus said in that expressionless way of his. He had shown little of any emotion in the time I had known him, and what little embers lived on in there had surely been quashed the day the persecutions took everything from him. 'The Herdsman turns to penance at last. He understands his sins... now, at the end.'

'Then he *is* dying?'

Glaucus' mouth almost moved into a sad smile. 'He has been dying from the moment he turned Diocletian's mind towards the foul attacks on my kind. But his flesh? Yes, it rots and falls from his bones. He has even commissioned the building of a tomb-palace at Romulia in Moesia. He talks of nothing but what lies... beyond.'

'How long: days, months?'

Glaucus sighed. 'He is prone to exaggeration, as we both know. His blight has been with him for a long time already.'

I recalled the distended, ashen-skinned form I had faced last in the Alpine passes, when I had herded him on out of the West after his failed attempt to dislodge Maxentius from Rome. That was two years ago and still he clung to life.

'But I do not doubt his fear that this summer will be his last.'

With a grunt and a shuffle, another voice interrupted: 'This one and the other rider are hounds of the Herdsman. We should throw them in the cells,' Krocus muttered from the edge of the room.

'I would readily agree,' I replied, speaking over my shoulder, 'were this any other being from the East.'

'You cannot think of travelling into his lair, Domine,' Batius gasped from the other corner of the room, having remained silent since finishing his meal. 'Remember the horrors we saw in Nicomedia? Remember all you risked, all you went through to escape it?'

I imagined the world once more, riven in three. Me, Maxentius, Galerius. It seemed that the great board was poised to lose one piece. Were Galerius to die, what chaos might ensue from the Herdsman's mutts: Licinius and Daia? Despite his loathsome nature, Galerius was still the most senior of emperors. With his dying and repentant words, might he set aside his grievances and bestow order upon the warring world? It was a slim hope, but a stirring one.

Still locked in that gaze with Glaucus, I replied: 'Only a fool would accept such an invite. Yet... I cannot afford to spurn it.'

'Then what is it to be, Domine?' Batius asked.

The fiery anger from before came back to me as I recalled the Herdsman's threats against Mother, his subtle hints that Minervina and Crispus would fall at the end of his men's blades, his gleeful overseeing of the brutal Christian executions... that snowy night when he tried to have me killed in the dining hall of Nicomedia's palace. I imagined him in this new tomb-palace at Romulia... shivering and alone. It shames me to say the image conjured a dark smile onto my lips.

'Let him rot,' I said in a low growl, then stood and strode from the room.

14

MAXENTIUS

ROME, 1ST MAY 310 AD

Time did little to diminish my grief. I spent the long, cold winter mostly staring silently at the door of my son's mausoleum at the new villa on the Via Appia. In fact, I was rarely in Rome and even then only when some matter became urgent enough that Volusianus would come out to the villa and drag me back to the Palatine. Then, when the job was done, I would be straight back to the maudlin peace of the new villa and Romulus' mausoleum – a tomb within a tomb.

I think I started to worry my villa's staff when they kept having to urge me back to my *triclinium* for food. They would invariably find me sitting on one of the huge blocks of masonry from the unfinished *hippodrome*, staring through the bars and into the gloomy interior of Romulus' sepulchre.

Euna, the ageing nurse, had come to the villa with young Aurelius, and the poor twisted lad was the only thing able to tear my attention from the resting place of my older son for even a moment. But never for long. For I could only hold so long a conversation with my younger boy before the tears came and I had to look away. I was truly lost.

I had paid no attention to Valeria during the winter, which, looking back was a failing I should have attended to. Despite that one crack in her icy armour in the room of our dead son, she had remained silent and cold, isolated and unwilling – unable? – to share in my grief. But then, I knew not what icy knives were turning in her own heart.

It was the kalends of the month, and finally the weather was changing. The winter had been unforgiving in its cold and bitterness, and the spring to which it had given way was little better. Filled with sleet that gradually transformed to unremitting rain, it had waterlogged the land, dragging all joy and humour from what was traditionally the season of hope. It mattered not to me, of course, for it snowed in my heart regardless of the outside weather.

Two days earlier the rain had stopped, at least. The ground still squelched and the sky still gloomed with dark grey ribbons of threat, but the air was warmer and the builders, who had by necessity withdrawn during the inclement months, were now once again raising the two great towers that would mark the ends of the carceres of my new private circus. The sounds of chiselling and hammering echoed across the landscape and drowned out the approach of the small party such that I did not even realise I had company until they planted themselves between me and that dark doorway into despair.

I blinked and looked up.

Valeria?

It seemed so unbelievable that my distant, loveless wife might deign to visit me that I actually rubbed my eyes to be sure that I had not simply drifted off to sleep on that block before the tomb. No. It was really her. And behind her, Volusianus.

I frowned. My wife's face might be implacable, but her eyes were racked with emotion which in itself was such a phenomenally unexpected thing that it actually snapped me out of my moody oblivion and made me pay attention. Volusianus' face, in stark contrast, was energetic – I might have even said gleeful.

'Valeria?'

'Father's health is failing.'

I scratched my head, trying to pull my thoughts together, wondering how she knew what was going on in the court of Constantine before it struck me that she was talking about her father and not mine. Her father, the all-powerful emperor of the East, *truly* ill?

That explained Volusianus' face.

'Galerius is ill? How ill? *Dying?*'

I tried not to sound enthusiastic over the possibility that my greatest enemy in the world might be suffering. Valeria's expression suggested I'd failed. Probably 'Dying' had been a touch too far.

'Critically, I am told. My stepmother informs me in a rather curt and unpleasant letter that Father is suffering endless bleeding from an infection in his belly and that whatever the physicians do to try and cure it continually makes it worse. She does not believe he will live to see another winter.'

I sat silent, staring. Despite the hole in my heart that echoed the hole in the tomb before me, the news made me want to stand and praise Apollo and Aesculapius for inflicting that most foul abomination of a human with something so dreadful and seemingly incurable. I am not by nature a vengeful or ruthless man, but when it came to Galerius, I had found I could wish him a thousand such deaths and retain a good conscience. I could easily have cheered on that blood loss. No, I'd never have made a Christian, would I? Valeria stood before me, her body soberly clothed, her soul naked.

Her eyes were the heralds of her heart. Her face might be a marble cast, but her eyes were filled to overflowing with fear, anguish, loss and perplexity. Galerius may have been the most appalling human being this side of the Styx, but he was still her father. How many times had I overlooked the endless faults of my own sire before I finally broke, and even now some small part of my soul urged me to heal the rift between us, even though I knew he would kill me, had he the chance. Parents have an indefinable hold on our souls.

So do children. I recognised in the swirl of emotion within Valeria's eyes some dreadful mirror of what had been happening to me since Romulus' death. Worse, perhaps. She had lost a son, and now stood to lose a father too.

Volusianus was almost vibrating, waiting for me to cheer or leap upon this new hope. He was going to be disappointed.

Swallowing the righteous pleasure that Galerius' suffering brought, I kept my face straight, my voice grave, and I rose, placing a hand upon each of Valeria's shoulders. Something had changed. Months ago she would have shrugged off that gesture with some sharp, icy comment about my manhood. Now, she looked into my eyes and I could see she was almost as lost as I.

'I am sorry, Valeria. Truly I am.'

And I was. I was sorry Galerius was not already dead, yes, but I was also sorry that she had to go through this.

Her eyes hardened. 'You hate him.'

There was no denying that.

'Yes. I hate him, as he hates me. But I do not hate you, Valeria. I never have, and so I am sorry.'

'Hm,' she replied curtly, her lips a straight line as she fought her longstanding instinct to be harsh with me, even in the face of my sympathy.

'You wish to go to him?' I asked quietly.

'My stepmother advises against it.' Her voice trembled as she spoke, and I knew just how deeply this was hurting her.

'What can I do to ease things, Valeria?'

Behind her I caught sight of Volusianus, who was scowling. He wanted me to celebrate the news, not to play the supportive husband. Galerius' illness was a victory for the West, whether the West be mine or Constantine's – or both. Volusianus would want me to stand in the forum and announce the news to the people of Rome, to give them hope, and to denigrate our enemy. He would want me to proclaim that the illness was a fitting punishment sent by the gods. I could quite imagine, given that bloated sack of offal's history, that the Christians who had suffered under his persecutions would now be claiming that their 'all-powerful God' had visited his vengeance upon their oppressor.

Valeria suddenly cast her eyes downwards, and when they rose once again to meet mine, there were tears on her cheeks – the first I had ever seen, I think.

'It is too much, Marcus.'

Marcus? My given name?

'First Romulus, and now Father. It is too much.'

And, brushing aside years of division and iciness, I pulled my wife towards me and wrapped her in my arms, crushing my own satisfaction that my enemy was dying as I held Valeria in a tight embrace, listening to her sobs as she shuddered again and again in my grasp.

And I was crying now too. For Romulus. For a closeness with my wife that I had never felt while our son was alive. For the fact that finally, at the last, she had shown a connection to the boy. For the world of what was not, but what could have been. I felt sure this bond could not last, but for that single morning it was the most important thing in the world.

And as we stood there in each other's arms, surrendering to grief, Volusianus, his face full of disapproval and irritation, turned and marched away.

15

CONSTANTINE

The warring gods of those dark years always agreed on one principle: when they relieved me of one trouble, they were swift to burden me with another, darker and riddled with sharper thorns.

The day began in my bed. Alone, enjoying the warm comfort of the soft sheets and light woollen blanket, yet loathing the absence of my loved ones. I had been out on the edge of my empire all winter and had intended to return to Treverorum by spring, but I still had a month or more of dealings here to contend with before I could be with them again: *Fausta, Crispus, Mother,* I thought with a sad pang in my breast.

'Domine!' a Cornuti sentry woke me with a hoarse cry. I nearly fell from my bed and dashed my head on the cold stone floor, such was his tone. 'The tribes are at the gates of the great fort!'

My befuddled mind was suddenly as sharp as a blade dragged abruptly along a whetstone. I glanced to the closed shutters, the gossamer veil there billowing gently in the spring morning breeze that crept through a slight gap. Outside: silence.

'The horns? Why are the buccinators not signalling the alarm?' I gasped, leaping to my feet and striding over to bash the shutters open. The bright sunlight, pastel-blue sky and mild air hit me like an ill-timed, playful slap. I saw the sea of Colonia Agrippina's red-tiled roofs, the murky green ribbon of the Rhenus, interrupted only by the dark timber bridge leading to the great grey titan of Divitia on the thickly forested far bank. I could now hear the gentle sounds of citizens ambling around the streets, the easy song of nature and the tumbling Rhenus. But not one raised voice, and no sign of movement or frantic action over on Divitia's battlements.

'They come in peace, Domine,' the Cornuti warrior added awkwardly only after I had made something of a fool of myself. I swung to pin him with a demon's stare, then old Lactantius stepped into view behind him, beaming smugly.

'All is well. The tribes have learned well the teachings of the true Lord. Come, see,' he said, beckoning me.

This was not the dark, thorny trouble I spoke of, you see; this was the sweet moment that only hardened the cruel blow that was to come.

A short while later I was dressed in boots and tunic, saddled on Celeritas' back, with Lactantius, Batius and Krocus and a pair of Cornuti walking with me as we crossed the Rhenus bridge.

'They emerged from the forest this morning, Domine,' the soldier who had woken me said. 'Marsii, bearing not arms and ire, but with mules laden with sacks of silver and trinkets.'

It was a tribute I had neither solicited nor expected. Indeed, the Second Italica legion operated a double watch on Divitia's walls, so certain was I that the establishment of my great fortress would provoke a reactionary assault.

'It is genuine,' Krocus said. 'I was there when they came. I recognised the men who brought the fineries into the fort. Chieftains and sons of leaders.'

Life had taught me to treat every gift with a suspicious eye. Was this the exception?

'They deposited the treasures by the foot of the eastern gates... then left, melted back into the woods,' Batius agreed, somewhat bemused.

'They say you are invincible, Domine,' the escorting Cornuti added.

The comment stoked a thousand memories. Among them, the bloody battlefields of Persia, the Carpi warriors on the Danube who nearly butchered me when they caught me alone, detached from my legion... and the assassins: the wicked blades of Galerius and Maxentius.

I looked down at him and erupted in a hard, lasting laugh that helped purge the memories – particularly the last one. 'They once said my father was invincible when he campaigned in these lands. He bettered the Alemanni in a great battle on the meadows of Lingones... but only a moon previously those very same dogs had chased his army from the countryside and back to that city. Yet the gates were shut, barred from the inside by the townsfolk. They certainly didn't think he was invincible then. The Alemanni were bearing down upon him and still the citizens refused to open the gates to let him in lest they be unable to shut them again in time to keep the barbarian horde out. Instead, a goat herder decided to lower a rope and leather harness used for lifting animals down from the battlements to hoist him up. And so the great Constantius Chlorus was hauled to safety like a prize hog!'

Batius and Krocus chuckled in unison, each recalling fondly their old master. Then they recognised the harmonious nature of their reaction, scowled at each other and looked in opposite directions.

The great, double-leaved gates of Divitia's western gatehouse groaned open as we came to the far end of the bridge. The iron-grey interior was dotted with men of the Second Italica, and in the heart of the vast grounds sat a trio of wagons and a bemused group of shaggy pack mules, the sacks on their backs betraying a tell-tale glint of precious goods. One of the mules was particularly weary-looking, with a mean eye and a bite missing from its ear. One of the Italica soldiers approached the beast to take a look in the bags it carried, only for the creature to take a sudden fit of pique, braying at him. As the legionary fled, the mule loped after him, chasing him in circles, biting at his buttocks, much to the amusement of the other legionaries nearby.

The mule cast a look at those men as if to ward them off, killing their laughter, then returned to its pack.

'Did Priam of Troy not once receive such a gift?' I said with a mirthful glint in my eye and a degree of respect for the brave mule.

'So I've heard,' Batius said with a chuckle, 'so when we get drunk tonight… we should keep an eye on that shaggy brute.' Then he glanced sideways at Krocus. 'I mean the mule, not you.'

Krocus was about to explode with some retort when Batius reaffirmed: 'We will be celebrating this turn of events, yes? With wine… yes?'

I sensed Krocus reflect Batius' hopeful look, and heard Lactantius groan wearily.

'Triple the wine rations tonight,' I said, but took care to add with a hard tone: 'but the double watch remains.'

* * *

It was deep into the night and the off-duty legionaries of the Second Italica were in a fine state of merriment. They sat by the porches of their long stone barrack huts, toasting bread and cheese on their braziers and toasting themselves and each other with the rich, red wine from the stores. There were ruddy faces etched with smiles in every direction. The men still on duty on the walls impressed me with their resolve: not one breaking their sentinel-like watch over the dark forest to glance behind them and down at their comrades in the fort interior. But I had promised them their share too – so long as they did their stint on duty.

Batius, Krocus and I sat on a stone bench by the Principia, drinking cups of warmed soldier wine. We chatted of old times – mainly about my father, for it provided a common ground for my two most trusted men to meet upon. I almost sensed Father's shade by my side, so vivid were each man's tales.

'A warrior, a leader,' Batius said solemnly, taking another mouthful of wine. 'That day the Alemanni chased him back to Lingones,' he said, nudging me, 'he only ran after trying to hold a bridgehead for six hours. He was plastered with blood and shaking with fatigue but still he held out until he saw there was no hope and no sense in him and his remaining few men dying.'

Krocus grunted in agreement, raising his cup. 'He was a fine man. Gone too soon.'

I thought of Father's achievements: keeping the West stable, shunning the persecutions at the risk of Diocletian and Galerius' wrath, forging a small but solid army utterly devoted to him – a force that was the foundation for my accession.

'If the gods have their wits about them, then he will be walking with them,' Batius said.

Krocus looked up, a slight wrinkle on his forehead. 'The gods?'

I sensed the subtext: *Which gods?*

But Batius did not take the bait. 'Whichever of them awaits beyond—' he lifted his hands as if to gesture to everything around us '—Mars, Wodin... the God of the Nazarene Christ.'

A scoff escaped my lips. Batius and Krocus looked at me, befuddled. The pair could not fail to love my father and his memory, but then they had not been at the sharp end of his ruthless ambition. 'He walked out on his wife and his boy.'

Batius' eyes closed slowly, as if realising his blunder. 'Domine, I didn't mean—'

'He left us with a home but little coin. He took with him my mother's confidence and sense of purpose. He stole a piece of my heart the day he deserted us. He left me dazed and mystified, drove me to seek out the grimmest of replacement paragons in his absence. I only ever took up place in Galerius' court because Father left us! He *drove* me to that whoreson!' I tossed the rest of the wine from my cup, suddenly annoyed by its heat in my veins.

'Constantine,' Batius said, his voice like a whisper.

Few people used my name these days. It took me back to my youth in a single breath, when big Batius was a young bull of a soldier. 'Fathers seldom avoid mistakes. Mine liked to drink, morning, evening, all night. He beat me and my mother.' The big man clenched and unclenched a fist as if recalling painful memories, then growled like a mastiff: 'For a time.'

'And how many sons can truly say they idolise their fathers?' Krocus mused dryly. 'Most follow the examples of other men: generals, gladiators, great speakers or bards... men whose dark sides they can choose to ignore.'

I noticed a welling of tears in the Regii leader's eyes and realised that this pair knew the truth and knew it well. I suddenly felt foolish and laughed to let the tension ebb. 'Fathers,' I proclaimed, pouring a fresh cup of wine for myself then holding the vessel aloft.

'Fathers,' Batius and Krocus said in unison. 'Bastards and heroes!'

Now you may recall the dark, spiny trouble that I said was to come and flatten my day. At this late hour, there was little time left for its advent. But come it did. And as with so many problems in recent times, it came on the back of a horse, carried by a rider. Not a cut-throat horseman from Maxentius' realm; not a cloying herald from the lands of the dying Galerius… but a rider of my own, from Treverorum.

The din of the hooves on the Rhenus bridge brought all eyes, drunk or otherwise, within Divitia to the western gatehouse. The gates swung open to reveal the horseman who arrowed towards us at the Principia. He almost fell from the saddle before the stallion had stopped.

'Domine!' he gasped. All memories of childhood evaporated with that cold, hard, weighty appellation. 'I knew it was not true,' he gasped, searching me as if to make sure I was real.

'What in the name of all the gods are you blabbering about, man?'

'Maximian has stoked a great fire! He announced in the forum that you had been slain out here by the tribes. He proclaimed himself your successor… and even took to donning your purple cloak as he spoke.'

I felt my skin harden into a shell. For years, the man had slumbered by my side. He had played the role of father-in-law well, and some days I almost forgot just how shrewd and scheming he was. I had installed him as Governor of Arelate and entrusted him to watch my southern borders for me, yet he had thrown my trust back in my face. He had once tried this trick in Rome to displace his very own son. Now he dared to try it in my lands, while living under my sheltering arm?

'A small force backed him, but the legion stationed near Arelate refused to believe the news, demanding evidence. He lost his nerve then, and upped and fled the city, but not before taking with him many wagons laden with the contents of Arelate's treasury.'

Batius gasped.

'That is the hub of our gold and silver store, Domine,' Krocus said.

I nodded, keeping my eyes on the rider. 'And now? Where has he gone? My family...' I said, the words instinctive.

'Your family are safe, Domine. Your mother, your boy and Fausta are in Treverorum, and that city has gone untouched by Maximian's treachery. He has fled to Massilia. The men of his loyal cohort have barricaded the walls of the city and made it their own. They blockade the roads there and trade in southern Gaul has ground to a halt.'

My blood felt like fire. *Fathers!* Fausta's sire or not, the man was a wolf. And the last thing I needed right now – on the cusp of stabilising my realm, was a gnashing predator, right at its heart.

I turned to Batius then Krocus. 'Leave a cohort stationed here. Have the rest of the men prepare to move out at dawn. Maximian has made his last mistake.'

16

MAXENTIUS

For over a month I tried to pull together the maelstrom of everything that was happening around me. It was as if I were being torn to pieces by my own heart, which wanted to lurch in so many directions... or occasionally to stop altogether.

I was still consumed by such soul-crushing grief for Romulus that whatever else happened in my life, it was always tainted by that numb ache, and rarely did a night pass where I did not cry into my pillows. I tried to turn to Valeria. I had seen an odd moment of hope in our sudden embrace following the news of her father's illness, but after the initial shock wore off, she became distant again, unapproachable.

And then there was the world *outside* our family.

There was Volusianus, who constantly hovered like a hornet, expecting me to do something important, when I found it hard enough even to manage the inane and mundane. And because of his ever-present shadow, I could not forget that Africa still held out against my rule, that Zenas was still unable to bring that great southern beast to heel, no matter how great the resources I sent him.

And I was never able to forget the threat my old friend Constantine posed in the north, nor the threat in the East. Galerius may be riddled with rot and dying a well-deserved death in his charnel palace, but his mastiff Licinius was ever picking at the border of my own lands regardless.

And the Christians, too. I had thought that the change in their leadership that I had imposed would quell those issues and, for a time, things had been quiet, though what I had thought to be peace had turned out to be merely silent trouble. That difficult sect was once again rising in terms of both voice and anger.

And to cap it all, Anullinus' troublesome brother Gaius Annius had returned from a posting in Sicilia – with middling success at best – and now pestered me for a position of import in the city. I had half a mind to oust the current Aedile in charge of the city's latrines and appoint Gaius in his place. A 'shit job' was the common joke.

You see? Everything for which I had no real interest or love picked at me and demanded my attention, while everyone that I loved and needed consolation from had turned from me or left me.

I felt curiously solitary for a man who lived in a city of a million people and ruled over them from a palace of a thousand servants.

I made my mistake at the festival of Fors Fortuna. I had been hurrying through my work so much one morning that I had unwittingly appended my name to an invitation to a private social engagement. Once I realised I had confirmed my intention to attend, I tried to rectify the matter, but Volusianus persuaded me that the bad public feeling such a move would create could be very harmful. And so I had, with due dread and irritation, alighted from my carriage at the town house of the senator Lucretius Ballator.

A prime example of the more odious, obsequious and generally verminous end of the senatorial scale, Ballator had been the man I had left quivering and quailing in the forum four years earlier, when I had almost been mobbed by a riotous crowd. He had not improved over time, and my accession to the purple had merely changed the title by which he addressed me, not his unpleasant manner.

I spent the first hour of the occasion swanning around the *domus* trying to be the emperor they all wanted to see and speak to. Ballator was somewhat off with me, though that might have more to do with Volusianus and the eight Praetorians in togas who moved among his guests for my safety than with my own actions. Everyone wanted to make themselves known to me, and many wanted to elicit my opinion on something or make veiled hopeful requests. None of them were interesting or entertaining.

Nor was the entertainment. Gauls cannot play lyres, apparently, and certainly one horse-faced young woman from Leptiminus could only drive animals back into their deep burrows with her warbling song. And as for the wrestlers... well I shudder even at the memory. Had they tried some of those eye-watering moves at the Olympic Games in the old days, Greece might have collapsed even sooner.

The gathering was not a banquet or formal meal so we were not tied to one place and consequently, in the end, I sought out peace and quiet wherever I could. Despite the summer heat, a thin veil of cloud had drawn across the city as the evening descended, and soon a gentle patter of rain began to rattle off the roof tiles and plip-plap into the impluvium pool of the grand atrium. The guests massed into the warmer rooms and left the atrium to the gentle rain. I spied the dozen or so folk who had been taking the air rushing in from the garden, shaking their heads with a fine spray of water. And I saw – and seized – my chance.

As I emerged into the wet gardens, two of the toga-clad Praetorians followed me, but I stopped them on the doorstep and told them to go inside. They were unhappy, but I smiled and laughed, asking them what predator I might find in such a well-tended walled garden in the heart of the city.

What predator indeed.

I walked out into the extensive grounds, enjoying the fine patter of rain on my face. It would take an hour in this light drizzle for me to even feel wet through my heavy toga, so I strolled, enjoying the freedom that the gardens brought.

I almost bit through my tongue when a voice murmured right behind me.

I had wandered beneath an arbour covered with thick vines, which the rain had yet to penetrate and where a marble seat lurked. The voice had said '*Domine*', in a sultry, sibilant hiss. Startled, I turned, bringing up my hands defensively.

A woman stood behind me. She was a little older than I, though not much. I think she was pretty. I *hope* she was pretty. It was rather hard to tell in the patchy shadows of the gazebo and with white lead on her face and the elaborate coils of a carefully constructed hairpiece atop her head. Certainly her *shape* was attractive enough, and the gauzy stola that she wore left me in no doubt about that. It bordered on scandalous. I started again, recoiling a step from her closeness, as I recognised her from the initial introductions. This was Lucretia, Ballator's wife!

'Really, Domine,' she said in her exotic voice, 'do I look like I might harm you?'

I realised my hands were still up to ward her off and dropped them, flushing.

'And where might I conceal a weapon if that were the case?'

She made a point of accentuating every curve with movement so that I could be sure she was unarmed. I was beginning to sweat and seemed to be having difficulty swallowing.

'You like what you see?'

I coughed a non-answer. Her forwardness was astounding and most un-Roman. In my better days I would have been horrified at such behaviour. That night? Well, let's just say that I was at an all-time low ebb.

'I... er....'

She chuckled, and there was a hoarseness to the laugh that I found awfully enticing.

'It would appear that of all Rome's nobility, only you and I are alive enough to enjoy the feel of water trickling upon our skin, Domine.'

I was grateful that the shadows of the arbour would hide my crimson cheeks.

'I... er... I needed some air. The guests can be... er... cloying.'

'They can, Domine.' She smiled, taking a step closer again, so that I smelled the exotic oils and rose-petal perfume in which she had liberally doused herself. It was heady, bordering on eye-watering. She could have anaesthetised small animals with her scent. 'And few can be as dull-witted and tedious as my husband. I was surprised you accepted his invitation. Surprised and *very* pleased.'

She took another half step forward and I made some kind of strange strangled noise.

Lucretia... My mind furnished me with rumour. A little ditty I had heard somewhere.

> *Lucretia likes them young and strong,*
> *She doesn't care for right or wrong,*
> *She's had the public in the street,*
> *And even the Ravenna fleet.*

I blinked in revulsion, panic, excitement and desire. Somehow, suddenly, I found it very easy to see a truth behind those words.

I raised a pointed finger to admonish her and almost leapt back in shock when she closed her mouth over the digit and licked my finger. I couldn't believe the audacity of the woman. She was a Roman matron with a respectable husband. Of course, he was an idiot, and unpleasant, and boring, and she knew all that. But she was in his house. And I had a wife. I had...

I pictured Valeria, the icy maiden with her back to me. I saw myself over the past month standing outside the door to her suite, wishing she would even look at me, wishing I could feel her embrace to help me deal with the dreadful, grief-filled loneliness.

I kissed her.

It was the most impetuous thing I have ever done. I have invaded nations, sent men to their deaths and claimed a throne that some would say wasn't mine to claim. And yet nothing felt as wrong, illicit and dangerous as that kiss.

She had desire. I had need. They were not the same thing, but they fitted together like a puzzle.

Half an hour later, she lay on the bench with a rosy glow, feeling the first drips of rain beginning to make their way inside the covered gazebo, so helpfully hidden from view from the house, and splat on her sizzling skin.

I tried to brush down my hair, horribly aware that it probably looked like a bird's nest. My toga hung all wrong and without a body-slave to make the task easy I spent quite some time adjusting the shape so that it looked even remotely acceptable. As soon as I was upright, I felt ashamed and stepped out into the rain, where we could not see each other and the rain could flatten my coiffure and wash away my immorality. After long moments I decided that I would be all right returning to the public gathering. The sodden toga and hair would masque my activity and hopefully douse the worst of the rosy-oiled scent that I had acquired. I turned to scurry back and jumped again.

Volusianus stood, sopping wet, in the centre of the garden with an incredulous look, shaking his head.

I hurried over to him, mortified, trying to find the words I needed. He found his own first.

'That was stupid.'

No preamble. No acknowledgement of rank. This was like having Anullinus back in my life. In fact, it was so familiar and oddly welcome, that directness, that it washed aside my fear and left me calm.

'It was a reaction. Regrettable. Nothing more.'

As I started walking back to the house, Volusianus fell in alongside me. 'If word of this gets out – and it *will* get out, for Lucretia has quite a mouth on her, as I'm sure you're now well aware – then your reputation will crumble.'

'I think you overestimate the matter.'

He frowned. 'No. You *underestimate* it. The higher classes

of Rome could easily turn on you. Half your perceived legitimacy on that throne is through your *Romanitas* and your moral right. Lose that: lose your throne.'

I rounded angrily on him. I knew it had been wrong, but it had also been unstoppable. In my situation I could no more have resisted that tryst than I could have walked on the air.

'Volusianus, I am not about to apologise to you or anyone else for finding much-needed solace after months of solitary grief. If I need to apologise to anyone it is Ballator, and he must be used to this sort of thing by now.'

'Domine…'

'No.' I held up a hand. 'If you think this is dangerous or a problem, then *you* deal with it. You always know best, after all.'

I walked off. Jove, how I regret that ending.

Two days later, things came back to bite me.

I was working through my daily records, correspondence and so on. I had cause to pause, for I had just come across something that had surprised and saddened me. In the pile of paperwork was a report from one of my Praetors, pinned to the deeds of a house down below the Palatine, near the great Flavian amphitheatre. Anullinus' house. I was being asked by my administrators what to do with the property. I should probably have given the house to its former owner's brother, but the idea of having a man Anullinus disliked inheriting the place of his death seemed… wrong somehow. Inappropriate. His property went to nobody, then, and had stayed in imperial hands for a while. The recommendation of the clerk who wrote me the request was that the house be auctioned to help fill the treasury.

Somehow I couldn't. I kept thinking back on the day I saw his butchered body in the place. I felt a wave of anger at Volusianus, who was so clearly the culprit, but let it pass. Recriminations now would do more harm than good. But I couldn't let the house go. And I didn't want to live in it. And, in fact, I didn't really want anyone else living there.

I made up my mind. I would keep it. Nothing more. It would be my property, but would stay empty and unused for now. And because I felt sure that the ever-argumentative Gaius Annius would argue, I had his brother's house's value paid to his estate to ward off trouble in advance.

Satisfied that I had made an acceptable decision, I scribbled my answer down on the vellum, blew the ink dry and put down my stylus. I moved the document aside to my pile of completed work and looked down to see the effects of my recent tryst staring back up at me.

I blinked at the documents before me.

I rose and crossed to the door, opened it and shouted 'Artemas?'

My principal secretary came scurrying over, bowing, and I beckoned him back to my desk. I pointed down at the paperwork.

There, on the wooden surface, stood the deeds to seven properties, including a horribly familiar town house. The name Lucretius Ballator was scribbled atop them all. They were, like Anullinus' house before them, being placed in the imperial trust with recommendations for sale and queries about their fate.

'What is this?'

Artemas peered at the vellum sheets. 'Senator Ballator's estate, Domine, for your disposal.'

'Why?'

Artemas frowned. 'Criminals' property is *usually* taken from them, Domine.'

'Criminal?' I felt as though I were attending some kind of child's theatre, and gestured for my secretary to be a little more forthcoming and elucidating this time.

'Senator Lucretius Ballator, Domine. Murdered his wife two nights gone. A very big trial, but very quick. Not much need for a trial, really, since it was witnessed by the Praetorian Prefect himself.'

'Was it?' I whispered. 'Was it indeed?'

'Yes, Domine. The senator drove a sword through her in their gardens after the party on the feast of Fors Fortuna. Ballator denied it, of course, but with such a credible eyewitness as the prefect, the entire case was dealt with in brief and the sentence carried out this morning.'

I stared. Ballator? Confusion filled me for a moment. Had Ballator found out what had happened in the garden earlier that night, he might quite understandably kill his wife in a fit of rage. But I could hardly picture that wet sop of a man encountering rage, let alone wielding a sword. And why would Volusianus be there too? The answer, of course, was plain and simple, and this would not be the first time Volusianus had plunged a sword into a back to overcome a troublesome situation.

Guilt riddled me. Guilt that I had unwittingly put Lucretia in such a position. And guilt that I had equally unwittingly given Volusianus free rein to deal with the problem as he saw fit. I remembered Ballator. The very idea of him murdering someone was laughable. He would run away from a bad cold!

I made a mental note to pay Volusianus back for this sometime. Between this and the still-rankling murder of Anullinus, he was racking up debts of blood surprisingly fast.

17

CONSTANTINE

MASSILIA, SOUTHERN GAUL, 10TH JULY 310 AD

The sapphire sea around the great southern port city of Massilia was still, its surface smooth as oil. The low coastal bluffs were riddled with pits, caves and niches – the honeycomb of Christian catacombs within a bleak portent of what was to come. For atop the cliffs, a broad, iron line of men and siege engines faced the city's walls, their standards hanging limp in the stinking hot air, outlined by the unblemished summer sky. It was the first of the *dies caniculares*, you see – the sweltering dog days when Sirius rose with the sun each morning. Days that most men spent in shade or in the *frigidarium* at the baths. Days that turned wine sour and drove hounds mad.

Yet I had no choice but to stand in that noonday heat, outside the high, strong walls and gates with the few legions I could risk bringing away from my ever-more encroached-upon borders. The feather-helmed Cornuti, the bronze-scaled Lancearii, two cohorts of the Second Italica and the First Minervia formed the ox-horn line on the grassy countryside, barring any exit from the landward side of the city just as Caesar and his armies had done hundreds of years before.

Down below the shimmering cliffs, a small flotilla of triremes blockaded the fortified harbour – penning in two galleys and many trade *liburnians* stacked with salted fish, wine, oil, coral and cork. In truth, the blockade was paltry – as was my 'fleet' in those contested waters – but it was all I could do. I simply could not allow the bastard within Massilia's walls any route of escape.

I scoured the battlements, seeing the iron helms of the rogue cohort of the Seventh Gemina up there, quite rightly veiling all but their eyes and mouths – for they should be ashamed of their treacherous deeds! An ancient and once-proud legion. And to think it was my Comitatus of tribesmen whose loyalty had been doubted!

I was dragged from my fiery thoughts by squabbling voices nearby. A knot of legionaries were sheepishly reporting to Batius some problem with the hundreds of ladders we had brought up. 'Too short?' Batius seethed, his eyes flicking from the ladders resting in the grass to Massilia's battlements.

One legionary explained the man responsible for measuring the ladders wasn't the brightest, and had counted the required length using his fingers – of which he possesses only nine. Batius dragged his fingers down his face like claws. 'In the name of…' he gasped. 'You'll just have to bloody well stand on each other's shoulders when you reach the top.'

The big man swung away from them and stomped over to me.

'Trouble with the ladders,' he growled, wiping the sweat from his stubbled head. His eyes never ceased to appraise and probe the defences, occasionally flicking to the red roof of the Temple of Apollo, jutting from within, raised on the mound at the heart of the city. 'But it matters not: Maximian cannot hold Massilia with just a single cohort.'

'That's what I fear. He knows he is trapped here. Like any rat on a doomed vessel, he will right now be scampering in search of a way out. And Maximian is an extremely shrewd rodent.'

My eyes ran over the land-facing walls and the naval blockade again. No way out. Was I overestimating the old dog?

'If we storm the place we *will* take it,' Krocus posited. 'But only four centuries of his cohort are on the walls. The rest...'

'The rest are embedded within the city,' I finished for him. I had besieged and stormed towns before. I knew what lay inside – all of the men with me probably knew also: barricades of rubble and timber across tight streets; marksmen on the rooftops, ready to rain arrows and javelins on any down below; flagstones thirsty for blood. The cicada song sounded like a thousand screaming voices, and I felt myriad eyes upon me – those of my arrayed men and those of the treacherous legionaries on Massilia's battlements... and those most wide and terrified eyes of the trapped citizens, cowering, daring to peek over the parapet from a section of wall near the descent towards the harbour. Romans. People, many of whom would die today under the flashing blades of my forces. People who had neither supported Maximian nor solicited his presence. *Maximian,* I thought, seeing the fat drunkard's face, those hooded, presumptuous eyes. First his boy, Maxentius, had tried to skewer me on the end of a hired blade, now the old bastard himself thought he could wrench my hard-won station out from under me like a rug. A cold wind swept over my heart.

'Fall upon the city with everything,' I said, sweeping a hand across the array of stone-throwers, the two high wooden war towers and the somewhat squat ladders. 'Break the gates, take the walls, crush the Gemina scum.' I saw the watching citizens from the corner of my eye as I added: 'Do whatever it takes.'

Batius' face hardened in determination. 'It will be done.'

The big man turned away and howled, snatching up a standard. 'Cornuti, *for-waaaaaard!*'

His cry was joined by a hundred other commanders and the thousands in their ranks and then drowned out by a dozen keening horns and the eerie groan of stressed timber as the war towers rolled forward, rocking slightly on the uneven grass. The din was joined by a steady thunder of marching boots and clanking iron as my legions advanced behind the towers, their armour glinting like the scales of a giant fish. The Gemina legionaries on the walls bristled, turning ballistae up there to train them on my forces, bending bows and lifting spears, just waiting for the range to be good.

I felt my heart rap on my ribs as the onagers creaked and croaked, wooden arms bent back and loaded with man-sized rocks, crews looking to me and my standard bearers to give the order to loose the great catapults. I raised a hand, one finger extended. I saw what would happen were I to drop it: the rocks hurtling through the air to shatter the parapet and stain the fine summer's day with a storm of dark dust and ruined bodies; the swaying war towers would follow up to engage the walls near those weakened points, the legions flowing up the wooden steps within and pouring onto the battlements, the blades being drawn...

A thick clunk and a grumble of timber – not from any war machine – halted me, finger still raised. My eyes stared, unblinking, at the tall, arched, bronze-strapped city gates as they parted. I saw Krocus stagger back a few paces and fumble to draw his sword – his first instinct to protect me.

'A sally?' he gasped.

And a sally it was, but not of soldiers. Instead, a tumble of citizens came forth, in rags and robes, faces white, wide and tear-streaked. A few hundred of them. They wailed, they fell to their knees facing me, they threw up their hands in plea and panic as a maw of Cornuti spear tips corralled them. I saw behind them in the shadow of the gateway two Gemina legionaries sprawled and still, one stained red, a quartet of young men lying crumpled beside them, their simple citizens' garb equally sullied with ripped flesh and lifeblood. The battle for the gates had come from within.

'They're giving me the city,' I said, the words spilling from my lips like an escaped fancy.

At once, the Gemina legionaries on the battlements heads' flicked towards the gates, craning to see what had happened. In moments, they knew, and they disappeared from the parapet in a heartbeat, back into the maze of stockades and traps they had no doubt riddled the streets with.

The gates were open, but the fight was still to come.

If I thought for a moment that the opened gates meant the battle was all but won, I was horribly wrong. My legions edged through the broad main way under a hail of sling stones, spears and arrows from Maximian's Gemina men posted all around the rooftops. I moved with Batius under testudo of Cornuti shields, creeping towards each building to let a handful of men slip from the shield-shell like passengers disembarking from a ship and slip inside the palaces and temples. Moments later, the screams of close combat sounded from up on the rooftop and Gemina bodies would plummet and splash like over-ripe cherries on the flagstones. At one juncture, we found ourselves at a crossroads, with four tall marble halls surrounding us, the archers atop each gleefully emptying their quivers down upon the perfect killing pit into which we had wandered. I saw the Italica men stranded in open space, ballistae on the rooftops spitting down upon them, ripping great troughs of red through their ranks, screams of the dying biting at me like crows.

'With me!' Batius yelled, waving sixteen Cornuti men with him into the ballistae-topped building, the clatter of their ascending bootsteps and yelling and smashing of iron sounding from the stairs.

Inspired by the big man as I had been since boyhood, I called to another group. 'The archers,' I barked, pointing up through cracks in the testudo to the century of bowmen stationed on the rooftop adjacent to the one Batius was tackling. We streaked across a stretch of open space, arrows whacking down around us and one clanging from my jewelled battle helm. The cool shade and the close echo of the building's interior was like a slap to my senses. I swung my eyes to and fro to adjust to the dimness, and a Cornuti man was swift to shoulder me clear of a thrown spear. I saw the culprit – a Gemina legionary on the mezzanine. Without thinking, I plucked the thrown spear from the post it had smashed into and turned it upon the thrower, the lance sailing up there and taking the soldier in the breastbone. He doubled over the mezzanine with a gurgle and mouthful of blood and hung there like a wet garment. As we sped up the stairs towards the roof I glanced at the dead man – the dead *Roman* – and realised what a step I had taken... what a black step down a night-dark road.

But the chaos of the fray engulfed me again as we emerged onto the sun-bleached stone roof and confronted the archers.

The bowmen loosed at us in panic but I was quick to raise my shield, peppered with arrows a trice later. Then the shield became a fist, breaking limbs smashing faces, my sword sweeping out at the archers. They wore mail, most of them, but they stood not a chance against my hardened regiment. It was with a savage triple-hack that I drove the officer among them from the edge of the roof, his scream cut short when he burst across the edge of a fountain down below, staining the water red.

Panting, snarling, I felt the dark road in my mind grow darker, seeing corpses of my kith littering the sides of the way. War is never glorious, nor sweet, but this was the most galling of clashes I had ever endured. And the worst was yet to come.

'Domine!' a Cornuti centurion, down on the street below and leading the testudo, cried. 'The way to the temple hill is almost open.'

I followed his gaze to see the rising street and the crude barrier that had been erected across it, made of tipped wagons and crates, topped with a thick watch of Gemina legionaries. 'Onwards,' I rasped, waving the small knot of Cornuti with me back down to street level. I almost collided with Batius down there, he emerging from the ballistae building at the same time as I stumbled from the archers' eyrie. The big man's face was whiter than sand, yet he was not injured that I could see. 'Batius?'

He looked at me, through me, his eyes wide.

'They're holding firm,' the Cornuti centurion howled back down the rising street, cupping a sword slash to his shoulder, staggering. The Gemina on the crude barrier were not for moving.

'Batius? I need you now,' I croaked, clamping a hand to his shoulder. 'As always before.'

He seemed to snap from his odd spell at this, nodding albeit shakily. But on he came with me as I joined with the main body of the Cornuti again and we surged uphill. The Gemina men screamed in defiance, crouching, spears and swords levelled.

A spiculum thrummed through the air and skewered one standing atop the wall of wagons through the belly. The soldier's mouth opened in a silent scream as his guts burst from the wound like an infected boil pricked by a pin, and he toppled onto the alley floor with a crunch. The other two Gemina men launched their missiles in return before a ruck of my legionaries forged against the wagon wall, which wobbled, swayed and eventually toppled. The Cornuti ranks surged across the fallen vehicles like a river shredding a dam, slaughtering the Gemina in their hundreds before racing on up the lane towards the city forum. I led the Lancearii in their wake up that crimson, corpse-strewn street, each of those javelin throwers speckled in red and with just a few missiles left – the rest embedded in the fallen, broken traitors' bodies scattered throughout the city. On we went up the slope towards Massilia's heart: the echo and clatter of boots rapped like scattering birds in the tight street, then fell away as we poured out into the great open square around the Temple of Apollo.

'Where is he?' I demanded, my head switching in every direction. My legionaries had the square; there was no doubt about that. The surviving eighty or so Gemina soldiers were kneeling at the ends of Cornuti spears, sweating, gulping, mouthing prayers. They now saw the folly of taking Maximian's bribe. But where *was* Maximian? I saw nothing but empty, echoing colonnades, mockingly silent, staring statues and an incongruously cheerful, babbling fountain.

A few of my legionaries emerged from within the temple, shaking their heads. How could it be? My forces had swept into the city brutally yet methodically, being sure to close in on this point from every direction. Maximian *had* to be here. Had he resorted to scuttling through a water tunnel or the like to evade me? No, surely not, for the old cur was no longer spry or thin enough for such a feat. I looked all around me. He had to be in the city somewhere, for the walls were mine, the gates were...

My gaze snagged on the open end of the forum and the terraced descent to the harbour. Over the mosaic of red tiles and white marble, I saw only one thing: the postern gate down there by the coast road. It was the one spot my legionaries outside had left unwatched. Beyond it, on the coast road, was an odd sight: the tiny forms of two soldiers, running alongside a plump rider on what looked like a badly struggling donkey. The soldiers carried sacks with them, and I saw the sparkle of what looked like golden sand dropping and spilling from their burdens as they went. Coins – coins from my stolen treasury.

I heard a low growl then realised it was my own. 'With me!' I barked.

Someone brought Celeritas to me, handing me the reins, and at once I was at a spearhead of men. We cantered down the broad, flagstoned way to the harbour, then out the postern gate. We caught up with the fleeing trio easily, and I dismounted into a run while Celeritas was still moving at a gentle trot. The pair of Gemina legionaries now dropped their sacks of booty and turned to face me in fright, faces agape in horror but their well-practised arms going for their swords at once. Steel sang as I tore my spatha from its sheath and swept it up. One of the Gemina mongrels fell, his face and shoulder cut deep. Batius blocked a wild blow from the other then drove his blade hilt-deep into the cur's guts.

Just ahead, the labouring donkey brayed and the well-fed snake on its back turned his head, face drawn and eyes bulging. I rushed forward and hauled the bastard down. He fell from the saddle onto his back with a weighty *thud*, coughing and retching, blinded by the tossed-up dust.

'You fat skin of wine!' I roared, snatching at the folds of his collar and hauling him up a few inches off the ground, nose to nose with me where I crouched. 'You dared to steal from me? Have you not learned – have you not seen enough of me over the years to understand?' Hatred throbbed through me as I saw a reel of memories: the wicked games of Diocletian and Galerius; their beguiling of Father, convincing him to abandon Mother and me; the countless deaths during the persecutions and the threats to my loved ones... the threats to me; the complacent demands that I should relinquish my title and my territory to them. 'Nobody will ever take from me again. *Nobody!*' I cast him back down then dashed the hilt of my sword on his mouth, sending his head snapping back with a crack and staining his teeth red. Then I positioned my sword tip at his chest. 'This is it for you... this is the end!'

It was a dark, nightmarish world for those few moments, but as my muscles tensed and the blade quivered, ready to split his breast and ruin his heart, I heard a voice that hauled me from the brink.

'Father, no!' I looked up, the spell of fiery hatred sideswiped by the word.

Little Crispus came running down the hill path from the grassy flats outside the city's land walls. I blinked, certain I had succumbed to madness. But no, the top of a newly arrived wagon jutted from the crest of the slope behind him; here he was, my dark-skinned, broad-faced boy, the lasting echo of my love with sweet Minervina. His expression, however, was one that I hoped I would never see again. His face was twisted, mouth wailing, eyes disbelieving.

'Grandpapa!' he cried, arms flailing as he fell down the last few steps of the descent to skid onto his knees beside Maximian and throw his arms around him like a shield. I remained there, frozen, the sword point still hovering at my foe's breast, my dear son just inches from its edge.

'Constantine, no!' another voice wailed. I knew who it was without turning back to the dirt path on the hillside. Fausta fell to hug Maximian also, weeping, her arms cradling her shaking father, her glassy eyes searching my face. 'Please, Constantine... no.'

After an eternity of struggle within, I stepped back, the quivering spatha falling limp, the tip dropping and finding a berth in the dirt. Maximian let out a rattling breath of relief.

Does that make me a merciful man, I ask you? Or perhaps you might think me a weak man – a fool, even? Neither bold nor ruthless as a true emperor should be. But damn, I defy you to be there as I was, to look your beloved and your progeny in the eye, see their tears, hear their heartsick weeping, and not acquiesce. If you think otherwise, then it is you who is the fool. And if you doubt me, then you will soon see you were wrong to do so. Bold, aye. Ruthless, utterly. For it was only a stay of execution I granted the old bastard.

That moment outside Massilia would prove to be the eye of the storm, a storm that would erupt again all too soon when Maximian finally faced justice... a storm that would change the world.

18

MAXENTIUS

I stood by the parapet of the Palatine, looking down upon the miserable Christians gathered beside the Circus Maximus. I had put those frowns on their faces that very morning, but better frowns on their faces than firebrands in their hands.

I had been dragged from my grief at the villa back to the Palatine to hold another meeting with the leaders of that troublesome cult, for even an emperor must put aside his personal problems sometimes for the good of his people.

Marcellinus had been destructive in his time as the Christian leader, and I had hoped that Eusebius would be a better choice, but the ensuing months of street warfare, burned temples and general trouble had proved me wrong. Where Marcellinus had taxed his lapsed worshippers, Eusebius preferred to humiliate and abuse them and somehow believed they would smile and take it, the idiot. So I had sent for the leaders of both warring parties and had them dragged into my presence where I had berated them angrily, threatening them with *damnatio ad bestias* even before settling upon the course of exiling everyone who purported to lead and denying them the right to raise a new Pope until I found one of whom I approved.

And that would likely prove to be a rather long job. I spent most days still wallowing in my pit of despair and would hardly give up my sweet misery for the troublesome Christians. And so there, below me, the gathered cultists watched their leader in dismay as he shuffled miserably along the street bound for the emporium and a ship for anywhere that wasn't Rome. Good riddance to the troublesome runt.

I was dressed in tunic and *paenula* only, the stifling heat of a Roman summer making a toga far too unpleasant, but I still had one badge of office upon my person – my imperial sceptre. In truth, I had meant to leave it in the aula regia after that irritating meeting, but had been in such a mood when I stormed out that I had forgotten and now, as my disposition calmed and the ire gave way once more to hollow anguish, I found myself irritably tapping on the parapet with the priceless sceptre.

'What happened to the man I brought Africa?'

I spun in surprise at the dark tone and rather blunt words of Volusianus. The man was standing a dozen paces from me in his uniform, armed and with a scowl of disapproval like none I'd ever seen him wear before.

'You forget your place, Prefect,' I snapped angrily, though in truth I was more concerned about his intentions than his lack of respect. History was replete with Praetorian Prefects who had slipped a knife into one emperor or another to advance their own career, and Volusianus was slowly acquiring a catalogue of butchery. Still, Volusianus' sword remained sheathed and he wielded only an old-fashioned centurion's vine stick.

'Don't try to put me in my place, Maxentius. Not when

we're alone. I would defer and fawn to the emperor I came to Rome for, but he seems to have gone, sunk in the Tiber along with his boy, leaving only a ghost of his former self.'

I blinked in surprise. No one had spoken to me like this since...

Since another Praetorian Prefect, Anullinus, had dragged me from my quiet villa life and thrown a purple cloak across my shoulders. I slumped again. Even my anger was tempered these days by my loss.

'Go, Volusianus, before you say something we both regret.'

'My arse, Maxentius,' he snapped, and I turned, frowning. 'Prefect...'

'No,' he retorted. 'You are the Emperor of Rome, not some moping actor in a Greek tragedy. It's time you stopped mooning about like some lost sheep and took the reins of your empire again. Remember, we are in a dangerous situation, beset by enemies, and if you cannot lead Rome, then perhaps you should lock yourself in your son's mausoleum and let someone else carry that sceptre?'

I felt my blood boiling quick and hot, partially with the anger he was stoking in me, and partially, deep down, with the personal shame born of the fact that I knew in my heart that he was right. I had for days now been wrestling with the need to force myself back into the world, but grief is like quicksand – the more one struggles to free oneself from it, the stronger its hold.

'You don't know what you're talking about, Volusianus,' I barked angrily, turning my back on him again – grief claiming my anger and enfolding it once more.

'Don't I? What do you really know about me, Maxentius? That I governed Africa? That I am a competent military man? Have you ever met my wife? No. And I doubt you even know her name. I suspect you don't know that she stays at our country estate nursing our baby son with tear-stained cheeks that have been unrelenting since our eldest boy died at sea eight years ago. Tears that only strengthened when our only daughter fell to the pox the month before her wedding. You are so wrapped up in your own little lake of misery that you can't even give thought to the possibility that you are not alone. That other people have gone through this before. And now it's time to decide, Maxentius, whether you are Emperor of Rome, deserving of my respect and a title, or just a grieving father who lets his broken heart rule his once-sharp mind.'

I spun, gesturing angrily with the sceptre. 'You don't know…'

'Yes I do,' Volusianus snapped. 'But some of us do not have the luxury of letting our grief control our lives. There is too much to do. You used to pride yourself on your Romanitas, Maxentius. You were going to be a Roman like those men of old. Well those men of old swallowed their problems and got on with it. They put the state above themselves – at least the *good* ones did. You wanted to be an Augustus, or a Trajan or a Marcus Aurelius. But you're becoming a Tiberius or a Caligula, driven mad with grief. Is that what you want? Will you be an emperor damned in memory, the last to rule this city?'

I lashed out without intending to. The priceless sceptre would have caught him around the cheek and drawn blood, but Volusianus was ready for me. His vine stick came up and blocked the swing, turning my sceptre aside, and then he was coming at me, like a killer, his eyes afire and that stick jabbing.

I had trained with his *doctores* among the Praetorians, and with swordsmen hired for the purpose in my youth. I may have rarely taken up arms in my life, but that does not mean I did not know how to. But the shock of this attack and the strength of it took me utterly by surprise and I found I was stepping back along the parapet towards the library doors, repeatedly passing the shade of the columns rising up from the low wall. The onslaught continued, that vine stick lunging and swiping, and I had no time to recover myself and press back, for it was all I could do to turn the blows aside.

We reached the end of the colonnade and Volusianus paused, his eyes narrowing.

'Are you a ghost, Maxentius, or a man?'

'I… am… an… *emperor!*' I roared, and stepped forward, pressing my own attack now, that sceptre swinging and jabbing, his vine stick flicking this way and that expertly, parrying my blows. We had almost reached our starting point once more when the truth of the situation sank in.

Volusianus was smiling. Not the vicious smile of a killer as I'd thought to see, but the slightly smug smile of a victor.

'Glad to hear it, Domine,' he said.

I stopped, panting, my arm shaking with the effort of the attack and the reverberation of repeated blows and parries. I felt at one and the same time numb and alive, cold and afire, angry and elated.

Domine.

The clever bastard.

'Was that true? About your children?'

'I was raised not to lie to the emperor,' Volusianus said quietly, and a haunted look briefly passed across his face before his smile returned in force. '*That* is the man to whom I brought Africa. *That* is Imperator Maxentius, Emperor of Rome. Good. Thank you, Domine, for I was beginning to worry about finding a successor.'

I almost lost my temper again at that comment, but catching the glint in his eye, instead I burst out laughing.

'Gods, Volusianus, but you know me better than I know myself.'

A lot like your predecessor, who you killed in cold blood, I added in silence.

'Rome needs its emperor as much as ever, Domine,' he replied quietly.

'I'm not sure how to do it, Volusianus. How to escape the grief. It's all well and good you making me angry enough to overcome it, but I cannot live with such anger permanently just to keep the misery at bay. And at night, alone, it will always come back.'

The prefect tucked his stick into his belt and reached out, grasping my upper arms in a manner that would see most people beaten for insolence.

'You will learn how to control it in time. Grief is like a *camisia*. You put it on when the day's business is ended and you retreat into the comfortable dark. You wear it at night, and then, in the morning, when the world needs you, you remove it and replace it with the apparel of command.'

I looked upon Volusianus with a respect I'd not felt for some time. Here was the man who had guided and supported me, rather than the man I'd been wary of since the death of Anullinus. I felt a faint touch of light – an element of positivity that had been missing from my life for some time.

'Is it possible?' I asked, more of myself than of my prefect.

'It is. The pain never leaves, Domine, but it can be suppressed and controlled.'

I nodded. 'Then perhaps it is time to concentrate on our problems. My tutors as a child told me that there were no unsolvable problems, just undiscovered solutions, and

I firmly hold to that belief. And if there is a solution to every problem, then there is a solution to the Christian one. Perhaps I can shed the camisia of grief for the daylight hours and find that answer.'

The world had changed for me again. I knew that the road ahead out of my pit of grief would be long and difficult, but I had taken a step on it, and that first step is always the hardest.

19

CONSTANTINE

MASSILIA, 23RD AUGUST 310 AD

I glanced around the dank, grey walls, streaked with green algae and lichen. The air was heavy with decay and stale with the breaths of the many who had perished down here. Iron grates and thick-doored cells clung to the sides of the corridor, whimpers and maddened chants came from within.

Two Cornuti flanked me as I strode along the dim passageway, and I felt guilt lick at my mind again, its tongue spiky and unforgiving. How many men had breathed their last down here – men of whom I had no knowledge, yet had been cast into this netherworld in my name, sentenced by my officials? The tongue lashed again: forget the dungeons – just how many men had died at the end of my sword or the swords of my legionaries in recent years? Where would it end?

The torturous chatter ended when I came to the bronze-strapped oak door at the end of the corridor. The cell keeper fumbled with an ancient-looking ring of keys and unlocked it. I had my guards remain where they were while I stepped inside.

The mouldering stink was worse in here, with no airflow

and little light bar afforded by the tiny grating high up on the ceiling, through which fingers of burnished-gold sunlight stretched across the cell and formed a grid on one wall, dust motes lingering in the shafts.

Below sat a sorry heap, head in hands. His silver hair was overgrown, tangled and greasy. A spiky grey beard festered on his chin and his hooded eyes were almost shut, so weary he looked. His body seemed saggy, merely skin and emptiness instead of the cushioning of fat he had enjoyed in his better days. And his garments – if one could call them such – were a ragged mess of urine stains and grime. Maximian, one-time Augustus of the West, embodiment of Hercules, equal of Galerius and chosen man of Diocletian, was broken.

Even that day when he had fled Italia after trying to usurp his own son – who was a damned usurper himself, among many other things, I will remind you! – when he had come before me in rags and stricken with hunger, he had still carried that devious sparkle in those hooded eyes. I knew then I was taking a snake into my home. But I did it for Fausta, you see. What a fool I had been to let the asp have such freedom. He had won my trust in stages, advising me shrewdly, putting himself second to my cause and – loath as I am to admit it – fuelling my ego, titling himself as my patron and assuring me I was the true master of the West. Perhaps I should have sent him away that day. Perhaps I should have struck his sorry head from his shoulders. I looked once more around the cell. That it had come to this was as much my fault as his.

'Ah, Constantine,' he said in a low, tarry drawl, not looking up.

It took me by surprise. No appeal for mercy. No attempt to negotiate his release. His pleas had been grand at first. *Give me a century of soldiers and a carriage, a team of stallions and a wagon of comforts, supplies and money enough to furnish me with a new country estate in Hispania.* In reply I had given him a hard, silent glare. And as the days drew by, he seemed to realise that mercy and leniency were not guaranteed. *Give me a boat, a few body-servants and a sack of wheat and I will sail far, far away,* he had begged me at the start of the new moon. Silence had been my response again. Silence to cover up the truth: that I could not bring myself to do it – not out of pity for the old bastard, but for the love of my wife and my boy. It was a choice of poisons, you see: to slay my father-in-law and estrange my most beloved, or to let him live in some dank gaol forever – perhaps one of the island prisons – and lose the respect of my people. But today, I had the impossible answer, at last – one that would free me from the poisons.

'You really thought you would win, didn't you?' I said. 'You thought you would come here and muster support, somehow, somewhere – take the West from me.'

Maximian's age lines deepened. Odd: where was the grovelling, the anger, the shrewdness?

So I continued, sure his usual demeanour would return. 'So great was your zeal that you chose to rush to this of all cities. Massilia, the city by the sea, famed for its wine. An odd place with ancient customs: where by a simple vote of the senate... any man within these walls can be commanded to end his own life.'

Nothing. Not a twitch, blink or gulp.

'Is that what you desire?' he said at last. 'Then bring me a blade. It is what you wish, isn't it?' His tone was flat.

What was this? I stared hard at him for what felt like an eternity. The fiery chamber roared within me, reignited.

'Then so it shall be. Before the September moon wanes,

you will fall upon your sword. Before then, make peace with your gods.'

I stood and swung towards the door, rapping thrice. It opened and as I made to leave, I paused. An odd feeling crept across my back and shoulders: that chilling sensation I had experienced at Colonia Agrippina when the assassin from Rome had been watching me. I imagined Maximian's eyes narrowed hatefully upon me, the old asp alive and plotting his next move.

I glanced over my shoulder to see his head was merely lolling again. Had I imagined his gaze on my back, the devious sparkle reignited in those hooded eyes? Or had he merely been quick to look away? But damn, it would make things so much easier were he to try something. The scourge of fire within grew fierce. I left the prison, my mind in pieces, hearing the thick clunk of the cell being locked behind me as I went.

I ascended into the bright, warm, sunlit afternoon, the heat of the day like a blast from a baker's oven. Massilia's sweltering streets and markets were everything the dungeon was not: alive with colour and noise – shouting traders, braying mules and playing children and the clank and clatter of the taverns and markets. Aye, the carrion hawks and flies had had their feast, and the streets had been washed of blood. I headed not back to the imperial villa near the heart of the city – for a short time before I came here Maximian's home – but up the winding, paved path to the sun-bleached bluffs above the harbour, my two guards moving with me like my shadow. Those heights, the rock face riddled with the Christian catacombs, were quiet and still, apart from the calling of the gulls. A place to think.

A few women stood there, by the entrance to one cluster of

caves and niches and a small Christian shrine – deliberately inconspicuous. The women wore robes and shawls over their heads. They reminded me of Mother, and it pained me to think of her back in Treverorum. Yet more moons had passed since last I was by her side.

When they saw me, and the two silent, ironclad Cornuti warriors flanking me, they left, heads down as if caught in some criminal act. I wanted to tell them they had nothing to fear and could continue their worship, but I sensed I would probably only terrify them more if I engaged.

The persecutions were long gone, but still their echo resounded in these parts. I realised that it probably always would. Thousands of years might pass, yet still tales of the grim edict and its consequences would be told. And perhaps those days were not entirely consigned to storytellers yet: I had heard a worrying tale from a wine merchant – a story about the goings-on in Rome. It seemed there had been some set-to between the Christians and the imposter who called himself overlord of that famous city and all Italia. Fires, riots and sedition. Maxentius had seemingly banished the Christian Popes from his realm. I remembered the days when we had stood together in Nicomedia. Maxentius had been colder towards the Christians than I and that was understandable given he had not grown up under the wing of a Christian mother and a devout tutor. But never, *never*, had he held the executions and public torture of the persecutions in anything other than contempt. But this was worrying news.

Was my one-time friend truly the changeling that recent events suggested? First assassins and now preludes to a fresh wave of condemnation of the Christians? And what would Maxentius make of my current dilemma? He had chosen to exile his father rather than kill him for attempting usurpation.

He had passed the problem on to me, sowed the seed of all that had happened here at Massilia. A spark of anger rose within me – was there no end to the affronts the southern pretender could throw at me?

I climbed a little higher. Up on the cliff-top, I saw another Christian shrine – little more than a simple stone altar exposed to the sky. By it sat a lone figure, cross-legged. Bull-shouldered and stubble-scalped, skin glistening with sweat, wearing just a threadbare military tunic.

'Batius?'

The grizzled veteran looked up, a long blade of grass in his teeth and his eyes wide like a boy caught somewhere he shouldn't be.

'Domine?' he said, trying to stand, spitting out the grass.

I waved my palms downwards to put him at ease, and he sat once more, chewing the grass blade again. I hadn't seen him much in the month since we had come here. He had spent the first few days after taking the city roaring drunk – nothing unusual really, but he had been quieter than usual after the wine had faded from his mind.

He said nothing and I respected his silence. I sat by his side and both of us gazed out across the silky-still waters of the *Mare Internum* for a good hour. It reminded me of the days in my youth, at the villa in Salona where the big man would take me into the Dalmatian hills to run, climb and spar with wooden swords. After a morning of hard work, we would often sit under the shade of a willow tree overlooking a gentle brook. We would eat bread and drink stream water, chatting and joking, then there would be a silence like this – a comfortable, shared moment of serenity.

'Do you think about them?' he asked, the sound of his words like a pebble tossed into a still pond.

'Them?'

'The Gemina lads,' he replied, drawing the grass stalk carefully from his teeth and replacing it again, over and over. 'I trained them, you know – the cohort that took Maximian's bribe.'

'They were traitors, aye, but they fought like lions,' I mused, recalling the bloody battle to take Massilia's streets. I could tell Batius was far from finished.

'I… I even spent a night with one young lad's mother,' he said. A sad smile crossed his craggy, broad features. 'Never came to anything.' He shrugged and grew owl-eyed for a moment. 'Never does. But before we parted for the last time I offered her some coins, to make life easier until her son brought home some silver. She stayed my offer and asked one thing instead: that I look after her boy and see him home safely.'

I saw a glassy sheen well in his eyes – eyes that had seen the horrors of battle in every corner of the world: living men peeled of their skin, heads cleaved open by axes, bowels spilled into the earth. Batius was not one for tears.

'I said I would. Now I never had the right to say that,' he argued, his gruff voice tightening. 'I'm the Tribunus of the Cornuti, not the Prefect of the Gemina. Once their training was complete, I had no part in their careers. I wasn't there to ward off Maximian's advances to them.' His head dropped, shaking from side to side. 'But I was there to punish them. I was there, spatha drawn, when we stormed the streets. I saw him up on that rooftop with the ballistae. I only realised it was him as I drove my blade into…' He stopped, his lips clasping together tightly and his empty fist clenching and shaking. 'He whispered my name to me as he slipped away. I'd never held a blade against a Roman until that day.'

I placed a hand on his shoulder and shook it gently in reassurance. 'Then you walked the same dark road as I,' I whispered, recalling the bleak emotion of that day. 'What choice did you have, Batius?' I said. *What choice I?* I added inwardly. 'You did not wake that morning intent on killing the boy. You were doing only what was right – grim as it was – for our cause. Think how many more would have died had we hesitated and let Maximian hold the city and potentially draw more support.'

Batius seemed torn between my logic and the deep, gnawing guilt within. *Guilt?* I glanced at the Christian altar and realised the big man hadn't come up here for silence. 'Mother and Lactantius have had your ear, I see?'

He looked up, understanding my meaning. 'Aye.' He nodded with a weak laugh, then shot a glance up to the skies. 'May Mars stay with me on the battlefield, always... but Lady Helena tells me stories about the Christian ways and I could listen to her day and night. And Lactantius? The old bastard is like a mangy dog with a bone. Yap, yap, yap.' He moved his hand like a hound's mouth. 'Then I realised some of his nonsense had sunk in. Guilt, conscience, forgiveness. I don't know if I understand it all, but I thought that up here I might find... *something.*' He raised a meaty finger and pointed to a dip in the grassy cliff-top with a sour look. 'Then I come up and *he's* here.'

I craned my neck a little, seeing a conical iron helm and a tuft of auburn hair. 'Krocus?'

'The hairy bastard was up here. He moved down there when he saw me.'

I could have laughed were it not for the look on Krocus' face. From here I could just make out his forlorn features, searching the ether just as Batius had been. He, too, had been

subject to Lactantius' endless lectures. I rose and glanced at
the two men so diametrically opposed in their personalities
and values, then at the altar: a stony, silent rib underpinning
some sort of bond between them. Tenuous and nebulous, but
a bond nonetheless.

One of my earliest memories returned to me then: Mother's
words to me on the night of the storm in Naissus.

'*What brings a man to war, Mother? What brings a man to
choose his god?*'

'*That is for each of us to find out, Constantine. That is the
journey we each must make.*'

The following day ended with a hot and balmy sunset.
Fausta, Crispus and I enjoyed a meal of salted red mullet
and rich, strong wine as the sun began to set, flooding the
dining chamber with rich orange light. My boy seemed to
have gotten past the moment where he came across me with
my blade at his grandfather-in-law's heart. At least on the
outside, he was my lad again: playing, singing and hiding in
and around the Massilian villa.

Fausta was another matter. She ate in silence. I had wanted
to speak to her this morning but I had awoken to find her
gone from her bedchamber – opposite mine. All afternoon
I sought a private and appropriate moment to talk with her
and tell her what had occurred the previous day at the cells.
But how do you tell your spouse that her father is to die at
your command?

I gave her a sideways glance, noticing again a difference in
her appearance. She seemed somehow less coltish. Her arched
brows were carefully trimmed and her face was painted
subtly – enough to highlight her fine features but not so much

that it would mask them. And she wore a white gown tightly trussed around her waist and scantly covering her chest. Her swollen bosom had me rapt for a heartbeat or two – damn, what an unfortunate time to be ruled by one's loins! But it was undeniable that in my recent years of distraction in the Frankish woods, on the Rhenus and solving troubles like these, that I had not noticed her change. The shrewd, playful girl who had walked into my life six years ago was like a lost memory. She was still shrewd, definitely, but she was most certainly a woman now.

When we were wed, three years ago, I had vowed to her that I would only lie with her when the time was right. Now, today, with all that was going on, the time was most definitely *not* right.

'When will we return to Treverorum?' Crispus asked, scattering my thoughts. 'I miss Grandmother, and I have so much to tell her. And Lactantius has promised me more lessons – I like his lessons.'

For an instant, I saw the image of Batius doing that yapping dog impression and almost exploded with much-needed laughter, but Fausta snapped before I could: 'Finish your meal, Crispus. Then prepare for bed.'

'But, Mother, I—' he started.

A cold look from her was enough to end the argument. I felt a great distance between us at that moment. It was as if her overly scornful words were fashioned to scold Crispus and scourge the memory of his true mother, dear Minervina.

Crispus did as he was told. Then I made eyes at the slaves and soon it was just Fausta and me, alone. It was an odd moment, for I expected her to turn her iciness upon me. But it was as if a candle had been lit within her. She sighed and tilted her head back as if to catch the last of the dying orange light. I noticed a glimmer of perspiration on her cleavage, and cursed myself when she caught me looking. One of her eyebrows arched more than usual. 'You do know that it *is* fitting for a husband to look upon his wife,' she said, 'in that way?'

The hot night air swam around us like sultry breath.

'Fausta...' I began. But I ask you again: how does one turn the subject to the fate of their spouse's father? Tell me – how can it be done?

'And I am beginning to wonder if you do not prefer the company of men in the evening. Batius and Krocus – which one is it?' Her tone was gently mocking, playfully slapping away my attempt to broach the more serious and pressing matter.

I laughed despite myself. When the laughter faded, I dropped my head. In my time I have looked the Persian *Shahanshah* in the eye, I have stared down the Gothic *Iudex*, and I have looked into the heart of evil itself, holding Galerius' gaze until he – the foul Herdsman – flinched. But I could not look my wife in the face as I said it:

'Maximian will die before the waning of the September moon. He has been offered a noble death by the senate – the chance to fall upon his own sword... and he has accepted it.'

Silence. I half expected a cup or a plate to come hurtling over the table and smash upon my head. Nothing.

'And so do I,' she said calmly.

I looked across at her, dumbfounded.

'When I arrived here at the end of the siege, I pleaded with you not to split my father's heart with your sword. But I have had time to understand what happened here, what he did. His heart is black.'

Such stark words. Yet they lifted me, the burden of guilt easing.

'He has lied, cheated and plotted against his own kin so many times. He cannot be allowed to do so again.'

'Then you,' I started, 'you agree with the senate's decision?'

'I agree with *your* decision, Constantine.'

Silence. She stared at me for some time like a beauty from an ancient fresco. 'Do not make me say it again,' she said. With that, she rose like a seductive dancer, the full splendour of her silk-clad curves captivating me as she made to leave the dining hall. I dug my nails into my palms, angry that my loins were interfering with such a grave matter.

I shot up, chair spinning away behind me, and paced over behind her to rest my hands upon her shoulders, my eyes fixed on her side-turned head. 'Fausta, if there was another way...'

'Be strong, Constantine, with him... with me,' she said, turning away but leaving a lingering and sultry gaze on me for a moment. The effect was explosive.

I caught her and swung her round, the sweet rose scent of her perfume catching in my nostrils and her teeth and eyes bright in the dying orange of sunset. My hands gripped her waist, soft, full and warm. 'Be *strong*? By all the gods, Fausta, you know that were he not your father he would be dead already. Do you know how many Roman soldiers I struck down on the streets of this city? Damn, I will not be accused of weakness!'

'No? Then treat your wife as a man should.' She pressed her body against mine, the vibrations of her rapid heartbeat mixing with my own. A coil of dark hair fell from the nest of it pinned atop her head, and she reached up to tuck it behind her ear, looking into my eyes coquettishly, gently biting one half of her lower lip.

All the fires of doubt of the month past were vanquished as

I cupped a hand behind her head and pressed my lips to hers – warm and soft. We took a few steps backwards until she thudded against the wall. I could taste the fresh wine on her soft tongue as we stumbled to the bedchamber, interlocked, entangled. We parted roughly as she shoved me onto the edge of the bed, pulling off my tunic and kneeling to prise off my boots, then stood again, reaching to the nape of her neck to untie the slim cord of silk that held her gown in place. With a shrug of her shoulders, the robe drifted to the ground around her ankles. Proud since the moment she had first pushed against me, my loins now felt set to burst.

She shoved my shoulders and I fell onto my back. Then, like a vision, she crawled astride me. She shuddered, upturned breasts quivering, nipples hard as I entered her. She whimpered at first, and a warm trickle of blood darted across my thigh. I was her first, I realised, feeling momentarily foolish that I could have forgotten. But her discomfort was fleeting, swatted away by the fiery, animal passion that seemed to be ablaze within her. Few moments in my life have been as wondrous as what followed, and as she bucked and writhed upon me like a horse-breaker I cried out and so did she. On it went, ribbons of her hair spilling loose and lashing to and fro with our frantic motion, both of us riding near the cusp of climax yet never wanting it to end. It was, I thought, no doubt a shared catharsis after such a dark and uncertain time – a purge of the tensions that had gripped our relationship since that last day of the siege.

At that very moment, as if that memory had been conjured to life from the force of our lovemaking, steel flashed before my eyes. Suddenly, everything was still, the passion halted, the promise of climax vanquished... the iron edge of a dagger at my throat, the hilt firmly clasped in Fausta's hand.

'Fausta?' I whispered, my manhood shrinking.

She glared down at me, her body slick with the sweat of passion, her eyes baleful, shining like cold jewels. 'I already knew about your plan for my father. I visited the dungeons this morning, at dawn.'

Suddenly the balmy night air felt glacial. I recalled again how I had awoken that morning to find her absent from her bedchamber.

'He told me tales from my youth, reminded me of the days of play and joy, of his love for me. He asked me if I could stand by the side of the man who was about to order his death.'

I searched her eyes, but they were growing harder, colder.

'He told me that I could save him. I laughed when he said that, pointed out that you were at the helm of countless legions. How could I, a lone woman, stand between the great Constantine and his wishes? And he reminded me of the day in Syria when I was but a girl, playing in the shallows of the Orontes. *I made you a toy boat out of reeds,* he said. I splashed and played all morning with that boat. But when I waded out of the shallows at last, I heard a shushing noise… something sliding through the grass, towards me. I turned to the sound just as a blunt-nosed viper struck out at me: *But with a stroke of my sword I cut off its head, and the danger was gone,* Father said.'

The dagger pressed a little further into my throat. Was it sweat or blood trickling down the sides of my neck?

'He asked me now to save him. He asked me to kill you, Constantine, to behead the snake. And so here we are.' The blade pressed in even more. I saw my troubles vaporise, knowing that death was about to usurp them all. Her eyes were bulging in madness. 'Do you understand what that feels like? My father asking me to kill my husband… and if I don't, my husband will execute my father?'

Her slender arms tensed, readying for the thrust that would saw open my windpipe, spatter her naked body in my lifeblood. It all ended with a great wail. Her hands shot up to cover her face. The blade tumbled from her grasp, rolled off the bed and clattered to the stone floor. She slid from me and onto her knees.

Stunned, I rose gingerly, barely believing I was still alive.

'There *were* days of play and joy,' she wept. 'But they were with Mother. Father was absent for all but a handful of days of my youth. Mother was little more than a useful concubine. And the story about the viper is true… but it was not my father who cut off its head, it was a guard – who also made me the reed boat. Father was absent that day and most others. He was never there for me.' Tears shot down her face as she looked up at me. 'I cannot do what he asked me to.'

I stood, ablaze with anger. 'Perhaps you should have. For now there is no chance for him. He has plotted against me for the last time. He will die… *tonight*,' I spat, 'and with not a shred of honour!'

20

MAXENTIUS

ROME, 24TH AUGUST 310 AD

Seven days had passed. Just seven days, and already I was regretting exiling the warring priests. Rather than, as I had hoped, the bulk of the Christians resolving their differences in the absence of that pair of argumentative morons, it seemed that the two had actually each been a unifying force for part of their troublesome sect. Now, instead of two groups of Christians kicking each other in the streets, there were reports of half a dozen different groups, some Lapsi, some not, all busy beating each other senseless with no focus. How they expected to ascend to their heaven was beyond me when they couldn't even agree on how to eat bread. I could only assume they planned to climb to this 'heaven' on the backs of their suppressed brethren.

It was ridiculous. I had begun my experience with their kind back in Nicomedia alongside Constantine, reviling the persecutions and admiring the Christians' strength, wondering how the emperors could not find a way to fit that strength into their world. Now, after years of exposure to their sect – and *being* one of those emperors – I was starting to think that Diocletian and Galerius had begun burning Christians purely out of exasperation, for there seemed to be no way to make them happy.

I had tried so hard in Rome to integrate them into the fabric of society and, to the everlasting credit of the Roman people, they generally welcomed their Christian fellows. There was little trouble from those who followed the true gods. All the trouble came from other Christians. They were simply incapable of being settled and happy and integrating themselves anywhere. I think if you left the entire sect alone on an island they would argue and fight until only one man was left. And then he would probably start to argue with himself.

I rant. I apologise. In telling this tale some factors are more important than others, but some, despite their relatively minor influence in my life, are simply too infuriating to let go of. And to some extent my exasperation – which you can discern through my manner – was what led me to my decision. Even in the depths of the darkest winters there are days of blue, after all.

I had tried over the last seven days a hundred different ways to control the Christian violence and, like a leaky wine sack, wherever I pressed on a hole the pressure and violence simply squirted out somewhere else. In the end, I appointed a praetor with the specific remit of trying to keep a lid on the boiling pot of Christian dispute. I did not envy him. In fact I paid him highly and offered him the chance of a future consulship if he just succeeded in not burning down my city. It was only after I'd left that summer that I realised I'd forgotten to set the condition that persecutions were not an option. Fortunately he was no Galerius, and the streets remained free of burning Christians, except in those ridiculous cases where they'd done it to each other.

I felt as though a yoke had been lifted from my shoulders when I entrusted the task to someone else. And my burdens lifted further still on a crisp, warm morning under skies of azure and amid the happy hum of bees and the unusually sweet song of birds. One might even have thought the world itself was trying to improve my mood. The constant ache of Romulus' loss stayed with me like a lost limb, or a background ache that has become so constant that it rarely makes its presence known.

As usual, Valeria was keeping to herself as she fretted over her father. That brief connection between us after our son's passing seemed to have been just a unique and unrepeatable event. I could not allow my thoughts to linger on that sad state any more than on Romulus, though, for such recollections threatened to drag me back into that mire of despair, and there was too much to do to allow such a thing.

Volusianus was grinning when he came to me. I lounged back on a couch in my bathhouse, listening to gentle pipe and lyre music after my morning cleansing rituals.

'We regain border posts, Majesty,' he began, by way of greeting.

'And a joyous morning to you too, Volusianus. Now, what was that?'

'Our borders to the north-east, Domine. Word has reached the city this morning that three of our border posts that had been taken by Licinius are once more in our hands, and there are efforts afoot to take three more back. Licinius has left the region, pulling out much of his military. The Sarmatian tribes are pressing on the Danubius to the east, and with Galerius wallowing in crapulence in his new half-built palace, Licinius had no choice but to run off and deal with the problem. As soon as the enemy shifted east, your commanders in the north made the spur-of-the-moment decision to retake the border. Good men, thinking for themselves and not waiting around while they sent to Rome for permission.'

I smiled. Good news was enough of a rarity that I almost thought to hold a festival to celebrate it. 'And if Licinius is away long enough, might we...?'

'Yes, Domine. We could recover our border entire. And without even the need for reinforcements. The pressure to the north has eased drastically.'

My smile widened. How long had it been since I had shown my teeth in anything but a rictus? 'And with Constantine busy attending to the troubles my father caused him, he's not looking to take advantage of the situation, I presume?'

'Word has it that Constantine remains in Massilia raging over your father's latest betrayal, Domine. Messages coming from the north are tangled. Some say your father has carved out his own territory and holds it against Constantine. Others that he has already been defeated and imprisoned. Some even say Constantine languishes in a cell at your father's command, though that seems far-fetched. The truth is veiled, but the result is the same: Constantine is busy.'

'Good. Thank you, Father. I rarely had the cause to say that when you were here, but you're doing me sterling service in Gaul!'

I chuckled to myself and poured a celebratory cup of fairly strong wine.

'No Licinius. No Constantine. The Christians passed on to that poor blighter of a praetor. What *will* I do with my day? Do I not have anyone to worry over?'

Volusianus laughed. 'It's a rare day. No one, I suppose, Domine. Unless you count Zenas and Domitius Alexander, of course...'

He straightened sharply as he realised what he'd said. I was in a good mood so rarely these days, what with a strangely absent-yet-present wife, only the hollow memories of my son and endless difficulties on the border and in the city. Yet I *was* in a good mood. And without thinking, he'd said the one thing that might just kill my optimism. Oddly, it didn't even penetrate the shield of my humour that morning.

'You are absolutely correct, Volusianus,' I said with purpose, sliding from my couch and hopping from foot to foot on the hot floor while I tried to locate my wooden clogs. Slipping them on with relief, I stretched, risking my towel falling to the floor, and clapped my hands on my Praetorian Prefect's shoulders.

'Then it's time we finally dealt with the problem. For the first time in a year we have the leisure to pursue such things however we wish. Come on.'

A half hour later, I was dressed and ready for the day. Volusianus had hung around outside my door with an odd mix of excitement and nerves. He was unused to a content, active emperor these days, and I think I caught him unawares. I swished out of my suite in my best purple and gold tunic with a perfect, pristine toga, wearing a gold circlet on my brow and looking as imperial as any man who ever trod the Palatine. Of course, I wasn't *on* the Palatine. Not quite yet. I was in my villa by the Via Appia, close to my son's tomb, where I liked to be, especially in the summer when the streets of Rome smell of sweat and shit and startled animals. But for this, I needed to be in the city, albeit briefly.

Volusianus had arrived with a century of Praetorians and as we hurried out to the villa's drive, where my horse was being made ready, I narrowed my eyes and examined the men. They looked good. Not just glittering and smart, like they should. They looked like soldiers.

'Your men appear suspiciously martial, Volusianus?'

He smiled. 'With the troubles in the north and the revolt in Africa I've had the men of the Guard and of the Urban Cohorts all on constant training, cycling through a century at a time. This lot will have marched hundreds of miles in the last month or so.'

'Good man. They look like soldiers, not statues. That's what we'll need.'

'For what?'

'For Africa.' I grinned and leapt onto my horse. Well, *struggled* onto my horse, but with more gusto than usual. If you know a good Roman saddle you know you can't simply leap into it without risking eunuch-hood on one of the horns.

Volusianus frowned. 'We, Domine? I had assumed you meant to send *me* to Africa to sort out Zenas' mess?'

I swung my horse about, hauling on the reins with purpose. 'I am sick of the city at the moment, Volusianus. Sick of the ghosts. Sick of seeing Gaius Annius hovering hopefully outside my aula regia. Sick of being alone. Sick of Christians. Sick enough that even war-torn Africa looks favourable. Romulus' tomb can spare me briefly, for he will always travel in my heart. I shall go to Africa and end this Alexander myself.'

He looked less than convinced, and my grin widened even further. 'If you're very good, Volusianus, I might even let you come.'

Laughing, I trotted off through the gate and began the three-mile ride into the city. The Praetorians, though surprised, fell into order with perfect precision and were quickly around and behind me, Volusianus catching up last.

'You really mean to go to Africa?'

'It will make the people proud. An emperor who takes the field is always popular with his people.'

'I don't remember that being the case with Gaius Caligula!'

I rolled my eyes at Volusianus. 'Say what you like, you shall not change my mind, nor spoil my morning. Once we enter the city, I will take one half of this century with me to the Capitol and the Campus Martius. You take the other back to the fortress.'

'Why, Domine?'

'I want you to select the three best-trained cohorts of men at your disposal and kit them for campaign. They will report to the *Navalia* at dawn tomorrow for embarkation. Make sure, also, that there are adequate vessels to take us to Ostia, and send a rider of the *cursus publicus* to Misenum. I want the rest of the fleet docking in Ostia as soon as they can to take us to Africa.'

'And you, Domine?'

'I go to secure divine support. The Christians might not be able to work anything out with their God, but I know *our* gods well, and I know what to do.'

At the baths of Antoninus Caracalla, beyond the Porta Appia, the prefect and I parted ways, he heading north across the Caelian and Oppian hills to the Castra Praetoria, still grumbling about how my true place was in Rome, I headed north-west towards the heart of the city.

In the same way, I suppose, that the Christians cannot begin to think how to live their lives without the approval of their single God, we true Romans must needs seek the divine endorsement of Jove on our endeavours, no matter how many other gods we might consult. For Jove is not only father of gods, and 'greatest and best' as all know, but he is the also benefactor and proud overseer of all that is, and ever will be,

Rome. His is the temple at the heart of the most important site in the city: the Capitol. His sanctuary rises on the hill like a fortress of piety, with a commanding view of Rome. Within, his statue stands proud and divine, and his priests interpret his will for the benefit of the people. Among them, foremost in the telling of things, are the *auspices*.

The auspex in particular who I saw that morning was not the most impressive of specimens as far as humanity was concerned. He had a limp – I think one of his legs was slightly shorter than the other – his left eye kept wandering off to the side as though it were becoming bored and searching out new entertainment, and he was clearly as deaf as a tufa block. But the thing is: the gods look *within* us, not at our skin. And though this man was rather unsettling to speak to, he clearly was beloved of Jove.

'Imperator, how may we help you?' he asked in a croaky voice.

'I seek great Jove's approval for a campaign to retake Africa, priest.'

The man nodded three times as though mulling it over, and then croaked, 'What?'

'I wish to reconquer Africa and seek the approval of mighty Jove,' I tried again, slightly louder.

'No. It's no use. Try my other ear.'

Some days this would have driven me mad with irritation – Rome seemed to have a habit of doing that these days – but nothing could ruin my mood today. I grinned and leaned uncomfortably close. He smelled of over-spiced mutton and strong wine.

'I SEEK JOVE'S APPROVAL TO RETAKE AFRICA!' I bellowed into his ear.

As I straightened, I realised every face in the temple

– probably everyone atop the Capitoline hill in fact, had turned to me. Ah well, news of my plan would soon have reached across the city, for I had no intention of delaying. The Praetorians in their protective arc around me watched the public carefully, but I was pleased to see only nodding approval among them. Now if only Jove felt the same…

'No need to shout. I'm not deaf in *that* ear,' the priest grumbled.

'My apologies,' I chuckled.

'What?'

'Oh, for the love of… Listen, can you seek Jove's approval for me?' I yelled.

'Come with me.' The man beckoned. I followed him as he stepped out of the front of the temple and into the balmy summer air, loaded with the smell of desiccated faeces from every gutter and alleyway. Yes, Africa would be nicer than Rome in high summer. The strange old auspex looked up into the sky, his eyes picking out details.

'No eagles,' grunted the priest. 'Shame. But in summer they tend to avoid the stink of the city. Still, I think Jove has already pre-empted your visit, Domine. Are you the sole commander in this campaign, or will there be more?'

My brow furrowed. Well, potentially three, I supposed, what with taking Volusianus along and Zenas being over there already. Although I might remove Zenas from command unless he proved to have good reason for his failures thus far. I sighed. 'Three, at this time.'

He nodded. 'As it happens, I saw three crows last evening, swooping south across the Capitol and making for the countryside. I thought it odd at the time, since they flew in a direct line, as though a sword sent by Jove was slicing through the sky. I wondered what they were trying to tell me. Now it is clear that they were Jove's foretelling of your campaign. You are *meant* to travel to Africa, Domine. It is meant to be.'

'And we have Jove's blessing?'

The old man frowned for moment. I actually thought he'd not heard and was trying to work out what I'd said, but then I realised his head was slightly tilted and he was listening to something. Finally he smiled. 'Can you hear the lilt?'

'The lilt?'

'What?'

'THE LILT?'

'Yes. The lilt of the song. Even the ravens are singing songs of joy. There is no discord. There is no lack of harmony. And…' He chewed on his lip. 'There is more, I think. You seek victory in Africa and the way you are going about it, you should find it. But you should also find something else. *Further* harmony. Further *peace*. Something entirely beyond the campaign can be put right by your journey. Yes. Go and fight your war and win with the blessing of mighty Jove. But watch for other things while you are there. Be alert. Be shrewd. Be clever. And you may find more than you dreamed of in Africa.'

I left with a frown of confusion, yet in high spirits. After so long wallowing in failure and difficulties and pain, it seemed as though the gods had begun to smile on me once more. One day maybe even the Christian one would, if only he could get his own worshippers in order.

From the Capitol I took my escort to the temple of Neptune by the river in the Campus Martius. It is a sensible thing to seek Neptune's support in any sea journey, especially one with so many ships and men over so many miles. I had hoped for his blessing – and, indeed, I received it – but with the result of my prior visit to the temple of Jove I fear I would have even laughed in the face of Pluto himself and carried on with my plans.

Zenas had failed long enough. It was time to restore my domain.

21

CONSTANTINE

MASSILIA, 24TH AUGUST 310 AD

Fausta's weeping filled the halls of my Massilia residence. A slave appeared with my boots, a light tunic and a waxed cloak, which I threw on. Without a look backwards, I left, stepping into the billowing night storm.

Thunder pealed and rain billowed around Batius, Krocus and me as we strode through Massilia's soaked streets with splashing footsteps and a martial clank of iron from the ten Cornuti escorting us, spear tips glittering with every shudder of lightning. Rain battered from my men's helms, drenched my hair and my bare head. From the lamplit cracks in shutters, confused, anxious faces peeked out, knowing something grim was afoot.

We entered the dungeon, where the stink of damp was rife. The full fury of the storm fell away but the dull, demonic roar of thunder outside was almost amplified by the subterranean vaults – as if angered that we had dared to take shelter from it. And the hiss of rain outside turned into a trickle as the many cracks and holes in the dungeon stonework spewed tiny streamlets of water down the walls and along the corridor floor. The cell door at the end was black one instant, then illuminated by a flash of lightning that lit up the whole corridor. Without discussion or delay, we strode forth and the cell was opened.

Inside, I found Maximian on his knees, shivering and panting, two Cornuti swords on his throat, his hands bound with rope. He looked up, his sweat-damp, tousled hair plastered across his face. I could see the manic glint was back in his eyes. It had only ever been hidden.

'She's lying,' he snapped. 'Bring her here and you'll see.'

The feeble claim almost had me laughing. 'I asked you to make peace with your gods,' I spat. 'Instead you poisoned your daughter's mind.'

Just then, Maximian saw the thick loop of rope Batius held. His eyes widened. 'You cannot! I am an emperor... I was... I was the master of...' His words tailed off, his head dropping.

I approached, crouching on one knee to be level with him. Memories of my youth – so foul so often – suddenly seemed to glow and call out to me like a lost friend: the day I arrived, at Father's side, in Treverorum to see the great Maximian ascend to Diocletian's side. I recalled that first time I had seen him, painted silver and strutting on the plinth of Treverorum's old basilica. I was but a boy, naïve and ill at ease in the presence of him and his then co-emperor, the now long-decrepit Diocletian. So mighty were they both, that day... 'These are your last moments,' I said firmly. 'Use them wisely.'

His shoulders rose and fell with deep, full breaths, and after an age, his head nodded in understanding. 'Very well. When next you see Maxentius,' he said at last, 'tell him...'

My eyes grew wide, my breath stilled. I was rapt. *Maxentius*. I saw him and me in our youth again, Maxentius building his wooden city and me offering him words of advice like an elder brother. *Damn the past,* I thought, blinking hard to stave off a wave of sudden and sharp grief. I wondered then what Maxentius knew of his father's fate... of *my* decision. The boy who had once called me his hero and his saviour would now know me as the slayer of his father. Would this be the cutting of the strained, gossamer-fine threads that still stretched between us?

'Tell him...' His head rose again, a grin broadening his flaccid features like a snake's hood. 'No, *sing* him the song... the song of battle.'

My heart grew cold. So this was the last hiss of the asp who once called himself Hercules.

'You know it well, don't you, Constantine?' He held up his bound hands and wagged both forefingers at me. 'You sing him that song, when you finally meet him again: the ballad of battle, the melody to which men die. For it is in battle that this will end for one of you.'

The storm clashed again as if to underscore his proclamation.

'You realise it's down to you and him now don't you?' he went on. 'Severus is long dead. Your father too. I am to die. Diocletian is a virtual shade, muttering about cabbages as he wanders alone and forgotten in his vast Dalmatian palace. Galerius is a diseased, pus-filled boil – soon to burst and seep away into the earth. Yet each of us once thought we could harness the beast of empire. Each of us at one stage sought to do what was right and proper – to honour the gods and our country. And, *boy*, let the gods be the ones to judge us! Take my life, but you and my son should ask yourselves this: when the last of the old emperors are gone...' the hooded eyelids descended until his eyes were but slits '...will you do better than any of us?'

A baleful silence was rent by another clap of thunder and a shiver of lightning.

'Domine?' Batius said in a low burr, holding up the loop of rope. Not one person in that cell needed the big man to elaborate.

Maximian's head flicked to Batius then back to me. 'My boy slew Severus just like this,' he stammered, nostrils flaring. 'And it is his path and yours, would-be emperor, to kill old leaders like us. To take the poisoned mantle as your own.' A feral sneer twisted his face. 'Only to become the prey of the brave young lions of days to come. You are but a single breath of an immortal plague...'

One of the Cornuti raised a hand to strike him but I lifted a finger to stop the soldier. Maximian and I shared a gaze until, like the lightning outside, he lurched suddenly in my direction, teeth bared, face ferocious but neck extended like a soldier pleading for a swift end. 'Do it... but hear Jove's wrath!' he snarled. Lightning scored the darkness, casting his manic form in blinding white for a heartbeat. '*Do it!*'

The thunder above and the thunder within my breast crashed in step. I flashed a look at Batius. For him, there was no doubt or hesitation about taking *this* Roman's life. The big man's face was like a shard of granite as he swiftly looped the rope around Maximian's neck then drew the ends tight, yanking it back, his oak-like arms bulging. I closed my eyes, hearing the breaking of vertebrae and the awful sounds of a man fighting for that one more breath he will never attain. Finally, I felt the dull vibration of his body toppling lifelessly to the cell floor.

As the storm raged high above, I sensed the great board shift once more, another piece gone, so few remaining.

It is in battle that this will end for one of you! the freshly risen shade of Maximian screamed in my ear.

I was sure then that I heard Fausta's wailing carried on the storm. And in the blackness behind my closed eyes, I saw the face of the dead man's son: Maxentius. My old friend stared back at me, eyes glacial, expression flinty.

I had no choice, old friend, I mouthed.

But such words were useless now. The storm had begun in earnest.

22

Carthage.

How much trouble, throughout the history of our great empire, could one city be? This great African metropolis had been a thorn in Rome's side countless times over the centuries. From the days of Hannibal and Scipio and the wars that crossed the sea and ravaged the world for decades, down through the fated Gordian usurpers' last stand there, to my late autumn campaign, Carthage seems to attract trouble of the worst sort.

I think that to some extent we swept in and stole Zenas' glory. I know I had ranted again and again over the months about the Christian officer's apparent inability to put the African revolt to rest, but in fairness, by the time Volusianus and I crossed from Sicilia with our force of Praetorians, my young general had settled most of Africa, driving back Domitius Alexander and his scant remaining forces, penning them in the cities of Carthage and Utica. The revolt would have ended by winter even without our intervention and, despite his deference, I could see how truly irritated Zenas was that we had come to interfere in his campaign just as he had been about to conclude it successfully.

Four cohorts remained loyal to Alexander in proud Utica some twenty miles north-west of us, and Zenas was there now, pressing on the walls and forcing them into an ignominious surrender. The arc of coastline that surrounded the city there would be battered constantly by siege engines mounted aboard the fleet, and I had little doubt that they had more than a day or two of resistance left in them. Zenas had taken the lesser siege, I think, just to prove he could still achieve a victory on his own. That left Volusianus and myself with Carthage, where Alexander remained with six cohorts. Volusianus was doing the actual commanding, of course. This was *his* world. He knew Africa and its people. He knew Carthage down to even its tiniest alleyway. And he felt the need to win back for me what he had once given me entire.

But the forces we led here were still mostly those who had fought for a year and a half under Zenas, and they remained loyal to him and rather unsure of us. I had solved the issue by taking on Zenas' right-hand man, Miltiades, as a senior officer in support of Volusianus and myself. Miltiades was a Christian like Zenas and tremendously popular with the forces, and he served as the perfect cushion between the new commanders and the extant army. In fact, over the best part of a month as Zenas pressed on Utica and we slowly squeezed the life out of Carthage, I had come to truly appreciate Miltiades. He seemed odd as a military man, and not because of his adhering to that odd, insular cult. He was a gentle man and a humorous one, given to expansive gestures, almost unreasonable clemency and an unshakable belief that everything would work out for the best. Such traits in a commander should realistically sound the death knell for an army, but somehow in Miltiades these ingredients just meshed perfectly and created a popular and talented officer.

Even now, as Volusianus and I watched the rosy fingers of dawn clawing at the tops of the hills of the Carpis Peninsula to the east, preparing for what would be the last day of the African revolt, I knew that Miltiades was on the far side of the city with half a legion, busily moving his siege towers and ladders into position to make his move where the great aqueduct touched the city walls. And I had no doubt that he would acquit himself well in the coming hours, too. Miltiades would move to breach the city there, at the high point. He *wouldn't*, of course. No one could. The triple land walls of Carthage were infamous and impregnable. Since the days of Scipio they had never been breached. And even with the paltry defences Alexander could call on, it would take a force ten times the size of Miltiades' even to attempt it. But that was not the point of his assault. Miltiades had a very specific remit: attack Carthage with great noise and violence and pomp... but try not to actually lose many men. For the *real* attack would come the only sensible way: by sea.

My trireme bobbed and lifted on the gentle waves, sitting amid a fleet of more than twenty warships, between them carrying a full legion's worth of the very best men in Africa, cohorts drawn from the Praetorians and the Third Augusta, and numerous centuries from other less prestigious units. Miltiades had assured us that it would work. He would draw the defenders to the triple walls facing the isthmus while we sailed from our hidden anchorage and made directly for the port, which presented an open access to the city as long as it was not adequately defended.

Our ships had moved into position during the night and anchored to the south of the Taenia peninsula, which had been occupied by the great general Censorinus during the first great siege of the city four and a half centuries ago. There we had lurked throughout the hours of darkness, praying to Neptune and any god we could name that we would not be spotted by some wandering shepherd. We would be visible from the city the moment we moved out of hiding, so we had to make sure our timing was right. We prayed again also that Miltiades could persuade Alexander's men that his was a true push to take the city.

I glanced off to the north. Somewhere around that headland lay Carthage.

'When we enter the city, do not get caught up in the fighting,' Volusianus murmured next to me. '*Domine*,' he added, with an afterthought of etiquette.

'I have no intention of doing battle directly. But you are a senior commander and too valuable to lose, Volusianus, so I might pass back the same advice to you.'

My prefect turned a hard face to me. 'Respectfully, Domine, I do not intend to get myself killed, but I have a score to settle with Alexander, and I will rip his head off with my bare hands before this day is out.'

I was about to reply, but my words would have been drowned out by the sudden blast of a cornu from the ship's rear. The call was taken up by the other ships in the fleet and I glanced once more to the east. The eye-watering globe of the autumn sun had put in an appearance, its white arc bulging up over the hills behind Carpis across the bay. The ships were suddenly moving with impressive efficiency, gaining speed within moments as they rounded the headland and began to race up the coast for the city whose harbour entrance lay a single mile north of us. As the fleet thundered on, the *auletes* aboard each vessel piping their tune to keep the oars rising and dipping in time, I prayed. I prayed to Neptune and to Mars and to Jove and to Hercules. I prayed to Sol of the Syrian east and to Minerva and *Mithras*, and even the Christian Christ, that Miltiades had made enough noise to pull Alexander's army to the land walls. Because while the ports represented a ready access to the city, the Carthaginians had been far from stupid, and with adequate manpower on the defences, the run into those ports would be suicide, facing the artillery on the tower tops.

Closer and closer we surged. I watched the wide-stretched arms of the sea walls – a single line of fortifications unlike those triple monstrosities on the land side – spread wide, urging us into the bosom of Carthage. I was keenly aware that those heavy towers that rose up on the walls each bore ship-killing artillery, and that six of them were within range to pound the life out of anything passing through that entrance. And then there was the long, wide commercial harbour, bounded to the east by another wall, punctuated with identical armed towers. And at the far end lay the military port, which would be a horrendous proposition, for it might hold as many triremes as we had in our fleet, and we had no idea about the size of the naval power in the city. We would heave to in the mercantile port and not run the risk of pushing into the military one.

I could see small figures now atop the towers. They were waving frantically. A huge, deep, booming horn call went up. Warning spread throughout the city. Good. If they were sending out the warning now, then that meant they were not already prepared for us. Still, I winced and clenched my teeth as the first ships closed on the harbour mouth, and I almost exploded with the release of pressure as they slipped between the towers and into the unprotected quay. Moments later the fleet was flooding the port of Carthage, each ship expertly manoeuvring to a berth. The boarding ramps were run out even before the ships were secured, and the men of our most elite forces pounded down the timbers to the dock side.

Each unit formed up under their commander in a matter of heartbeats and as soon as they were ready moved off into the city. I had no idea how they knew what they were doing, but the specific goals and directions had been set by Volusianus, who had governed the province from this city for years and knew exactly where to send his forces to secure Carthage. I stood with the prefect as the men of my loyal army saturated the city, brushing aside any civilian stupid enough to get in their way. They were under strict instructions not to kill the population, although I was personally not above a little ruination and salting of the earth, given the fact that this city had thrown its support behind my enemy. Still, great Caesar himself had gone far through magnanimity, and I would emulate him if I could, though hopefully not to the same conclusion.

Our ship docked swiftly, somewhere in the middle of the fleet, and the century of Praetorians on board filed out onto the dock and awaited their commanders. Volusianus gestured and our horses were led down to the flagged stonework. We followed and mounted, and then took to the streets at the heels of my loyal guardsmen. A commotion was now rising throughout the city. Alexander's men had clearly discovered that they had been duped and were rushing back in bulk to face the threat that was already in the streets. The port had mustered some manpower from somewhere – probably naval personnel – and the artillery on the towers were starting to find range, aiming for the ships invading their city. They would be too late now. Most of the troops were in the streets and half a cohort was already moving like a swarm of ants up the sea walls, securing towers and gates.

Fighting in the streets is a dirty and abhorrent business, and I consider myself fortunate that we were not with those units that met Alexander's rebel cohorts in the narrow ways and alleys of the city. It would have been a bloody business and even with the best will in the world, civilians would be killed. But Volusianus and I had different goals. Our century of men moved from the port and made directly for the Byrsa – the hilltop acropolis that dominated the city from its very centre. For though the citadel walls and been gone since the time of Scipio, the Byrsa was still where the governor's palace stood, and my Praetorian Prefect felt certain that Domitius Alexander would be found there, cowering and fretting, and not with his men at the city walls.

The Byrsa is a high place, and the journey to it from the port is an arduous, strength-sapping climb. The palace of the governor – the palace of the *traitor* and *rebel* – stood at the very crest and was a grand affair, as befitted a man with such power. It was a three-storey structure with a great colonnaded front.

And it was defended. Alexander had kept back at least a century of men, and they were now formed up in a shield wall, preparing to hold the building against their rightful emperor. The sight annoyed me. It perhaps made me arrogant and reckless. As the Praetorian centurion bellowed for his men to charge, I drew my own blade. Somehow I couldn't sit back and just let this happen – I had to be part of it. Volusianus was in no position to argue me down, since he had also drawn his sword and begun to move forward.

I would like to say that I was heroic and dashing, that I rode in with my men and played my part in the end of the revolt. Certainly my very presence heartened the men, so that is true in a manner. But the simple fact is that my Praetorians were better trained, better equipped and enjoyed much higher morale than the enemy. The attacking force, even wearied from the climb, fell upon the defenders like wolves upon lambs, tearing into them. Blood flowed across the flagstones in a growing pool. I did manage to put blade to flesh somewhere in the melee, for my sword was running with crimson once it was over. As the Praetorians moved among the rebel legionaries, dispatching the wounded, I stood and shuddered. Blood had sprayed up each of the columns along the building's front, giving it an eerie, otherworldly look. Volusianus was on the move a moment later, the centurion pulling together the remaining men of his unit as we stomped into the palace.

Lucius Domitius Alexander was not hard to find. A heavy-set man of middle age with a curly beard and short, almost severe haircut, he stood in the centre of the peristyle garden, his toga of white and purple looking suspiciously imperial to me. He had a spatha – a long cavalry blade – in his hand. If he'd had any remaining guards with him either they had fled or he had sent them away. I could see slaves and servants cowering in the corners of the garden, but Alexander stood proud and unrepentant.

'Domine.' He nodded at me as I entered. Volusianus' knuckles were white on his sword hilt and I could see his eyes narrowing.

'Domitius Alexander,' I replied quietly. 'What did I do to you that you would rebel and take Africa from me?'

I had not meant to ask such a question. It just somehow slipped out.

Alexander shrugged. 'Nothing personal, Majesty. A man cannot serve two masters and while they say you are a good man, *good* men are unimportant. *Strong* men matter.'

'Strong men like Galerius?' Volusianus snarled, crossing to a low marble bench and table upon which sat a few wax tablets, a stylus and a fine leather purse. As though he knew already what he would find, my prefect used his free hand to sweep up the purse and loosen the strings before tipping its contents to the table. I wandered across, frowning, fascinated. As I had thought when I saw them tumble, they were eastern gold aurei, bearing the image of that bloated sack of worms Galerius.

Alexander shrugged again. 'I was appointed by Constantius, but he is dead and I have served Galerius faithfully for a lifetime. Should I overturn decades of loyalty for an upstart, just because he's a good man? My conscience is clear, son of Maximian.'

'You intend to fall on your sword?' Volusianus snarled. 'Hard with such a long blade. Or will you fight me?'

Alexander looked down in surprise, as though he'd forgotten he was holding the sword. With an odd smile, he threw it casually across the lawn. Volusianus, his eyes flashing, stepped forward and brought up his own sword, swinging it wide with impressive strength. In that instant, Alexander screwed his eyes shut and waited for his end. Yet the prefect twisted the blade as he swung, so that the flat steel connected with Alexander's skull, rather than the edge biting into it. The rebel governor fell to the ground, groaning, and Volusianus, his teeth bared in a feral expression, gestured to the centurion.

'Bind his hands.'

'I don't want a prisoner,' I said quietly.

'I'm not taking him prisoner, Domine,' Volusianus grunted. The centurion produced a long piece of leather thonging from somewhere and wrapped it around Alexander's wrists, yanking it so taut that it bit deep into the flesh, binding his hands together tight enough that the flesh began to turn purple immediately.

'You stinking piece of Galerian filth,' Volusianus snarled, then spat a wad of phlegm into Alexander's face. As the groggy captive swayed, recovering his wits from the head blow, Volusianus bellowed, 'Rope!'

A soldier quickly produced a length of rope, which he and Volusianus formed into a simple slip-knotted noose. Alexander suddenly seemed to be coming to his senses and realised what was happening. His eyes widened in panic. 'No!'

'Hold still, you shit,' snapped Volusianus, dropping the noose over the rebel's head and pulling it taut. He handed the rope to the guardsman and pointed up to a fine piece of decorative stonework, which included a set of holes through the pediment above the columns. Two soldiers held the struggling Alexander, while the Praetorian threaded the rope through the hole with some difficulty. Then four men grasped the cord and, at Volusianus' command, hauled on it.

Lucius Domitius Alexander rose jerkily from the ground, shaking and gasping, clawing at the rope that was already tearing into the flesh of his throat. He rose in bounces and jerks until his feet were at chest height, where he stopped, as the Praetorians tied off the rope. We all watched the rebel who had cost us a year and a half of peace in Africa dance the dance of strangulation. He bounced and thrashed and shook and swung, clawing, his eyes bulging as though they might burst from his head, his tongue, purple and swollen, emerging from fat lips as he slowly gave way to the final journey, though with no coin beneath his tongue that journey would not be across the Styx.

There was a strange crackly noise and then a sigh, and the smell of freshly voided bowels as a steady stream of urine trickled down to the paving beneath him. The foot kicked and twitched, and finally fell still.

Africa was ours once more.

I could have stopped the brutal execution. Perhaps I should have. The man had only done what he thought was his duty, and what could be more Roman than that? But somehow I just didn't want to. He thought I was a good man. I wasn't *that* good.

'Now I have to decide whether to burn the city to the ground,' I hissed, still angry, despite myself, my eyes sliding to those Galerian coins.

Two days later I was sitting in that same palace when two pieces of news reached my ears, one welcome and one that shifted the world beneath my feet.

Firstly, Zenas brought us the news that Utica had fallen. The revolt was truly over. Zenas had approached me nervously, as though expecting to be upbraided or reprimanded for his failures. But I was in the oddest of moods, and I embraced the young officer like a lost brother, whereupon he almost wept with gratitude. I chuckled as I saw Miltiades in the corner of the room nodding his approval at the gesture.

A strange mood for sure. I was elated, for we had retaken Africa. But I was also uncertain. I had seen the faces of the people in the city since it fell. Though they had not thus far suffered my wrath for their support of Alexander, I could see they resented my very presence and that they had been returned to the fold of my imperium. I could quite imagine that within a month of our departure for Rome, another rebel would rouse Africa against me.

And the optimism I had felt since that morning when we decided to mount this campaign had faded, consumed by the knowledge that I would soon be returning home. Rome was my heartland and the home of my soul, and yet these days it was just a city of dead children, cold wives and unreasonable cults.

'I am all in favour of razing the entire city in the same manner as Scipio,' I grumbled. 'And transferring the seat of government to somewhere else. Perhaps Thysdrus or Hadrumetum. The citizens here seek only to do me ill. And Carthage's history is not illustrious. Hannibal. Gaius Annius. Now Alexander. It attracts enemies and lunatics, clearly.'

Volusianus cleared his throat. 'We have found huge amounts of Galerius' gold in the coffers of leading men in Carthage and among the African military. Your enemy more or less *bought* Africa from under you. The people here have grown wealthy and fat on Galerius' beneficence. They will eventually come to realise that the animal was just using them, and they will come to see you as a liberator. But give people time. Blood still runs in the streets and the memory of a year and a half of warfare is all too fresh.'

Zenas nodded. 'It will take time, Domine, but Africa will settle again.'

'We don't *have* time,' I rumbled. 'We devoted huge numbers of men to the suppression of this revolt and we have been more than lucky that my opponents to north and east have been too busy to take advantage of the situation and push into Italia. But we cannot expect Licinius to be held on the Danubius forever, and Constantine...'

I trailed off as I once more saw in my mind's eye my old friend. 'I still cannot believe that he will come against me, but we cannot afford to be complacent. We need to take the troops home and move them north where they will be required in due course. And that means leaving Africa unwatched. Can we afford to do that at a time when further revolt is not an impossibility? And while burning Carthage to the ground might remove the bulk of the rebel spirit, and would certainly make me feel better, it could equally spark a whole new rebellion.'

'Domine, might I make a suggestion?' Miltiades stepped out of the shadowy corner of the room and approached the dais upon which I sat. I pursed my lips and nodded. 'Well, Domine, the people of Africa are resentful as they can only see as far as their purses. They remember the gold that flooded in from the East and know that Galerius will now send them no more because of you.'

'I am aware of this,' I hissed, but without real anger. There was something about Miltiades' face that soothed me. Perhaps it was the warm colour – he was descended of the Berber tribesmen local to the region, and the glowing tone made his white smile and bright eyes seem all the more warm and pleasant.

'They cleave to the memory of Alexander and of Galerius' gold,' he went on. 'If you wish to truly settle them, you need to change those memories. You need to remind them that Alexander was not a champion for them, but a servant of Galerius and his Tetrarchy, as was Gaius Annius in his time. And you need to remind them what Galerius' gold actually *means*.'

'Which is what?' I had no idea what the man was driving at.

'Africa has the largest population of Christians in the West. My people are everywhere in this province – in the army, in the government, traders, nobles, sailors and even spies. And while the world watched in horror what the emperors did to my people in Nicomedia and in Rome and the north, few people outside Africa seem to realise that the persecutions were worse here than in most provinces. This land was *brutalised*. Utterly. And who was it that ravaged the Christians of Africa? The very man who now pays them to make war on an emperor who has levied no such violent decree. You want a way to win the population, Domine? Remind them that Galerius burned and tortured them. Ask them if their blood money is worth *that*?'

I blinked. Was it that simple? I knew that the Christians were numerous here, more so than in Italia or the north. But I had not ere considered them influential enough that they might turn the tide of imperial power. I smiled at Miltiades. Astoundingly, after two years of finding the Christians nothing but trouble with their endless infighting, it seemed as though they had handed me the means of recapturing Africa's heart.

'Miltiades, you are wasted with the Third.'

And he was. I had decided there and then that this new advisor would come back to Rome with us, where he could be much more use. Some of my lost positivity began to return then, only to be punched out of me a heartbeat later. I heard the shuffling of feet and looked to the door, where a prefect of unknown name stood, travel-worn, sweating and with the bleakest of expressions.

The hairs standing on the back of my neck in anticipation, I threw a question at the man with my eyes.

'Domine,' the officer said, his voice croaky and dry, 'I bring unhappy news.'

Well I'd already anticipated that much. I waved him on with a finger.

'Reports have come in, Domine, from Ancharius Pansa of the frumentarii. Your noble father, the former emperor, has perished.'

Perished? An odd choice of word. Not 'died', as one might announce a fat old drunk's body finally giving way to his habits, or an older man passing in his sleep. 'Perished' carried an edge of menace. Of violence. I felt a strange swirl of emotions wash through me. Oddly, the first was the urge to cheer for the freedom my family and I would finally feel. But that swiftly gave way to regret for the way my father and I had parted, to horror for the realisation that I was now the *pater familias* of an entire imperial line, to hollow acceptance of the inevitable and to cold uncertainty of what had truly happened. He had been at Constantine's court, along with his daughter, my sister. One emotion had been noticeably absent from my torrent of torment, though that would not last for long.

'How, perished?'

The officer glanced at his feet, readying himself. I could picture him and the other men tossing dice to decide who would carry these tidings, and this man's face as he lost.

'Domine, according to our reports, your father sought to heal the division in the West by taking Constantine's realm from him and uniting it with your own.'

'Laudable,' I said quietly. '*Uncharacteristically* laudable. Go on.'

Another braced pause. 'He held Massilia against Constantine, Majesty. But the pretender's armies were too strong. They overran him and he was captured in flight. He was imprisoned, Domine, in a dank cell. The... Constantine visited him, it is said, and gave him a sword, commanding him to take his life.'

I slumped back.

Commanded? By a man who, like me, had claimed the purple against the will of the Tetrarchy? How could a *usurper* justify commanding one of the few true reigning emperors of Rome to kill himself? The very idea of my old friend passing a sword to the man who had ruled so long alongside Diocletian and telling him to fall on it was insane. He had no right. No authority...

And there it was. Anger. I had parted with my father in it, but it seems he had sought to solve my problem for me. We could have ruled the West together as father and son, perhaps. But no longer. He had been condemned like a cur, for all his death might have happened by his own hand, by a man who claimed to be noble. Noble! I would show my old friend. My father might have died like an animal, but he would be remembered like an emperor! I snarled, feeling purpose filling my veins once more. I would announce a permanent end to persecution in Africa, denigrating Galerius in the process, shower the province with largesse, and then return to *my* city, where I would deify my father to spite the man who'd murdered him.

Rome was calling once more, and suddenly I felt a little more able to handle her.

23

CONSTANTINE

GAUL, 19TH OCTOBER 310 AD

I left Massilia on the ides of October, riding north with my retinue and a cohort-strong escort of legionaries. Summer had been eaten up by grey skies and fresh winds. The rolling countryside of southern Gaul was still green and beautiful, but peppered with patches of light frost and dew. In truth, it could have been raining fire and I might not have noticed for, as I swayed on Celeritas' back, I could only gaze through the ether and into eternity, blind to my surroundings.

Fausta had left for Treverorum the morning after the last embers of Maximian's funeral pyre had died to grey ashes, taking Crispus with her. It seemed that she preferred to nurse her grief in isolation... and perhaps it was for the best. For even now I still felt pangs of fury about that moment when she had tricked me, lured me to our bed and then threatened to slice open my throat. She had assured me of her loyalty, and I accepted that. But something was gone, I realised. Our love lay broken like a clay slab. Smashed by the memories of her blade at my throat, and of her father's brutal end.

On the day they left, even young Crispus had seemed so withdrawn: I found him in the peristyle of Massilia's villa the morning before he left, throwing a hide *harpastum* ball into the air and catching it forlornly – his 'grandpapa', with whom he used to play, absent. He had kissed me wetly upon the cheek and wrapped his arms around my neck when I stooped to be level with him, but his eyes struggled to meet mine, and his face – as with any child's – failed to mask his inner feelings. Sadness and confusion at what he had been told: that his grandpapa was dead and it had been my doing.

A deep, unrefreshing sigh spilled from my lungs and I stroked Celeritas' grey mane. He nickered and shook his head as if my touch was a bothersome fly. I chuckled without a grain of mirth.

We crossed a heath then the road led us through a range of foothills and pine woods. As we passed through that maze of hills and trees, my mind continued to wander in a labyrinth of murky thought. It was mid-morning when I was torn from my introspection by a strangled belch.

'Begging your pardon, Domine,' Batius said, ranging alongside me, eyes red and watery, thumping a fist against his breastbone then belching again – long and serrated, like the hinges of a heavy wooden door in desperate need of lubrication. 'It's that barley beer they were selling in the waystation last night.' He pulled an expression that suggested he had not enjoyed one of the eight cups he had drained. 'Does wicked things to the guts, it would seem.'

A noise like an irate goose sounded just ahead. I saw Krocus – one leg lifted a little from his saddle before he settled again, clutching his belly. The Cornuti marching behind and downwind of him clamped hands over their mouths and noses and uttered curses, appalled.

My mood brightened just a fraction. 'You and Krocus did well – sacrificing yourselves like that, drinking the only barrel of it between you, letting the rest of the men drink the wine,' I noted.

'Hmm? Well, it was only right. That hairy bastard had the lion's share, though.'

I recalled the two in the tavern beside the waystation – rocking back and forth with laughter as they shared ribald tales with one another and the rest of the legionaries. It had distracted me last night and again I smiled with a genuine spark of cheer. Batius would never admit it, but he and Krocus were almost in danger of tolerating one another.

'How will you handle things when we return to Treverorum?' Batius asked, squinting along the pine-walled road.

My smile vanished, thoughts of the storm that had been unleashed with Maximian's last breath rising again. 'I will gather the senate, the nobles, the priests, my generals,' I said with a greater confidence than I felt, looking down the road with Batius, knowing the empire – the world – was approaching a dark precipice. 'I will tell them what happened at Massilia, though I am sure there are few in all of Gaul who do not already know. *Then* we will talk of what is to come.'

Batius shrugged and pulled a granite-hard soldier's expression, straight ahead, then drew a wineskin from his bag – looped over the saddle – and popped the cork, taking a long pull on it before handing it to me. 'It will be a troubled road, Domine. But I will be with you every step.'

I took the skin and drank deeply. Once, twice, again. I drank more than my fair share as we rode, I must admit, but the warm, tart wine fairly eased my troubled head, temporarily as always, but eased all the same. Batius and I talked mutedly of our shared past, and it comforted me when he reminded me of the better times – the good things I had done in my years.

It was noon by the time we came to a pine-edged glade at the roadside, the lush green grass freckled with wild white narcissi. And at the heart of the small clearing was an ancient shrine: a small ring of marble columns topped by a dome – the circular room enclosed within the columns no bigger than a hut. The stonework – grey like the sullen sky – was veined with ivy and moss, and starlings had made a nest in the eaves.

'A temple?' Krocus said, slowing his horse to fall level with Batius and me. His bright eyes narrowed and he stroked his fiery beard. 'A house of Sol Invictus?'

I saw, toppled in the grass, a statue of an athletic, beardless, naked youth clutching a bow. 'Apollo, a close cousin.' Despite the swell and sway of the rival faiths in those days, it was an odd sight to see a statue of a once-great god broken and seemingly forgotten like that – and his temple in a state of neglect.

I noticed a small brook running through the clearing and a thicket of ripe plum trees at the glade's edge too. I slowed, realising the next waystation and chance of rest was several hours away.

'Halt!' I heard one of my commanders shout from up ahead, looking back and reading my actions and my thoughts.

'Slake your thirst, water the horses, eat,' I affirmed, dismounting.

I heard the dull rustle of iron and as they gladly obeyed, filing off the road and into the mouth of the clearing, unbuckling helms and setting down spears, shields and kit, I noticed a few cagey glances from my men. Bar the various wine sessions, they had been oddly quiet since Maximian's execution. To hear the dialogue that went unsaid in their minds: have we backed a false king, an emperor slayer?

I turned away from them, eager to find a moment of silence. I found myself drawn towards the shrine, like a magpie to a gemstone. The penumbra within that tumbledown sanctuary seemed to call to me. A moment of quiet reflection might well help balance my thoughts, I reasoned as I strolled towards it.

I heard the soft thud of the soldier's boots jogging across the grass behind me. 'Domine, shall I send a rider ahead to the waystation to have them prepare beds and hot meals?' a man called after me. But a gruff shout from Krocus – who had read my mood as accurately as Batius – halted the eager-to-please soldier: 'The emperor wishes to be alone.'

The murmur of the soldiers' voices fell away and was replaced by the babbling brook and a gentle breeze soughing through the woods. The shrine stood there before me like an open question, a staring stranger. Now the wine was in my veins, that is true, and my mind was already maudlin from my chat with big Batius, and perhaps that was responsible for the stark turn in my spirits that was to come.

I paused before I entered the temple, opting to pour the remainder of the wineskin into a small votive font – long dry – by the opening. The nesting starlings sang as I stooped to enter the low doorway. Inside was a floor of crispy, russet leaves and a squat, storm-grey altar, worn and spotted with patches of emerald and cream lichen. I knelt before the derelict altar and felt a great sadness fall upon me, sensing all of this broken, hateful world I had helped to create. Death, loss, dread... much of it my doing. Roman instinct almost brought words of worship to my lips, but I refused to speak to the gods. All of the dark times had come about under their auspices.

My head lolled and I closed my eyes.

I must be forthright and admit that it was my weakest moment, for I questioned whether things might not be brighter for all had I not risen in my father's wake and taken the purple robe. I had always believed I was the most valorous of all the imperial contenders, but what use is undying valour, if it is used only to perpetuate war? Were it not for my rebuttal of the Carnuntum Edict and its call for me to swear undying fealty to the loathsome Galerius and relinquish my station to one of his underlings, then perhaps the strife would be over: the Herdsman and his hounds would surely have gone on to end Maxentius' rebellion and preside over a united empire. And would the endurance of a foul leader be a fair price to pay for peace? Some may say so. After all, many more had died in the few clashes of this civil strife so far than had ever perished in the Herdsman's abhorrent persecutions.

Doubt seized me in its talons like a bald rook, shaking every droplet of belief from my heart. I saw my unending efforts like a strained rope, fraying, ready to give. I even imagined what words I might use to seek peace with Galerius... to offer submission. In the darkness behind my closed eyes, I saw Maximian's shade racked with laughter, I saw my father behold me, ashamed. In that stark, black void I sought out no god, but I made a plea to the infinite darkness. *Guide me. Show me what is right.*

Bleak silence followed, broken only by a breeze that moaned gently through the forgotten temple's eaves. It lasted for an eternity, and my vigour drained with every passing moment.

Then I felt an odd, weightless warmth upon the back of my neck, like a gossamer veil. I opened my eyes and lifted my head. Through the cracks in the limestone chamber walls and the ring of columns, sunlight had flooded into the shrine, bathing my back, casting my silhouette on the altar. I turned to the low doorway, ducking and emerging into the small portico. The autumn sun had broken through the veil of clouds, bathing the pretty glade in its light.

Handfuls of my men turned to me. I could not allow them to see how close to breaking I had been in the shrine, so I adopted a false but well-practised stance, affecting pride and confidence. But then, just as I made to step out from the portico and into the sunlight to cross the glade towards them, I was almost blinded when a shaft of white light – like that cast by a blade in a noonday desert battle – flashed across my face. Blinking, I realised it was the sun's rays, reflected from the thin film of wine I had poured into the font.

I took one more step forward, but when I caught sight of my soldiers not just looking at me but *staring*, I halted. Their mouths had fallen agape, and they were owl-eyed as they beheld me in some sort of awe, pointing. It was as if I had sprouted wings!

Those who had not yet noticed me emerging from the shrine were soon alerted by their comrades and within a trice, each of them too regarded me as a man might look upon a strongbox of jewels. Batius' lips moved as he mouthed some instinctive prayer and stared at me. Krocus dropped the rag of bread he had been eating.

I saw how all eyes hovered on my breast, and glanced down. There, that blinding, dancing light had settled upon my bronze scaled vest.

The letter X, repeated thrice, hovering, shimmering. The number thirty. I realised now what had happened – what my men had seen: As I had emerged from Apollo's temple, this chimeral radiance had passed down over my head like a laurel wreath, and now it hovered over my heart.

Had I been alone, the moment might have passed just as that brief spell of sunshine that was quickly swallowed up by a white cloud. But the men had seen it and taken from it something that would guide me sharply on my journey hereafter. It was their belief in me that quashed my self-doubt on that, the bleakest of days. And they would be with me thereafter, to the bitter, bloody end.

Just as Maximian's shade had foretold.

24

MAXENTIUS

ROME, 26TH DECEMBER 310 AD

I turned over one of the newly minted copper coins in my cold, stiff fingers, flipping it again and again, reading each face repeatedly as if they were new to me every time.

My father's profile looked more stately and calm than ever it had in life, veiled and with a crown of laurels. It was a generous likeness, for sure, but it was still most certainly him – as he had been at his height, not bitter and wicked, bloated and worm-ridden in a Gaulish cellar.

Divo Maximiano Optimo Imperatori.

Despite my deification of the old man in the temple and minting coins in remembrance, and despite my generally unexpected care of his memory, that was still a laughable phrase. *Divine Maximian, best of emperors.* As if *any* of this current flock who claimed the throne around the empire could claim such a title, myself included. Sitting in the tablinum in the late winter's cold sunshine, surrounded by the busts of the greatest men of Rome's thousand years – Augustus, Trajan, Vespasian, Marcus Aurelius – I could hardly compare any living Roman to the heroes of old. But propriety is what it is, and Maximian had in the end done more good for the empire than harm – not for family and friends, but for the state – and so he did not deserve to disappear into the endless night unsung. I had granted him the traditional honours of an emperor.

The coin's reverse flashed in the sunlight – an image of an eagle with spread wings and the simple legend *Memoriae Aeternae* – to his eternal memory. I wondered if people a hundred years hence would even know his name. But then, would they know mine? I was maudlin, I admit, and it was not just the fault of the coins or the death of my father.

Volusianus cleared his throat to remind me he was there and I looked up with expressionless eyes at the man I had elevated to the consulate in the coming month for his achievements. He had not yet laid down the control of the Praetorians and, though he would have to, I felt certain he would be best suited remaining in that post.

'It's fine,' I said, tossing the coin to him. His arms unfolded in an instant and his hand shot out, grasping the coin mid-flight.

'It is incendiary,' he corrected, without thought to address me with an honorific. He sounded oddly disapproving of the coin, considering his belligerent stance on my old friend. 'Constantine might well take it as a slight, you realise?'

'Let him,' I grunted. I didn't particularly intend to rile my old friend with the commemoration of the man he had killed, but I was damn well not going to condemn my father just to preserve the fragile peace. After all, Constantine wouldn't come for me – I *knew* that still, despite Volusianus' constant muttering to the contrary. No, my old friend would be quietly offended off in his western eyrie, and our uncomfortable status quo would go on, for while neither of us enjoyed this situation, neither of us could countenance declaring war on the other.

'Miltiades is waiting for you in the garden,' Volusianus said quietly.

Wonderful. As if I'd not suffered enough advice and coddling from Volusianus. As I stared off into steely sunlight, my Praetorian Prefect made to leave, but paused at the door and then crossed the room once more, kneeling in front of me. His face was such an uncharacteristic picture of concern it rather took me aback.

'*Why* honour your father? He is hardly deserving and you know it. And while it irks me to counsel any course that might satisfy Constantine, I cannot agree with the deification of that old snake.'

I sagged slightly. 'Do you know how much strength hate requires, Volusianus? I just don't have the energy to hate the man, and without hate I am left with acceptance. I've not had more than a fingernail's worth of strength or energy since the day...'

Since the day Romulus died. That was not *quite* true, of course. I had returned to Rome from Africa full of fresh purpose, sure I could take on the yoke of leadership once more, but without Romulus to return to, it had fallen somewhat flat, and without the distraction of a military campaign on which to concentrate, I had quickly slid once more into gloom.

'Why do you insist on staying in this place?' Volusianus muttered. 'It is not healthy. You have the palace of generations of emperors on the Palatine, and a new villa of unsurpassed quality on the Via Appia, yet you wallow in this haunted townhouse like a mourner. It is not right. It's not good for you, Domine.'

There – an honorific at last. Perhaps fearing to bring to my attention the scene of his crime, for in this very house one of my closest advisors had killed the other. I began to grit my teeth at the memory, my ire rising to eclipse my shroud of despondency. I forced the anger back down and after a hundred heartbeats without an answer, Volusianus sighed and rose, backing away with a bow and leaving the room.

I sat in silence for some time. I stayed in this house because Miltiades had suggested it, and like almost everything the African said it seemed like a good idea when spilled through his lips. This house, at the foot of the Palatine, across from the greatest temple in the world and the amphitheatre of the Flavians, had belonged to Anullinus, and I'd still not let the place go.

Well, I was here because of Miltiades' advice, and I could not leave him standing in the small perfect garden all day, could I? I rose, nodding my respect to the busts of great men I had had brought from the palace to keep me company in my solitude, and made my way out into the December chill, pulling my toga tighter around myself.

Miltiades was standing there next to the small fountain, watching the play of water, shivering badly. Rome in winter was a far cry from his familiar Africa. He looked up as I approached, and bowed his head respectfully.

'Domine.'

'Miltiades. What brings you here?'

'You have been curiously absent from public life for two days, Imperator. I fear for your disposition when that happens.'

I *had* been absent. Not 'curiously', though, I would have said. Quite expectedly, in fact. I had had my heart torn out by the loss of Romulus, lived in a constant state of uncertainty as to whether I could even open myself to Valeria, suffered a brief respite while concentrating on the downfall of Alexander, only to entirely miss the golden opportunity for catharsis the auspex had told me to expect, and then returned to a troubled city. As for my disposition...

I laughed with no humour at all. 'What would you have me do? I attend to the business of state. Young Aurelius is off by the sea with his tutor, Romulus is... gone. Valeria might as well be. Social occasions are hardly leaping out at me.'

Miltiades stepped directly in front of me, eyes narrowed as he peered into my face.

'You have been in this house ten days now. How does it make you feel?'

'Cold,' I shivered, pulling my toga even tighter.

'You dissemble, Domine. *Talk* to me. How does this building make you feel?'

I frowned and folded my arms, remembering my rising ire back in the office. 'Mostly angry,' I replied simply. 'At Anullinus for leaving me when I still needed his help. At Volusianus for being the man who dispatched him, and for being too valuable to me to punish. At a world where I am not allowed two advisors who can work together.'

'Good.'

'Good?'

'Yes.' The African smiled indulgently. 'You have spent far too long feeling morose and put upon, sad and hollow. These are negative emotions that can only do you harm. But there are, strangely, negative emotions that can do you good. Anger is one. Fear is another. Frustration, too. These are emotions that are generally caused by evil, but which spur a man into action rather than driving him to solitude. And that is what you need, Domine. All those who know you of old tell me that you were a young man of spirit and of optimism. That you dreamed of building and restoring. That the very reason you agreed to take on the purple robe in this city was to put right a floundering world in which the Roman people suffered. Now they no longer do so because of the work you have done on their behalf. But suffering moves from heart to heart like a canker, and in healing the city and its people, you have taken on their pain and their sadness. Now it is time for you to let that go.'

'But how can I?' It seemed an impossible task.

'Give your suffering to me, Domine. I can take it.'

I shook my head, not so much to say no, as to try and clear it of the endless conflicts it seemed to contain. Miltiades gave me an oddly knowing smile.

'You came to stay in this place when I suggested it, and in doing so left your villa and the tomb of Romulus. I am sure I do not need to remind you that you used to break down even upon losing sight of that mausoleum. Now for ten days you have not seen it, and yet you have not run back. You are beginning to accept things, and with acceptance comes ease. Now revel in the anger you feel in this place. Anything that overwhelms the sadness and the urge to retreat into a shell.'

'But I still have no one to turn to. No one but *you*, I mean,' I added with an odd pang of guilt.

'Go to your wife.'

'My *wife*?' I said, startled. 'That will hardly ease my suffering.'

'Do not underestimate the human heart, Domine. You have suffered long and hard, but you must remember that the lady Valeria has suffered also. She has lost a son and now, if word is to be believed, she is in danger of losing a father. And she cannot turn to her husband, for there is a chasm between you. One of you must build the bridge, and you, Domine, are the builder, are you not?'

I blinked. As I mentioned before, everything that passed

this man's lips seemed like a good idea. It was partially why I kept him close. Unlike most of the Christians I had come across, who seemed determined to suffer endlessly for their cult, Miltiades seemed filled with the need to build, grow and support, and that was something sadly lacking in my life in those dark days. I simply nodded. I couldn't find words to reply, and I just turned and walked from the garden. I didn't see his face, but I would be willing to bet a chest of gold coins that he was smiling indulgently at my back.

Half an hour later I was in the imperial palace, which had never been much to my taste, but had remained home to Valeria in her frosty misery. I found her standing on the old Tiberian balconies, overlooking the forum. She was alone, and I realised with a guilty start that in over a year I had only ever seen her alone. Was this a trick of Miltiades? Such sudden revelations?

She turned as I emerged from the doorway and I could see that she had been crying. Something new crested within me to break down the shell of sadness I habitually wore, but this time it was not anger. It was sympathy. Without words, I crossed to her, walked around in front, putting my back to Rome and the world that threatened to weigh me down, and I enfolded Valeria in my arms. I stood there for some time, holding tight to that ice-cold figure, and then the most unexpected thing happened. Her arms reached around me and mirrored the clasp. We embraced, and a decade of ice seemed to melt as we warmed each other.

Damn you, Miltiades, if you aren't the shrewdest man I ever met!

25

CONSTANTINE

Augusta Treverorum, 30th December 310 AD

I stood by the tall, arched window on the mezzanine of Treverorum's mint, gazing into space. An acrid tang of furnace smoke hung in the blistering air. Smelters worked the ovens on the floors below, melting down old silver coins, coins sporting Maximian's image on one side and mine on the other – all merely to produce a new batch of monies of equal value for no gain. Why? Well, the coinage *had* to change: for one thing, no longer could I lean on Maximian's noble lineage, now that I had ended my father-in-law's life. But that wasn't all. My teeth ground as I recalled the sight in the days after we returned to Treverorum: my soldiers dragging the hidden money chests from the cellars of Maximian's villa.

It had been the old bastard's final slight! In his years at my court, it turned out, he had been hoarding a slice of my coffers – intercepting taxes and working with venal administrators to line their private treasuries and his. When those corrupt administrators had been brought before me, many of my courtiers demanded their deaths in forfeit. They might have thought me lenient or soft in letting the curs live, but they hadn't seen the innards of the British tin mines that I instead sent the felons to: like the guts of a giant, slumbering beast; eternal darkness, toxic air and space enough only to scurry like rats. Those wretches would live for a few years in such squalor there, I reckoned, in chains, scraping endlessly at the seams, losing their sight and then their minds.

My top lip twitched: their fate would have been fitting for Maximian too. But it was too late for that: he was gone – and the old rogue would no doubt have blocked the mine tunnels with his flaccid body anyway. This thought made me laugh, or snort in derision at least. I glanced around the mint: re-minting the coins was my final retort, my way of grinding his memory into the dirt.

One smelter brought a barrow of round silver planchets up the ramp to the mezzanine, where my minters were seated cross-legged before me, taking advantage of the light from the window. They worked in a steady, slow rhythm, each lifting a single blank silver planchet – still hot from the smelting process – from the barrow with tongs, placing the unmarked disc upon the anvil die mounted on a post between their knees, then aligning the opposing trussel die over the disc like a stake, before striking down with their hammers.

Tink, tink, tink...

Three more silver denarii. The trough in front of the artisans now bore a small ridge of the currency, each and every coin bearing my profile and my title... my true and rightful title.

Augustus.

Aye, Augustus. For that was my title, my station, my birthright. No more self-doubt; *that* had been shed in the odd shrine on the road from Massilia. Augustus I had been proclaimed by my father's troops when he died. Augustus, a title Galerius had tried to deny me. Augustus, I would remain.

I stepped forward, lifting one still-hot coin from the pile, tossing it over and over in my hand, seeing my effigy there once, twice, thrice... then it landed on the opposite side, embossed with the face I had chosen to replace and besmirch Maximian's with: that of a long-dead ruler. Claudius Gothicus – conqueror of the barbarian hordes over forty years ago. Ruler of a united empire. One of the last true emperors before the rise of Diocletian and his toxic Tetrarchy.

The idea had sat awkwardly with me at first, when my advisors had put it before me in the planning room at the palace. But they had drawn up a convincing argument: firstly, I needed to repaint my lineage, replace the vacuum left by the dead Maximian; secondly, they plied me with rhetoric, strong oratory insisting that my father had the blood of Claudius Gothicus in him and thus so did I. The case was well argued, citing nieces and marriages who could be traced back to a forgotten brother of Claudius Gothicus. In my heart of hearts I knew it was unlikely – for Father's mind was twisted and tormented by the very lack of such noble lineage – so much so that he had estranged Mother and me to marry into the Tetrarchic line. Yet I embraced my advisors' theory. Why? Because the very fact they had tried to piece together my lineage like this demonstrated how devoted, how utterly loyal, they were.

And that all came back to the happenings at the broken shrine. The small knot of men who had witnessed the laurel wreath of light passing over my head had not been slow in spreading the word. The citizens and the legions far and wide had heard the tale: their emperor had been crowned in divine light at the threshold of an ancient shrine. The pontifices and haruspices of Treverorum, of Avaricum and Lutetia Parisiorum took leave of their temples to gather at my court. These oft-self-absorbed priests and diviners wore looks of wonder as they beheld me and asked me to recount the story. Even the Christian bishops, Maternus and Ossius, had journeyed to Treverorum to ask me what I thought it might mean... or, as it played out, to *tell* me what it meant. The numerals of light that had passed across my chest – *XXX* – foretold of a thirty-year reign for the one chosen by the Christian God. Now the clerics of the old ways were none too pleased at the bishops' proclamations, insisting instead that Mars was behind it all. But despite their difference, they were engrossed, intrigued, taking up residence in my palace for the month. They were *with* me.

I tossed and caught the coin again and looked from the window, across Treverorum's frosty rooftops, to the palace, rising high above all else. Up on the balcony there I saw a lone figure, swaddled in black, outlined by the unbroken white clouds. The wintry breeze lifted her hair gently as she stared into eternity, or maybe just into the very recent past. With my crowning at the shrine, I had won the hearts of my people, it seemed, but that of my young wife remained adrift.

I turned from the window and flitted down the ramp, leaving the mint to walk through the bitter winter air, feeling the eyes of the many on me. The two Cornuti – my ever-present shadows – came with me as I made my way back to the palace. I wasn't even sure why I was returning there: to try to converse with Fausta again? But what use when these days our conversations were so very different from times past. Prosaic, without emotion and skirting around the death of her father. And Crispus was taking after his adoptive mother, the light rarely in his eyes now.

Inside the palace gardens, I stopped by the skeletal orchard, recalling the earlier days when I helped Fausta and Crispus pick pears. The memory of their lilting chat and laughter brought a melancholy upon me.

'The fruits will bud again,' a voice said.

I turned to see old Lactantius shuffling towards me. 'Things will be right, given time,' he said, making eyes at the balcony and the black shape that was Fausta. Crispus was with her now, and I saw him looking sadly down at me through the balustrade's green-veined marble pillars.

'She is lost to me,' I said flatly. 'She is no fool. She understands why I did what I did, but knows also we cannot be what we once were.'

'She does not understand you,' he corrected me. 'Few could. In truth, only the handful of men who have ever been burdened with the imperial purple might. Give her time, Constantine. Time will blunt her grief.'

'Nearly five moons have passed!' I snapped. But I noticed his attentions had wandered, an eyebrow arching at the new coin I was still toying with in my hand.

'You disapprove,' I stated, no hint of a question about it.

'For once, no,' he said, taking the silver denarius and holding the side with the face of Claudius Gothicus up. 'These will travel far and wide and tell the world: Constantine is no black offshoot of the Tetrarchic weed, of the foul persecutors. Your father resisted Tetrarchic policy. You, Constantine, can smash it, consign its dark legacy to the dust.'

A frisson of pride shot through me. 'You could have been a fine general.' I smiled.

'I choose to spar with words, Constantine.' He grinned. 'When Diocletian formed the Tetrarchy, he boasted of the *concordia*,' Lactantius said, 'the unity it would bring.'

I thought of the civil strife that had racked the empire in the time since: outrageously debased coinage, famine, power struggles, men being burned alive and peeled of their skin in the name of faith and empire, riots, cities in flames. 'And the Tetrarchy failed, utterly.'

Lactantius nodded in contemplation. 'As have the Tetrarchic gods. Jove, Hercules – their time has passed. The era of the four emperors has shown that. Where was the favour of either divinity during the wretched decades we have both lived through?'

'I refuse to believe concordia cannot be attained. This empire knew peace and greatness once before and it can be so again,' I insisted.

'Of course it can,' Lactantius laughed gently. 'Don't you see? *You* can be the one to change the world. Virgil, the great bard, once preached about the birth of a child who would bring peace to the earth.'

I tried to interrupt with a dismissive laugh but he held up one taut finger to silence me, then continued: 'But you must ask yourself: where might concordia be found?'

I smiled dryly. 'You led me into a maze once more, old tutor, a maze that ends at the feet of the Christ, I suspect.'

Lactantius' gaze was probing, searching. 'We all wander in a maze, Constantine. Where each of us will emerge, is down to our actions, our choices.'

I recalled from my boyhood my own words to Mother on the night of the storm. *What brings a man to choose his god?*

Lactantius, damn him, seemed to hear my thoughts. 'Your men – the ones who were with you at the shrine. What did they see when you emerged from its door?'

'A message from a god,' I said.

'*Which* god?'

My mind walked backwards until I remembered: the staring, awestruck eyes, the whispering lips. 'They each saw different gods. Krocus thought it was a shrine to Sol Invictus. Batius knew it was Apollo's temple, and he seems certain it was the sun god's blessing. My legionaries whispered words of worship to Mars, some to your Christ, some to Mithras, even.'

'And who is Sol Invictus? God of the sun? Is that not Apollo also? And does not Mars Neton wear a radiant crown? Mithras too – is he not the God of the light? And would it surprise you to know that the rays of the sun are thought to be the light of—'

'Of Christ himself,' I finished for him, knowing well the oft-repeated mantra.

'... falling every night as he did on the cross and rising again the following morning?' Lactantius concluded with a hint of a smile.

'The sun holds the hearts of many, it would seem,' I shrugged in agreement.

'Unity,' he whispered, then leaned a little closer, '*Concordia*.'

PART 4

Iacta alea esto
(Let the die be cast)
– *Plutarch (attrib: Julius Caesar)*

26

MAXENTIUS

I had spent much of the twenty-day journey in the company of Valeria. Firstly on board the ship from Ostia around the west and south coasts of Italia and across to Dyrrhachium in western Moesia, and then in the covered wagon from there across the hard, dry rippling landscapes of my enemy's domain to our destination. Only for the past few days had I taken to riding a horse at the front of the column.

I had felt a shudder as our ship landed, knowing that I now travelled openly in lands controlled by, and loyal to, the dreaded Galerius. In fact, I had shivered almost constantly through the latter stretch of that journey, as though I were walking brazenly through the cave of a slumbering bear. We had encountered numerous military units that in previous years I had seen chased back from my lands with their tails between their legs, and half expected to be stopped and executed offhand by them, but Valeria and her missive were enough to see us past any checkpoint, and we had even spent recent days with an escort of Galerius' own soldiers.

I had felt an odd wrench once on the journey, when one of my escorts informed me that we were passing the great imperial city of Naissus, but would not be stopping. Naissus, I knew, was the city where Constantine had been born, and dark, troubled thoughts of my old – former – friend assailed me all that day and during the fitful dreams of the following night. From Naissus we had taken a more northerly path alongside some unnamed river on a recently constructed road, stopping to overnight at a place called Timacum before rising once more and following a narrow, ancient route above a winding stream to our goal.

I wasn't sure what I'd expected from Felix Romuliana, but whatever it had been it certainly wasn't what faced me as we crested the rise and I beheld the great palace of my enemy.

I fear I have leapt ahead of myself. Forgive me. Galerius was dying. There had been rumours abounding now for so long that many considered them to be just that. And judging by the dreadful descriptions of his ailment, we had assumed them to be, if not fictional, then at least blown out of all proportion. And then the letter had arrived in Rome, and we had learned the truth of the matter. Galerius was on his deathbed – this from his own mouth, apparently. And he had called for his daughter to visit him before his passing.

I had actually tried, very carefully and very obliquely, to persuade Valeria not to go. Galerius had all but foisted her off on me those many years ago and had shown precious little interest in her progress throughout our cold marriage. I could count on one hand the number of times he had even sent missives to her in almost two decades. And now, just because he was sick and frightened, suddenly he began to show an interest in her. In truth, who was I to argue, given my own complicated love – hate relationship with my father? But despite his apparent lack of care, Valeria still bore a daughter's love for her father, and she would not be dissuaded.

And because that embrace with Valeria to which Miltiades had driven me had healed so much of the dreadful rift between us, for months now she and I had begun to live tentatively almost as man and wife once more – a situation I could never have imagined coming about, and one that had finally blunted a little the edges of my grief over Romulus. I would not let her return and face the fat old monster alone. Perhaps it was less noble than that, in truth. Perhaps I thought that I had finally found the wife I had hoped for when first we were paired and now feared her staying in Moesia and my being left alone once more. Whatever the case, I decided I had to accompany her on her journey.

Volusianus tried to persuade me not to go, of course. Walking into my enemy's lair of my own volition? How stupid was I? But in the end, since I would no more be dissuaded than Valeria, he came along with a unit of Praetorians as my escort.

Other news reached us en route as we passed through imperial way stations and *mansios*. Galerius had issued an edict from Romuliana, calling an official end to his long-term persecution of Christians. The East would finally know the peace that the West had experienced for years. Peace? No, perhaps not that, remembering the endless infighting of the Lapsi and the warring Christian sects. Not peace, then, but at least a lack of oppressive fear from the authorities. Freedom to worship openly. Welcome news I suppose, but while the forgiving and the naïve thought it a sign of the emperor's mellowing and his largesse, I saw it as a desperate man facing his final days and suddenly panicking that he had backed the wrong chariot in the race. An anxious penitent trying to put things right, in case the Christian God took a disliking to the man responsible for such bloodshed among his followers.

I still think I was right. Galerius was an oaf and little more. There was less forgiveness and love in him than in a block of tufa, and Romuliana only supported my theory of his bet-hedging policy.

But it was not this empire-shaking news that unsettled me, so much as the discovery that a similar letter to Valeria's had been sent to the old bastard's former protégé. Constantine had also been summoned to Romuliana. My heart was in my throat. Had I known that before we left Rome, would I still have come?

Regardless, we finally reached the great new palace of Galerius in late spring, the strong scent of red helleborine and wild green-winged orchids drifting on the near-still air. I had heard this place described variously as the emperor's death palace, the world's most sumptuous mausoleum, the golden dungeon, and much more. They were all wrong. Yes, Galerius had built it when he discovered he was ill and had clearly intended to live out his final days here, but there was more to it than that. The road we were following was old. Very old. This hillside was far older than Galerius' palace. And it was a high place – one of those that carries an atmosphere of ancient sacraments. There was a feeling there that this was the continuation of something as old as man itself.

No birds sang at Felix Romuliana, I noted. Not even the ever-present Moesian woodpeckers or the goshawks I had seen performing their spectacular sky dance over every hill throughout our journey. No birds at all. No bees hummed either. There was no rustling in the grass. It was as if life shunned the place. Or perhaps the *place* shunned *life*?

But for all that, it was not a mausoleum. If anything, it was a *fanum* – a temple complex. And it was enormous – as large as my new villa on the Via Appia, and more so.

Romuliana rose impressively from the high ground – a great white edifice in the greeny-grey. Whatever it had been constructed of, it had been whitewashed heavily and gleamed in the spring sun, immaculate and pure, its red-tiled roofs only giving counterpoint to the glory of the white walls. The whole complex was surrounded by a wall some thirty feet high, each side of the deformed square punctuated by six projecting towers – huge things, among the largest I had ever seen, each pierced by dozens of perfectly glazed windows. A high gate was almost hidden between the central pair of towers, and we were making for it at our guide's directions, but my gaze was drawn to the side of the complex and beyond. Behind the place, and visible only briefly from a rise before we turned to approach the gate, was an ancient circle of standing stones such as those in old Gaul of which dusty academics speak. And beyond even that I could see a high hill, upon which stood a great tetrapylon gate and a huge, circular mausoleum. Interestingly, a second identical mausoleum was taking shape, surrounded by workmen and wooden scaffolding.

I didn't need to ask. It was said that the emperor's mother was buried here, and clearly Galerius was preparing to rest beside her.

Again I felt a chill as I passed through that gate. I was in the spider's web now. In the bear's cave. And the evil old bastard wouldn't even need to be able to heave his worm-ridden carcass out of his bed to condemn me to death here.

The huge gateway opened into one of the most glorious ensembles of Roman architecture I have ever seen. In a clever use of space that fitted the topography, the buildings were not all aligned to grid as one would consider normal, but juxtaposed at interesting angles, such that nothing quite sat as expected and the visitor was constantly kept on his toes. Everything was arcades and colonnades and high walls of many windows. And all of it was whitewashed like the outside, with similar red-tiled roofs.

I was always a keen student of architecture, as I've noted before, and I could pick out certain buildings without explanation. A huge bath complex at the far end, identifiable by its curves and chimneys. Two great ornate palaces. Stables, guard quarters and, what struck me as surprising and informed to some extent my opinion of the place's purpose – a number of temples. Two in particular rose above the rest, and I could see that one was a temple of Cybele – the Great Mother – from the *fossa sanguinis* before it – the pit where worshippers of that most ancient and terrible deity could bathe in the blood of the slaughtered bull. The other temple was, I believed, consecrated to Jove.

In addition to his edict for the Christ God, Galerius had tried to hedge his bets by adopting a place of ancient spirits and so honouring Jove and the Great Mother. It all screamed of a man trying to please all the gods who might have a hand in his afterlife. Had I not been *where* I was, for *what* I was and to meet *who* I was, I might have laughed.

As we stopped outside one enormous building palace lackeys came forth, offering to help me dismount, aiding Valeria in her descent from the carriage, taking the horses away to the stables and the like. As I stamped life back into my feet, Valeria alighted and looked around with the most complex expression born of curiosity, fear, sadness and hope in varying amounts. This was the land of her family, and it was as much a home as she could ever imagine, and yet it was also the place where her father would be buried, close to her grandmother – a monument to the fact that they were gone, or soon would be. I crossed to her and put my arms around her, trying to take away some of the fear and sadness, though my eyes were roving the area, searching for something. I half expected to see Constantine or one of his men strolling around without a care in the world. Nothing, though.

We were shown into a palace proper and through beautifully decorated rooms to a lobby, where I was told my escort could go no further. I caught the tense, disapproving look in Volusianus' eye, but shook my head. I had come this far and I would see it through.

Leaving the Praetorians under the watchful eye of Galerius' household guard, I escorted Valeria – just man and wife in the palace of the most powerful enemy I had ever made – to the great door where two more soldiers stood.

Valeria proffered them the note from her father, and a guard took it and bowed his head while his colleague opened the grand, red-painted door, studded with bronze lions.

The room beyond was surprisingly Spartan, given the rest of the place, and I was rather taken aback. Galerius and austere were not two words I had ever expected to use in the same sentence. In the centre of the room was a bed of enormous proportions. Atlas himself could have lain comfortably in that bed, and even coupled with Titanic Phoebe therein. Galerius was almost lost in the thing.

I smelled the emperor before I saw him. He reeked not of death, nor even decay. In truth it was the most foul odour I had ever encountered – a smell that made death and decay seem sweet by comparison. He lay naked as a babe amid purple sheets of silk and linen. Only a single fold of plum-coloured bedsheet covered his modesty, and that – I find it hard to fight the revulsion enough to describe it – was stuck to his flesh with something dark that had seeped through the material and glistened wetly on the outside. The smell increased as I approached and I wondered how long a man could reasonably hold his breath without passing out.

Valeria seemed not to be suffering from it, or perhaps her grief was strong enough to override it. I cared nothing for the man, and felt only revulsion at his presence, which only added to my hatred of the odour.

The head turned to face us, as though he'd just realised we were there, though we had been in the room for two dozen heartbeats now. His face was greasy – waxy, pallid and grey, bags under his eyes voluminous enough to hide a pomegranate within. His eyes were bulbous and yellowed. In short, he was the sickest-looking man I had ever seen; had ever even *heard* of. The dreadful tales of his condition were not exaggerated accounts. If anything, they downplayed the horror.

I was gagging as he spoke.

'Va... Valeria? Child.'

'Father.'

Valeria edged closer to the bed. I wished for nothing more than to leave the place. The old emperor cast a sickly, unpleasant smile at his daughter, then his gaze slipped to me, and something of his old power and ire returned as his lip curled.

'You would bring this u... usurper to my san... sanctum?'

'Father, he escorts me. The way is long and dangerous, and he is my husband. Once you must have thought him worthy, for you gave me to him.'

Galerius looked me up and down and his power seemed to drain out of his open wound, his figure deflating once more. 'He is not wel... welcome in my house. He shall not be h... harmed while he is here with you, but should he enter my do... domain *without* you, I will have him s.... skinned. Out, son of M... Maximian. I have no wish to l... look upon you.'

I gave him the most unpleasant smile I could muster, attempting to carry all the smugness of a man who was hale and hearty looking at an enemy who was not, and turned. 'Find me outside,' I said to Valeria, and strode from the room. In truth, I could not leave the place fast enough. I had almost vomited several times at the smell, and I would relish being able to breath something that wasn't filled with the stench of his bloated near-corpse.

I opened the door, stepped out into the spacious lobby, and froze.

Constantine stood, freshly arrived, at the far side of the room.

While I was dressed in white and purple court clothes as was wholly appropriate for an emperor accompanying his wife, he was in military uniform, looking ever the veteran. He was older, more worn, and haunted about the eyes I think, but he looked masterful and in control of himself. I envied him that, and wondered what he saw when he looked at me.

Gently, I closed the door behind me, shutting out the murmured conversation of Valeria and her father. I noted with some irritation that Constantine had clearly entered the building alone, not like I, escorted by my Praetorians. He had, however, surrendered his weapons.

I struggled. I fought against it, but I must certainly have appeared apprehensive and uncertain. Even as I masked my churning stomach with a veneer of cold calm, my emotions raced. It had been so long, and the world had done its best to drive a wedge between us. I constantly hoped deep in my heart that we could bridge the gap that wedge had made, but I was unsure how to do so, or even if it could be done. Did he see me as an enemy now? Did he believe it was me who had sent the blade to his throat? If so, how could I hope to reason with him? I spoke before I had even decided what to say, banal words of fact. No emotion.

'Valeria is with him,' I said. The first words I had spoken directly to my old friend in many years.

'Then I will wait,' he replied, equally flatly. 'Father and daughter deserve time, no matter who the father is.'

I gave an odd smile. It felt very strange after all this time and all these chasms between us to be talking as one man to another with even a hint of civility. Words had to be chosen carefully now. A bridge had to be built carefully, with bricks of just the right shape and size, lest we be plunged into the cold waters of chaos when it collapsed. Nothing confrontational. Nothing political. Nothing personal. It had to be something light. A breaker of the winter ice. A joke, perhaps? And at the expense of a mutual enemy. Surely that would fit the course of bricks I had to lay?

'Take many breaths of good air before you go in,' I warned him. 'The stink of the old monster is unbelievable.'

'I have already encountered the stench.' Constantine laughed. 'I arrived yesterday and have already been insulted and abused once.' And suddenly, despite everything, I could see hints of my old friend before me. The years had fallen away and we were the same comrades who had rescued Romulus from the burning granary. 'Besides, he always stank.'

'Not like this,' I said, feigning gagging. 'An open sewer full of corpses would be a nosegay next to this.'

'So more like Severus, then?' he prompted with a mischievous smile.

I chuckled. 'Or like my father,' I retorted, and with those ill-chosen words all humour and ease fled the room, leaving us facing one another in an awkward silence. Damn it.

Wrong-shaped brick. I felt the bridge begin to crumble as dust fell and the water below yearned.

'I am sorry it had to be done,' Constantine said. 'Not sorry that I did it, but that it needed to be done at all.' Remarkably diplomatic, really. I doubt I'd have chosen my words so well.

'It is regrettable that you were put in that position in the first place. He should never have come to you. I should have had his head struck off when he tried to usurp me. My advisors called for it, and I almost did. He was my father, for all his faults, but I should have killed him cleanly then.'

A tense pause.

'Why, then, did you dignify the old snake with deification?' my old friend said, and the temperature dropped just a little again. Dust scattered from the shivering, half-built bridge.

'He was an *emperor*,' I snapped. 'And for Rome, not a bad one. There have been worse who have made it to Olympus. Perhaps he did deserve to die, but that was not your decision to make.'

'He hated you,' Constantine said with disdain. '*Despised* you. You should have condemned him, not deified him.'

'This from a man who murders his father-in-law like a common criminal?'

Constantine's face hardened as he straightened. '*This* from a man who sends knives in the night like a common criminal?'

I felt my blood heating, my temper fraying. No matter how much I liked to consider myself a temperate, sensible, cautious man, there was ever that streak of my father in me that reacted badly at times like this.

'And here we are,' I said icily, as I searched my vocabulary for something that would cut him and put him in his place.

'Here we are,' he echoed.

It was one of those moments where the world hangs in

the balance. Where destiny spins on a knife-point. Could the whole span of our lives have turned out different if I'd managed to control my ire that day? I do not know. All I know for sure is that what I did say was probably the worst thing I could have said in such circumstances...

27

CONSTANTINE

FELIX ROMULIANA, 30TH APRIL 311 AD

'The hook-nosed killer who nearly opened your throat... *was*... my... man,' Maxentius snarled at me. 'Yes it was one of my hot-headed courtiers who sent him, and I chastened him for it. I almost had the flesh lashed from his back for it,' he continued through clenched teeth, his face twisted and creased like a wolf's. He was tall now, tall and regal, with the air of a leader. In truth that scared me more than anything else. Gone was the boy. Gone was the friend. With his next words... all but gone was hope.

'But I wish... I wish I *had* sent him after all.'

The stark oath echoed around the tall lobby, striking and dying in the high eaves only after an eternity. Sickly sweet and wholly inappropriate white curls of incense smoke coiled from the cracks in the door leading to Galerius' death room, thinning into wisps between Maxentius and me. So absurd: me and my one-time friend in the bowels of the Herdsman's Golden Dungeon, that friendship now drawn tight like the last sinew holding a head to a body. Never has the future been so riven in so few breaths. My blood turned hot like the August sun.

Now I must explain: I had travelled to Romuliana with great caution, to give the Herdsman his last audience, but also to once and for all assert my secession, just as Lactantius urged me to – cutting all ties with the Tetrarchy: gods, emperors, legacies... everything. What kind of fool, you might think, would wander into his enemy's lair? Well, two whole legions of mine were poised at the Danubian port town just a short march away, brimming on the hastily armed ships of the Classis Germanica. More, an entire cohort had escorted me to the northern gates of this sparkling grave.

Yes, if there were to be any acid words exchanged, it would be with the putrid, decaying Herdsman. And the cur had not disappointed. In the Augustus of the East's death chamber, he had beckoned me to him. I approached cautiously, stooping to put my ear within arm's reach of his rubbery, flaccid lips. He merely prised his mouth open like a crack in a stinking shell, his brown, rotting teeth and grey, receding gums parting and his blue tongue lashing once to whisper in my ear with a breath that reeked of rotting flesh: *Pretender.*

So yes, I had come prepared for some vicious, barbed assault, but not from my boyhood friend. I didn't even know he was to be there. When first I saw Maxentius step from Galerius' death room I was filled with admiration for him: as brave if not braver than me for coming to face the man he had directly humiliated in battle just a few short years ago. My next thought was of how I might build bridges with my old friend. I was prepared to humbly explain why I had ordered his father's death.

But now? Now madness had me. Even through the cautious first few words I had exchanged with him, and during that brief and golden moment when we both laughed – when, against all the fates, it seemed like we were young again – I knew the flames were taking hold. Often people cite me for my temper more than anything else. But damn, that day I proved them all right.

I held up a finger and jabbed it across the room like a bowman taking aim. 'Say it again, false prince.' I trembled with fury – almost echoing Galerius' taunt to me just a short while before. Was this the bullied becoming the bully? I took a step towards him. I did not plan it, but it shook him. He stepped back, shaking. Anger, fear? I wondered. Then he halted and his nostrils flared, his shoulders broadening like a man who would back away no more. But still I came at him.

He braced, his eyes alive with fire. 'And what of Italia and Africa? How many years have I, this false prince you speak of, ruled those lands? When Severus came, when Galerius came to take Italia back from me, I crushed them, sent them and their proud, gleaming legions back to these lands.' He said this as if Galerius was not even in the same province, let alone the adjacent room. 'You? You – disinherited by your own sire, unworthy of the purple – have tangled with knots of barbarian raiders and no more in your northern bogs and heaths. Look upon yourself in a polished shield, Constantine, before you next curse another.'

It was like a vase of pitch landing upon a roaring fire. The accusation stuck to me, melted my last semblances of control, consumed me. 'You did not defeat Galerius: his armies were rife with disease and lacking grain and water by the time you marched out to meet them. Even then it was only your snake of a father buying the venal hearts of Galerius' regiments that secured victory for you! Your triumphs are fed to you by the hands of your generals. Like a dog... a *dog!* Your father was a mongrel. You are but a weak pup – with none of his guile and all of his failings.' I came to within a finger's width of him, nose-to-nose. 'Once I thought you a friend, but I was wrong. You have been a bane to me, Maxentius. A dark, vile bane…'

My head dipped and I glared at him like an angered bull. 'You remember the first time we met in Treverorum's halls? That day, I should have helped Candidianus kick you into your grave.'

I saw the merest flash of something deep in his eyes. That frightened boy, lost within. But with a screech of iron, the boy vanished forever. He lurched backwards, drawing his sword in one fluid motion. The tip hovered at my throat. He glowered down the blade's length. I tilted my chin up and glared back.

Absurd confidence on my part, you might think? Well, Batius and Krocus were only a room away. With just a shout I could have them in here and they would butcher Maxentius, even if he did strike me down first. It was the logic of a barbarian, and I see that now.

It was the creaking of the death chamber door that broke that terrible moment. Two of Galerius' Joviani legionaries had emerged. They beheld us standing there like that, and I heard one of them chuckle darkly.

Maxentius and I looked at them, seeing the pair and – beyond – the rotting heap that was Galerius on his charnel bed, his grey head turned towards us on his pillow, his decaying maw open in an executioner's smile. His shell of a body jounced as a racking, hollow laugh sailed out, wrapping around us like a colony of bats.

My eyes switched back to Maxentius and his to me. Rivulets of cold sweat ran down his face, wide-eyed, aghast. I realised my demeanour was identical. Had we been drawn here for just this purpose? To slay one another before our greatest foe? The Herdsman could take no blame were we to fell one another.

I stepped away first, then he.

He sheathed his sword.

Without a word, we parted, leaving the tomb of Galerius from opposite ends in heavy, swift strides.

The Herdsman had been denied his spectacle. Soon after, he would breathe his last.

But for Maxentius and me, there would be no such mercy.

28

MAXENTIUS

We had not yet reached Rome. Gods, but we'd not even left Moesia and Galerius' lands before the news overtook us. We were occupying a lofty mansio by the seashore on the edge of the sprawling port city of Lissus at the time, the entire building having been commandeered for my imperial party.

Galerius – the Herdsman, Augustus of the East, successor of Diocletian, hero of the Persian wars and Emperor of Rome – was dead. Mere months ago I would have given out gifts at such news, struck commemorative coins, festooned my halls with gay garlands and put on a month of games in celebration. Now? My wife's father had died, and with the anticipation of her mourning went any will I had to feel joy at the old bastard's passing.

Moreover, while Galerius had at times been an evil obstacle in my life, he had of late been more a nagging background ache, while my path was now obstructed with a new hurdle: an enemy who had once been the closest of friends.

The courier bowed awkwardly, having delivered his tidings, and backed out of the room to seek lodgings in the town. As he disappeared, I gestured to the two Praetorians on guard duty also to leave us and to close the door. I was chewing my lip against the possibility that Volusianus might bounce happily into the room, rejoicing at the news. That would *not* go down well.

Valeria stood next to me. For a long moment after that door closed and an odd silence descended, she stood still and wordless, staring into space. I actually worried briefly that her mind had become unhinged at the news. I dithered. We were closer than we had ever been, even when Romulus was conceived. We were almost a true man and wife, now. And this was a strange, critical moment. The wrong word or gesture here could undo everything that had been built these past months. Twice I started to reach out with an embrace, trying to comfort her, only to falter and drop my arms once more. I expected wailing grief, but she wasn't crying. She was silent and still.

Finally I walked around and stood facing her. She continued to look through me and into the heart of nothing, and her face was contemplative. Is it not odd how opinions and memories of people change when they die? That fat old trout who had tried to usurp me and fled to my enemy had become my father once more in death. I wondered what Valeria was feeling about her own sire. Finally, unable to take the silence and stillness any longer, I reached out and clasped her upper arms.

'Valeria?'

When she glanced up she was pale and serious. She looked a little like the Valeria of old – the ice queen who had so chilled my life. But there was one important difference, and I could see it in her expression. Her icy anger was not aimed at me. This was a new and intriguing development and, while

I should really have continued to soothe her, I found I had nothing to say until I knew what was in her mind.

'Valeria?'

'What will you do?' she asked quietly.

I was rather taken aback by the question. 'I suppose we should have some sort of commemorative festival. Games, races, that sort of thing. And sacrifices, and probably some coins with your father on one side and me on the other. You know.'

'Not about Father,' she said, a single tear forming in the corner of her eye at the word.

'What?' I was utterly confused. My gaze slipped to the door, which had crept open quietly to display the shape of Volusianus, perhaps trying not to intrude while feeling the need to approach. Valeria's voice called back my attention.

'*Constantine*. What will you do about *Constantine*?'

Again I floundered. 'I... don't know. What *can* I do? Certainly nothing until I get to Rome. Valeria, your father...'

'...is dead, Imperator,' Volusianus said, stepping into the room and bowing respectfully first to Valeria and then to me. 'He was the last true claimant to Diocletian's legacy. Now there remains only you and Constantine, Majesty, and a few sundry wastes of flesh in the East. Galerius' passing will leave a huge hole in the governance of the empire.'

I had expected fury from my wife for the rude interruption and was therefore all the more surprised when she nodded. 'That hole will be filled soon,' she said, adding her voice to Volusianus' song, 'and you are my husband, so you should fill it. Long I have wished your fall, largely because you were my father's enemy. Now I have only you, and I would see you rule, Maxentius.'

Volusianus drifted close, lining up with Valeria like a shield wall. 'Daia and Licinius are dogs,' he snarled, 'yapping and sniffing their privates. Only you or Constantine can hope to take true control of the empire now.'

The pair of them were suddenly animated, Volusianus wagging his finger to emphasise his words. 'The Tetrarchy has *failed*, Domine. Rather than promoting ordered succession, it has bred the belief that anyone can carve off a piece of power for themselves. A band of dogs remain, biting at each other's throats. See how Diocletian's dream has died? The Tetrarchy will diminish until only one claimant remains, and he will be a *true* emperor, as once ruled supreme, like Augustus or Trajan.'

Valeria, nodding, added, 'That emperor should be you.'

I blinked. I had not heard my wife opine such on the subject of the throne before and had clearly not been aware of how keenly she understood matters. 'Valeria, my claim to the East...'

'Is unimportant!' she snapped, and Volusianus nodded, taking up the argument. 'Before anyone can claim total dominion, they must have mastery in their own lands. Neither you nor Constantine can hope to challenge the East while you face each other. And you will never again be allies. You know that now. So you are faced with a very simple truth, Domine: destroy Constantine, or he will destroy you.'

A chill ran through me. I was outnumbered and caught in a pincer movement of opinions. Volusianus had said things like this to me before, but never Valeria. And while the prefect had always been animated and sometimes convincing in his arguments, they had never before sounded so coldly, logically reasoned like this. I had no time to marshal my thoughts, though, as the prefect was off again.

'Domine, Galerius was the last of the truly ordained,

righteously worshipped claimants to the purple. He was selected in official succession and rose through the role of Caesar correctly. The lady Valeria is his daughter and therefore carries some small right to claim imperial lineage. She is married to you, who are the direct heir of a man who was once Augustus with Diocletian himself. You were brought up at court, with the *expectation* of the purple. You were *groomed* to rule. No one in the empire has even *half* the claim that you have. Daia is a caretaker. Licinius cannot even rule that small portion he was given, for you and Constantine defy him. And Constantine? His father was Augustus for a *year*, Majesty. A *single year*.'

'Truly,' Valeria leapt in, picking up the attack. 'He has no noble blood, just a crude bumpkin family from some provincial backwater. And Constantine himself? He was never expected to hold power. Can you not see he was groomed to be a soldier, not an emperor? No, Constantine has far less claim than you.' Her voice dropped to a conspiratorial whisper even though we were alone. 'Some even say your former friend was not born of Constantius' wife at all, but of some whore of a camp follower. Did you never hear that? Better that way, anyway. His mother is a *Christian!*'

She almost spat the word.

I really had no idea how to take it all. I was dumbfounded, my eyes slipping from wife to prefect and back repeatedly.

'So what do I do?' I asked them. They seemed so sure, so full of hard truths and logic, and to see the pair united was a force to behold.

'Send spies to his camp,' Volusianus said. 'Fortify the borders. Perhaps seek an alliance with Daia. That way you could keep the East in check while you deal with the north.'

Valeria threw out a hand so forcefully that I actually

flinched. 'Constantine rides on his military reputation and that of his father. Ruin him. Rumour travels faster than an arrow, and aimed correctly it can do a lot more damage.'

I stared.

'Volusianus,' she said, turning to address directly the man she had been supporting, 'the emperor wants you back in command of the Praetorians where you are most useful, and he wants your five best spies sent to Constantine's domain. Three in Treverorum and two at his other major military centres.'

As the prefect nodded I stared at them. So this was my next step then? My reinstated Praetorian Prefect and my wife were planning my future together...

29

CONSTANTINE

AUGUSTA TREVERORUM, 21ST JUNE 311 AD

The meeting chamber was ablaze with fiery tirades, barely concealed threats and hectoring cries that would not have been out of place on the battlefield. Seated at the top of the crescent of marble steps upon which the disputants raged, I let my head sink and raked my fingers through my hair. Memories of Galerius' stinking charnel manor plagued me. But gone now was the Herdsman. Gone now was the liberating sense that, despite all my acts, there was another being in this world who was more dogged, ruthless and loathsome than I.

Since Galerius' passing, I had heard tales of widespread celebrations across the empire entire: stories of cities exploding with cheer and clouds of colourful petals; praising old gods and new for seeing that the bloodthirsty Augustus had breathed his last. The citizens of my one-time eastern home, Nicomedia – rumour claimed – had even taken the bold step of defacing the statue of Galerius at the port by etching Christian symbols upon the marble. What a legacy, I thought. A man who had set out to become master of the world, and who would be remembered forevermore as a monster.

Now, it seemed, every eye in this world had turned to me.

'The Herdsman is gone,' Prefect Baudio of the Second Italica roared. 'The purple cloak has fallen. Your ranks long to march for you, Domine, to make it yours!'

'Strike south!' Hisarnis cried. The iron-haired Bructeri leader was now shorn of his beard and distinctly Roman-looking, even wearing a muscled cuirass over a tunic and sandals. 'Chase the whelp Maxentius from Rome and make the West your own, then turn the legions to the rising sun and crush the vermin there.'

The officers near the bullish prefect erupted in a chorus of guttural cries.

I thought of Maxentius, of his blade at my throat by the door of Galerius' death room. Just as his sister had held steel to my neck! Who could I trust in this world if he and she could press a blade to my neck like that? My anger rose like livid sparks from a smith's furnace. I imagined my legionary ranks grinding Maxentius' stolen soil under their boots. I envisioned myself throwing him to the ground, pinning him there with a lance, demanding he explain himself.

Once, I would have done anything to help you, to protect you. Now, you are a bane, Maxentius… a bane!

'The fruit is ripe, Domine,' said Vitalianus, a decurion of my *Protectores*. The rider had remained silent on the issue until now, but I could see the light in his eyes as he spoke – enchanted by the prospect of taking the unharnessed empire.

'It is time,' Krocus agreed, trying to keep his voice level.

'Your generals speak in harmony,' a white-haired noble who now called himself a senator insisted. 'And your council will support you. Rome's occupation is an insult to us all. Take it… *take* the West… then take all of the East. All you need to do is give the word, Domine.' He hunched forward, rounding his shoulders like a watching crow gathering its wings in readiness for flight, beak primed to persuade me further.

I looked past him, above him and the many faces, seeing a ceremonial bronze shield mounted on the wall above the opposite marble steps. On its tarnished surface was a sullen face. An ageing face. A dull reflection of myself staring back at me. Something Maxentius had said to me at Romuliana came flooding back.

Look upon yourself in a polished shield, Constantine, before you next curse another.

I looked across the sea of proud faces. The empire *was* leaderless; Maxentius *did* hold Rome and the south illegally. One word was all they sought, but I felt my heart teetering on the edge of the debate. Once the word was given, there would be no turning back.

'War will bring death,' a voice said, cutting through the chamber like vinegar through oil. I looked up, fighting the absurd urge to laugh. Bishop Maternus held a finger up as if to keep the spell of his contrary – if rather obvious – statement alive. 'The thirty-year reign granted by God must be a righteous one… one not stained in blood.'

Then his crony, Ossius stood, his grey, rubbery lips parting and his tarry voice adding: 'You clamour for legions to march, for Romans to march upon Romans… like *carrion hawks!*'

The many generals bristled at this, the senators too. But most had trouble refuting this stark reality. The bishops had come to Treverorum nearly a year ago. I had welcomed their arrival as a sign of growing support. But they had long outstayed their welcome and they were irritating to say the least. Yet this was something new, something different.

'On our emperor's word, a hundred thousand souls might

live… or die,' Maternus insisted. 'Think of this when you scream for the legions to march!'

I was grateful for their interjection, but then I saw the sparkle in their eyes: the barest glimmer that made me wonder – were they going against the swell of opinion altruistically… or merely because they saw a chance to draw closer to me at the expense of the others?

So I turned to the last two faces in the great chamber, the only two who I could trust to help me make my choice. Batius sat by my left, Lactantius next to him. The pair said nothing, but I saw the looks in their eyes. A more convincing argument than all the chamber occupants combined: power-hungry noblemen, glory-seeking generals and oily clergymen. Batius gave the slightest shake of his head.

'Roman blood on Roman swords,' he said softly so only I could hear. 'Is that what you wish to be remembered for?' I could hear hesitation somewhere in his words, but weak and nascent at best.

I knew that I would not submit to the calls of the prefects and the senators. Not today. But would they understand? Hard-eyed men. Ambitious men. With an empire up for grabs, might some see themselves as bolder, better men to take it? I eyed them with an equally hard gaze, standing, breathing deeply and reminding myself I was their master. But before I could move my lips to speak, the chamber doors burst open. A pair of Cornuti stumbled in, escorting a hawk-nosed officer in dusty armour, holding underarm a helm with a solid gold fin. Now I would have normally dismissed and admonished the fellow for his hasty and abrupt entrance, but that day I welcomed the hiatus he offered me. I invited him to speak by means of an arched eyebrow.

'Domine! There are stirrings beyond the south-eastern

borders,' the visitor said, striding into the chamber to stand at the foot of the ring of steps, looking up at me.

And you are? I almost said. But Father's shade lent me a hand, reminding me of his impossible knack of remembering the name of almost every single soldier under his command. I narrowed my eyes for a moment. *Crossus Gavius... Vindex,* I realised, recalling one memo among thousands reporting his promotion to the post of Prefect of the I Martia Legio, watchers of Gaul's south-eastern border forts.

'Go on, Prefect Vindex.' I noticed his face brighten at the use of his name.

'Licinius has crushed the Sarmatians,' he said.

'The steppe lancers have been defeated? That is some achievement.'

'He has held games and triumphal processions in the eastern cities. But it is his latest move that will trouble you more, Domine. He now positions his freed-up armies closer and closer to the West,' Vindex replied.

'He taunts you! Turn the legions east: march into his lands and trample him,' one noble shrieked like a gull, 'before we have another Herdsman to deal with!'

They were bent on battle, I realised.

'War with Maxentius must take priority!' a pontifex snarled.

'Ha! You speak as if you know the realities of war,' a general barked over him.

I swung from the gathering, stalking up to the high window, to stand on the sun-soaked balcony replete with a table, a wine jug and cups. I felt their gazes upon my back, heard their whispered exchanges, heard the babble of the streets outside and the buzzing insect song of the countryside beyond become an infernal, rasping din. I tried pressing forefinger and thumb together... to no avail, for my thoughts only spun faster and fierier. Only one truth held through it all: the delicate balance of the empire remained. Licinius, Maxentius and I. It would take a brave man, perhaps a foolish man... maybe a wicked man... to move first.

'The legions are to remain where they are,' I snapped over my shoulder, pouring neat wine with a tremor in my hand and drinking a cup in two great, untasting gulps, then swinging back to face them all. 'The council is over. Now leave me.'

Their voices erupted again in a din the likes of which I have rarely heard in civilised climes.

30

MAXENTIUS

H *orror vacui.*
Aristotle once said that. 'Nature abhors a vacuum.'
And so she filled it for me. The continual background fear of
Galerius was gone. The cold dismay with which I had suffered
a façade of a marriage was gone. Indeed, with the rekindling
of a real marriage and the constant support of the insightful
Miltiades, even my ever-present pain at the loss of Romulus
had become a more bearable ache. Constantine had pushed
me into ire, but now, *he* was gone back to his northern rat-
hole. The city was calm, Africa was quiet, the legions at rest.
And so into this agreeable dull nothingness came once more
the cult of the Christ.

It had been almost a year since I had gone through that
ridiculous sequence of putting self-involved, self-indulgent
dullards in charge of that troublesome group. Things had
become so quiet that, with the culmination of the African
campaign and the death of Galerius, I had almost forgotten
entirely about the matter. Eusebius and Marcellus had both
stood in my aula regia and looked me in the eye while treating
me as though I worked for them. I had no idea what had

happened to them after they had been banished. They had left the city and my entire domain, and might well now be dead. Two less argumentative crows picking over scraps on the street. The strange lapse into silence that had ensued had been so nice I had not noticed it.

But now, it seemed, that silence was about to be filled with squabbling voices once more. Indeed, I could hear them outside the door, tearing strips off each other in the corridor. I sighed. Apart from the few Praetorians around the room, I was accompanied only by Volusianus in his military garb and Miltiades in a toga. Since I had brought him back from Africa the man had become something of a fixture in the court. He had fallen seamlessly into the ways of Rome and had become counsel to me on a personal level every bit as much as Volusianus played political and military advisor. The irony that while the Christians of Rome caused me endless difficulties, one of their own number had become a crutch upon which I leaned had not escaped me.

The Praetorian hovered by the door, awaiting the command. I chewed my lip and reminded myself not to lose my temper, no matter what happened. The deep-seated ire that I had inherited from my father was often troublesome. It had led me to precipitous action with the Christians before and most recently had almost driven Constantine and I to blows in the East. I ground my teeth as I habitually did now when my old friend's name popped into my head, but forced him from my mind and concentrated on the matter at hand.

'Admit them.'

The door opened under a Praetorian hand and two parties entered in parallel lines as though trying not to touch each other in case they caught something. It was impossible to tell who was who. The group on the left, which filed to one side and gathered in a cluster, consisted of half a dozen people in poor, plain clothes with sad, mournful expressions, gathered around a rather pompous-looking portly man in a rich tunic and cloak. He leaned on a shepherd's staff that seemed to me strangely at odds with his clothing. The other group, who gathered at the far side and stood suspiciously eyeing their opposite numbers, consisted of ten men in drab grey robes gathered about one tall, gaunt fellow with a beak of a nose who leaned on a similar staff and wore silk! *Silk!* I could already feel my temper fraying at the sight of them, and promised myself that I would attempt to make this the briefest meeting I had ever held.

'I understand you both seek boons of me? Which of you are these so-called Lapsi?'

Yes – the whole lapsed worshipper issue was still raging strong in my city. Are these Christians not unbelievable?

The fat man bowed. 'Emperor. I am Statius, the leader of our poor beleaguered people, appointed by the will of...'

'Fine,' I cut him off, turning to Beaky. 'So you are?'

'Majesty, I am Vivianus, the current bish...' he realised instantly that I had not officially agreed to any Pope, any bishop of Rome, and changed tack. 'I am the highest ranking of the Christian priests of Rome, and these are the synod with whom I confer.'

Oh good. More than one of them. I felt the ire growing again, especially as I watched the hate-filled glances pass between the two groups. Miltiades in one of his many quiet moments of parable had taught me that his religion was one based on peace and forgiveness, though I had yet to encounter either to any great length among their people.

'State your case, Vivianus.'

'Majesty,' the beak-faced one began, his voice sibilant and

irritating, 'it has long been our goal to bring together the Church of the Lord Christ in Rome under one all-encompassing shelter, brothers and sisters in faith, such that...'

Ire. Rising.

'You are not standing for public office, Vivianus. You have no need of grand speeches. Talk plainly, man.'

'I seek, Majesty, the freedom to deal with the internal matters of my people without the pressure of imperial authorities weighing upon my hand such that...'

'You want me to let you do as you like. Got it. Thank you. Statius?' I added, turning to the fat one as the crest of Vivianus fell.

Statius was beginning to sweat. Good.

'Majesty, we are subject to constant pressure from these old fools. They will not attack us in the street, or burn down our churches anymore, because the Urban Cohorts are swift to respond, but they harass us and make our lives hard in every legal way possible. We are poor and without the network of the holy fathers, and we have no way to defend ourselves but with our poor, scarred fists...'

'And when you do, the cohorts take a dim view,' I summarised for him, noting to myself how poor he really did *not* look.

Silence fell. I huffed. 'So there is an unspoken warning – or possibly even threat – here that unless your groups are allowed to deal with one another without my interference, things will probably blow up into violence?' I lunged up from my throne angrily, leaping three steps towards them and wagging a finger. Every last supplicant took a step or two back, nervously.

'Let me remind you all that the reason none of you can even *shit* without my cohorts being there to weigh the result is because, when left to your own devices, you were killing each other wholesale and burning down portions of my city. And when I tried to let you have a Pope to sort things out yourselves, each one we tried just made matters worse. I have had it up to here,' I snarled, drawing a finger across my throat, 'with your entire sect. Under one man you kill each other. With no leader you kill each other. Under two men you kill each other. My soldiers try to *stop* you killing each other and you actually *petition* me to let you kill each other again? How is it that there are any of your people left? How have you not fought yourselves to mutual extinction? They say the empire is gradually filling with Christians, but I swear for each one of you that appears two more kill each other.'

I stopped and realised I was trembling. I had lost my temper in exactly the way I had planned not to. And I had been more acerbic than was truly necessary, but I think all the frustration of Romulus, of Constantine, of Galerius, of Anullinus, had got the better of me and found an outlet. One thing was certain: no plaintiff in that room was going to open his mouth now until I told him to. I forced myself to calm and strode back to my seat.

'Here is my conclusion: the meeting is over. You will all return to your places of work or residence and you will await an official edict. I will mull over the matter and consult very learned men before I decide how to proceed. But until I release such an edict, any single one of you who causes trouble will be thrown in the Carcer to stay there until you rot. Do you understand?'

In the silence there was a meek chorus of nods.

'Do you *understand*?' I bellowed.

A hurried bark of acknowledgement. I nodded curtly. 'Get out of my sight.'

I waited until the Christians were ushered out by the Praetorians, gave a quick nod to Volusianus, who would see them off the premises to add a level of militant authority to their ejection, and rose again, pulling my toga tighter where it had loosened as I lurched angrily about. As I reached the rear door and the guardsman pulled it open, Miltiades appeared at my shoulder with his infuriatingly pleasant smile.

'Congratulations on not crucifying anyone, Majesty.'

As I walked I cast an arched brow at him. He chuckled. 'I preach the art of forgiveness and tolerance and even *I* might have been tempted to have that lot beaten.'

Despite myself, I laughed. Miltiades was that almost unique thing in Rome in those days: a Christian who spoke sense. Halfway along the arcade beyond the door I stopped and turned to look across the garden. The octagonal fountain at the centre had been there since the days of the hated Domitian, but it still delighted as it burbled happily amid the well-tended bushes and flowers. The ground fair sizzled in the summer heat and bees hummed about the plants. It was idyllic and did almost as much to calm my mood as the man beside me had.

'I am vexed with it all, Miltiades.'

'I can see that, Majesty.'

Always *Majesty*. Never *Domine*. Their sect reserved that title for their god. It often irked me, though for some reason not with this man.

'I don't understand your people, Miltiades.' I hurriedly held up my hands with a smile, attempting to forestall a lesson. 'Don't preach, though. I just cannot fathom a people who when faced with threats from every direction cannot even stop fighting each other long enough to defend themselves from outside. If I let these men deal with their own troubles there will be a bloodbath. But if I continue to exert control over them I run the risk of turning into an oppressor like my forebears, and the resulting pressure will probably build to an explosion anyway. No matter what I do I seemingly cannot prevent the coming trouble.'

I spun to the man, my expression oddly pleading in a manner I'd not intended.

'What do I do, Miltiades? What would *you* do?'

He did not immediately answer me, which was a good thing. I knew that when the man focused on a problem rather than trotting out a reply, his solution would be worth hearing – he was one of those people. Finally, amid the chirrup of birds and the hum of bees, Miltiades once more spoke sense to me, and began to solve my problem.

'I would take the matter into my own hands, Majesty. I would not leave it to them, and I would not leave it to fate or time. Moreover, I would not hand it to any one of them to deal with, for each has his agenda. I would, if I were you, make some grand gesture of inclusion for the Lapsi. There are things that can be done. Perhaps the return of their confiscated goods, payments for lost livelihoods, the rebuilding of places of worship. And it will have to come from the Church. The Christian authorities of Rome will have to be seen to do this. Then the Lapsi will feel welcome and part of the brotherhood once more. The trick then lies in making the Church authorities happy to comply, but that should be easy. It is the nature of most men when given a little power to indulge and seek more material gain. Sadly I see that even in my own people who supposedly eschew such wealth.' He smiled at me. 'I refer not to yourself, of course, Majesty, but to those who claw for position in a hierarchy.'

I chuckled good-naturedly. It was almost impossible to take offence at Miltiades.

'So appeal to the Lapsi with a gesture of inclusion, Majesty, but appeal to the authorities' baser nature. Build a few extra churches for them, fill their coffers beyond that with which they pay the Lapsi. Let them have some open festivals in the streets. Maybe donate something to the Church on a personal level. You will be surprised how easy they are to buy off. Once all this is achieved there will no longer be such a thing as Lapsi, just one coherent Church who owe you a favour.'

I was shaking my head in wonder. Such a simple, elegant solution. I laughed aloud and started to walk again, but I had changed direction now. 'You are a subtle and clever man, Miltiades. You were wasted in Africa.'

With the man gently murmuring more and more thoughts on the details of his plan, we strolled through the palace until we reached the Palatine libraries. Here we were close to the slopes of the hill and the acrid smell of the summer city began to insist itself on the nostrils. I could hardly wait to get back out to my villa once the day's business was done, but the palace was still the best place to meet with supplicants.

The library was cool and dark and I sauntered inside with Miltiades still expounding on the Christian issue behind me. I ambled across to a large ornate cupboard inlaid with ivory from Africa and bent to open the doors. Miltiades hardly seemed to notice what I was doing as he continued to define his 'grand gesture' but when I withdrew the cupboard's only contents and thrust it at him, he stopped mid-flow and blinked.

He stared at the Papal robe in my hands. It had rested in this dark place for almost a year since it had last adorned the shoulders of a man appointed by both emperor and Christian authorities. This time they had no say in the candidate and he was not even a priest. I suspected they would argue about that, but a man who could come up with an elegant solution to the Lapsi issue could easily calm concerns over his appointment. One thing was damned certain: for the first time I felt absolutely sure about handing that robe over. I knew I had the right man to lead his sect and yet stay within my domain peacefully.

'Majesty?'

'Take it, Miltiades. It's waited for you for a year. You've helped heal me from a broken wreck back to a functioning husband, father and emperor. Now do it for your people and my city.'

He continued to stare in awe at the robe and my confidence in my choice grew stronger still. The others had all almost leapt to take on the robe. Miltiades was dumbstruck. As he stood there in silent reverence, I rounded him and placed it across his shoulders myself. He was the first Pope to have his mantle laid upon him by the hand of an emperor.

I rounded him again to face him eye to eye and smiled. 'Go enact your plan with my blessing.'

He nodded dumbly, apparently not trusting himself to speak, and accompanied me from the library. Outside I paused for a moment to allow my eyes to adjust to the light, and as they focused, I spotted a solitary figure leaning on the balcony of the Palatine's great exedra, looking out over the Circus Maximus and the Aventine Hill beyond. The air here was cloying and dusty as Rome always is in high summer, and I was surprised to see Valeria here. I gestured to Miltiades to leave me and, as he hurried off full of purpose, I crossed to the railing and leaned next to my wife, once again revelling in the fact that I could do such a thing. Just a year ago we had been separated by such an icy gulf that I could never have imagined this. When she placed her delicate hand on my folded arm, I felt a thrill.

'Have you burned them all?'

I studied her face for a sign of ferocity – Valeria was no lover of Christians, for sure – but could only find good-natured ribbing. I smiled. 'Miltiades has the problem well under control. I think we have seen the last of it.'

'Good,' she replied, 'for I have other news you might find less sweet for your ears.'

I felt that familiar shadow across my heart. What bad tidings were coming now?

'You will remember that I told you of rumours that had sprung up about Constantine's parentage?'

I nodded mutely. The rumours of which she had apprised me in Lissus, on our return from her father's palace. That Constantine was the son of a whore and not of the rather pleasant lady I remembered from our time in Nicomedia. I had heard the rumour myself, though only spoken in soft voices in the still of a private place. It did not do to defame an emperor after all, even if he did not rule your city.

'It seems that the rumours are taking root everywhere,' Valeria said. 'My maid has seen slogans painted across the city's walls, labelling Constantine an illegitimate whoreson. Poets and lyricists are incorporating the rumour into songs. And questioning his parentage will cast doubt on the legitimacy of his claim to the purple, too.'

I pursed my lips. It was something of a surprise that the tale had become so public and open so quickly, even with Valeria and Volusianus propelling it, but it made little difference now. 'In all honesty, I cannot truly consider that poor news. Constantine no longer holds such a place in my esteem. Let him rage and rant when the rumours reach him. I am rather surprised, though, that such dangerous talk has become so popular in Rome from a single arrow of rumour aimed at Constantine's domain.'

'I would look no further than your closest officers for that,' she replied with a sour expression.

Volusianus. Yes, this had all the hallmarks of his rather unpleasant and underhanded methods. What my calculating wife might have used as a surgeon's blade to incise Constantine from the body of the West, Volusianus had turned into a sledgehammer with which to pound the empire entire. I frowned as a thought occurred to me. 'Why do *you* consider this news sour? I thought you *advocated* all-out war between us?'

'Of course I do, husband, but on *your* terms, not *his*. You gather your armies, march into his lands and take the West from him and your name will be on the lips of every citizen from Britannia to Africa. And you can drive the campaign to your advantage. But if Constantine is goaded too much? Well, the man is a peasant, and peasants are rough and simple. He will bridle at the insults and if you push him too far, he will gather his armies and come to Rome. Then you are fighting on *his* terms.'

I nodded vaguely, uncertainly. To me, Constantine was not the peasant of which she spoke, but she was absolutely correct about his moods and strengths. He would react and it might well be violent and precipitous. I could hardly upbraid Volusianus for his foolhardiness when the arrow had been loosed by Valeria's order. Word was out now and Constantine would hear it soon enough, which meant that if I dissembled, apologised and backed down, I would appear weak. I could foresee escalation of the trouble in the coming months, but there was nothing for it now. Words had been spoken and we were committed.

Whatever ties with Constantine that had remained in tatters these past months were now well and truly severed. My old friend was no such thing anymore.

Unless something miraculous happened, it would come down to him or me.

31

CONSTANTINE

AUGUSTA TREVERORUM, 20TH JULY 311 AD

The messenger fell to his knees as if succumbing to the baking-hot sun. A sultry breeze passed over the palace's rooftop terrace, casting the fellow's thin hair back. His dry lips moved wordlessly, unable to repeat the statement that had seen me rise up from my seat like a scorpion's tail.

'He said... what?' I demanded once more, my voice tremulous, my vision shuddering with each beat of my heart. A fire spread across my skin and an invisible, choking hand squeezed my throat. For all the world, it was as if I had been taken back to that day of my youth in this very city, long before it was mine: when Father had publicly taken Theodora as his highborn wife, estranging Mother and me.

The messenger was now paler than Persian sand and shaking like me, though with fear instead of anger. 'He... he said... he... he...' the poor fellow tried and tried again, but he could not repeat the message that had struck me at the first time of airing like a Frankish axe to the breast.

Helena is no noblewoman; she was merely a concubine. Thus, the mighty Constantine is but the spawn of a whore!

'He said... he—' The fellow's words were mercifully ended

when Batius' ham-like hand settled on his shoulder. The messenger almost leapt from his robe with fright, but the big man quickly soothed his fears. 'The emperor does not need to hear it again,' Batius said, 'but your swiftness in bringing this to his attention will not be forgotten – and it takes a brave man to bring bad news to the imperial palace. The *Magister Officiorum* is looking for an assistant, and I will see to it that your name reaches him,' he continued, opening the terrace door to let the relieved man make his escape inside the palace's cool halls. Batius remained at the door for a time, back turned, scratching his sweaty, stubbly scalp, and I knew he was composing himself. He had been like an uncle to me back then in my younger days. I would not be so easily mollified now.

'Does he know how hard I have worked to resist the calls of my council?' I snarled. 'Does he? How could he do this?'

Aye... *he*: for this outrageous spite had come from the tongue of Maxentius. On that day when my father had shamed me, Maxentius had been there. Batius and he were the only ones to offer me kind words, to spare me the hard, mocking eyes cast by the many other gull-like nobles there that day. Now, it seemed, he had not merely turned his back on me... he was goading me, slandering the ones he knew I dearly loved.

Batius turned now, his face long, scars and age lines picked out as ribbons of shadow by the stark sunlight. 'I doubt he even knows that message made it onto a scroll, Domine, let alone that it reached you here.'

I raked my fingers through my thick curls of hair, eyes sweeping around the terrace, a single breath held captive... then, with a roar, I swept a hand across the table, scattering the empty and half-empty wine cups and plates there across the tiled floor – some bouncing through the balustrade and toppling off down into the gardens. Once the din had faded, I shot an accusing finger out, as if Batius was to blame. 'Even if he never *spoke* those words, he let the message travel across imperial lands. What do you expect of me? To *forgive* him?'

'Not in the least,' Batius replied, utterly unruffled by my behaviour – he had seen my tantrums as a boy when we used to practise sword fighting together, and he looked at me now as he had done then. I know now that my conduct that dog-hot morning was barely forgivable. Two jugs of wine – drained before noon – and the sticky summer air had mixed to boil my mind before the unfortunate messenger had arrived. Yet Batius stood there like a granite bluff, his only sign of emotion the sadness in his eyes. 'However this found its way to you, we must now accept that it has.'

'It has not *just* travelled to me though has it, Batius? Rumours and more scrolls, the messenger said, all across my realm and that of Maxentius. How can I pacify my tribunus and my prefects – proud generals who only demand that I let them fight for me – or the carrion gulls of my senate, now?'

'Because you know there is still a crumb of hope,' the big man said.

'Is there?' I scoffed. 'If there is then it is only a worm-infested morsel, dangled from the tarnished gods of the Tetrarchy,' I spat, Lactantius' musings fuelling my convictions.

'While there remains hope of avoiding war with Maxentius, you must embrace it,' Batius persisted. 'Fight one another, and you will hand the world to Licinius. Fight one another… and our spathae will be stained with Roman blood.' He hesitantly shook his head, gazing through me. 'That cannot be the way… surely?' he questioned the ether.

'I cannot let this go unanswered,' I snarled through gritted teeth. 'He. Called. My. Mother. A… *whore!*'

'Someone in his *camp* did,' Batius tried to correct me. 'The same person who ensured the slur was spread far and wide like a blight. Did you not say it wasn't Maxentius but one of his retinue who had organised that cut-throat to strike at you in Agrippina?'

'He claimed so,' I scoffed, 'as would any man caught with their hand on a bloody knife.'

'And what if it was not a claim, but the truth?' Batius took a step towards me.

'Scribe!' I yelled, pouring myself a third cup of wine to the brim.

'But, Domine,' Batius added, 'Maxentius is not here. We cannot establish what is behind this slur. Before we respond we should think carefu—'

The slap of the scribe's sandals cut Batius off. The hunched, sandy-haired man seemed oblivious to the crackling atmosphere on the terrace, and halted between Batius and me, looking at us each in turn, a wax tablet in one arm and a stylus in the other hand.

'This is the tale of Maxentius, False Prince of the South,' I began, swinging away from the table, gulping at my wine in between strides to and fro. The scribe's eyebrows arched, suddenly aware of the toxic situation he had just strolled into. His stylus scratched and tapped at the wax in a woodpecker-like fashion. 'A proud man, but neither of purple blood, nor a Roman.'

'Domine...' Batius tried to halt me.

'He sprung from a Syrian womb, where his mother often used the hot desert nights to lure men to her home.'

Batius slid a hand over his weary face, rolling his eyes and muttering an oath skywards.

'Soldiers, fishermen, beggars... all have known the mother

of Maxentius. Of course, the Tetrarchic gods intervened to ensure that it was Emperor Maximian's seed that spawned the boy Maxentius. Who could question them, after all? Have Jove, Hercules and Mars not brought contentment across Roman lands?' I laughed once without humour, Lactantius' preachings echoing piercingly in my head now.

The Tetrarchic gods have failed: Jove, Mars and Hercules have fallen – look at the glorious ruin in which their followers wallow. Shun them, Constantine – just as you have shunned their lineage. I drew out a coin from the batch newly minted. Now they sported an image of me not as an emperor wearing a wreath, but as a greater being, nimbate, just as I was that day at the tumbledown shrine. A shiver of pride struck through me.

'Have those gods not bestowed upon us the empire of today?'

'Domine!' Batius tried again.

But I threw up a hand, threw the rest of my wine down my throat, and threw caution from the balcony. 'Make a hundred copies of this,' I demanded of the scribe. 'Have them sent to Britannia, to Hispania, all over Gaul. Send them to the East… and send riders south too: cross the mountains into Italia and nail this message in the market squares of the Padus valley cities.'

A knot of slaves shuffled onto the terrace, bowing their heads and averting their eyes, eager to give the impression that they had heard nothing. But that was just the thing: right then, I wanted them to hear, to talk, to spread the affront – to make Maxentius feel for himself the shame he had caused me. Then I saw the duo whom the slaves were escorting. The reed-thin Maternus and the slack-lipped Ossius. The bishops, whose visit for a 'month' had become a permanent residence.

My eyes narrowed to crescents and I offered them a faint nod. I noticed that Maternus was wearing a fine silver pectoral – a recent acquisition – draped over his white robe.

'Domine,' they replied in unison, offering full bows from the waist.

I glared at them until they shuffled nervously.

'The last time we spoke, we talked of the will of God,' Ossius said at last.

You did, I thought.

'God has spoken to us again,' Ossius said. 'He fears that His flock is in great danger. The... False Prince of the South...' he said with a self-congratulatory smile, 'presents a dark threat.'

I could have laughed long and loud were it not such a grave matter. It was all I could do not to stare at them agog. They had beseeched me to ignore the senate and the legionary commanders not a moon ago.

'The thirty-year reign was divinely granted, Domine, and it must be... protected. Were the legions and your hardy forest regiments to mobilise and march south,' Maternus said, 'then God would be content.'

'Would He?' I said, stepping towards them. 'Would He really?'

The silver cup in my hand bent in my tight, powerful grip, a splash of wine leaping from it. Batius must have sensed the flames rising within me, as he stepped between me and the bishops. 'Your advice is noted, though you should seek appointment or await a senate session in future,' he said, gesturing to the tall doors leading back inside.

'God's will transcends the senate, soldier.' Ossius smiled, the words dripping with superiority. 'As we have discussed.'

Batius lost his soldierly stance for a moment. 'Aye,' he agreed.

The bishops left, and I realised the scribe had too. The dark slur on Maxentius was already on its way to the scriptorium, perhaps even now being copied out by the scribes there, and would soon be on its way to the corners of the empire. I was gripped for a moment with a fiery dread. *What have I done?* Then I recalled the smear that had prompted it:

The mighty Constantine is but the spawn of a whore!

I swung round, seeking a target for my ire, when *another* meek man emerged from the shady palace interior. A rider: slight and coated in dust – I knew them all too well these days.

'What?' I roared.

The rider gulped. 'I bring word from the frontier forts of the south-east. Disguised Licinian scouts were apprehended in the market towns.'

'Scouts?' Batius said, his eyes narrowing. '*Licinius'* scouts?'

The big man and I shared a look. It was less than a moon since I had banked on at least a season of respite from the East.

'Aye. It seems that Licinius is ready to invade the West imminently – sees your territory as a riper prospect than Maxentius' – and right now he plots an invasion of southern Gaul. Several of his legions have been sighted, at camp near a weak spot in our border in Noricum. The morning before I left to ride here, they were marching north-west... to penetrate your realm. An act of war, Domine.'

I beheld the rider for a trice, then swung away, booting the poor table across the terrace with an ox-like bellow. 'Muster the Comitatus,' I snarled at Batius.

32

MAXENTIUS

ROME, 30TH JULY 311 AD

I felt muscles straining and pulling. I have seen soldiers fight and train many times in my life and most can maintain their strength and agility for quite some time, but any man not trained by a centurion or a *lanista* who tells you he spent half an hour hacking at a *palus* is a liar. Twenty strikes is all it takes to drain the last reserves of power from your arm and to increase the weight of the sword exponentially with each blow, such that it soon feels as though you are trying to throw a trireme.

I had stepped up my exercises with the Praetorians since coming back from the East. Something about that nerve-racking sojourn in the lands of my enemy had made me feel that I needed to be more capable of my own protection, and who better to train the emperor than his own guards, the elite of the Roman military?

Shoulder muscles screaming at me, I lifted the heavy blade once more and jabbed at the palus. The tip struck the timber and the reverberation up my arm almost floored me.

'Fifteen more and you can rest, Domine,' reassured the grizzled centurion with the impressively scarred nose. *Fifteen* more? *Two* would be pushing the bounds of my endurance.

'Fifteen is not possible,' I gasped between breaths, pulling back my arm and feeling the sword drop almost to the ground.

'You're an emperor, sir. The son of emperors and protector of Rome. You can do it.'

It was a good effort at enthusing me, but I was flagging beyond hope.

'Think of something that enrages you, sir,' the centurion said, coming close so that his voice sounded low and menacing. 'That's what I tell my lads if they seem to be wanting for drive. You'd be surprised how much energy anger lends you.'

Angry. What made me angry? The problem with the Popes and their flock had all but gone away. Africa was settled, and Licinius, while he was on the move, seemed to be concentrating on the north and ignoring me. There was one thing, though I was trying very much not to think about it unless I had to. Even thinking about why I wasn't thinking about it was enough to start the blood coursing and before I'd even realised it, the tip of the blade had come up again.

'Constantine,' I hissed under my breath, imagining that broad, honest-looking face with its mop of curly hair before me on the battered wooden stake. I slammed the tip of the sword into his visage, imagining it breaking bone and shearing muscle.

'Bastard son of a whore,' I snarled, pulling back the blade with reserves of strength of which I'd been unaware, tapped through focusing on my northern opponent. Remembering the previous day, when the rumour had first reached Rome and quickly spread through the streets like a conflagration, I roared and slammed the blade in once more, deep into the centre of Constantine's smug, lying, slandering, malign face.

'My mother,' I snarled, slamming in the sword again. Not my dreadful horrible father who, though I'd deified, I still reviled. The man who had made my youth so difficult and had almost done for me as an adult. No. Constantine, who knew first-hand how awful my father was, had left the old fool's shade alone and instead attacked the good name of my mother!

Slam.

My good, pure, loving mother!

Slam.

This from a man who had been my friend.

Slam.

A man I had almost called brother.

Slam.

A man who *was* my brother-in-law!

Slam.

'My mother!' I bellowed.

Slam, slam, slam, *slam*.

By the time I finally ran out of strength, I had hacked and chipped a huge shredded section of the palus away, and oddly what remained was faintly reminiscent of a grinning skull. I howled and smashed the sword into it, fury driving me even as it began to abate.

The other Praetorians in the garden had stopped what they were doing and were staring at me. The training centurion reached out gingerly towards my sword.

'That was more than fifteen, Domine.'

Sweat was pouring down my face, streaming into my eyes and half-blinding me. My hand was shaking wildly as it gripped the sweat-soaked hilt of the heavy blade, which slowly dragged itself back down to the ground. I felt utterly drained. Of course, I was blaming Constantine for something that might not have come from his own mouth. After all, equally unkind words that had struck him had actually come from

Volusianus. Indeed, if I was going to be angry with anyone, it should have been my Praetorian Prefect, for it was he who had started this slinging of insults. But it was done, and now the pendulum of hate was swinging with heavy inevitability.

I let the centurion take the sword and stared down at my shaking hand, gripping and releasing a fist to try and stop the trembling. Turning to leave the garden and visit the baths to clean up, I spotted Volusianus in the doorway and the fist gripped again. I fought a powerful urge to use it to break the prefect's nose. The anger was going now, though, most of it driven into the wooden stake at sword point, and leaving only empty resignation. I walked across to the doorway, accepting a towel from a slave and wiping the worst of the sweat from my head and face.

'Good work, Domine,' the prefect noted. 'You could stand your ground among the Praetorians these days.'

'What is it, Volusianus? I'm tired and I need to bathe.'

The prefect huffed and I noticed a twitch appear in his lip for just a moment.

'I am concerned, Domine.'

'You're always concerned about something. Make yourself clear.'

'The treasury, Domine. It drains rapidly.'

'It is in the nature of treasuries to drain. If the *Aerarium* is running low, top it up from the *Fiscus* treasury – my personal funds are more than adequate and can be drained a little. And there must still be money in the Military Aerarium, too. Just have the officials move the money around to make sure there's enough.'

'Imperator, there is *not* enough. The Aerarium is almost empty. One of the priests at the temple of Saturn said there is so little metal in the vaults he's worried the whole temple will float away. Priests have a peculiar sense of humour, I know, but if even the priests are concerned...'

'Move it around,' I repeated wearily. 'Make Gaius Annius a *quaestor* and let it be his problem. He's desperate for a job. So long as he doesn't leave my personal funds empty.'

'Your own Fiscus is not so healthy, Domine. You already authorised the praetor in charge to release extra funds for the military, which, I expect you can guess, means that the Military Aerarium is also thinning alarmingly.'

I paused, throwing the sodden towel to a bench. 'Then where is the money going? We had enough a few months ago.'

'Your damned Christians, Domine. You restored all their property, built new churches and repaired old ones. Their property, which you restored, was a significant portion of the treasury, and has been ever since Diocletian first seized it. And your Pope—' he spat the word with distaste '—Miltiades, is still asking for more. We cannot give him any more money. We cannot afford to give him what we already have!'

'Volusianus...'

'Domine, we are supporting a massive army, bigger than those in the north and the east. It costs a huge amount to keep it active and ready, yet we cannot afford to cut down. Our forces are what stop Licinius, Daia and Constantine from simply walking into Rome and plucking you from the throne. And we're still paying off the extra grain we had to buy in during the African revolt. Years of excess shipments cost a king's ransom and we have been fortunate indeed to be able to pay our dues slowly over time. And the fortification of the north-east. That does not come cheap. Even with the army doing much of the work, a substantial financial outlay is required. We're going to have to find some more money soon, and you have to stop giving it to the Christians.'

I sighed and turned to the doorway.

'I'm going for my bath, Volusianus.'

As I stalked irritably off into the dim interior of the building, I could hear Volusianus in the doorway shouting after me like some peasant in the forum.

'You have to do something about it, Domine. You can't just ignore this.'

But I did. That was exactly what I did.

33

CONSTANTINE

NORICUM, 15TH AUGUST 311 AD

The world was silent as I looked over the sea of chill dawn mist, streaked with pale fingers of first light. Dark islands of pine and crags of grey rock jutted from the fog. The brume clung to my skin, wetting my dry lips, droplets now and then running down the gilt nose guard of the jewelled helm gifted to me by Hisarnis then splashing onto my scale vest as my heart crunched, over and over. For a moment I dared to believe that I was the only soul present in the hills of Noricum. Until Celeritas snorted, breaking the silence.

The wall of soldiers – the six regiments of my Comitatus – stretched out before me on the low ridge shuffled, unnerved by the sound, each sparing just a trice and a glance to attribute it to Celeritas before returning their eyes to the languid sea of mist.

Days like this I knew all too well. Silence shattered by a foreign, jagged howl, or some tribal horn, moaning like a demon then shrieking like a hawk… and then the denizens of the wild woods would spill from the mist, come for me and my men like wolves. Today, it was different, and more chilling than ever… for it began not with a groan from a barbarian tusk, but with the long, fulsome, stirring song of a Roman buccina. The noise searched within my armour, within my skin… shook my very marrow.

To a man, my Comitatus braced and bristled. On my left: Krocus and the Regii, Tribunus Ruga and the Ubii, Batius and the Cornuti. On my right: Tribunus Scaurus with the Petulantes, Tribunus Micon with the Lancearii then Hisarnis and the Bructeri – all of them at once roused by the awful prospect of what lay ahead. Battle-twisted miens, staring eyes, puffing breaths… and their lips, moving over and over in prayer. And, by all the gods, I was asking the divinities the same questions: *is this right?*

But they came at us before the gods could answer. And they came like a silver storm. Six of Licinius' eastern legions – strong and fresh, some adorned like peacocks with tall, brightly dyed plumes and all charged by some homily from their commanders. They surged up the damp slopes at us like the horns of a bull, causing the earth to shudder under us. With a thrum and a whoosh, a cloud of slingshot and arrows spat up at us, battering into our shields, punching into flesh. Only a hastily thrown-up Cornuti shield spared me having my eye dashed out by a thrown stone. At that moment, I was sure this was divine retribution: for drawing such a small force of my own here in haste, to bring Roman iron upon Roman flesh… the gods *had* answered.

'*Spiculae!*' Batius thundered as they came to within fifty strides.

'For your emperor!' Hisarnis screamed as the line entire raised their iron-tipped javelins.

'For the *true* emperor!' yelled Ruga.

'For the Sun… for the true God!' Krocus howled.

I glanced across at the fiery-bearded warrior, a shiver rushing across my skin.

My wall of men exploded in a refrain the like of which I've never before heard. I swear the mist itself peeled away such was their voice. They hurled their spiculae with gusto, the lances sailing through the air and plunging into Licinius' front ranks with a staccato thunder of wet thuds and puffs of crimson mizzle. Men were knocked back, javelins harrowing their chests, legs kicking out before them. One took a lance square in the neck, the tip plunging on down into his chest. I gawped at the fellow as he sunk, eyes staring... at me... through me. At once I was sure the answer of the gods lay in the fellow's dying eyes. This was wrong... so wrong.

But a voice – familiar and unheard for some time – cut through the air and into my doubts. 'Take the bastard's pig-heart!' Licinius shrieked. I saw him, down at the foot of the ridge slope, ringed by his archers and slingers and well clear of my men's javelins and sheltered under trees in case we turned our bows upon him. His pudgy face was purple with misplaced righteousness, and the fine armour and high-plumed helm clung to him as ill-fittingly as a stolen silk cape on a beggar's back.

As our eyes met, so did our forces. With a din of shields and iron, visceral screams, the sharp *snap* of shearing bone and the swift *rasp* of tearing flesh, the cur's forces hammered against mine, just three of my ranks standing between me and their blades. Celeritas stumbled backwards and the Cornuti bunched around me as Licinius' legions pushed. A spear's length in front of me, one of Licinius' men rose, lifted by the broiling iron swell, to slide across the sea of heads. He was limp as a rag toy, and I soon saw why: the back of his head was gone and the last strings of red-grey matter trailed from the cavity. I saw four of my veterans cut down by a gleeful century of easterners, saw swathes of Ruga's men falling to their knees in cries of pain. I heard Krocus, holding the left, cry out, and saw there Licinius' lot surging round his flank, pouring against his rearmost ranks. Then a wet death cry from my right: the same sight there, Hisarnis' oldest warriors sinking under plunging blades as Licinius' men wrapped around that side too.

I twisted to the ala of leather-helmed, mail-shirted equites gathered behind me – five hundred riders, each wide-eyed and eager like their mounts. 'To tame the bull, we cut off its horns,' I snarled. 'With me!' I heeled Celeritas towards the right, pulling my spatha from my scabbard, feeling the earth quake as my riders surged to keep pace. We fell into a rhombus-formation like the head of a spear then sped for Licinius' battle-giddy men.

As I trained my lance on the neck of a Roman soldier, I saw Mother in my mind's eye, saw tears on her cheeks. *For one God, for them all, hear me: of this, I have no choice*, I mouthed as we plunged into their ranks. My spear snapped back and jarred as I tore out the throat of the soldier. A swathe of bodies were carved asunder as we stampeded on into their midst like culling herdsmen. From somewhere in the blackness of my mind, I heard Galerius' death cackle once more – as if he was amused at my taking on of his old moniker. My sword juddered as I took the head of a legionary, my shoulder jarred as I thrust the tip down into the torso of another, my mind grew cold and numb as I hacked the arm from a third.

Hot, wet blood spattered us... but we did it. Damn what any man might say... *we did it!* We cleaved off one horn of Licinius' bull. When we peeled back and headed for the left, the men assailing Krocus and the fierce Regii there needed no more than a glance at us – charnel-red, steam rising from the gore upon us – to know they were done for. The bull was on its knees.

I heard enemy war cries turn to screams of pain, saw men plunging to their knees, smelt the waft of opened guts and fear-loosened bowels. The regiments of my Comitatus erupted in cries of victory even before the eastern legions peeled away in headlong flight. My eyes swung to the treeline down below as they did so. Deserted – the fog swirling where Licinius had been as if a spirit had sped through it. Gone to safety before the day had even fully turned against him. The rumours were true, it seemed: Licinius had the riches and resources Galerius had left him, but carried none of his predecessor's charisma or mettle.

And we were alone again. I found myself standing on the blood-stained ridgetop, panting, having slid from Celeritas' back in a stupor.

'He rides back whence he came, Domine,' Krocus rasped, spitting blood from a broken-toothed mouth.

'This is a momentous victory,' Ruga panted, staking his sword in the ground to prop his weight against it.

Hisarnis' helm slid from his head, his short, matted hair glistening with sweat. 'The eastern dog is whipped, and all will hear of it.'

I stared at the carpet of bodies around us. Romans, all of them. I looked up and met Batius' eye. Now I truly know how he had felt that day at Massilia, and I fully expected the big man to react as he had done then. But this time his face was hard, untouched by emotion, or at least caging it well within.

'Roman blood on our swords, old friend,' I whispered so only he could hear as I wiped a rag across my blade.

'So fate would have it,' he muttered, then looked to the rising sun, squinting. 'So God would have it.'

I beheld him for a moment: his craggy, broad features, and

a light in his eyes. 'We killed scores of our kin today, Batius. All told, many hundreds, nay thousands, lie still.' All around me I saw the men of my Comitatus issuing prayers. Some to their old forest gods, many to new. Some, even, fell to one knee and plunged their sword in the ground, head bowed... towards me.

Their acclamations were growing in a crescendo, tears were welling in my eyes... and then it happened. It was a moment that changed everything. I didn't realise it then. If only I had...

The branches shuddered in the spot down from the ridge – where Licinius had been. I froze, at first expecting fresh eastern legions to rush us. But instead, I was treated to the sight of Licinius himself reappearing once more, tumbling head over foot, booted back towards the ridge by one of Krocus' men. He rolled over and over in the damp bracken, his cape twisting and entangling him, his plumed battle helm falling away from his fiery-red, flabby face. Batius, Krocus and I set off at once, skidding down the ridge side, picking our way between the fallen men until we came before Licinius. He rolled to his knees before me, clutching in panic at his bare head in search of his fallen helm.

My soldiers formed a ring around him. 'I found him taking a piss in the trees, so I ran his two guards through and brought him to you, Domine.'

I might have laughed were it not such a grim moment.

'Constanti-C-C-Constan-C...' he stammered.

A few of my men laughed. I raised a finger to silence them. 'Are you trying to beg for your life?'

His lips flapped silently a few times before he made do with a hurried nod of the head.

In reply, I prised my jewelled battle helm from my head

and drew my recently cleaned spatha. Licinius' pig face grew moon-like, his eyes like those of an owl, fixed on the blade as I brought it to rest at the side of his neck. 'Maximian knelt before me, at the last,' I said in a low burr. 'At least I allowed him a moment to make peace with his gods. You, not so.'

As I swept my sword back, readying to strike, we were treated to a dull, wet rumble – like the sound of soldier porridge being spurted from a pig skin – and then the most horrific stink. Steam rose from Licinius as he stewed in his own faeces. It only strengthened my resolve all the more, and I drew my sword arm back a fraction farther for a harder, cleaner strike. But at the last, when I had set upon slicing his head off, he blurted out: 'I can give you something – something far greater than my head.'

I said nothing, simply staring at him, blade hovering. At last, I gave him the slightest rise of one eyebrow as an indication of interest.

'All this t-time, you have been pegged in the north-west. W-with Galerius and me in the East and Maxentius in the south, you have been unable to act against one for fear of the other falling upon your exposed flank.'

'Very perceptive,' I growled.

He shook his fat, pudgy head. 'No more,' he said, 'I can swear to you that I will not interfere should you choose to deal with the false emperor in Italia. My armies will never move against you, never set foot in the West again. All this... in exchange for my life.'

I heard my men's voices rise in excitement as they realised what this meant. It was like a sudden cage of fire, leaping to life. It was a gift I did not want, but one I was compelled to accept.

34

MAXENTIUS

I stood on the gleaming wet steps of the temple of Jupiter the Thunderer high on the Capitol, towering above the forum, the damp white robes of the pontifex maximus – the city's chief priest – draped piously over my head and reaching down to the floor as my arms stretched up from the folds, offering devotion to the father of Rome.

Behind me, inside the temple, I could hear the messy business that always followed a sacrifice. When the great deed had been done and the religious observations seen to, someone had to come and clean up the viscera, skin the beast and butcher it ready for the feast. Choice parts of the animal sizzled in a brazier, filling the temple with the overwhelming smoky stench of charring meat. That was one of the reasons I had hurried through the last parts of the ceremony and wandered out to the porticoed steps and the relatively rain-fresh air to be found there.

Gods. Sometimes, despite my role as the empire's chief priest, I wondered rather irreverently if gods were worth all the effort. I had seen precious few instances of divine intervention in my life, and even fewer for the general good. And yet I seemed to be at one temple or another in the city every few days overseeing a sacrifice or a blessing or some such. Zenas had once opined to me his bafflement that a city whose people seemed to spend every day of the year celebrating one god or another actually managed to get anything done, let alone conquer half the world. Of course, one might put that down to the will of the gods, but I had my private doubts about that too. After all, the Persians, the Goths, the Sarmatians, the Franks – all these peoples we had fought over the years – they all had their own gods, didn't they? And if we won our great empire through divine will where were *their* gods? No. Steel, muscle and will drove the state. Gods gave so little compared to what they were given.

Yet despite my misgivings, I kept my hands raised to Jove the Thunderer, worshipping under an open sky as was only right, despite the ceremony having been carried out inside due to the misty rain that had settled over the city. Even on my least pious days, I revered the very fabric of Rome, and that fabric was stitched together with the threads of religion and tradition.

Had I needed an indicator that something was wrong with Rome, I might have bitterly noted that in good years, when I stepped forth from the temple and raised my hands, intoning the ritual words, the people of Rome would be crowding the forum, heads turned skywards, cheering me and celebrating with me. Today there were plenty of people in the forum, despite the wet weather, but precious few were even concerned with my presence.

I finished my prayer, my voice barely loud enough to roll across the Capitol's summit through the endless muffling of the rain, let alone carry down to the public in the open spaces below. Falling silent, I peered down at the crowds, feeling rather underappreciated and sour. If this was the reception I got at the city's greatest temple, I was very much in two minds as to whether I would bother with the Aventine temple to Juno that afternoon or leave the duties there to some lesser pontiff.

My bitter musings were interrupted by a roar from below. Frowning, I squinted into the misty rain, across the square on the Capitol with its small pool and shrines, my eyes scouring the forum until they fell upon a knot of citizens in the open space between the temple of the Divine Augustus and the Basilica Iulia. Something was happening there, the people surging this way and that as if involved in either a brutal wrestling match or some rabid dance. I couldn't see what they were doing at first, the distance being great and the air filled with endless mizzle. Then I caught sight of a brightly painted figure amid the crowd, larger than life, that broad, handsome-in-a-rural-kind-of-way face staring up at me in an accusatory manner.

Constantine.

One of the many statues I had commissioned almost three years ago to celebrate his marriage to my sister – a futile gesture at reconciliation and the binding ties of family. I had since learned that all family ties did was destroy one's freedom. Yet somehow, despite everything that had happened – even though I had grown to despise what Constantine had become: a man who had defamed my mother and killed my father – it had never occurred to me to have the statues of him removed. Even the one in my aula regia that I passed on a daily basis and that sat at the heart of my palaces. I should have removed them all, really. We Romans are fickle with our heroes – always have been. Over the centuries an emperor's image might be found on every street corner, and then the

Praetorian Guard would draw their blades. The next day the throne would be worn smooth by a new worthy backside and those many busts and statues would be either torn down or reworked to resemble the latest usurper.

Yet Constantine had remained. All across the city his wide, deceiving face smirked out at me. Why *had* I not ordered them removed? Still, the public seemed to be tearing one down right now. I watched that wide, country-boy face vanish into the press of people as the statue snapped at the ankles and fell, probably crushing some rabid nobody. Why they had suddenly taken it upon themselves to destroy him, I couldn't say, and I was torn by conflicting emotions at the sight. Part of me was furious that my people would tear down my creations, no matter their nature. Part was abhorrent that the people would destroy the image of an emperor, even if he was now our enemy. A large, seething, wicked part of me was glad they had done it and wished I was there, stamping hobnails into the painted face of the man rumour said had entered into an alliance with Licinius. And the small part that still filled with nerves at the thought of confrontation was grateful that they had done it and not me. Conflict within; conflict without. Conflict everywhere.

The folds of my white robe were starting to become saturated and I felt the rain drip from the end of my nose. Perhaps it was time to go back inside.

I turned and the lictors who stood in neat lines to either side, keeping citizens away from the imperial person – or at least there to do so had there *been* any citizens on the Capitol – turned on their heels like soldiers, preparing to follow me wherever I went. Two figures, though, had emerged from the rain around the corner of the temple and were scurrying towards me. Volusianus was dressed in his toga, but you would never meet a man who carried such a military bearing even in civil dress. He wore the white robe like a cuirass, and the clacking and scraping of military boots beneath the hem complemented the bulge near the armpit where a sword hilt showed through the toga. Behind him was Zenas, similarly dressed in a toga yet managing to look less like a soldier and more like a politician. Both men wore scowls and I knew from their looks alone that trouble had raised its ugly head again. They wouldn't wear such faces for the smashing of a statue. Indeed, Volusianus had advocated just that more than once.

'Domine,' Volusianus began in respectful tones, aware that he was standing before a temple to our greatest god and surrounded by very edgy lictors.

'What is it, Volusianus?'

'Have you heard the rumours yet?'

I frowned and my gaze slipped to Zenas, who had turned an equally furrowed brow on his companion. 'Respectfully,' the Christian said to my Praetorian Prefect, 'that is not the most urgent issue here.'

'It is the *only* issue here,' snapped Volusianus angrily.

'The provocation to war is less important than *rumour*?'

The prefect turned on Zenas, more or less ignoring me now. 'The "*provocation to war*", as you call it, Zenas, is the direct result of the rumours, and something that should have been done years ago in my opinion.'

'That, Volusianus, is because you want war without understanding the consequences. We could...'

'AHEM!' I barked, silencing the pair of them, leaving them standing less than a foot apart as though about to butt heads, glaring at one another. It was so reminiscent of Volusianus and Anullinus in earlier days that it set my teeth on edge just to look at them.

'Domine,' Volusianus said again, flashing a warning glance at Zenas, 'there is news.'

'Rumour,' corrected Zenas, earning an exasperated, angry snarl.

'*Rumour*,' the prefect repeated, 'has reached the city concerning your noble father.'

My father? My father was dead. Had been now for quite some time. And even I, who had had him deified and minted coins in his memory, might baulk at applying the term 'noble' to the fat, usurping martinet who had ruled my life with not even an echo of love. Still, I was interested. I nodded for him to go on.

'It seems, Domine, that what we understood of your father's passing was only part of the story. The men we have in Constantine's court have gleaned more knowledge. It seems that the truth is darker. Your father was not permitted to end himself honourably as we had thought. Constantine, it seems, made an example of him. It appears that he was garrotted, in public. Gasping out his last breaths as the cord bit into his throat while Constantine's barbaric soldiers, his shaved barbarians in Roman tunics, leered on from the square.'

I narrowed my eyes. 'I spotted rather a lot of "*appears*" and "*seems*" among your words, Volusianus. You do not sound sure.'

'Domine, this is coming from the mouths of our own men. From the frumentarii. From Ancharius Pansa, in fact, a man with an unparalleled knowledge of subterfuge, infiltration and intelligence gathering.'

'If the men we sent to Constantine's cities are sending us back information, why do I hear nothing useful about troops and supplies and political divisions, just rumours of personal attacks? Why are rumours abounding in Rome about he and Licinius when I have had no such confirmation?'

That being said, with my recently so-tarnished opinion of my old friend, I would not put such a thing past him. Garrotted in public? That was no way for an emperor to die. I saw him in the eye of my mind, collapsing to his knees on the stone of Massilia's forum, blood sheeting from his neck. Then I saw once more the painted face of Constantine falling into the crowd. Suspicion filled me, and I pursed my lips, drawing in a deep breath.

'Is there the slightest chance, Volusianus, that this information has reached the Roman people before it reached my own ears.'

The prefect had the grace to look a little embarrassed 'The lady Valeria once reminded you, Domine, that rumour travels faster and is more damaging than any arrow. She urged you to blacken Constantine's reputation and set me to the task, but it would appear that he is doing the job for us.'

'You are sure of the truth of this?' I asked.

'Sure? No, Domine. I can say nothing for certain that has come from another man's lips, but I have no valid reason to doubt it. Do you?'

Zenas was almost vibrating with urgency, and I switched my gaze to him, an action he took as permission to address me.

'They are tearing down Constantine's statues and smashing his busts.'

'I saw it in the forum just now.'

'Domine, it is happening all across the city, like a wave of hatred.'

'Rumour?' I prompted Volusianus darkly.

'The spies bring us other information, Domine. But this is... incendiary.'

'Constantine will learn that his statues are being smashed.' I shrugged. 'Given his own acts, I hardly think he can stand on some moral high ground and take offence. Could he confront me over the matter, I might retort with a question as to how many statues he had raised to his brother-in-law across his cold, wintry empire. No. He has no right to be offended. In fact, perhaps we should enact a law restricting his image. We might destroy all his images, even the ones in my own palace. Why should the plebs have all the fun, eh?'

Zenas paled. 'Domine, do we really want to push Constantine any further? Word will reach him of this violation and he will feel honour-bound to do something about it. If you will not stop this destruction, then you must prepare for war.'

'Constantine is not ready for war.'

Volusianus now rounded on me. 'How can you say that, Domine? He rode forth with an army to scourge Licinius and, if what we hear is true, bound the dog to him. If there *was* a treaty of non-aggression between himself and Licinius, Constantine would no longer need to fear for his other borders and would be at liberty to turn his attentions to you. Worse yet, what will happen if Licinius decides there is much to be gained from *joining* Constantine in marching on Rome?'

'Licinius' army outnumber Constantine severely. If he has beaten the dog then it was through trickery and deceit, not strength of arms. If Licinius was shrewd, Constantine's head should now be bouncing around on the tip of a Licinian spear. Also, our army is bigger than either Licinius' or Constantine's, and *no one* could trust Licinius enough to invite him to join them. No. Constantine, even if he wanted to come for us, couldn't do so yet.'

'Even if Constantine and Licinius do not join together, what value is our huge army if the pair take turns at us, like crows at a hanging body.' Volusianus sighed. 'Domine, I told you that the spies bring us other news also. Men from Constantine's armies are beginning to concentrate in southern Gaul, and only a fool would think this a deterrent to Licinius even if these rumours we hear are false.' I scowled at the implication I was being foolish, but he was in full flow now. 'Constantinian scouts have been seen in the passes of the Alpes. You cannot imagine they are there to enjoy the mountain air and some of that fine Raetian cheese? Constantine masses men at our border, and we provoke him.'

'I thought that was what you wanted?' I snapped rather harshly.

'Yes,' Volusianus barked in reply, forgetting his honorifics in his irritation. 'Yes, I advocate severing all ties with your brother-in-law. I advocate driving him mad with hate and anger, because angry, hateful men make mistakes. And I advocate war, because until you are undisputed master of the West you will never be able to face Daia or Licinius. I advocate war. A war of extinction. And it will be cruel – Roman against Roman – legions butchering legions, yet it is necessary. Yes, I agree with all of that!'

I was leaning back as though a hurricane had emerged between his teeth.

'But,' Volusianus spat angrily, 'not without being *prepared*. We are not prepared for war. Our armies are spread throughout Italia and Africa, concentrated in the north to some extent, but even then spread out to ward off attacks from any side. And we should be drawing defensive lines, fortifying cities. Choosing battlefields for when we need them and clearing out the populace from danger zones. We should be building defensive systems. In half a decade, Hadrian built a stone wall eighty miles long with fortresses, milecastles, ditches and crossing points. We have more men in the north than he had in Britannia and they do nothing but train. We might not have that sort of time, but they should be preparing the region as best they can.'

'Though we might not wish to push the men *too* far, Domine,' interrupted Zenas, earning another black look.

'Why?' I asked.

'Because pay is scarce. It filters into the more important veteran units first, and those in places of high value. But there is not enough to pay every man each month, and there is the constant threat of dissent.'

I rounded on Volusianus. 'Why am I finding out about this now?'

My prefect gave me a bitter look. 'With respect, Domine, I warned you about precisely this two months ago. You paid the Christians off and that drained the treasury. Left too little to pay the men. Now your Christians—' he nodded, sneering, at Zenas '—are happy and fat and wealthy and our borders tremble under the angry boots of unpaid soldiers.'

'Then we need more money,' I said decisively. Volusianus almost rolled his eyes at the statement of the obvious.

'Money has to come from somewhere, Domine,' Zenas put in. 'That inevitably means from the people in the end, and the people are already heavily taxed. The buildings, the walls, the army, the war – everything has cost the people dearly. I must warn you against further taxation.'

I felt my frustration growing as I shook the water from my head covering, then was unable to settle the soggy wool back into its position. I fought with it for a long moment and then with a bark of anger threw it down to hang among the other folds, allowing the cleansing rain to wet my scalp.

'Then give me another solution. We need money but you advise me not to raise any.'

Volusianus harrumphed and looked at Zenas. The two men seemed to have some silent conversation, carried out through their eyes. The younger Christian sighed and shrugged. 'War.'

Volusianus chewed his lip for a moment as I frowned, then nodded slowly. 'Maybe that's the only way. Maybe we *don't* prepare any more, after all. If we prepare, we give Constantine more time to ready himself. Perhaps we simply move the bulk of the forces north and commit? Try and take him while he is equally unprepared?'

'What?' I frowned. I knew what they were saying, of course, but it seemed incredible, especially given how Volusianus in particular had been advocating precisely the opposite mere moments ago.

'War, Domine,' Volusianus said, receiving a nod from Zenas. 'You cannot afford to pay the troops, and tax is no solution. Taxing the rich will destroy your support and credibility. Taxing the poor will risk revolt. Taxing the outlying regions might send them running to your opposition. Tax is not a viable option. But if we went to war with Constantine now, the army would be too occupied to worry about missing pay for a month or two. And by the time things had been settled and we were in control of the Alpes and southern Gaul, the troops would be inevitably fewer, while our funds would have grown through plunder. Hardly an elegant solution, Domine, I grant you, but a solution nonetheless.'

I blinked. War? Was he mad? Save on troop wages by killing off my army in a war in the mountains? No. I still did not believe Constantine would come for me. Even if the desire was in him, the practicalities were lacking. He couldn't. He wouldn't manage it. He wouldn't dare. And I would not go down in history as a man who launched a civil war, killing Romans and family in the process. If that had to happen, Constantine would have to start it.

'No.'

'Domine, I fear you do not have the luxury of too many options. Besides, when Constantine hears of this destruction of his images, he might well decide we are far more of an enemy than he had thought and come for us. I admit that I was wrong to advocate preparation just now. Strike first. Licinius would sit on the periphery and watch. He and Constantine might have a pact of non-aggression, or they might not, but either way he would not waste men if he can let others do his work for him. He will let us deal with Constantine. I am certain of that.'

'No. Never.'

Zenas was nodding along with Volusianus now, which was a worrying development and a sure indicator that I was making the wrong decision. But I still made it, even aware that I was probably being unwise. I could do nothing else. I would not start a civil war with my brother-in-law.

'That is my final word on the matter. No to war. Shuffle around some troops if you wish. Set them digging ditches and raising ramparts if you think it will help, but we will not march beyond our territory. I will speak to my treasury officials. We will work out the bare minimum of funds we require and I will have a blanket tax put on the entire empire. The load will be borne equally by all and will be the lightest load we can make it. The people will understand. It is for their security, after all.'

'Domine, this is folly,' Zenas said quietly but urgently.

'It may be, but it is also my command. I shall have the tax levied urgently and we will get the money to the army within the month. And if you are worried about such a fictitious build-up of men in the south of Constantine's domain, Volusianus, take the three legions covering the major Italian ports and send them north to Verona and Aquileia. They can support the troops on the border.' I saw Volusianus winding up for another tirade and turned my back on him, throwing my sodden robe over my head again and fussing angrily at its positioning as I snapped my fingers to the lictors and we stomped off.

It was the wrong decision, and I knew it. It was also the only one open to me.

I took out my anger on the seven busts of Constantine I found on the Palatine, and that grand statue of him in my aula regia, smashing marble until my knuckles bled.

35

CONSTANTINE

We returned from the clash in Noricum to Treverorum in the dead of night. I had dispersed the regiments of my Comitatus to their nearby base forts and billet towns along the way and entered the city with just Batius and a century of Cornuti in tow, to a man soaked by billowing, relentless mizzle. Nobody but the gate guard noticed our return... just as I had hoped. I had sent scout riders ahead to tell of my victory and that terms had been reached but I had expressly demanded that no assumptions were to be made, and certainly no plans to be formed in my absence. Not yet. Not until I had had a chance to think.

I took the quiet but firm salutes of the palace gate guards. Good, I thought: And then... I caught one of the sentries flashing eyes at the other – eyes brimming with excitement and anticipation of triumphal celebration. I pinned him with a look that had the effect of two glowing copper rods, almost nailing him to the stonework of the gatehouse.

'You have something to say, soldier?' I growled, my voice not nearly as ferocious as my glare.

The soldier nodded anxiously, licking his lips before

saying in almost a boyish whisper: 'Is, is it true, Majesty? Has Licinius thrown open the way to Italia... a clear road for you to topple the Tyrant of Rome?'

'You make it sound like such a simple matter, soldier.'

'Domine,' he agreed with a gulp then stood rigid, not daring to meet my gaze again.

I rolled my eyes at a thoroughly craggy-looking Batius and bid him goodnight as he headed off to his nearby villa. I entered the palace grounds, dismissed my pair of Cornuti escorts and clattered through the high halls until I came to my bedchamber, throwing off my robes and boots and collapsing onto the soft bedding. Through my open door and across the corridor I could see the locked door of Fausta's room. Apart from that fraught moment when she had been on the edge of slicing my throat open, I realised, we had never shared a bed and likely never would. I, the true Augustus of the West, master of millions, had never been more alone. The warmth of the woollen blankets and the cool comfort of the silk sheets were no replacement for a companion, and I could only think longingly of the bygone nights with Minervina. Of her naked body cupped alongside mine, of the scent of her skin, of the heat of her against me. Such taunting memories faded at last, gradually obscured by the silvery threads of sleep.

It was a restful, deep, and much-needed slumber. Blackness, unspoilt. But after some time passed, I realised there was someone in there with me. A distant, tiny figure. I willed myself closer to it. Someone familiar? As I drew close I saw that it was my first spouse. She was as hale and striking as ever I had seen her. Her sweet, dusky, heart-shaped face lifting in a radiant smile, her ample curves accentuated by a red gown. In her hands she clasped a simple, wooden token – imprinted with an emblem of a fish, the symbol of her faith.

'Minervina?' I croaked, reaching out with a shapeless hand across the ether of the dream. My beloved wife, little Crispus' mother... she had come back.

I rose and moved towards her, soundless syllables escaping my lips, tears streaking my face. 'How can this be?' I managed to utter. At that moment, I was unaware that this was the strange netherworld of sleep, you see. And when I came to within a pace of her I saw that it was not as I thought. This was not Minervina. For her eyes shone like distant stars – touched with something that was not of the realm of men. As my realisation arrived, her smile faded and her expression darkened. 'Who are you?' I whispered, suddenly wary.

'I am whatever you wish me to be,' she replied, her voice a deafening whisper that rushed all around me like a gale. She changed then, like the shadows cast by a candle on a wall, becoming another: tall, hale, proud, draped in a toga... 'Father?' I croaked, falling to one knee. Indeed it was him in every aspect of appearance – as he was before the canker worked its claws into him... as he was when I was a boy. But still... still those eyes were not of a man. And from his hands, a shield sprouted like a flower opening to the morning sun. A battle spear appeared in his other palm and on his head he wore a tall, gloriously plumed helm. A vision of Mars!

'Who are you?' I demanded.

'That is the question you must answer,' it replied. As it spoke, it changed again, and lanced me through with a shiver of fright, for there before me was... *me!* Clad in bronze scale, eyes glowing like coals still and on its head, on *my* head – a wreath, a wreath of *light!* It was just as I had been on that day at the ruined shrine of Apollo.

'The way is clear. The journey must commence. Show them the truth, Constantine, bring them together...'

'What does this mean?' I croaked. But the vision was fading before me. The darkness lightening. At once, it was as if the invisible ether below me was whipped away: I was falling. Flailing, I swung my arms out at the grey all around me and a terrible scream permeated the nightmare.

I woke with a start, sitting bolt upright, my sheets tangled around me, stuck there with sweat. My scream echoed and died to nothing. Daylight streamed in through the shutters which I had neglected to secure the previous night. There was a moment of silence where I ran my fingers through my unwashed hair and across my unshaven jaw. I could not shake the image of the molten-eyed being from my dream, a shiver dancing down my back.

Then from the streets came the most unwelcome din.

'All hail our glorious emperor, all hail Constantine!' one voice blared.

A chorus of cornua erupted to put music to the cry, then drums thundered. Men and women cheered and sang. I heard the splash of freely offered wine and the clack of cups, smelt the tang of roasting boar and the never-ending shriek of laughter. Stumbling from my bed and throwing a sheet around my waist, I stepped gingerly onto the balcony. The rains had ceased overnight and now the streets were awash with celebration.

'Licinius has been routed! The world will soon belong to Constantine,' one fellow howled before closing his eyes and draining an entire jug of wine as if to punctuate the claim. In the alleys I saw the writhing forms of rutting couples. Less than an arrowshot away, screened from such debauchery by the city walls, a Christian gathering stood in a cemetery meadow and sang around the graves. Songs to their God, songs of celebration.

On the rooftops all across the city and the *vicus* outside, I saw dancers and acrobats, women tossing petals down on the revellers below.

'Fine morning, Domine,' Batius said from behind me.

I swung round to him, startled. 'No triumph, I said. No plans, no great proclamations!'

Batius shook his head. 'You know as well as I do, news like this cannot be put to one side.'

I spun around, swinging back a leg with the intention of booting a clay pot, halting just as I remembered it was actually thick marble. 'Drunks I can abide.'

'Glad to hear it, Domine,' Batius said with a hint of a smile, patting the drinking skin that hung from his belt.

'But tell me... pray to all the gods... tell me that somehow *they* are remaining calm and at bay.'

'They?' Batius said.

'The nobles, the priests, the bishops!'

But a cry from the corridor behind Batius dashed all my hopes in one pompous outburst. 'This is a glorious day – a *most* glorious day!'

I heard the drumming of sandals and boots stomping along the corridor, growing louder along with the polyglot babble of the self-important. I shot Batius a pre-battle glare then threw on my military tunic and stepped into my boots, stomping past him to the door. There, in the passageway, a pack of dreadfully familiar faces were striding at haste towards my chambers. A pontifex led them, a dark-robed Rex Sacrorum by his side, his face in shade, the wide cowls of his cloak rising and falling like the hood of a cobra. The temple haruspex hurried to keep pace with them. Upon seeing me, their faces brightened like cats who had just spotted a plump mouse in a corner.

'Domine!' the pontifex gushed, throwing his hands up in salute and celebration. 'We have matters to discuss. *Urgent* matters.'

'Not now,' I growled under my breath and turned away from them to pace off down the corridor. But they followed, unabated.

Batius, reading my dismay, was quick to step out before they could reach me, tossing a white cloak around my shoulders and gesturing towards the great meeting chamber. 'Give audience to them,' he whispered. 'Hear them out at lea—'

His words went unfinished as we passed an adjoining passageway, and caught sight of the two less-than-homesick bishops, Maternus and Ossius, vulture-like, swooping towards me. 'God has shown the way. Licinius is broken. The road to Italia beckons. Now the south will shudder. Rome can be liberated. The ordained thirty-year reign can begin with a holy victory. The tyrant Maxentius can be brought to heel like Licinius!' Ossius pronounced as if it issuing a decree.

'The south *must* be dealt with, Domine. They say Maxentius tosses busts of you down on the ground and laughs openly,' Bishop Maternus wailed dramatically.

The two factions, eternally opposed until now, came together in the confluence of corridors, pursuing me, harrying me, braying in demand. I stalked on down the hallway, determined to defy them.

Then, up ahead, I saw the meeting chamber doors. But waiting there was a cadre of men in cuirass and soldier garb. Baudio, prefect of the Second Italica. Vindex of the First Martia. Micon of the Lancearii. Krocus too. My generals turned from their huddle, as one. Their faces were stony, resolute. They came towards me like a third pincer.

'This opportunity cannot be passed up, Domine. Trade and travel have ground to a halt,' Baudio said. 'The great roads all over the empire are blocked with armies, restless, eager to use their blades or put them down. They wait for your word!'

'Maxentius has an army three times the strength of mine,' I snapped, barging past the generals like a cavalryman breaching an infantry line.

'But your legions are skilled and strong!' Bishop Maternus shrieked as the three bands pursued me. 'It will be the final step. A swift, decisive end to the Tyrant of Rome's reign.'

I cast a look over my shoulder at the bishop. 'Do you know what happened to Galerius and his armies when they marched into Italia? Many times more numerous than mine, his legions were annihilated there. I witnessed the few who survived as they fled in defeat.' I batted my chest. 'I saw them crossing the wintry passes of Noricum. Men staggering through the frozen wastes, little more than skeletons, eating tough roots, skin bruised with blackened and untended wounds. And so very few of them, so very, very few.' I leaned a little closer. 'Thousands fell on the hills of Narnia, cut to pieces by Maxentius' army. And those poor beggars who staggered past me in the icy ravine? I saw it in their eyes: many of them would have gladly traded fates with their dead comrades.'

'You are... afraid of him, Domine?' Bishop Maternus said, his tone dripping with triumph, his eyes shining like the many precious trinkets he had acquired in recent times.

I ignored the others and glowered at Maternus. 'Maxentius has defeated Severus, repelled Galerius, ousted his worm of a father. He has nearly one hundred and twenty thousand soldiers. He holds a chain of formidable, ancient fortified cities of Italia. He has Rome, a city he has wrapped in high walls... damn him!' I spat, thrusting a fist past a now less-cocky Maternus' face and into the wall right next to his head. In my mind's eye all I could see was the wooden block city the boy Maxentius had built when first we met as youngsters. My words... my own damned words!

If you hold the greatest city in the world – a glittering jewel coveted by all others – the first thing to set your mind to is its protection. Your city lacks walls. High ones. Strong ones.

'Licinius has pledged to stay out of western affairs... but...' I began, shaking with rage, 'does that mean we must pounce on the chance to paint the West in Roman blood? Do you know how many legionaries we sliced down in Noricum? How much more blood must be spilled to please your gods?' I snarled, halting at the great doors and turning to eye the pincer-arc of bishops, generals and pontifices together.

'Domine, perhaps... perhaps you should consider the idea,' Batius said.

'You too, Batius?' I almost wept.

'I do not relish the slaying of Romans. But I fear that to hesitate will bring more bloodshed in the longer term. Does that not make it a lesser evil? Your reputation soars, Domine. Your armies venerate you as a god. They are ready to mobilise in full.'

I thought of that dream from just a short while ago. The memory of falling almost had me grabbing the walls for balance. My breath grew short and my throat narrowed. It was a panic like that which had beset me all those years ago, on the day my father had forsaken Mother and I. I swung away from them, barged the meeting hall doors open and swept inside. Swiftly, I spun on my heel and threw them closed again, seeing the faces of the mob gawp in surprise.

Quick as a lion, I pulled the ornate bronze locking bar on this side across the doorway, shutting them all out.

With a thick clunk, there was silence.

For that moment they were mute. I couldn't even hear the clamour from the streets. Soon enough though, I heard the buzz of instruments and laughter from the carousers out there, and after that the horde beyond the door erupted in a chorus of protest. Some beat their fists on the doors, others simply wailed their case over and over.

I turned away from the doorway and trudged to the semi-circle of deserted marble steps. I plodded to the table stocked with wine and poured a cup of it from a jug. One cup became two. Two became five. Soon, I found myself in an absurd counsel with my own thoughts... and a thousand ghosts.

I looked around the chamber, seeing Father, Galerius, Severus gazing back at me. Maximian too, wearing the rope that had choked the life from him as if it were a *torc*. The steps were filled with an army of dead men who had at some time been part of my life. Not one of the curs offered the slightest hint of support, each simply staring, empty-eyed, right through me.

I let my head loll to escape their imagined stares. When I looked up again, my head now swimming with the wine, the counsel of shades had adjourned. Instead, I saw just Maxentius. Not the boy with the toy wooden city, but the stern-faced man I had to confront. He said nothing, but his eyes said everything.

I laughed wryly and took a long, deep drink of my wine. I stood and climbed the steps to the high, open arched windows, standing in one of the small balconies to gaze over the autumn day. The song of triumphal joy continued unabated from the streets – straw effigies of the vanquished Licinius now being hoisted in the forum. The green hills beyond the walls and the meandering teal ribbon of the River Mosa sang a song of tranquillity. For all the world it seemed that a better time had come, and to all those in the streets and farmlands, I wished for it to be true.

I turned my gaze south, seeing the distant hazy blue countryside fade into the azure infinity of the sky. Somewhere far beyond lay Italia. In that ancient land the manipulative pup who thought himself my equal resided – still – in Rome. His hectoring words from Romuliana swarmed and stung at my wine-addled mind. Another desert-dry chuckle. Another mouthful of wine. Teeth grinding. Angry heat spreading over my chest.

'Does it ever feel to you, old friend,' I said, the once-genuine term dripping with spite, 'that we are destined to meet again, in very different circumstances?'

Silence. I wondered if, right now, Maxentius stood on the balcony of his unlawfully occupied city, up on Rome's famed palace hill, spiting me in return. Silence continued. For a trice, I imagined myself on the warm summer zephyrs, spirited south to Rome, striding up the hillside to enter the palace, taking it as my own, claiming it as I perhaps should have done long before now – as the baying pack beyond the doors demanded of me. It sent streaks of dread and desire through me – fire and ice.

My gaze fell to the palace gardens. I wish it had not. Down there sat Mother, Fausta and Crispus. They played and sang, my boy leaping and spinning as they clapped. It was how things should have been for me. Now? Now it looked like another man's life. This fine balcony had no bars or cage, but I felt like a prisoner all the same. I swear I heard Maximian's shade cackle behind me. When Fausta looked away from the play and up at me, her face grew impassive, like a mask donned to protect the wearer, and I felt the sun setting in my heart.

Loss comes in many forms. When I lost sweet Minervina to the cold hand of death, all those years ago, I at least had the chance to embrace her one last time – after her body had been washed and anointed by the Christian priests – to kiss her forehead, comb her hair and to pay her the respect she was due with a fine funeral. This was loss of a different kind. There would be no embrace, no kiss, no proper end. And if only I had known then what a wicked road remained for her and I to tread…

I barely noticed the pair entering the hall from a small side door – directly connected to my map room. Batius waited at the bottom of the steps while Lactantius climbed the stairs to come alongside me.

Lactantius. Surely the voice of reason. He stood with me in silence for a while, gazing over the countryside.

'I had a dream last night,' I said sadly, breaking the silence at last. 'A god stood before me.' Then I shook my head and corrected myself: '*all* the gods.'

As I told the story, Lactantius listened intently, his eyes narrowing in interest and widening in wonder. 'With whom did I speak, old tutor?'

The old fellow's eyes grew misty, as if a great realisation had settled upon him. 'You spoke with the Divine Mind,' he said, 'the will of God, Constantine, of the one and only God.'

I frowned, confused. '*The* God. Which is *the* God?'

He smiled and his eyes sparkled. 'The one who has watched over you. The one who has elected you as his chosen child, just as Virgil foresaw. You have survived many grim times, Constantine. Wars uncountable. Galerius' court! You fled across the empire alone in the dark heart of winter. You took your father's place at the helm of the West and have been its true steward ever since... and I believe it was all for a good reason.'

Because it was my right! I roared inwardly.

'God has guided you to this moment. Because you are the one who can bring peace at long, long last. Sometimes, peace can only thrive in the absence of the wicked. Your old friend is not wicked – I sincerely believe that. But his cadre and the beast that his realm has become, truly is.'

My heart sank. I realised now that Lactantius too was minded like the mob at the doors. 'Peace? By starting a war?' I snapped. '*Another* war?'

'The war began long ago. The son of God said the end of the world will come: a clash that will be the end for many, many souls yet it will also bring peace at last. Be sure you are on the right side, Constantine. The time has come to choose.'

'Time?' I said, remaining with my back turned at the top of the steps.

Time! the counsel of wraiths hissed all around me, unseen.

The doors of the meeting chamber shuddered with renewed banging and unruly shouts from the pontifices and bishops in the corridor outside.

'The legions crave your word, Domine,' Batius added. 'The empire is on the edge of disaster. Galerius is gone. Loathsome as he was, at least he provided an air of authority, a modicum of stability to the East. The West at least needs such a man at the helm. With Rome, with all Italia and Africa firmly in your guiding hand, Licinius and Daia would never dare challenge you again.'

'A guiding hand?' I mused, seeing a soldier's hand, clasping a blade, steel and knuckles soaked with blood.

Conquer or be conquered! one of the shades whispered in my ear.

I felt their gazes upon my back. Heard the babble of the streets outside grow clamorous – shrieking revellers, thudding drums, cavorting masses. My head seemed set to explode.

Then I looked down on my family in the gardens below. At the last, I thought of my adversary in Rome, not as an emperor but as a man. Maxentius, his dead boy, his deformed tot and his strident wife. A tiny spark ignited within my breast. A last touch of warmth in a fast-cooling, dark cavern.

'Well, Domine,' Batius asked, 'what is it to be?'

36

MAXENTIUS

'We need to get you to safety, Majesty,' said Ruricius Pompeianus, leaning on the low wall in front of the great bronze statue of Titus Seius, who looked down his nose at us from metallic horseback, as noble as a Roman could be, and clearly disapproving of what I'd done to his city.

From the vantage point of this parapet on the Capitol I had a good view of the whole forum spread out between the crowded Palatine and the various great edifices of my predecessors that kept the *subura* region at bay. The view was not a sight to bring relief.

It had begun at the start of the month as mumbled protests, but had taken only days to become angry voices. At first I had dismissed it, concentrating instead on the news from the East. Diocletian had died. The man who had designed the destiny of Rome with his Tetrarchy, who had been the scourge of the Christians, the undisputed master of the Roman world and at whose signal men had risen and fallen, had died. And what a death. They said that he simply stopped eating and slowly starved to cadaverous waste, sick in both body and mind, ravaged by the knowledge of what had become of his intended new world. I liked to think that perhaps some of what had driven him to his lingering suicide was guilt over the burning of his wife, but even at his death I could not imagine that. As the realisation of his passing sunk in, so we were led to face the problems that still faced us in the living world.

Rome can be fractious and argumentative, and I had seen protests and even riots in my time here, but it had always been something we could resolve one way or another. This, it seemed, was something different. To resolve the religious crisis in my lands I had healed the rift among the Christians with money from the treasury. That had solved that problem but left us short to pay what was now a vast army. Thus I had exchanged potential trouble with the Christians for potential trouble with unpaid soldiers. Well, while I wanted rid of the trouble with the Christians, *no one* wants trouble with the army, and so, flying in the face of the guidance of my closest advisors, I'd taxed the Roman people extra to pay the army.

Now, the Christians and the army were both content once more, but the ordinary folk were outraged. It seemed I was in the midst of a great puzzle with no solution. I had three mouths to feed and only two cakes, so I kept passing them around for each mouth to take a bite. I could find no way to ease the tax burdens of the people, but that had not set me on the edge of panic the way unpaid soldiers or warlike Christians had. After all, if you have to anger a group, the ordinary person is surely the safest? Well I had thought so, anyway.

Now I was coming to understand just how wrong I had been. I had over a hundred thousand soldiers in my empire that I had mollified. There were perhaps a similar number of Christians, at a guess, who had now stopped burning each other's houses. But the ordinary people? There were over a million of them in the city alone, *ten times* that many across my domain. Disenfranchising young 'Gaius Plebeius Nobody' seemed safe enough, but *several million* 'Gaius Plebeius Nobodies' started to look like a threat.

Then, this afternoon, the threat had been made good. It was the end of the festival of *Compitalia* – the veneration of the crossroads, when honey cakes were given and statues and woollen figures adorned every door. A time of general goodwill and neighbourly spirits. As always, despite Volusianus' warnings, I had come to the Capitol to give thanks at the temple of Ops, the god of abundance and plenty. It was one of my lesser and more relaxed religious duties. I had entered the small temple, which stood somewhat in awe of the great temple of Jove that overshadowed it, an hour earlier. I had presided over the rites therein, pausing only briefly at an increase in the background noise of the city outside.

Then, before I had even uncovered my head, Volusianus had entered, cursing in a most impious manner. He and Ruricius had apologised to the small knot of officials who had been with me, and all but dragged me out of the place. I had been incensed, blustering and arguing. The pair, surrounded by Praetorians, had taken me over to the parapet and then let go of me. I had shouted angrily at them, demanding to know what right they had to manhandle an emperor. My ranting, though, had trailed off into a horrified silence as the noise around me made itself known, filtering into my angry ears above my own voice. I'd torn my furious gaze from Volusianus and cast it across the forum.

We were at war. At war with our own people. Or at least, that was how it looked.

With the two officers and their men close to heel, I ran

along the wall, past the doorway of the Porta Stercoraria, grateful that it was only opened once a year and right now remained resolutely locked, separating me from what was happening in the forum. I reached the wall at the far side of the gate where I had a much better view of the forum's open spaces, and my heart rose into my mouth, threatening to make me gag.

'We need to get you to safety, Majesty,' said Ruricius Pompeianus.

Bronze, immutable, Titus Seius stared down at me.

'Surely this is just a public nuisance that can be quelled as always?' I murmured, watching the seething mass of humanity down below and not even remotely believing my own words.

'Zenas has gone to try that. See towards the Flavian amphitheatre? And along the Vicus Iugarius?'

My eyes roved across the roiling mass of Roman citizenry to catch sight of two new groups moving onto the scene. The Urban Cohorts were approaching between the Temple of Rome and the Palatine. Good old Zenas had brought in his men to pacify the rioting crowds. I could see little more from this distance other than the fact that nearly a whole cohort of armoured men were moving in perfect unison. They formed a shield wall and began to push into the crowd. I couldn't see for certain, but I knew they would not be wielding swords. Zenas' men were usually armed with coshes. They would be laying into the people if need be, using examples to deter further resistance. It was not what I wanted to see for my people, but it could be worse. Zenas was ever a sensible man.

The second group, coming up the Vicus Iugarius from the river, was a unit bearing colours I didn't know.

'Who is that?'

'Moesian auxiliary unit, Majesty. They've been based in

the Castra Peregrina in the city for some time, as we didn't really know what to do with them. They've been with us since your father turned the tide at Narnia, but with them being from an eastern province, no one feels safe putting them somewhere they might have to fight their countrymen. Zenas has been using them to supplement the Urban Cohorts for a few months.'

I nodded. May the gods bless these men from Licinius' domain who were helping keep the peace in my city.

'Are we safe here?' I asked.

'For now,' Volusianus grunted. 'I've got men on all the points of access who can at least give us warning and buy us time. But we'd be better off getting you to the Palatine, as Ruricius said.'

'When I said "to safety", I meant the Praetorian camp, not the Palatine,' said the commander of the Imperial Horse.

'Surely things are not that bad?' I muttered.

'We'll know just how bad any time now, Domine. If this is going to be resolved without disaster it'll happen under Zenas.'

I stood, tense, with my two officers, leaning on the low wall and watching my city tearing itself apart. Below, close by, I saw several horrifying incidents born simply of the ready presence of such anger. Six men kicking another to death for no obvious reason. A child weeping over a mother trampled by the crowd. A cut-purse being dealt rough justice by the mob. Zenas was moving closer, though his unit was slowed by the press of the ordinary citizens.

'They're not giving way to him,' Volusianus noted. 'He's heading into trouble.'

The mob, pressed in by Zenas' cohort, were bulging out into other places now, and angry shouts were directed towards the six centuries of Moesian soldiers who were advancing cautiously, their round shields held out like a wall. An officer gave a command and the unit spread out, blocking the street and bracing, whereupon the commander yelled an order in thickly accented Latin for the public to 'cease this display and disperse'.

He was told to 'fuck off' in a hundred voices, and his anger at the lack of respect drove him to make the last mistake of his career. In response, he yelled at the crowd that he had 'better things to do than herd stupid, shitty Italian sheep' and that if they didn't disperse he'd 'put his boot up their arsehole to the tenth lace'.

Three men in the crowd jostled one another and exchanged heated words. Another man pushed forward and stepped out into the space between the crowd and the soldiers. Then another. Then half a dozen. And suddenly everyone was running, the mob of ordinary people hurtling along the Vicus Iugarius with violence in mind. I watched in disbelieving horror as the Moesian commander shouted for his men to hold as the tide of angry humanity ran at them, surging along the paving, crammed in by the high buildings to either side.

The Moesians were veterans. They were soldiers. They were armoured in steel and armed with coshes. But they were outnumbered by hundreds to one. I saw the crowd hit them like a wave crashing on the beach and within heartbeats they were lost from sight, submerged beneath the flow of rebellious plebs. Here and there I saw an auxiliary soldier struggling to raise his head above the surface and suck in air before he was battered and torn apart and vanished into the sea of bodies once more.

I stood in utter shock. Almost five hundred men who

had fought in wars for the empire, loyal to me to the end, had been utterly obliterated in mere heartbeats by the very people they were raised to protect. Volusianus was right – Zenas *was* heading for trouble. We *all* were. But the horror of the Moesians was not over. I watched in appalled silence as struggling soldiers were dragged from the crowd, battered and broken yet still fighting for their life. Men had found ropes from somewhere, perhaps one of the shops or stalls along the street-side, and were forming makeshift nooses, looping them around the damaged soldiers' necks and then throwing the ropes over any projection they could find on the building facades. The men were hauled, struggling, from the street where they dangled, kicking and thrashing, to howls of victory from the crowd. I was still astonished that this could happen in my city. I had seen civil disturbance before, but this was new. Horrible. Unbelievable.

The Moesians kicked and struggled until the life fled their eyes, and then hung there, as though staring up at me, dead and yet accusatory. What had I done? Was all this simply because I wanted to make the Christians happy again? Perhaps Diocletian and Galerius had been right? Were that troublesome sect poison to the state? Had they ruined Rome and led me to this?

No. Even through everything, there were Christians like Zenas and Miltiades, who had put the state and even my own welfare above theirs. Besides, Galerius had died badly, his fate decreed by Nemesis for his awful reign, and now Diocletian had rotted away, driven out of his mind by the ghosts of guilt and ruin. Such, apparently, was the fate of enemies of the Christians.

'Gods, no!'

The shock and disbelief in Ruricius' voice dragged me

back from my thoughts and redirected my attention. I almost echoed his words. How could this be happening?

Smoke was rising in roiling columns from the temple of Saturn at the heart of the ancient forum, not sixty paces from where I stood. Had this crowd lost its mind entirely? To turn on the state and the emperor was an appalling thing. To turn on the army that protected you was unthinkable. But to turn on the gods themselves? Smoke was pouring from beneath the tiles of the roof, and boiling out of the open doorway between the columns. It took long moments for me to be able to think of anything but the incredible sacrilege of burning a temple, and when finally my mind latched on to something new, it was oddly: *How do we stop this turning into a new Neronian fire and destroying Rome?* The answer to that was simple, of course: the temple of Saturn stood apart in an area of brick and marble and wide pavements. There was a minimal risk of fire spreading from there, though if the mob would fire a temple, it was not hard to imagine them starting conflagrations in more dangerous and flammable areas. But the thought that finally cut through all this and galvanised me was the realisation that the temple of Saturn also held the state finances. In the vaults beneath that venerable structure were the strongboxes that held the Roman treasury. Admittedly there was little enough in there now to attract even the attention of the most adventurous thief, but the message sent by the burning of the imperial treasury was clear to me.

I watched with little hope as Zenas struggled to push into the forum, but failed to make an impression upon the crowd. His men's clubs smacked into flesh and bone repeatedly, trying to stop the surging mob, but they were losing, and I was far from surprised when I saw them begin their orderly retreat from the fray. Bricks and tiles and anything else that came to hand were cast at them, and here and there men of the Urban Cohort were felled, being gathered up by their mates and dragged behind the protection of the shield wall as they pulled further and further back until they were lost to sight.

'Give me your permission to deploy the Praetorians,' Volusianus said in a quiet and oddly menacing tone.

'What?'

The prefect grasped my wrist and turned me to face him.

'Domine, Rome is poised on the brink of disaster. We need to regain control; to reinstall order, and we need to do it now. The crowd is just realising what it is capable of and what it has done. And when they understand that they have murdered a military unit and burned a temple with impunity, they will realise they can do it again, and might as well do, since they have already committed crime enough to damn themselves. Zenas' men are good at policing the streets, and that Moesian unit might have been good deployed as part of a battle formation, but the Praetorians are the best. They are trained for combat. They're used to it. Give me permission to bring Rome to order, before we lose the chance for good.'

I dithered still. The idea of deploying the Praetorians against people who were only revolting because I had taxed them too far was horrible. But my mind quickly filled with images of dangling soldiers and burning temples, and I was nodding before I'd even consciously made the decision. 'But with coshes, Volusianus.'

'Domine, that is the wrong decision.'

I blinked. Who was Volusianus to dictate to me? 'Be careful, Prefect.'

'Domine, look at how ineffective the Urban Cohorts and the Moesians were. A stronger deterrent is needed.'

I glared at him and waved him away irritably. Volusianus

bowed and turned, marching away. Only when he had been gone for some time did I realise that I had not, in the end, actually said 'no'.

'Are we safe here still?' I asked Ruricius.

'Short of being on the Palatine or in the Castra Praetoria, it's as safe as anywhere, Domine. Volusianus has left adequate numbers at each approach to the hill, and I have a unit of the Horse Guard stationed at the rear of the temple of Jove. If any move is made on the Capitol, we shall take you by horse down to the river. We are close to the Tiber Island. At the very worst we can hole up there for a time, with only two narrow bridges to guard.'

I nodded and watched the chaos below. Buildings were being looted. Plaques and statues were being smashed. Men were being killed. And it was spreading out from the forum along all the main thoroughfares. Soon someone would set fire to one of those rickety wooden insulae on the surrounding hills, and then Rome would burn.

I felt sick. This was my doing. Admittedly, I couldn't see a way I could have done anything any better. Had I dealt with the matter a different way, it would now be Christians murdering and burning, or rampaging rebellious troops seeking payment. But that was little consolation as I watched my people tearing apart their own city.

I sagged when Volusianus reappeared perhaps half an hour later, dismounting from a sweating horse, looking tired and fraught. He had ridden hard for the Praetorian camp and then back, having given his orders. It was no use now reinforcing my decision to allow only coshes.

'Domine, all will soon be under control. Watch.'

I did. For two hours, as the sun set over Rome – symbolism that did not escape my notice, either – I watched cohort after cohort of Praetorians emerge from one street or another, converging on the mass of folk in the forum. They were arrayed for war, blades out. I had known they would be, for all my orders. Volusianus had chosen to take my failure to say no in the end as tacit agreement, the damnable man. I watched as my own elite military marched on a crowd of angry, frightened civilians and began to butcher them like hogs on a feast day. No mercy was given, though I saw it sought often enough. My sickness only increased as time went on. At one point I actually vomited over the wall, down onto the roof of the Portico of the Olympian Gods. I felt numb. I wanted to give the order to stop it, but I couldn't. I could hardly speak. What had I done? What had *Volusianus* done?

The Praetorians butchered their way through the people of Rome until they met their peers and took firm control of the forum. Perhaps half the crowd escaped that bloodbath, fleeing through narrow ways and hiding in nooks. But by the time the sun set on that dreadful day, the paving of the forum had gone, hidden beneath a sea of blood and a carpet of butchered bodies.

'We have become monsters,' I said at last, turning a hollow look on my prefect. For the first time in my life I was grateful that Romulus was already playing in the Elysian fields and not here to see what his father had done. He would have been ashamed. I know *I* was. I had taken the purple not out of self-aggrandisement, and not through desire to rule, and not even through jealousy at those promoted above me – or not *solely* through that, anyway. I had taken the purple to save Rome, and instead I was destroying it. Was this how so many of history's damned emperors had begun? Well-meaning mistakes and impossible choices? Was this what had cursed the memory of Caligula? Of Domitian? Of Commodus? Of... Diocletian, perhaps?

'We are *not* monsters, Domine,' Volusianus said quietly. 'We are men doing what must be done to keep the world working. And this is no time for weakness.'

'*Weakness?*' I whispered, astonished. 'You think expressing horror at all this is *weakness?*'

'Fortify yourself, Maxentius, Emperor of Rome. What you see down there is only the *beginning* of the horror. I know that you refuse to accept it, but the truth is that Constantine will come for you. He has to. He has cowed Licinius, but only with a united West can he hope to stand for long against the East. The Praetorians can control Rome...'

Yes. I could see that. At the tip of a sword.

'...but it is time to look north. We garrison Aquileia and our border forts in the mountains and the flat lands to the east, but what we need is to fortify the Western Alps now, before it is too late.'

I simply stared, shaking my head. What had we done? What had we become?

I learned the next day that over six thousand Roman souls had been dispatched by Praetorian blades that evening. Why should Rome tremble about the possibility that Constantine might come, when they had an emperor here already murdering his own people?

It was the last winter.

And it felt like it.

EPILOGUE

CONSTANTINE

26TH JANUARY 312 AD

I closed my eyes. For a time, I was a boy again, talking with the young lad I had just met in Treverorum's halls. Maxentius was his name. He was a likeable sort: shy, thoughtful and true. Together, we built a wooden town, both of us happy to be distant from the ceremony ongoing elsewhere in the city. It was a graceful, fleeting moment of calm, of peace... of hope. Then I heard the wail of a thousand voices...

The blistering cries of Treverorum's military men upon whose shoulders I had risen to the purple; the harrowing moans of the wraiths who haunted my every waking thought – the wretched, tormented Diocletian now among their ranks; the taunts of the ethereal, divine being who stalked my dreams. The will of God, Lactantius had called it. The din became piercing, all-consuming until, like a mirror dropped from a high tower, the reverie of my young self and the boy Maxentius shattered, leaving me alone in the blackness.

Now, I heard only one voice. Mother, her laments echoing through the palace's high, lonely corridors. I had tried to explain to her: a strong man can resist his peers, his generals, his holy men... but no man can defy a god. Yet still she wept – for me and for my soul.

He was once a brother to you. You will spend eternity in flames!

With a gasp, I opened my eyes, and that dark netherworld was swept away by an icy tempest. It roared around me, keening, a storm of white enshrouding me, scudding horizontally on the ferocious bora winds, stealing the breath from my frozen lips and nostrils. Hisarnis' golden, jewel-studded battle helm once again rested upon my head. For I was not in the palace of Treverorum, you see. I had made my choice.

Crouched on one knee, the blizzard scourged me like a torturer's whip, furrowing my bear cloak, turning my flesh numb. Below the high ridge upon which I knelt and a short way south I could see two lonely stone towers, protecting the white-floored pass, scantly garrisoned, the purple banners caked in driving snow. The way that would take us into the Cottian Alpes. The mountainous route that would lead us into Italia. The road to Rome.

My one-time brother had neglected to bolster this track. Why? Perhaps because he had assigned his armies to the easterly Julian Alpes instead, in fear of Licinius – despite his vow never to set foot in the West again – turning upon him there in support of me. I wanted to believe that, you see, but deep down, I knew the truth. Hatred had grown between us, but even to this day, I know that he didn't believe I would do it...

I rose from my knee to stand tall, turned to my side, looking across my small cadre of stony-faced, white-flecked generals up on the ridge with me – Krocus and Batius side by side, eyes hard, hands on the pommels of their swords – down to the vast iron war machine that waited, halted and concealed, a mere arrow shot north of the pass. Forty thousand soldiers, enchanted by my every word. Ready to make battle in the throes of winter – that most un-Roman of war seasons – a tactic as Frankish as the regiments of my Comitatus down there among my legions. I looked at my numb, blue-tinged hand. To raise it meant there would be no turning back. To raise it would be to shatter everything Maxentius and I had once been, forever. For this war would end only when one of us lay cold and dead. The other would be master of the world...

Up went my hand. And chopping down it came, like a battle standard.

Historical Note

Part 1 – The collapsing world of the Tetrarchy

Following the Carnuntum conference, as it is named and which we dealt with towards the end of the previous volume, there followed three years of tension in the West (and indeed in the East, though that is not the focus of our tale). The retirement, both voluntary and forced, of the former Augusti left a dangerously unstable world with a pack of claimants loosely bound by a system that was already in a state of collapse. Galerius and Daia in the East could follow the Tetrarchic system well enough, but unfortunately the West had three claimants, each to the title of Augustus with no junior Caesar. Constantine held the north, Maxentius the south, and Licinius loitered on the eastern borders seeking advantage wherever he could.

The world this created could hardly be considered stable. In the northern regions the tribes hovering on the periphery pushed and picked at the Rhine borders, forcing Constantine to tend to them repeatedly, yet due to their changing attitudes to Rome and the spread of Christianity in the region they conversely also supplied Constantine's world with a ready force of manpower for both military and agricultural matters. In addition to constant tribal difficulties, and the ever-worrying presence of hostile emperors in the East, and rival claimants both to the south and in the central regions, Constantine also faced difficulties caused by his father-in-law Maximian, whose forced retirement had clearly rankled and who had spent the time since then brooding and planning a return to power. Having failed to do so at his son's court in Rome, he had fled to Constantine's lands and attempted to take power there.

In the south, Maxentius faced his own difficulties, juggling financial and social issues and walking a fine line between different potential disasters. The end of the Christian Persecutions did not herald the era of peace one might expect, but rather left the strong young sect with freedom to cause more and more trouble, mostly among themselves, but with effects that spilled over into the wider landscape. Adding to this the revolt in Africa, which must have proved considerably more difficult to put down than expected due to the sheer length of time involved, the southern claimant was largely too wrapped up in his own troubles to spend much time worrying about his opponents elsewhere.

The death of Galerius remains one of the most startling and gruesomely described demises in ancient history – thought to be a form of cancer that 'devoured his genitals'. But beyond the death itself, the ramifications of the passing of the main player in the surviving Tetrarchy threw out what remaining political balance there was, and left the claimants with little choice but conflict. Galerius' presence must have been an oddly unifying force, since he remained the most powerful enemy of both Constantine and Maxentius, and his absence would leave them without a major mutual enemy (Licinius being much less powerful than his master). The old emperor died in agony in his palace at Felix Romuliana (which still exists). The visits by Constantine and Maxentius and their meeting at the palace are our own creation and not attested in sources, though such things are entirely possible as the terminally ill emperor languished there for some time and there are hints that he was preparing himself to face what came next.

Thus the political, military and social landscapes of the West were somewhat in turmoil throughout those years. It is into this cauldron of troubles we have thrown our characters, attempting to guide them within the bounds of known and accepted history while attempting to divine the truth of their actions and motivations with the heavy application of logic and common sense and a touch of adventure and derring-do.

Part 2 – Maxentius

Maxentius from 308 to 312 AD faced immense difficulties. Sources paint a picture of a man who was no friend to Christianity, but then the sources are almost uniformly Christian, and are therefore clearly biased towards Constantine, and were bound to damn his opposition. Tellingly, they are equally derogatory of Galerius and Licinius. From the early fourth century comes a peculiar anecdote involving the martyrdom of Saint Catherine of Alexandria, which is fanciful to say the least and we have discounted it, excluding it from our tale. Yet despite the view the Christian writers paint of him, the facts show something different. Maxentius allowed the Christians to elect a Pope after the banning of the institution under his predecessor. He returned the Church's property, ultimately contributing to his own downfall.

And in his retinue were men of power who worshipped as Christians. Strange as it may seem, the humorous sequence of events described here, with Pope after Pope failing to solve the problems and being exiled by Maxentius, is based upon historical fact.

The African expedition is interesting. History tells us very little about what happened other than that Maxentius sent Volusianus and Zenas to deal with the usurper there. Most of the detail of these events, therefore, are our own interpretations, down even to the locations of the major action. There is no reference to Maxentius being there at all, though for the sake of our tale and the continued points of view of the protagonists, his presence was the only way for us to adequately relay the importance of the rebellion and its resolution.

On a side note, since the removal of Anullinus's brother Gaius from his position in 307, we have had Zenas in overall command of the Urban Cohorts. A full list of the prefects who actually commanded that force between 306 and 312 is available, and numbers eight people. We have chosen to leave Zenas in control, however, rather than introduce a series of characters who would have little bearing upon the plot and would vastly increase and complicate the cast list.

Without a doubt, the most important event during this time in the personal life of Maxentius was the death of his son, Romulus. The young man's tomb at his father's villa is still visible beside the Via Appia, south of Rome and next to the circus that Maxentius built. The precise cause of Romulus' death remains unknown, though it is recorded that he drowned in the Tiber. The effect of his death upon his father might be expected by the reader anyway, but it is made clear by the grand monuments dedicated to him (the mausoleum, the temple in the forum, the statue voted by the Governor of Sardinia) and by the young man's deification and commemoration on coins. How Maxentius dealt with this issue remains unknown, though he went on ruling his empire and facing off against men likely more powerful than he, so he must have found a reservoir of inner strength from somewhere. We have made this a Christian advisor in the form of Miltiades, Rome's 32nd Pope and the last Maxentius would meet. Miltiades was a native North African of Berber descent, a Christian, and a Roman citizen, an interesting combination that fits into our tale like a piece in a jigsaw puzzle.

Lastly, the sequence of events that led to Maxentius' downfall is to some extent an echo of what is widely regarded as the decline of the Roman Empire. With an increasing shortage of funds compounded by religious unrest, crumbling borders, the inclusion of neighbouring tribes, endless usurpations and rivals, there was little Maxentius could do to halt the snowballing troubles. By the end of 311 he was, as they say, robbing Peter to pay Paul, and something would have to give. It did in spectacular fashion with the deaths of thousands of Roman citizens at the point of Praetorian blades, one of the darkest moments of Maxentius' reign and the apex of his troubles. While we have laid the blame for this, like other matters, at the feet of Volusianus, history attributes the massacre to Maxentius, adding to his notoriety.

Whatever the truth, Maxentius' world was truly crumbling by the dawn of 312, and he was now faced with the greatest threat of all: Constantine.

Part 3 – Constantine

Constantine, like his southern rival, found no shortage of troubles in the spell between 308 and 312, a period when he was at once hailed as Augustus of the West by some and denounced as a false emperor of ignoble lineage by others.

Initially, his most persistent threat was not the rival Roman factions pressed against his domain of Gaul, Hispania and Britannia, but the ever-troublesome Frankish tribes who saw themselves as honour-bound to make war at every opportunity, and frequently flooded across the River Rhenus in small packs and occasionally in confederate multitudes. The Bructeri were but one of the troublesome Frankish peoples, and we have chosen them to illustrate Constantine's policy, which emerged in these years. Rather than fighting endless battles in an unwinnable war, he opted instead to offer clemency and alliance to the tribesmen: a space on Roman soil to call their own in return for fealty and conversion to the Roman way of life. Such measures relieved the pressure on his over-raided and under-tended grain fields, allowing Roman citizens to gather harvests without threat of barbarian attacks – and for their newly settled Frankish allies to join them in these endeavours.

Ultimately, the men of such tribes – the Regii, the Cornuti, the Bructeri, the Petulantes and the Ubii – would emerge as fully-fledged Roman regiments classed – perhaps confusingly (hence our choice not to use the term) – as auxilia. But these regiments were not the sub-legionary-quality auxiliaries of previous centuries; instead they were hardy and fierce, on a par at least with their legionary equivalents and favoured by Constantine who installed them as a private 'Comitatus' of sorts. These auxilia forces retained their tribal names but fought in the Roman way, and sometime later would become the basis of the famed auxilium palatinum (palace regiments).

The late Roman writer Zosimus attacks Constantine's policy of drawing many legions away from his borders (sometimes referred to as a 'defence-in-depth' approach). This account tends towards caricature, for the conventional legions had been splitting into smaller, ad-hoc units since Diocletian's reign and earlier. Old-style legions of over five thousand men had by Constantine's time proved insufficiently mobile and flexible to meet the rapidly changing threats of the fourth century. Pertinently, in an age of civil war, bolstering a central reserve could be considered as a prudent strategy.

Concerning the religious make-up of Constantine's army: by 311, his legions were certainly not universally Christian, just as Maxentius' were not all pagan. There were a growing number of Christians in his forces, however. It seems that in this era a 'just war' psyche was developed to win over doubters and allay their misgivings over violence and bloodshed.

Constantine's vision at the broken shrine of Apollo (Apollo Grannus, to be precise) is little understood, although one outcome of the event was the divination of a thirty-year reign for him. More importantly, it seems to have moved him further down the road towards an appreciation of the power of an all-encompassing God, one which all of his subjects could genuinely believe in. It also served as a metaphor supporting his break from the now-toxic gods of the broken Tetrarchy (Jove and Hercules).

His later vision of an unnamed God, loosely identified as Mens Divina (the Divine Mind), is even less understood, but seems to have nudged him on past another milestone in his 'journey' – be that political or pious.

Regarding the death of Maximian: Constantine was

enraged by his father-in-law's attempted coup, but actually showed some mercy once he had regained control of matters. One version of events has it that, having stormed and retaken the city of Massilia, Constantine at first allowed the one-time Augustus a period of reprieve, only for Fausta to become entangled in some devious plot of her father's to assassinate her husband. Ultimately, this consigned Maximian to his fate, which appears to have been death by suicide (hanging) or maybe strangulation by the hands of another.

On a side note, the siege of Massilia did actually see – as we have described – Constantine's bungling siege engineers mis-measure the height of the city's walls, resulting in what must have been the rather comical sight of his legionaries having to stand upon each other's shoulder to reach the battlements.

Constantine's clash with Licinius at Noricum is fictional, but it brings about the factual occurrence of a pact arising between the two in late 311. This was the key – maybe or maybe not the one that Constantine had been seeking – to smashing the deadlock: with Licinius backing away, Constantine could realistically consider an assault on Italia.

And it is there we shall resume in the third and final volume of our saga with a tale that became the stuff of legend... and changed the world.

CONSTANTINE

MAXENTIUS

Glossary of Latin Terms

Aerarium – The imperial treasury.

Ango – A barbed javelin favoured by the barbarian tribes east of the Rhine.

Ambulatum – Legionary 'manoeuvres' training.

Apodyterium – Bathhouse changing rooms.

Armatura – Basic legionary training with sword, shield and javelin.

Armilustrium – A late-autumn festival in honour of Mars, where soldiers would ceremonially stow away their weapons over winter.

Aula Regia – The emperor's palace.

Auletes – Naval flautist tasked with playing tunes to keep the oarsmen synchronised.

Ballista – Roman bolt-throwing artillery that was primarily employed as an anti-personnel weapon on the battlefield.

Biga – Racing chariot.

Buccina – Curved horn used by the military for signalling and issuing of commands.

Bulla – Amulet worn by Roman boys until their coming of age.

Camelopardalis – Giraffe.

Camisia – An undergarment or nightshirt.

Carceres – The starting gates at a racing circus.

Comitatus – The elite regiments of the Roman army.

Concordia – The Roman Goddess of Harmony, and more generally the principle of harmony.

Cornu (plural cornua) – 'G' shaped horn used in imperial games and ceremony.

Cursus Publicus – The empire's state-run system of couriers and transportation.

Damnatio Ad Bestias – The sentence of death at the jaws of the circus animals.

Doctores – Military drill sergeants.

Domus – Home.

Dux Militum – Duke of the Armies, a lofty position in later Rome.

Fanum – A temple.

Fossa Sanguinis – A trench in a temple where sacrificial blood would collect.

Francisca – A Frankish throwing axe – typically tossed across the ground – capable of breaking bones and disrupting legionary formations.

Frigidarium – The cold room in the bathhouse.

Frumentarii – The shadowy school of imperial spies and assassins.

Harpastum – A Roman ball game.

Haruspex – Individual trained in divination by reading the entrails of a sacrificial animal.

Insula – Roman apartment block, often of many storeys, with shops in the ground floor.

Iudex – The leader of the Gothic tribes.

Kathisma – Greek term for the imperial box at an entertainment venue. Cf. *pulvinar.*

Lanista – Gladiator trainer or owner.

Lapsi – Those who renounced Christianity under pressure from Roman authorities.

Liburnian – A small, swift and nimble galley with just a single bank of oars.

Limes – The limits or borders of empire.

Magister Officiorum – The 'Master of Offices', one of the most senior bureaucratic posts in the empire.

Navalia – Roman military port.

Paenula – A poncho or raincloak.

Palus – A stake used for sword practice.

Pilentum – A lady's carriage.

Protectores – An elite corps of bodyguards dedicated to the emperor's personal protection.

Pulvinar – Latin term for the imperial box at an entertainment venue. Cf. *kathisma*.

Quadriga – Ceremonial chariot towed by four horses.

Quaestor – Title applied to men in various administrative posts in Roman government dealing with finance.

Rex Sacrorum – The Priest/King of Sacrifice.

Sestertius (plural sesterces) – A large brass coin.

Shahanshah – The Persian 'King of Kings'.

Sol Invictus – 'Unconquered Sun.' Later Roman Sun God adopted from the eastern regions.

Spatha – Double-edged sword, longer than an old-fashioned gladius, originally a cavalry weapon.

Spiculum (plural spicula) – Throwing javelin of the Roman infantry, replacing the earlier *pilum*.

Subura – The slum region in the city of Rome.

Tartarus – The deep abyss of torment to which the souls of the sinful dead are condemned.

Testudo – Formation where infantry place shields around all sides and overhead of their unit, thus providing protection from missiles from all directions.

Toga Virilis – Plain white toga adopted by male Roman citizens when they come of age in their teenage years.

Tribunus – By this period in history, the term 'prefect' was used to denote a legionary commander, but 'tribunus' was still used at times to denote high-ranking officers.

Triclinium – The dining room of a Roman household.

Tubilustrium – The spring ceremony where the Roman army was declared fit for war.

Vexillatio (plural vexillationes) – A detachment of legionaries from the main body of their legion.

Vigiles – City watchmen, who acted in the roles of both police and firefighters.

About the authors

SIMON TURNEY is from Yorkshire
and, having spent much of his childhood visiting
historic sites, he fell in love with the Roman heritage
of the region. His fascination with the ancient world
snowballed from there with great interest in Rome,
Egypt, Greece and Byzantium. His works include
the Marius' Mules and Praetorian series, as
well as the Tales of the Empire series and
The Damned Emperor series.

www.simonturney.com   @SJATurney

GORDON DOHERTY is a Scottish author,
addicted to reading and writing historical fiction.
Inspired by visits to the misty Roman ruins of Britain
and the sun-baked antiquities of Turkey and Greece,
Gordon has written tales of the later Roman Empire,
Byzantium, Classical Greece and the Bronze Age.
His works include the Legionary, Strategos
and Empires of Bronze series, and the
Assassin's Creed tie-in novel *Odyssey*.

www.gordondoherty.co.uk   @GordonDoherty

For one to rule,
the other must die...

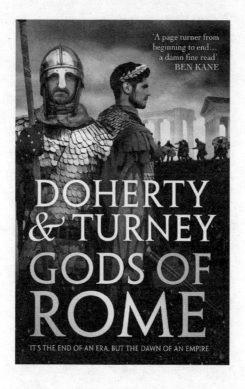

Read *Gods of Rome*, the final book in
the Rise of Emperors trilogy.